# RULES OF OUR OWN

## RULE BREAKER SERIES

## J WILDER

*To batteries and birth control.*

# AUTHOR'S NOTE

**Disclaimer: Kindly be advised that I shall absolve myself of any obligation to address any unanticipated familial expansions that may arise as a consequence of engaging with this literary work. It is strongly recommended that readers exercise their own discretion in family planning while navigating these pages.**

Join <u>Jessa's readers' FB group</u>. **ARC SIGN UP EXCLUSIVE**. You'll get updates on Lucas and Piper's book creation and all kinds of fun extras. I'm dying to hear what you think!

I met River, Alex, and Mia way back in 2019 while writing what would be Rule Number Five. I didn't set out for them to fall for each other. I thought they'd be friends at first, but the further the story continued, the more they just kept sneaking themselves in. Practically screaming at me to do their story justice.

I still almost didn't write this book. To say I was nervous would be an understatement. There's a lot of hype to live up to and anyone who knows me knows I'm an anxious mess 99% of the time.

**Note:** There are WAY more sex scenes in this book than I set out to include. Sometimes the author just has to follow the story, and that's where they wanted to go.

This is also a hockey romance in the loosest sense of the term. They are hockey players but the book doesn't revolve around hockey.

Happy freaking reading!!!!!!

**Trigger Warning: Domestic violence. Manipulation, threats, scare tactics from an asshole controlling ex. Fuck you, Jason. Fuck you!**

Content info: polyamorous relationship where all three members are equally in love with one another.

# CHAPTER 1
# MIA

"*NOW BOARDING for flight WS2371 from Ottawa to San Francisco,*" a woman's voice crackles through the cavernous airport's speakers. I can't miss this flight. Not when the next one's not for another four hours. Tonight's the first night of Piper and Lucas's destination wedding celebration, and we're supposed to be hanging out just us girls. No doubt involving copious amounts of alcohol, which, at this point, I desperately need.

I'd taken the early shift at the hospital—I'm a first-year intern, so my days are absolute chaos. Then, mistakenly, I thought I could squeeze in an extra hour of research on my Prosthetics For Kids charity. My *one more minute* had magically morphed into two wasted hours, leaving me in this mess.

"Are you listening?" Gerard's voice cuts through the phone.

I adjust my cell, pinned between my shoulder and ear. "Yes, of course."

"I'm serious, Mia. Two months, then I'm moving the funding to Eric's team."

"That's not enough time." My throat goes dry, and my steps falter as his words slam into me. When my local Prosthetics For Kids fundraiser took off, Gerard was the first to offer to back me financially. He works for AstroCore Holdings, a company that helps allocate funds to different charities.

I'd been over the moon knowing this was my chance to expand Prosthetics For Kids from grass-roots to national. He'd warned me then that his support depended on me figuring out how to expand my backyard fundraiser to a full-fledged charity. Which translates directly into raising money. One backer alone isn't enough. At the time, I thought, how hard could it be?

Hard. Really flipping hard.

"I'm sorry, Mia. It's not personal. I can't tie up funding in a charity that's not going to take off. You know this."

It's not personal, *my ass*.

Nothing in my life has ever been this personal. My heart drops at the thought of those innocent kids going without the help they need. I can almost feel their smiles slowly fading and see the anguish and worry return to their parents' eyes.

I weave through people waiting at their gates and grit my teeth. "I'll get it done."

"You better. This is your last chance," Gerard says, his voice steady, making it crystal clear he means it.

The phone goes silent.

My eyes sting, and I blink back tears. I'm going to need an actual miracle to pull this off. Unfortunately, praying hasn't resulted in any help.

Trust me. I've tried.

With the lack of divine intervention, I've been killing myself to raise the money. I've spent what feels like years of my life researching hashtags, trends, viral freaking sounds, knowing that social media's my best shot at making this work.

*"We are now inviting those passengers with small children, and any passengers requiring special assistance, to begin boarding at this time for flight WS2371 from Ottawa to San Francisco."*

I squint to see the gate sign down the hall, and my heart kicks up as I double my pace. With the change of speed, my suitcase goes from humming behind me to the cheap handle twisting in my grip.

Shit. Shit. Shit.

I give it a quick tug, trying to balance it out, but the hard plastic bottom catches the back of my heel.

*Argh!* I swallow my cry and bite my cheek against the shards of pain radiating through my foot. Every cuss word known to man flies through my head as I reach down and fix the strap of my Croc. I fight the urge to collapse on the ground, clutching my foot, and keep moving, hobbling as fast as I can.

There's a crowd of people at my gate, but instead of forming lines to board the plane, they're all staring toward the desk, which is currently blocked from view.

Relief washes over me, and I take a few calming breaths. I'm one step closer to my night of gossiping with Sidney and Piper while we put together decorations for her wedding. This is like Bridesmaids 101.

I've been hiding my exhaustion from my friends, even as I'm sliding toward total burnout—holding on by a thread—and I desperately need this. I squeeze between two men and scrunch up my nose at the overpowering scent of cologne. Please, dear God, don't let them sit next to me.

There's an attendant with perfectly pinned-back hair speaking with a man at the front. He's pleading with her. "You don't understand. My wife's having our baby. I don't know what happened. She's not due for at least three more weeks." He places both hands on the counter. "She needs me."

His tone shreds through my chest, and a desperate desire to do something, anything, squeezes my ribs.

The woman speaks into her microphone, "This man is trying to get home for the birth of his child. I'm calling for a volunteer to agree to being bumped to the next flight."

He looks frantic, hair sticking up, shirt half-buttoned, and his eyes dart through the crowd, begging for help.

People shift around me, but no one steps forward. The attendant looks at the man with sympathy. "I'm sorry, sir, but the best I can do is book you onto the later one."

His shoulders collapse inward, and the corners of

his eyes redden. His helplessness goes straight to my heart, and I step forward, knowing this means bailing on the girls, but I'll make it up to them somehow.

I move to his side, facing the attendant dressed in an impeccable blue suit, and slide my ticket toward her. "He can have my seat. I don't have a checked bag."

The man audibly inhales, and he looks between me and the attendant. I give him a hesitant look, worried I'm giving him false hope.

Her fingers fly over the keyboard, and she scans the screen before looking at us with a blooming smile. "I can make the switch," she addresses me. "You do understand you'll have to wait four hours for the next flight?"

"Yes. It's not a problem," I say immediately.

She nods and hands the soon-to-be father his boarding pass. "Enjoy your flight, and congratulations."

He turns to me, eyes watering. "Thank you," he says and wraps me in a hug. I pat his back a few times until he lets me go.

"No trouble at all. Congratulations."

With those words, he's off, rushing down the tunnel toward the plane.

A warm feeling settles in my stomach, happy with my decision.

"You were very generous," the attendant remarks, not bothering to look up from her computer.

I shrug in response. "It was nothing. Anyone else would've done the same."

Her gaze floats over the crowd of people finally moving toward the counter. She raises a brow and hands me a new ticket. "I'm not so sure about that. We'll see you in a few hours."

I make my way toward the waiting area and do my best to get comfortable on the hard plastic seat before pulling out my phone.

Sighing, I type in the group chat.

**Me: Missed my flight. Coming in late.**

My bestie slash university roommate is the first to respond.

**Sidney: Please tell me you weren't still at the clinic. I texted you two hours ago.**

**Me: No comment.**

**Piper: Sorry to hear that. Still coming in tonight?**

Even though it's Piper's wedding, I'm not surprised she's calm about me being late. If anyone understands my obsessive need to concentrate on the charity, it's her. As someone who works as a physiotherapist helping patients with new prosthetics, Piper's just as invested as I am. We've bonded over the years, and now I'm as close with her as I am with Sidney.

**Me: Just a few extra hours. Don't wait up.**

**Sidney: Please *eye roll emoji* We'll see you when you get here.**

**Me: *kissy face emoji***

**Sidney: Wait! This has nothing to do with Jason, right?**

Sidney and Piper hate my ex Jason with the intensity of a thousand burning suns.

The Jason who wants the house, the wife, the 2.5 kids, and the picket fence. The Jason who grew up with a silver spoon and a dad who sits on the board of my hospital. The Jason who never misses an opportunity to bring up the fact that he'd been the reason I landed my internship in the first place.

The same Jason who made me feel like an absolute piece of garbage.

He constantly complained I didn't prioritize him enough, and I couldn't even deny it. I'm not going to just give up my work because my boyfriend can't handle it.

Pretty sure he thought I'd cave eventually because after a year, he dumped me, calling me selfish.

Our breakup should've hurt, but the truth is…it didn't. Which is why when he flipped his script and started telling me he was sorry and we were meant to be together, I ignored him.

At the time, his texts came through every five minutes. They started with *I love you* and *I'm sorry*, then rapidly transformed into calling me a selfish bitch who wasted a year of his life. The trickle of guilt that I'd used him as a placeholder is the only reason he's not blocked. He was someone to fill the empty space in my life where a relationship should be. But I never gave him my heart. Not really.

Not when I'd made that mistake three years ago.

**Me: No. I think he finally got the hint.**

**Sidney: He better have. Pretty sure Jax is ready to murder him.**

**Piper: Yeah, Lucas too.**

**Me: Well, no murder necessary.**

I grab my backpack from the floor and drop it on the chair beside me, waiting for the next message to come through.

**Sidney: Alex and River flew in this afternoon. *winky face emoji***

A jolt flares in my chest. I don't know how I'm going to feel seeing them again, but if it's anything like the anticipation, I might actually explode. Nervous energy skates under my skin. I haven't let myself so much as think of them since I graduated from university three years ago. Anything more than that has me spiraling into things I wish could've been.

It only took one semester for my every thought to revolve around Alex and River. I'd fall asleep to good-night texts and wake up to good-morning messages. I didn't know it was possible for a person to consume your life that fast, let alone two of them.

At some point, our friendship shifted, and I swear you could cut the tension between us with a freaking knife. It all felt new, and fun, and meant to be. Until it didn't.

That last night at the bar haunts me. We were at the club, dancing, and things finally started to click into place. Alex grabbed my hips, and I caught my breath when he leaned down, and his mouth began to descend to mine. Time slowed, with each ticking millisecond bringing him closer.

I closed my eyes, ready to finally feel him against me, but his warmth disappeared. When I opened them, Alex was on the ground, holding his face, and River was standing next to me, fist clenched at his side.

I knew there was no way I could choose, and I refused to come between them. So, even though it felt like I was ripping my own heart out, I ghosted them both and didn't look back.

**Me: So?**

**Piper: So you haven't spoken with them since university.**

**Sidney: Don't even pretend like things didn't turn south. You three were inseparable, then one day you were crying in your bedroom.**

Of course she heard that. I'm not ready to get into it. Not when so much of it still feels like an open wound.

**Me: It was university. We were practically kids. Plus, we never even kissed. Just friends and all that.**

**Piper: Keep telling yourself that.**

We really were just friends. That's all I let us be. My eyes burn, and I fight against the memories. They'd balanced each other perfectly. Alex made me happier, lighter when I was too harsh on myself, and River knew when to sit back and just let me work through it. He offered the steady support I needed. Sometimes things are stressful. Hard. That doesn't mean I needed to give up. Unlike Jason, River understood that.

I change the subject, and I'm grateful when they let me.

**Me: Love you two. I can't believe you're getting married.**

**Piper: Believe it!**

I turn off my phone and pull out my laptop, determined not to waste a single second of this delay. As much as it kills me, I know there's no way I'm getting anything done once I get to Napa. Piper and Lucas are the closest thing I've seen to real-life soulmates, except maybe Jax and Sidney. There's no doubt in my mind this is a once-in-a-lifetime moment to support her.

*See? Not selfish.*

I ignore the small part of me that's relieved that getting in so late means I won't have to face Alex and River tonight after all.

# CHAPTER 2
# MIA

THE BACK-SEAT WINDOW fogs as I lean in, blurring my view of the resort. I missed my shuttle from the airport to Napa Valley and had to hire a private car for the nearly two-hour drive. I hand my credit card to the driver, and my fingers tap on my bouncing knee as I wait for the transaction to go through. It makes a loud beep, and the driver frowns at me.

"Miss, it's declined."

I fake a smile through my mortification and hand him a different one. "Sorry, wrong one."

He swipes again, and relief washes over me as the telltale chime from the machine signals it's approved. As a medical intern buried in school debt, I'm seriously broke, and after this trip, I'll be chowing down on nothing but ramen noodles for the next month.

There's no way I'd have been able to come if Lucas and Piper hadn't paid for my stay, and I can't thank them enough. I don't have long to dwell on it. My door opens, and a smiling doorman welcomes me.

"Welcome to Resort Bardessono."

"Thank you."

My breath catches the second I step out of the car, and the soft, lilting fall of water fills my ears. The place is gorgeous. No. Stunning. I breathe in through my nose, the scent of flowers, rain, and honeysuckle hanging in the air. I'm still gawking at the resort's modern architecture, which is somehow both modern and rustic, when a white Porsche rolls up behind me. The valet opens the door, revealing a vaguely familiar face, sending reality tipping on its axis. She's from one of those housewives shows that plays on repeat in the hospital. I dash my gaze away, praying she didn't catch me gawking.

I'm not in Kansas anymore, that's for sure.

I know one day as a doctor, this won't be unattainable, but right now, it's like a freaking fairy tale. I guess this is what happens when your friend's marrying an NHL star.

"Ms. Brooks," the bellman says, jolting me from my thoughts. "If you'll just come with me, I'll guide you through the lobby."

I reach for my carry-on, but another man dressed in a resort uniform gets to it first. "Don't worry, miss. I'll bring it to your room."

I swallow hard, not sure how to tell him I can't afford to tip. Instead, I grab hold of the handle and give him a smile. "I'd really rather keep it with me if that's okay."

He looks surprised but nods. "Of course."

I follow the first man through the entry door, and I'm immediately greeted by happy squeals. Both Sidney and Piper are waiting for me next to their guys.

Jax releases his arms from around Sidney's waist, running a hand through his shaggy brown hair and giving me a dimpled smile as Sidney skips toward me so fast you'd think we didn't see each other weekly.

Her dark hair's pulled up in a high ponytail that bounces with her steps, revealing the silver section underneath, and she's wearing a matching top and skirt set with a floral pattern on it. Her full cheeks are flushed, and she's smiling so widely her eyes crinkle at the corners. I've heard Jax call her a sexy librarian, and no matter how gross that is, it's undoubtedly true.

"I can't believe you missed your flight," she chides, but it's friendly with no judgment.

I shrug and stumble back as a weight slams into my side with an oomph.

Piper's bright golden hair frames her face, her glittering cornflower eyes lit up with joy as she wraps her arms around me in a warm embrace. She is wearing a thin-strapped white eyelet dress that is feminine and elegant, perfect for a wedding weekend.

Meanwhile, I'm in my purple scrubs with teddy

bear pins along the collar because I didn't have time to change.

Piper lets out an exaggerated sigh and steps back. "Thank God you're here. The guys outnumbered us all day. We had to watch hockey games. Old ones!"

Sidney laughs. She likes hockey just as much as the guys, but she doesn't contradict our friend. They'd grown closer over the years, even while living in different cities.

Jax plays for the Ottawa Senators and Lucas for the Boston Bruins, so they bonded over their guys traveling and the highs and lows of being WAGs. Which is a term I still can't believe they call themselves. Wives and girlfriends.

Lucas is tall and broad, with deep brown skin that stands in stark contrast to the petite and fair-skinned Piper. He wraps his arm around Piper's tiny waist, and his brown eyes shine as he looks at her lovingly.

Just like their personalities. Complete opposites, but a perfect fit. Once he's done nuzzling his soon-to-be wife's neck, he gives me a smile. "Glad you made it."

Jax wraps an arm around my shoulder and tugs me to his side. "Long trip?"

"Not a complete waste. I got a lot of work done while I waited." I shrug.

He barks out a laugh. "Of course you did. You know, most people would've gotten drunk at the bar."

"Since when have I been most people?" I reply,

reaching to mess up his already messy brown hair like I'd seen him do to Piper.

We'd grown close, living in the same city for the last few months, both equally happy to spend time with Sidney.

He laughs. "Just promise to relax for a while. You're getting stress lines."

My hand flies to my forehead, and I glare at him. "Listen, you—"

"Who did you sucker in to watch Crooks?" Sidney asks, wrapping an arm around Jax's back, deflecting nicely.

"Kid down the hall's watching him." Crooks, aka Crookshanks, is my orange tabby cat.

"Did you get an emergency contact number in case he's attacked?" Jax asks, fighting back a grin.

I roll my eyes. "What? She's sixteen. I'm sure she can handle one cat for the weekend."

"That would be true if your cat wasn't possessed," Lucas adds unhelpfully.

"He's not that bad. Stop exaggerating." I look between the three of them for backup, but they're all wearing matching smirks.

"Oh, yes he is." Jax holds up his arm, revealing the thin lines of scars. "Vicious."

"I told you not to pick him up. He doesn't like that."

"Oh, how could I forget. Don't pick him up. Don't touch him. Don't sit in his favorite spot. Don't breathe in his direction." By the time Jax is done, he's full-on laughing.

On second thought, maybe I should send the cat sitter a quick text.

"Okay, okay. Let's check you in." Piper grabs my hand, cutting me off, her smile a little too wide, and there's a suspicious-looking glint in her eyes as I follow her to the front desk.

The attendant welcomes me to the resort, and I tell her my name. She takes a second to search through the computer before her eyes meet mine. "I'm sorry, miss, but I don't have a room under that name."

*Shit.* Piper booked all of this, and I didn't even think to check. She's overloaded with wedding stuff. I should've known better. Piper squeezes my arm as if she senses my unease and says, "Check the villas."

I shoot her a look, saying she's insane. They're like ten thousand a night.

"Ah, there you are. I've got you down for four nights. Is that correct?"

I'm too stunned to speak, so Piper answers the rest of the concierge's questions. The woman slides a yellow bracelet over my wrist before I have time to process anything.

"This will give you access to your room and all other areas of the resort. Enjoy your stay."

The second we're away from the desk, I grab Piper's shoulders. "You can't be serious. It's way too much."

Sidney joins in, wearing the same mischievous look Piper had on earlier. "Relax, it's fine."

They're clearly up to something, but Lucas and Jax grab their girls before I can confront them.

"We'll see you in the morning, 'kay?" Piper calls out as her fiancé tugs her along to their room.

"Can't wait." She booked us a full salon prep day, and I'm seriously looking forward to it.

"Right this way, miss." The bellman latches onto my bag before I can get to it and leads the way through the maze-like paths. It's lit by a soft, warm glow, with a quiet and peaceful ambiance. The music from hidden speakers blends into the background, creating a tranquil atmosphere. Everything seems inviting and charming, providing an escape from everyday life.

A girl could get used to this.

We stop in front of villa number two, and I take a step back as my brain tries to process it. It's a stand-alone building the size of a small cabin, crafted with a mix of wood and steel that just screams money. "This can't be my place."

"I assure you, miss. It is. Just use your wrist pass."

The lock on the door clicks open when I bring my wrist to the small black circle above the handle, and I push it inward.

The bellman steps in first with my bag, and I grimace when he asks me if there's anything else I need.

Swallowing, I face the music. "I'm sorry. I don't have any cash on me."

"No problem, miss. It's all covered." He does an

almost bow-like gesture as he steps away and makes his way back to the lobby.

Well, that's a relief.

The room is large and airy, with the back wall lined with floor-to-ceiling windows that fill the room with moonlight. A large mountain is outlined in the background. The generous bed on one side looks as if it was custom-made, and there's a comfortable sofa beside it. A kitchen and dining area are tucked away in one corner, and a warm fire crackles in the fireplace. All the furniture is modern yet cozy and inviting.

The bed's covered in crisp white linens, and I don't waste a second stripping out of my scrubs. I kick off my Crocs, sliding off each sock before working at the knot holding up my pants. They hit the floor, where I shake them from my ankles, leaving me in just my lilac panties with a cat face on the front and *Tell your cat I said pspspsps* written across the back. I grasp the bottom of my shirt, grateful to finally get it off, when one of the teddy bear pins along the collar snags in my hair. I wiggle it from side to side, but with every move, it tugs my hair more. *Shit.* My arms are stuck above my head in the makeshift straightjacket, and I struggle to escape, only for the edge of the bed to clip the back of my knees, sending me sprawling backward onto it.

"Woah there, Kitten. You haven't even bought me dinner yet," a familiar voice says from a few feet away, sucking the air from my lungs.

I yank the pin out, pulling myself free, only to

realize I'm now in nothing but a thin tank top and panties.

Standing in the bathroom doorway, gaze roaming over every inch of my exposed skin with a cloud of steam billowing around him, is a nearly naked Alex Grayson, star forward for the Boston Bruins.

# CHAPTER 3
# ALEX

MIA GRABS the throw blanket from the bottom of the bed and uses it to hide her lower half and those adorable purple panties with it.

*Fuck.* She looks better than I remember, with her pale blonde hair semi pulled up and loose strands tumbling around her face that leave the tan length of her neck exposed. I should look away, but I don't. *Can't.*

I let my gaze dip lower over the top of her cleavage, exposed by her white tank top, then drag further down, swallowing as I catch on the curves of her hips barely hidden by her makeshift skirt.

It's been three years since I laid eyes on her, and here she is, laid out on my bed like my fucking dessert. If I'm dead, I don't want to be resuscitated because this must be heaven.

Mia's hooded green eyes travel over my bare chest, following the path to where my hand grips the front of my towel wrapped low around my waist.

Her throat shifts with her swallow, and her tongue sneaks out to wet her bottom lip. The action drives all the blood to my rapidly hardening cock. *Fuck*. My dick twitches, and a squeak of a sound escapes her lips as her gaze shoots to mine.

As if finally noticing she's still on the bed, she jumps to her feet, holding the end of her blanket in a death grip, and hisses, "What are you doing here?"

"Shouldn't I be asking you that? This is my room." I lean against the doorframe, a small smile pulling at the corner of my mouth as I loosen my grip and let the towel adjust an inch lower. Mia's eyes darken, focusing on my abs before she shakes her head.

"It can't be. My wrist thingie worked on the door." She holds up her arm, and I mirror her, showing my matching yellow band.

"Looks like we're roomies." I say it straight-faced, but internally, I'm reeling. It was one thing to know she was going to be here for the wedding, but it's a whole other thing to have her in our room. Her free fist opens and closes at her side, and she glances around the space as if looking for signs of an alternative reality. *Oh, Kitten, this is all real.*

She's still shaking her head in disbelief when the door beeps and River steps in. He freezes as he takes in the scene, then lifts one black brow. "Hello, Mia."

Fuck, he practically purrs her name, and she noticeably shivers. It brings back memories of the three of us dancing, her body pressed between us, before everything went to shit and she disappeared off the face of the Earth.

"Hi," she breathes out on reflex, distracted by the sight of him. She takes River in the same way she did me. His black hair is styled off his face, with a few loose strands dropping over his eyes, and he's rolled the sleeves of his crisp white oxford dress shirt to his elbows, revealing thick forearms that steal every ounce of Mia's attention. Even I have to admit he's a sexy fucker.

I clear my throat, drawing both of their focus. The intensity nearly knocks me off-balance, and I have to lean more of my weight against the doorframe. "So, Mia. What are you doing in our room?"

"This is my room." She points at her wrist again, and I smirk.

"I thought we already went over this," I say and hold up my wrist to show off the band.

"There must be a mistake." She taps through her phone, then lifts it to her ear.

I highly doubt it. Sidney and Piper looked entirely too smug when they announced River and I would be bunking together earlier. Pretty sure one of them mentioned the nice size of our bed.

I can't hear the other end of Mia's conversation, but with each second, her brows pull together, forming a line between them that I want to rub away, and she chews her thumbnail.

River steps further into the room, closing the distance between them, crowding her until she looks all the way up, and her mouth drops open slightly.

She thanks the person on the other end, eyes never shifting from his when she ends the call. Fuck, the tension radiates off them as he takes his time practically consuming her with his gaze. *Buddy, I fucking feel you.*

River's always been controlled and silent, but that's shifted over the past few years to a quiet dominance that makes you pay attention. I've caught myself on more than one occasion just waiting for him to say or do something. Just like Mia is now.

"Did they tell you what happened?" River asks, tone casual.

"Who?"

The corner of his mouth lifts. "The concierge. That's who you called, right?"

She slowly moves her head up and down in response. *Fuck, she is gone.* He takes mercy on her and steps back, breaking whatever hypnosis he put her under. A flush crawls up her neck. "They apologize for the inconvenience, but it's how the rooms were booked, and they don't have any others. I'm going to kill Piper."

I laugh, and warmth fills my chest when she glares. I've missed that fire.

"If I find out you had anything to do with this—"

River buries both his hands into his black dress pants pockets and rocks back on his heels. "You know we didn't, Mia."

Her shoulders slump, and for a millisecond, I think I see disappointment flash behind her eyes, and then she sinks back on the bed. "I'll crash at Sidney's."

I choke on a laugh. "Oh, yeah, I'm sure she and Jax won't scar you at all."

Her eyes widen, and my smile grows. "Come on. You're really telling me staying in here is worse than being in their room? You know Jax will totally fuck her while you're there. It's kind of their thing."

Her face scrunches up in disgust, drawing a full laugh from my chest. "Exactly."

"There's only one bed. I'm *not* sleeping with you."

*Sleeping with you* rings in my ears before I shake it out and glance up at River, who nods. "I'll sleep with Riv on the pullout. You can take the bed."

"Really?" She raises a brow. "You're really going to share a bed?"

"Wouldn't be the first time." I shrug, leaving out the fact that I'd been passed out drunk those times and letting her imagine exactly what we could've been doing. I rake my free hand through my wet, dirty-blonde hair. I'm still only in my towel and love how every time she looks at me, she flushes a little more. "Plus, I have the perfect solution. I'll build a pillow barrier to keep him on his own side."

River side-eyes me but doesn't contradict anything I've said. Instead, he opens the minifridge and pulls out three drinks, tossing me a beer before holding out a hard cider to Mia. "Do you still like this kind?"

"Yeah…" Her voice trails off. She seems as off-balance as I feel with this entire situation. The only one of us who appears unaffected is River, but I've known him long enough to know he's just hiding it better.

He nods and twists the cap off before handing it over. I watch her throat expand as she takes three deep pulls from the bottle before speaking. "Just one night, and I'll sort it out in the morning. Okay?"

"Okay," he replies evenly.

Considering she's been avoiding us since university, this feels too easy. Unease sits in my stomach, knowing how quickly she could disappear. She's done it before.

"Alex."

My gaze shoots to River's. "Yeah?"

"Come talk to me outside while Mia settles in," says the man that doesn't talk. But I know what he's doing, giving her a second to get dressed and let it all sink in without two giant-ass hockey players looming over her.

I grab a pair of shorts from my open bag and stand so I'm just barely blocked from her view by a high-back chair. I revel in the sound of her gasp when the terry cloth fabric hits the floor. If she keeps making sounds like that, River will need to tie me to the bed. A warm hum travels low in my gut, but I ignore it.

Once I have my shorts on, I grab my beer and follow Riv out the door, where we both lean our backs against the wood siding.

"I think Piper and Sidney are trying to kill me."

He lets out a long sigh and tips his head back, resting it on the wall.

"You and I both, buddy."

We're silent as the reality of tonight settles in. I'd planned on cornering her somewhere to get her to finally speak to me. Instead, she just walked right in and took my fucking breath away.

"Have things changed for you? Because they haven't for me," I ask and take another long drink of my beer and try not to tense up.

"No." River's tone is final, and I nod as dread settles low in my gut. We're still in the exact same position we were back at university, with us both wanting her and her refusing to come between us. I'd admire her for it if it didn't hurt so fucking bad.

I turn toward him and lower my voice, letting him know how serious I am. "I'm not giving up on this. Not when it's likely my last chance."

He faces me, one brow raised. "Neither am I. Will that be a problem?"

I slam my head back and wince when it connects to the villa behind me. "Considering that's how we lost her the first time? Yeah, that's a problem."

"What if it wasn't?" River faces the sky. "A problem." He seems tense. Maybe even nervous. He doesn't look at me when he says. "What if we share her instead?"

A jolt runs through me, and I freeze, a nervous energy buzzing up my arms and down my back. *Does he mean together? Do I want that?* I clear my throat. "What do you mean? Like having separate days?"

"No, not like separate days." River's deep, rumbled reply commands my attention, and I meet his intense black stare. The air around us grows thick, and suddenly, I crave what he's suggesting. *Fuck.*

We've casually shared girls before, but something tells me that everything would be different with Mia. Every dirty fantasy of Mia pressed between us has my pulse beating in my ears. Even the thought of seeing him fuck her has my cock stiffening, and I have to reach down to pin it under my waistband. The two of them are both so hot they'd be like fire together. "What if she doesn't go for it?"

River's gaze follows the path my hand takes before piercing mine, and he straightens, confidence returning with the set of his shoulders. "What if she does?"

"You serious?" I have to check.

Black eyes pierce mine. "Dead."

"Then we'd better start warming her up to the idea." My smile grows, and I know my dimples are showing when I turn.

All the blood drains from my face when I walk inside, and my breath catches in my chest. River barely covers his groan when he comes up beside me and sees what I do. Mia's standing backlit in the bathroom doorway, blonde hair cascading around her shoulders, in a gold slip nighty that grazes her thighs. The world could end, and I wouldn't notice.

"Bathroom's all yours." She travels to the bed and pulls back the sheet, acting like she's completely unaffected, but the goose bumps running up her neck give her away.

My gaze catches on the skin where her hem rides up while she gets into bed, and I take a step forward, only to have River grab me by the arm and haul me into the bathroom.

I'm totally fucked.

———

She watches River pull the foldout bed from the couch and lifts a brow. "The bed's bigger. I can take the couch."

"Not a chance, Mia," River says, voice firm.

She huffs and faces away on the bed, her covers pulled up over her ears as if she's afraid we'll see a single inch of her. Too late. A slow smile warms my mouth as I picture the little piece of gold fabric she put on for bed. I'm never getting that out of my head.

I strip down to my boxers and grab a few pillows from the sofa, lining them up in the middle of the pullout bed. It's significantly smaller than I thought now that I'm really looking at it. Couldn't be larger than a double on a good day. Hell, the thing may collapse under the weight of two grown-ass NHL players.

"You okay?" River steps up to his side of the bed and raises a brow at my pillow divider. We'd flipped a coin, and the lucky bastard scored the side closest to Mia. Still out of touching distance but no more than a few feet away. Are we a little creepy looking at her? Probably. Am I going to sit here and pretend I haven't been more than a little obsessed with her since senior year of university? Absolutely not.

My brows pull together in confusion. "Yeah, why wouldn't I be?"

He scans me over, and his features relax. "Do you want the sheet or the duvet?"

I bite my tongue against a smile at how this six-foot-four, two-hungry-fifty-pound man says duvet.

"Can't we just share?" I fold the covers back and get in and immediately realize the problem. My hand slides easily to the other side of the bed since my little pillow barrier is above the blanket.

"We can, but something..." River looks at my makeshift wall, and the corner of his lips lifts. "...tells me you're afraid we may accidently touch."

I roll my eyes and toss the pillows to the ground. "Hey, now, I'm just stopping you from cuddling me. You know how I hate that."

Quiet as always, he just shakes his head and snags the sheet, pulling it to his side and tossing the blanket my way. "Keep dreaming."

We both settle under our individual covers before River reaches over and plunges the room into darkness.

Whereas everything felt like a lighthearted joke a moment ago, all my senses feel magnified now. I wasn't kidding before when I said he and I had shared a bed before. But never like this, never stone-cold sober, and I'm hyper aware of the ways it's making me feel. And none of them are bad.

I'm a naturally curious fucking creature, and I've caught River looking at me enough times to catch my attention. Normally I can shake the thoughts, but there's something about feeling him shift a foot beside me that has my pulse kicking up a notch.

Having them both here is so close to every fantasy I've ever had. So fucking close it's almost painful.

Somehow, we've landed ourselves a do-over, and this time, we aren't screwing it up. This time, I don't want her all to myself.

# CHAPTER 4
# MIA

MY BREATH LEAVES me in a whoosh when the villa's front door closes. I've been pretending to sleep from the second I heard the boys wake up, listening to the quiet sounds of them getting ready before they slipped out.

I roll onto my back and press my palms into my burning cheeks. They'd been hot in college, with corded muscles and boyish charm. But that had nothing on them today. Alex still has a playfulness to him, but there's an undercurrent when he looks at me that threatens to take me under. It's like someone took his playfulness and made it sharp.

River's just as quiet as he used to be, but what he lacks in words, he more than makes up for in intensity. When he'd come up to me last night, it was like he sucked the air out of the room and replaced it with thick tension. I've never believed in that alpha male bullshit. Just a way for guys that can't get laid to justify their assholery. But I'll be damned if River's quiet dominance didn't have me freezing in place, eagerly listening for what he'd finally say.

It took hours for me to fall asleep. Each time I closed my eyes, the sound of their breaths filled my mind, and suddenly, the five feet to their bed felt like five inches.

I damn near moaned when I peeked and saw them both in matching black boxer briefs that left nothing to the imagination. They were both huge— my mouth watered, and my fingers begged to pull the fabric down. Even if it was just to see another inch.

Apparently, I'm a total perv because I spent the rest of the night trying to ignore the insistent ache between my thighs. It's still there, begging me to do something about it. I suck in a few breaths, running through rudimentary biology stats, trying to tamp down the lust quickly taking over. I huff out a breath. Biology's definitely the wrong thing to count on to keep my mind off these men.

I rub my thighs together, doing my best to ignore the dampness there. It's clearly been entirely too long since I've gotten laid.

Screw it. I'm an adult. Nothing wrong with taking care of this. I just won't think of the two very sexy, very off-limits guys staying with me.

I reach into the suitcase I'd left open on the nearby bench and pull out a small handheld fuchsia vibrator. *Please be charged.*

It hums in my hand when I press the button, and I swallow hard as I dip under my waistband. I try to imagine my usual, I really do, but my mind freezes on the images of Alex in a towel. But instead of him securing it around his waist, he lets it drop. His hard, veiny cock bobs, and my mouth goes dry.

I whimper as the vibration travels through my clit, bringing me closer to my release. I reach my other hand under my nightdress, hiking it up, and pinch my nipple. My thoughts shift, and it's suddenly replaced by long, thick, callused fingers, and searing black eyes meet mine as River rolls the bud between his fingers. Oh shit. I suck in breaths, so fucking close I'm trembling, barely coherent words tumbling from my lips. "Alex, Riv—"

"Fuck." A low groan comes from the doorway, and my eyes snap open directly into River's. Déjà vu from Alex in the doorway from last night, only *way* freaking worse.

A muscle works in his jaw, a pink flush across his cheeks, and his fist clenches at his side. For a moment of weakness, I want to keep going, but then reality snaps into place. My cheeks stain red, and I jump off the bed, my vibrator crashing to the floor as I flee into the bathroom, locking the door behind me before collapsing against it.

That didn't really happen. *Right?* Please, God. It's the lack of sleep. I'm hallucinating. Oh my God. I didn't say his name? Please. It's official—I'm never coming out of here.

There's a light tap on the door. "It's alright, Mia. I should have knocked. Completely normal. Don't be embarrassed."

His voice is steady with a hint of command, and I feel my heart rate even out. How the hell is he so calm?

I stay completely silent, determined to wipe this entire thing out of my memory and never think of it again.

"I'll see you later," he says before stepping away.

Not if I can help it. The first thing I'm doing is changing rooms, and then I fully plan on hiding from him for the rest of the trip. I don't release my breath until I hear the front door close. Even then, I wait another ten minutes before stepping out and freeze mid-step.

Sitting on my bed is my pretty pink vibrator that River must have picked up.

# CHAPTER 5
## RIVER

I DROP my bag on the floor next to where Alex sets up the barbell. The resort gym's huge, with all the equipment we could need and glass windows lining the entire wall, looking toward the mountain. Images of Mia, head tilted back, cheeks flushed, hand slipped underneath her panties, fucking destroys my concentration.

Never in a million years did I expect to catch her displayed like that. It took every ounce of my willpower to stop from going over there and replacing her hands with my own.

God, the sounds she made. Her gaze flicked up to mine, and for a split second, they darkened. I followed her tongue as it traced her bottom lip. My girl forgot. Forgot all the bullshit she put between us. For the briefest of moments, I saw the girl who used to look at me like I was the only one who could satisfy her. Like I was the only one who owned her.

"Hey, dickhead." Alex snaps his fingers in my

face and gives me a lopsided smile. "Where the fuck did you go?"

I raise a brow and stay silent. We'd been friends since AAA, so it's not like he expects some form of in-depth explanation. I keep to myself, and that's how I like it.

"Where's the speaker?" He sits and lies back on the bench, positioning his hands on the barbell above his chest. His back's arched, feet planted into the floor, and for the second time today, I force myself to look away.

"Forgot it." I step around so that I'm facing his head and hover my hands around the bar. Mia's thrown me off, and I'm struggling to pull myself back in line.

Alex laughs. "What the fuck do you mean *forgot*? That's what you went back for."

"I was distracted." Not a lie.

He eyes me for another few moments before huffing out a breath. "Whatever. I'll settle for your titillating conversation."

I spot him for ten reps before we switch out, and I take his place on the bench. The weights are heavy, but I need the burn in my muscles to keep my head from drifting to a certain blonde. Hair splayed out around her. Teeth digging into her lip…

My elbows buckle, and Alex grabs the bar, helping me safely rack it.

"The fuck is wrong with you today? You never space out." Alex asks with a laugh of shock in his voice.

I look him over. Sandy-blonde hair he'd cut short a few weeks ago and a lopsided grin. You'd never know he's absolutely vicious on the ice. I sit up and watch him as I deliver the news, and his reaction does not disappoint. "I walked in on Mia getting herself off."

He does a double take, mouth dropping open before he slams it shut. "Repeat that. I don't think I heard you right."

I lean forward and catch his pupils widening. "Mia was laid out on the bed, vibrator against her clit, while she pinched her nipple, head back, moaning what sounded like our names."

"Oh, fuck." Alex collapses on the bench beside me and stares at the ground as he processes what I told him. I wouldn't have said a word to anyone else, but the way his breaths are coming out in short, stuttering inhales, I'm glad I did. He tips his head back and blinks at the ceiling fluorescent lights. "She knows you saw her?"

"She does," I answer.

"Fuck me. She must be mortified." His eyes dance back and forth with his thoughts before a slow smile curves his mouth. "And horny."

Not expecting that, I jerk to face him. "How do you figure?"

"You're telling me that you walked in on Mia when she was about to come? There's no way that girl would risk getting caught again." His smile grows. "Which means she's out here aching."

A growl-like sound rumbles through my chest.

Fuck, I like the idea of that. Like her squeezing her thighs together as her pussy drips.

He knocks his shoulder into mine. "So what's the plan?"

My lips curve in the barest hint of a smile. "Now we drive her insane until she begs for us to fix her needy little ache."

# CHAPTER 6
# MIA

"SO, HOW WAS YOUR NIGHT?" Piper asks from beside me on her matching black massage chair, and I groan. I knew it was coming. Honestly, I'm surprised it took her so long.

My cheeks flush bright red, remembering my run-in with River not even an hour ago. I groan, covering my face with my hands. "You know I might kill you, right?"

"You can't blame her. It's really the resort's mistake," Sidney pipes in.

I scoff. "Don't you dare blame it on them. I'm on to you two. Just please tell me you have another room for me."

Piper grimaces. "Well, I would, but I'd be lying."

"You've got to be kidding me." My shoulders slump, and my head falls back against the chair. I turn to glare at Sidney on my opposite side. "What do you think you're doing?"

She fights back a grin. "What? Why do you think we had anything to do with it?"

"That look right there. That's why I think you did this," I say, pointing at them.

"Don't move," Susan, the pedicurist, warns, and I freeze in place. She's holding something that looks like a scalpel against my heel.

"Sorry." She gives me a small smile and goes back to torturing my feet.

I lean forward, looking at Shana for help. I barely knew her in university, but besides the guys, she's one of Piper's best friends. "Are you in on this too?"

"Girl, I really wish I was." She chuckles, resting her head against the chair and closing her eyes. She's wearing her hair in braids that she's rolled into a bun on top of her head.

Piper's hand closes around my forearm. "Don't ignore the question."

"What question?" A petite girl with green hair pulled into space buns smirks at us from the open door. "Sorry I'm late." She hands Piper a large paper cup, and the fresh smell of coffee fills my nose.

Piper removes the lid, blowing on it before taking a sip and humming. "Forgiven."

"Hi, I'm Misty." The girl sits on a stool in front of us, having missed the majority of the pedicure. We still have facials after this.

"She's the PR manager for the Bruins," Piper adds.

"Nice to meet you. Love your hair," I say, and she smiles before Piper starts in on me.

"No changing the subject. Answer the question. How was your night?"

"Fine." My thoughts immediately fly to the sound of Alex's towel hitting the floor as he was barely, and I mean just barely, blocked from view by a chair. He did it on purpose. I'm sure of it. Freaking guy always knew how to get under my skin. My already warm cheeks flame now.

Misty leans forward, eyes sparkling. "Okay, I need deets. Fill me in."

I groan. "Piper has me staying in a villa with Alex and River."

"The Alex and River I met yesterday? Damn," Shana adds with a knowing look.

"I'm sorry. I'm pretty sure anyone would kill to be in your position." Misty smirks. "Actually, do you want to switch rooms?"

The thought of someone else staying with them twists my chest, and I purposely ignore the feeling.

"You look a little red, Mia. Don't like that idea? Maybe feeling a little jealous?" Sidney says, and all four of the girls laugh.

"Not jealous. Just don't want to inconvenience your friend."

"Oh, it wouldn't be an inconvenience." Misty's voice drops low and is tinged with mischief.

Okay. I may be a little jealous. "That's alright. I'm fine."

"I'm sure you are," Piper says.

Desperate to draw their attention off of me, I switch to a topic I know Piper can't resist. "I spoke with Gerard yesterday. He officially gave me a time limit before it's over."

Piper jolts forward in her chair, startling the woman massaging her feet. She gives an apologetic smile before turning to me. "You've got to be kidding me."

"Afraid not." I suck in a breath, the weight of what I'm about to say pressing down on me. "It would take a miracle, and I'm all out of those."

Misty looks between us. "This is the charity Piper's been working on? The prosthetics for kids."

The idea for Prosthetics For Kids came after my first few weeks as an intern in the pediatric unit. There was a young girl in for a checkup after a transtibial amputation, where they amputated her leg below the knee. Even with what happened to her, she was a bouncing ball of sunshine that had the entire staff wrapped around her finger.

I overheard her parents worrying about not being able to afford all of the different prosthetics she'd need while growing up. The sheer injustice of it all hit me like a brick. The only thing the parents should've had to worry about was their daughter. Instead, they had this heavy financial weight hanging over them.

Within a week, I had a fundraiser started, raising money not only for her but other local kids in the same situation. It was a huge success, hitting national news, but it was a blip on what I wanted to do. Once the initial inertia was over, the funding ran out, and the entire thing fell flat.

At that point, I realized I didn't want to only help a few kids; I wanted to provide a solution to the problem as a whole. Which meant I needed money.

I'm not talking about a local fundraiser level either. I'm talking millions of dollars in fundraising to pull this off.

My shoulders slump in defeat, and I sigh. "Soon to be *was* working on."

Misty's brows pull together before smoothing out. "Maybe I can help. Give me a few days to sort through some ideas, but I can probably get the players to pull their weight into getting it rolling."

My chest tightens, and a grin grows across my lips. I'm really starting to like her. "That would be amazing."

"You know what else relieves stress?" She waggles her brows.

"I've got it covered, don't worry." I remember River's hooded gaze traveling down my chest to where my hand was tucked under my waistband and the loud vibrator filled the room. Dammit, I thought I was totally going to die from embarrassment.

"Come on. All work and no play keeps the orgasms away," Misty says, and even I can't stop myself from joining in on their laughter.

I have my share of toys, always finding it easier to guarantee I climaxed rather than count on a man. "Seriously, I've got it. Plus, I don't do randoms."

Piper smirks. "Who said anything about randoms? You're single, and you have two totally hot men literally in your room. You've got to at least sample one of them. It's not like it has to be forever."

My thighs press together, my panties growing wet as her words bring up memories of Alex and River in their boxers, climbing into the bed beside mine. I want to. God knows I do. The problem is I'm not sure I can do just a weekend with either of them. "Maybe."

Sidney whoops, a huge grin taking over her face. "I'll take that."

I huff out a breath, refusing to look at her, and focus on Piper. "I can't believe you're getting married in two days."

Sidney snorts. "I can't believe it took this long."

Piper rolls her eyes. "You're one to talk."

Sidney's mouth snaps shut, and a pretty pink flush covers her cheeks.

Misty and Shana both laugh at that.

"I honestly can't wait." Piper's gaze softens, and I reach over, giving her arm a quick squeeze.

The girls keep talking, but my thoughts drift to River and Alex. For once in my life, I want to be selfish. To take what I want for a change.

And there's no hiding that I want them both. Now I need to see if they're down for that. Judging by the way River punched Alex back in university, I'm guessing my chances are slim. That's not the risk though. The risk is how much it'll hurt to get on that plane and never look back when the weekend's over. Not when the last time nearly killed me.

They're my almost. Almost kiss, almost touch, almost something. Just almost.

When I'm looking for always.

# CHAPTER 7
## ALEX

FUCK ME. I wish I'd been the one to go back for that speaker. I still have a semi just from River describing Mia playing with herself. I know he loves that she's into toys just as much as I do. Falling asleep to the sound of her breathing was something else. It's more than being horny—there's an overall comfort I don't dare to name. I knew I was gone for her in university, but after three years, I didn't expect just being near her to have me so fucking undone. Because that's exactly what I am. A walking fucking disaster of hormones and emotions, bubbling to the surface. I'm not sure I'm going to survive this weekend if I can't get her in my arms. I'm also not sure I can get her under me and let her go. Again.

The first time had been like a knife to the gut, and I had no choice in it. This time, I know exactly what I'm walking into, and I can't fucking stop myself.

I walk around the path between the resort buildings and spot where the crew is set up. Jax, Sidney, Lucas, and Piper have already staked out a large area by the pool. They have their own gazebo and sitting area, no doubt costing a fortune. Even in a high-end resort, I've seen people snap photos of us. Hockey players aren't as famous in the States, but that doesn't mean people don't notice.

I approach them from behind, a cold beer already in hand, and pause just in time to hear their conversation.

"She's staying. Finally gave up finding another room." Sidney's voice travels to me easily from where she sits on a wide seat meant for one, curled up into Jax's side with her legs over his.

"Who's staying, Trouble?" Jax hands her a cool drink, and she rests her back against his chest, leaning her head onto his shoulder and settling into him before smiling at Piper across from her.

"Mia's staying in the villa. She's finally given up harassing the front desk to find another room."

"You mean the villa with River and Alex?" Jax laughs. "I should've known that it was the two of you."

Lucas tips Piper's chin up. "What did you two do?"

"I mean. I didn't do anything. The resort must have messed up with their rooms. I definitely didn't accidentally on purpose put them all in the same villa." She can't contain her grin, and neither can Sidney.

He holds his soon-to-be wife's jaw in his hands and arches a brow at her before a smile of his own cracks across his face. "How much did that cost me."

She shrugs. "Enough."

You'd think that would piss Lucas off, but if anything, his expression turns soft, like he's impressed with her.

"Just hope that it doesn't come back and bite you in the ass. There's history there," Jax adds while wrapping a strand of Sidney's hair around his finger before letting it go, only to do it again.

"Oh, come on. There's *almost* history there." Piper scoffs. "Those three are in desperate need of an intervention."

"By forcing them to stay together?" Lucas asks.

Piper blinks her blue eyes at him, and all of his focus is on her. Her voice is soft when she says, "You mean conspire to have your two best friends bang our bestie, preferably at the same time?"

He groans and drops his forehead to hers. "You said that entirely too innocently."

She shrugs. "Someone had to do it." She holds up her glass to Sidney, and they cheers. From what Jax has told me, while Piper and Mia were friendly senior year, they didn't get close until they started working together on the Prosthetics For Kids charity.

"All I know for sure is they were inseparable one night, then Alex showed up with a black eye the next day. Mia admitted to me that she fell for them both and refused to make them choose."

My breath catches in my chest as Sidney's words slam into me. Of course, I knew there was something special between Mia, River, and me, but hearing her confirm Mia's feelings is like a fucking blow to the chest. I'm not sure if it's excitement or devastation of the lost opportunity.

Sidney continues. "So she cut all ties and never spoke to them after that."

"There's only the one bed and the pullout couch. Who do you think's on the couch?" Piper asks curiously.

Lucas cut in. "I'd bet all my money it's Mia in the bed and River and Alex on the pullout."

"Is there something between them?" Sidney asks.

Even though we're all closer now, she doesn't know us the way Jax, Lucas, and Piper do.

"If you mean a fuckload of pent-up tension, then yes. If you mean has it gone any further than that, no. River's bi, but if Alex is, he's never done anything about it," replies Lucas.

I'm not ready to examine whatever's going on between River and me, but something is going on. I can't lie to myself and pretend I haven't noticed the slow build of something I haven't named yet building between us. Not that I plan to act on it.

I clear my throat, announcing my presence. The group jolts, and they at least have the decency to look embarrassed for being caught gossiping about us.

I take a seat between both couples, polish off the rest of my drink, and accept another from Jax.

"You ready for us to kick your ass next year?" Jax asks, a fucking smirk on his face. The fucker is one of the most competitive people I know. It's a miracle he found someone so perfectly matched in Sidney.

"You talk a lot of shit for someone who plays for a team who hasn't won the cup for a century," Lucas replies, and I laugh, some of the tension loosening from my shoulders.

"Yeah, but now they have me." I can practically hear Jax's grin.

Lucas rubs his hand down his face. "Cocky bastard."

I snorted, fucking loving all of this. There's a comfortableness when I'm with them. Something I hadn't felt before...before meeting River. Where the hell is he?

Jax relaxes into his chair, bringing Sidney back with him. "Okay, dickwad."

Piper busts out laughing. It was her favorite insult since they were kids, and Lucas hated it.

"Oh, you think that's funny, Killer." Lucas drops his face into the crook of Piper's neck and snarls. Her mouth snaps closed, and her hands tighten on his thighs.

Lucas carries on like he isn't groping his girl in public.

"You guys are gross."

Jax chokes on a laugh. "Just wait. This will be you soon."

A thrill shoots down my spine as my mind

conjures an image of Mia sprawled over me while we all hang out together. I shake my head. "Don't get ahead of yourself."

All four of them look at me like they know more than I do. Like, they're just waiting for my dumb ass to catch up.

River saves me from responding by dropping down in the free spot across from me.

"What are you talking about?" he asks. He's always been less quiet with us than with anyone else.

"Nothing," I force out, trying to be casual, but the way his right brow raises, I know I failed miserably.

"Okay." He tilts his head, drawing out the word. We've known each other since we were thirteen, playing for the same AAA team, and he's always been able to read me like a book. Back then, he was the only one to notice my family didn't come to my games.

Now that I think of it, it's probably when we started to treat each other more like family than friends. River's parents weren't around either. He didn't live with them, and they didn't bother making the few-hour drive to watch him play.

My phone buzzes, and I roll my eyes at the article my mom sent. Some new achievement my brother's done. It's not that I'm not proud of him, because I am. We might not be close, but that doesn't mean I don't respect the shit out of what he's done for the scientific research community.

No, what fucking stings is the only thing that's

ever impressed my parents is being intellectual, and I've always been just a jock to them. Fuck. Making the NHL barely deserved a call from them.

River watches me, and the muscle in his jaw ticks. I can tell he wants to ask, but he won't. He knows not to push it. That I'd rather pretend my parents weren't dicks than admit it bothers me.

"Heads up." River tosses me a new beer, and I catch it easily. He searches my face, and I give him a faint nod, letting him know I'm fine.

The group's silent, heads bouncing back between River and me like they're trying to decipher our silent conversation.

I plaster on a smile and tell a joke to divert the conversation like I always do. Being the funny one is just as much of a defense mechanism as it is a part of my personality. "Pips, I can't believe you're marrying this asshole. It's still not too late to run away with me."

"Say it again, I dare you." Lucas growls, pulling a laugh from me. I love fucking with him.

I ignore River's hot stare, tired of him reading my mind, and stand, pulling my shirt over my head with one hand. "It's too fucking hot. I'm jumping in."

I don't wait for anyone else before executing a perfect dive into the crisp liquid, letting it cool my heated skin. I stay down until my lungs burn and I have to fight against the need to take a breath before swimming to the shallow side and surfacing. The water hits just below my waist, and the warm sun already heats my exposed skin. I shake out my hair, then rake my fingers through it, pushing it off my face. River's sitting shirtless on the edge, feet dangling in the water, watching me.

Heat floods me, and I swallow hard, wondering if he can read all of my secrets.

# CHAPTER 8
## MIA

A FEW HOURS LATER, I tighten my deep green sarong around my upper waist and catalog my features in the mirror. What seems like permanent purple bruises underline my green eyes, and my string bikini cuts into the skin around my back. I survived the past few years with a single-minded focus, and the wear is starting to show on my face.

Where I softened over the years, Alex and River became defined. All chiseled jaws and rippling abs. Heat floods my lower stomach. It should be a crime to be that hot.

My fingers twitch to grab the cover-up I laid on the bed. The urge to hide is more than I want to admit.

My phone buzzes, and I grab it from the table. A text from an unknown number flashes on the screen.

**Unknown: Where are you?**

**Unknown: Answer me.**

I swipe to clear it. It doesn't take a genius to know

they're from Jason. His messages have become more desperate by the day. I never respond, hoping one day he'll get the hint.

I tuck my phone in my beach bag and rake my hands through my hair, clip it in place, then leave the villa, heading toward the pool.

Heat envelops me the second I step outside, and the loose strands of my hair stick to my neck. The temperature's going to be close to one hundred the entire time we're here, and I'm pretty sure my Canadian ass is going to melt. It's hot in Ottawa, a sticky humidity that makes you feel like you need a shower the second you leave the house, but it has nothing on the baking heat here.

Nerves dance under my skin as I replay Piper and Sidney's words the closer I get. That I could just enjoy myself. That it doesn't need to be serious. She pretty much told me to have sex with one of her best friends. I can't deny I could use the release though, and both River and Alex look like they know what they're doing. No, I know they'd know.

Am I asking for trouble? Absolutely.

Alex and River are the last people I should be thinking about, but I can't ignore the tension that's always wound around us, pulling me in until I don't want to get out.

There's history there I can't deny, especially since I'm the one who ended it. We started off as friends— sure, we got along a little too well, a little too close to be completely innocent. I knew then I was in over my head, but I couldn't help but fall headfirst.

Alex and River have been best friends for years, and I just snuck in and nearly detonated their relationship. It wasn't their fault I'd messed up and fallen for both of them.

I round the corner and immediately spot River. He's thirty feet away, standing next to Lucas, his dark hair wet and slicked back off his face, and he's wearing the barest hint of a smile. I freaking miss that smile. So rare that whenever he did, it turned me into a walking pile of goo. His deep black gaze flicks up to mine, and his smile grows.

I take a step backward, suddenly overcome with the need to flee. Who the hell am I kidding? I turn to head back to my room, where I can at least get some work done, and come face-to-face with a smiling Piper.

"Where do you think you're going?"

"I forgot I've got something I need to take care of." Not technically a lie.

She raises a brow and places her hands on her hips. She's wearing a similar outfit to mine, only hers is sky blue. "I'm not going to call you out for running away—I'm a bigger person than that—but what I will do is remind you that this is my wedding weekend, and you have no choice but to hang out with me."

"Aren't bride privileges exclusive to the day of the wedding?" I turn back to the gazebo, already knowing the answer, and she hooks her arm into mine, hauling me to a stop.

"Tell me what's really bothering you. Are you

scared about losing funding? Because if that's why you're turning back, I'll go to the villa with you, and we can dive in. But...if you're bailing because two gorgeous guys are eyeing you like dinner, you're coming with me, even if I have to drag you."

"They haven't actually shown interest in me."

Piper snorts and looks me up and down. "Something tells me you'll be fine."

"I'll have a drink, but I'm not interested in a fling with Alex and River." For all I know, they're still pissed about how things ended between us.

"Uh-huh. Let's go." Her tone lets me know she thinks I'm delusional. She tugs me along toward where Lucas is already watching her.

My gaze catches on Alex. He's pulling himself out of the pool, rivulets sliding down his tan skin and fluorescent green shorts hanging low on his hips. He raises a brow when I approach and runs his hand through his blonde hair, darkened by the water.

"Like what you see?" Alex asks playfully.

I shrug, hoping I look casual when internally, I'm anything but. "You're alright, nothing special."

Alex barks out a laugh and gives me a cocky smile that sends shivers up my spine. Even now, these boys hold entirely too much power over me.

"Glad you finally came out of hiding." He nods, eyes bright. He's always been larger than life.

I stiffen. "I'm not hiding."

He huffs out a breath. "We're sharing a room, and I haven't even seen you today. You're totally hiding."

"Don't remind me." I nearly lost my mind when

the concierge informed me that the entire resort's completely booked. The idea of spending the weekend with Alex and River both terrifies me and sends heat coursing through my body.

He wraps an arm around my shoulder and tugs me in for a relaxed hug. "Don't be like that. We're friends."

My chest tightens. "Are we?"

"We were once. Nothing stopping us from being friends again besides you." The playfulness drops from his face, and he tilts his head closer to mine. Serious Alex has always taken my breath away.

My cheeks heat, and I can't deny I missed them.

"Okay. Friends." My voice is almost a squeak.

"Maybe more," he adds, not bothering to hide the heat in his eyes before he jumps back in the pool, splashing me with water.

I'm too stunned to say anything and jump when Jax comes up beside me. "Hey, you look like you could use this."

He hands me a plastic cup with some kind of fruity drink, and I scrunch my nose before nearly draining it. I may not love sweet drinks, but at this point, I'd do anything to cool myself down. I wipe my hand over my mouth. "Thanks."

Jax grins at me, and I roll my eyes.

"What?"

"Not a thing," he replies, and I don't believe him for a second.

The girls all sit on loungers, soaking up the sun

while chatting idly. Sidney sits up. "Finally! Five more minutes and I was sending a search party."

"I'm not even late."

Misty looks between us. "Well. You're a little late."

Did I take longer than normal to choose my outfit? Yes. Am I going to tell them that? Not a chance.

"What is it, pick on Mia day?" I huff, dropping onto a lounger, and rest my head back.

Sidney's brow raises. "You're just too fun to rile up. Plus, you're supposed to be relaxing this weekend. Loosen up a bit."

"I'm loose."

She huffs, calling me on my bullshit. "You look like you're going to bolt back to your room at any second."

I force my shoulders to relax. "I just have a lot on the go."

Sidney turns serious. "Trust me. I know. You've been killing it. But you're working yourself too hard. I just don't want you to burn out. Take the weekend off. Enjoy Napa. Then I'll completely support you going back to your neurotic self. Deal?"

"Fine. Okay. You're right," I give in.

"What's that? Say it again."

"I said you're right. Now I need a drink."

The girls all whoop, but I'm distracted by a cup of amber liquid being passed over my shoulder. I look back, and a pair of near pitch-black eyes settle on mine.

River wets his bottom lip. "Grabbed this for you."

Holy shit. The way he's looking at me has my toes curling, and I have to restrain myself from twisting in my chair to get a better look at his naked chest. I wrap my hands around the cup, enjoying the cool sides against my heated skin. "Thank you."

Jax calls to him from where the guys gather, and River nods at him before looking back to me. "I'll talk to you later."

His voice is low and gravelly and sounds more like a promise than a statement, sending sparks dancing along my skin. I take a sip of my drink, hoping it'll cool me down, only to realize he'd grabbed me another cider. My cheeks flush, and I drain the cup without thinking.

"You should see your face," Shana says from where she drops into the seat next to me.

"Right!" Piper joins in. "Like, I'm going to need a fan over here. That was hot."

I glance over to where Alex and River now stand, and I can feel my cheeks warm. Sidney squeezes my arm. "Relax, see where things go."

Relax…ha. Does she even know me? I haven't relaxed in years. "I'll try."

She grins. "You better."

We spend the next several hours soaking up the sun before shifting to mingling around a few tables once the sun settles, taking the scorching heat with it. After a few more drinks that seem to magically appear, I'm feeling pleasantly buzzed and sway on my feet to the music.

I watch where Sidney stands tucked into Jax's side, and Piper leans her head back against Lucas's chest as they chat in a group. I'm so happy for them, but a teensy part of me feels empty that I don't have that same easiness in my life. They're all so sure of each other. Like it's fate that they met.

Goosebumps freckle my skin when the breeze picks up, and I rub my palms over my arms. Large hands cover mine before wrapping around me, and a chin settles on the top of my head. Alex's chest rumbles against my back. "You look cold."

If I was cold a second ago, I'm not now. I should pull away, but I let the steady buzz from the alcohol mix with his calming scent and rest my weight into him. A quiet voice at the back of my head tells me I wouldn't be doing this if I were sober, but the tipsy part of me doesn't care.

I've missed the way Alex's arms feel around me, and for once, I don't question it.

Jax walks up to us. "So, did you confirm your cat sitter's still alive?" He smirks. "Do we need to start calling hospitals to find the missing body?"

"I called. She's fine. He's not going to bite the hand that feeds him."

"Somehow, I seriously doubt that," Jax responds.

Jax and Alex carry on a conversation that I can't even begin to process as Alex's heat soaks into my spine. He's treating this like it's absolutely normal to hold me instead of the complete opposite. I don't bother fighting it. Instead, I take another drink.

I'll worry tomorrow.

My gaze travels, looking for River, only to find him already looking at me from where he's speaking with Lucas and Piper. Even from fifteen feet away, I can see his eyes are hooded, and the muscle in his jaw clenches. He doesn't look away, and the weight of it has me leaning harder into Alex. His arms tighten around my stomach, and he dips his head into the crook of my neck, sending shivers through me. He chuckles low, the sensation vibrating against my back. "You like him watching you, don't you, Kitten?"

I bite my lip, relaxing further into him.

"I'm going to go find Sid." Jax's low voice cuts in, and my gaze flies up to where he is smirking at us.

If I wasn't so buzzed, I'd definitely be embarrassed.

"You do that," Alex replies playfully, not bothering to deny the tension happening.

Jax has barely left before River moves. His steps are slow and calculated as he practically stalks this way.

"Relax." Alex nuzzles my neck, speaking directly into my ear. His hands splay until they cover me from ribs to waist, and the feel of his rough calluses against my bare skin has heat flooding my core. His grip tightens, pulling a low moan from my lips, and he stiffens behind me before pulling me back against him so I can feel his hard cock against my ass.

By the time River joins us, my thoughts are barely coherent. I tilt my head back as he looms in front of us, so close his chest grazes my arms I'd subconsciously wrapped around Alex's. A voice screams in the back of my head that this is exactly what tore us apart the last time. But even in my tipsy state, I can tell something's changed. Neither guy seems to mind the other's presence.

Oh my God. Are they on the same page?

Dark eyes meet mine, sucking me under, and I reach out, wrapping my hand around River's neck, no longer in control of my body.

"Mia, if you keep looking at me like that, I'm going to strip off that pretty little bikini and take you right fucking here." River sounds serious, and suddenly, I don't care about anything besides having him inside me.

Both of them.

"Promise?" Any attempt to be seductive is ruined by my hiccup.

River searches my eyes, which are already going fuzzy as the full force of the alcohol I've consumed hits me. He cups my cheek in one hand, lifting my jaw upward as he drops his mouth so close it grazes mine. "Ask us again tomorrow, and we're yours."

# CHAPTER 9
# MIA

A QUICK GLANCE at the clock tells me it's 1:00 a.m., and I'm still nowhere close to falling asleep. Not when the sound of their breaths draws all my attention. Their sofa-bed is a mere five feet from mine, and it's taking actual willpower not to crawl between them. I was kidding myself thinking I stood a chance sleeping in the same room. Not when the moon slips through the window and illuminates the hard contours of River's arms and chest. He's shirtless, because of course he is, and I can't stop my gaze from traveling down the smooth path of his abs to where the sheet loosely covers his hips. I feel like a voyeur staring at him while he sleeps, but I can't for the life of me force myself to turn. My buzz is long gone, leaving me with nothing but an incessant ache between my thighs.

I can just make out Alex's arm and shoulder blade where he's hidden from view. He shifts in his sleep, revealing more of his muscular back, and I swallow hard, ignoring the heat pooling in between my thighs. Why did they have to be so respectful?

River's face is soft with sleep. His long black lashes fan out on his cheeks, and his full lips are parted slightly. My breath hitches when sharp black eyes meet mine. I struggle to take in a breath as his gaze slides down my face, over my collarbones, pausing on the outline of my nipples visible through the thin satin fabric of my nighty.

He holds my gaze for several seconds, drawing every molecule of my attention until my skin warms and my heart skips erratically in my chest. Damn, I want to touch him, want to feel his strong fingers trail down my skin. I want to taste the indentation of his muscles, following a path down his abs to where I know a trickle of hair leads under his sheet. Curiosity is killing me. River's huge, tall, big hands, big feet... does that mean he's like that everywhere? My chest flushes, and my breath stutters with the thought.

It shouldn't be possible in the dim light, but I swear he's reading my mind, and he proves it when he runs a hand through his coal-black hair and rolls onto his back, letting me see where his hard cock tents the sheet. Warmth pools between my thighs, and I rub them together to lessen the ache.

River stokes a building fire within me as his hand travels down his chest underneath the fabric and grips himself. His head presses back into his pillow, and a low groan rumbles in his throat.

There's something indecent about this entire scene. Two men so close to me, driving me insane without a single word. Suddenly, I want Alex to turn, to witness what we're doing. River's abs ripple as he strokes his cock faster, shifting the sheet further down. A whimper escapes my mouth when it stops just before I can see him.

Alex groans and lifts onto his elbow. His sandy-blonde hair's wild from sleep, and his eyes widen as he takes in the scene. My breath freezes in my chest as I watch what he'll do. There's a good chance he'll freak out, but the tight coil in my stomach's begging him not to.

His gaze darts between me and where River's stroking himself, and a hint of a blush washes his cheeks. He visibly tenses before his eyes turn dark, and his tongue darts out to wet his bottom lip.

I have to fight back a moan when two sets of hooded eyes bore into mine, sending shivers down my arms and back.

The things I would do to watch them. For a few beats, I let myself bask in the heavy silence between us, tension pulling the air tight. Dammit, I want to say fuck it all and slide my hand between my legs as their gazes eat up every second of my release.

I trail my fingers down my collarbone and over the peak of my breast. Both boys don't bother hiding their groans. A tremble rolls through me. I've wanted this, dreamed of this for so long, but...

I want to scream when my senses come back to me and the cold reality of what we're doing snaps into place. I take a deep breath, close my eyes, trying to soften the erratic pounding in my chest, and self-preservation has me turning away.

My core aches, and my skin burns to be touched, begging me to turn back, but I fight against it. My ears are focused in on the rustling behind me, and for a brief second, I think one of them will force the issue.

"Good night, Mia."

A flash of disappointment tightens my ribs when River gets up and heads to the bathroom. He doesn't bother to close the door, and I inhale sharply when the sound of water crashing over him fills the room. After what I just saw, there's no doubt what he's about to do. I lie there, breaths shallow as I strain my ears to hear. There are several moments of near silence before the telltale smack of rhythmic skin on skin reaches me. I freeze, heart pounding in my ears as I listen.

I should pull the pillow over my head to give him some privacy. I should get up and leave. I should do a lot of things, but I stay still, unable to move. His grunt reaches me, and it takes a direct route to my clit. My skin's hot, and my lungs burn.

The mattress beside mine squeaks, and I roll over, my gaze immediately landing on Alex's. It's dark, the only light coming from the open door, but I can make out his eyes. They're blown wide, and his mouth is dropped open. We watch each other as we're both voyeurs to our friend jerking off.

There's another groan from the bathroom, the rhythm increasing, and Alex bites his lip, his gaze never leaving mine. His chest is bare to me, and my mouth waters as I take him in, his muscles twitching under my stare. The several feet between us feel like inches, like I could reach out and place my hand over his beating heart.

More noise comes from the shower, and Alex's hand digs into the sheet, his tendons flexing as he grips it between his fingers. The fabric shifts below his hips, and I can make out the contour of his stiff cock. *Jesus.* He's just as affected as I am. My body overheats, like they've lit a flame inside me that only they can put out. Alex's chest rises and falls at the same frantic pace as mine, anticipation burying in my stomach.

My pulse is erratic, my thighs slick, and my mind is lost as River's growl breaks through, pulling a moan from my lips.

A slow, sensual smirk pulls the corner of Alex's lips as he takes in my undone state. He leans in closer, voice barely over a whisper. "That was all for you."

Fuck. There's no way I'm surviving this.

The shower turns off, and I roll onto my back, eyes blank on the ceiling. Holy shit. What the hell just happened?

The bathroom light flicks off, and I pull the blanket up to my ears, the fabric uncomfortable over my sweat-slicked body. River's footsteps grow closer. His presence looms over me, and I have to clench my muscles to fight the urge to reach for him. I steady my breath in hopes of convincing him I'm asleep until he climbs into his bed, and the room goes silent.

I groan internally, knowing it'll be impossible to sleep. *Tomorrow, I'll get my own room.* I ignore the pinch in my chest, betraying the fact that it's not what I want at all. But I learned years ago we don't always get what we want.

# CHAPTER 10
## ALEX

SOFT SNORES ESCAPE Mia with each of her breaths, and her face is buried in her pillow, a small damp spot of drool underneath it. She's fucking beautiful.

I brush a strand of her hair behind her ear, smirking at the way she turns into the touch. I'd missed my little hellcat more than I'd ever admit. She stirs, her green eyes slitting open, and a warm smile pulls the corner of her lips. She looks so genuinely happy to see me that my heart aches the second she wakes fully and pulls away.

I clench my teeth and focus on the lamp beside the bed like I give a single shit about it at all. "Morning."

"What time is it?" She groans and throws her arm over her face, like an adorable vampire allergic to the light. Her hangover must be kicking in pretty hard. The sun's barely lightened the sky, but River opened the curtains that line the entire wall of our room before heading out.

"Early. Here, take these." I hold out two ibuprofen and a large glass of water. She sits up dutifully, taking the meds and gulping down water. I fight to keep my attention on her face, knowing damn well she's wearing her sexy little sleep dress. That thing is going to kill me.

"Why?" She closes her eyes for a second before they narrow on me. A thrill tingles down my spine. She's so fucking sexy riled up.

Determined to crawl a little further under her skin, I say, "Why what, Kitten?"

"Why did you wake me up before sunrise?" she hisses, proving her nickname.

I bite my smile, but I'm unable to contain it. "We've got a surprise for you."

That has her perking up. "What kind of surprise?"

"Nuh-uh. You're just going to have to see for yourself." I take the glass from her and do my best to tamp down my reaction when her fingers brush mine. This girl has no idea how much she fucking owns me. "Dress warm."

Her brows pull together, no doubt wondering why in hell she would have to dress warm in a place that's over a hundred degrees, but Napa's chilly in the morning. Especially where we're going.

She goes to speak, but I cut in. "You know, you used to trust me. It'll be fun."

Her gaze softens, and she takes a deep breath, her

hand rubbing at her chest. "I still trust you. Just give me a few minutes."

I ignore the way her words make my heart stutter and clear my throat. "I'll be outside. Don't take too long. We don't want to miss it," I say over my shoulder as I leave.

River's already waiting outside when I walk out. "She up?"

I take the to-go cup he hands me and breathe in the welcoming scent of coffee. "Yeah. Hopefully the pain meds kick in before we get there."

"She'll be fine. She was fairly sober by the time we passed out." River's dark eyes meet mine, and I swallow hard at the memories of last night. I adjust my sweats. I'm not attracted to men, but I can't deny I felt something last night. And if I'm being completely honest, it wasn't the first time. There's something about River that has my blood heating and my curiosity piquing. He's the closest friend I have, but I've never felt like we are brothers. Somehow, it's always been more than that. Deeper.

The door opens behind us, drawing our attention, and Mia walks out. My gaze travels up from her Adidas sneakers, over her leggings that hug her thighs, and lands on a thin white T-shirt. Yeah, that's not going to cut it. "I thought I asked you to dress warm."

She rolls her eyes. "Well, I didn't exactly pack my parka."

"Good morning, Mia." River nods, his gaze hot on her, and she takes in a shuddering breath. Fuck, he's got an effect on her. I'm looking forward to how that plays out.

She clears her throat. "Morning."

I hand River my coffee and pull my black hoodie over my head. I smile when it clears my face and I notice her staring at my abs exposed by my hiked-up shirt. A slow, cocky grin forms on my mouth. "There you go staring at me again."

"What. No—" A pretty pink flush floods her cheeks, and her eyes snap to mine. I laugh and tug the hoodie over her head before helping her pull her arms through.

"It's okay. I like it." I say, and lean over and kiss her forehead like I used to. She stiffens, but I just continue on like I didn't just overstep. River heads back into the room while I roll up her right sleeve until it's above her wrist and proceed to do the same on the other. She's frozen in place, brows pinched as she watches me. It's the way her eyes darken that gives me the confidence to continue.

I step back, and my mouth waters at the sight of my hoodie engulfing her.

Mia's gaze darts between me and River exiting the room, door closing quietly behind him. "So, you going to tell me where we're going?"

"Where's the fun in that?" River's voice is low and gravelly from sleep, and I smirk when her breath catches. After last night, I can practically feel the energy. There are so many things left unfinished between us. He tosses me another hoodie and I pull it over my head.

Entwining my fingers through Mia's I gesture to the parking lot. "Come on, the car's waiting."

She only freezes for a second before curiosity gets the best of her, and she follows me toward the front of the resort. River's trailing behind us, and I fucking love knowing my hoodie covers her perfect round ass.

There's a black Mercedes sedan already waiting for us, and I wave at our driver. "Andre, sorry to get you up so early today. Hope Mrs. Samson wasn't too put out."

Andre laughs and shakes his head. "This wouldn't be the first early morning bal—"

"I'll stop you right there." I gesture my head toward Mia. "We're keeping it a surprise."

Andre's eyes widen, and he smiles at her. "Lucky you."

"No hints?" Mia smirks at him.

"This will be worth the wait," Andre replies with no idea how right he is.

I open the door for her with a little bow. "After you."

She huffs out a laugh. "You're lucky I'm still half-asleep so I can't come up with anything to tease you with."

She gets in, and I grab the roof of the car, ducking down and leaning in close. "I can fucking assure you, you tease me just fine."

I walk around the car, ignoring her gasp, and get in on the other side. The seats are large and lined with a supple camel leather. She looks at me with round eyes. "I'm not a tease."

I raise a brow. "You're a little bit of a tease. It's cute."

River lowers himself into the back, pushing Mia toward the middle.

She scooches over but looks at him incredulously. "Aren't you going to get into the front?"

"No." There's that gravelly voice again. Goose bumps spread up Mia's neck when River's side presses against hers. We're definitely too big to all fit back here, and her entire left side presses against mine. She's still, mouth open, frozen. He reaches over her, pulls her seat belt, and clicks it in.

"Safety first." His mouth is so close to hers even I swallow.

*Fuck.* This is either going to be the best trip of my entire life, or my balls are going to fall off with how turned on I am.

Mia holds her coffee with both hands, tucking her elbows in while taking a hesitant sip. Once she determines it's not scalding, she tips it up. My gaze lingers on the way her throat moves with each swallow.

River huffs, and my eyes meet his. He just shakes his head, the tiniest hint of a smile curving his lips.

Playboy all-star NHL player or simp who gets turned on by his soon-to-be girl drinking a coffee?

Mia keeps her gaze straight ahead through the window, no doubt trying to look unaffected sitting between us. But by the way the heat from her thigh is burning into mine, I call total and utter bullshit.

Normally, I'd be respectful and never press this hard hitting on a girl. Actually, I normally give zero shits and just let them chase me. But Mia gets into her own head. She's amazing, caring, and selfless. She's a good fucking person, which is more than most people can say. But those qualities make her her own worst enemy.

I know why she left us, and it had nothing to do with not wanting us. After River punched me, she pulled away. Coming between us is just something she'd never do. She'd rather be miserable than ruin River's and my friendship. Unfortunately, she didn't calculate that we'd be fucking miserable too.

I'll admit, River and I were out for ourselves back then. There wasn't even a hint of what we want now. She left because we tried to make her choose. That is never happening again. She deserves everything she wants without having to choose, and I'm going to show her just how good it can be.

River wraps his hand around her knee, and his thumb and fingers span from one inside edge to the other. The car stops, but she's not paying attention. All of her focus is on where he touches her, and she sucks in a breath when he tightens his grip.

I lean in close, taking advantage of her distraction, and whisper in her ear. "He's distracting isn't he, Kitten."

Goosebumps explode down her neck, and her gaze snaps to mine, mouth slightly open. I could kiss her right here. Dig my hands into her hair and capture that perfect little mouth of hers. River would hold her in place for me as I worked down her body. From the way she's looking at me, I'm pretty sure she's thinking the same damn thing. I smirk and get out of the car, and her disappointed sound follows me out. Driving her crazy's half the fun.

River gets out and helps her with an extended hand. She's glaring at me the entire time, but then her eyes widen, and she sucks in a little gasp as she takes in the sight behind me.

There's a crowd of people standing in a large open field, all looking at the same thing. A large tarp-like fabric is laid out on the ground in a rainbow of colors, attached with strings to at least ten different large wicker baskets.

"We're going hot-air ballooning?" She looks between River and me with an almost innocent excitement.

I tug her into my side, unable to resist touching her. She doesn't pull away, instead leaning a little closer. "Surprise, Kitten."

# CHAPTER 11
# MIA

"MIA, right? Do you want to help get it started?" David, our instructor, is holding the far end of the empty blue-and-white-striped balloon for me to take. He's just gone through thirty minutes of safety instruction, which boils down to: Stay away from the edge, and don't touch the fire. "We're going to start filling it with cold air first, then add the heat to lift it up. I need you to hold it above your head so it expands properly."

David's young, early thirties tops, and has a lean physique you'd see most swimmers have. But he has one of those smiles that says, "I know I'm hot," which is a total turnoff. *Well, unless it's Alex. Why is it so hot on him?*

I glance back at the guys. River and Alex stand next to each other fifteen feet away. Both of their arms are crossed over their chests, and they're glaring at David. He's lucky his attention is on me, or

I'm pretty sure he'd be scared shitless. River takes a step forward. Or maybe *not* lucky.

I take the fabric from where David's holding it, and our fingers brush. My shoulders relax when there's no tingling warmth from the contact.

The balloon is thicker than I expected, some kind of nylon or polyester blend.

David smiles and says, "Okay, hold it up high until I tell you to let go."

I lift the heavy fabric above my head, grateful for Alex's extra-long hoodie that smells of sweet coconut and a hint of salt, which I've been ignoring. Loud fans turn on, and the balloon slowly starts to fill, so slowly that even with three other people helping, my arms begin to ache. *Come on, buddy. Tell me I can drop it.*

My muscles are just about to let go when River steps behind me. He's so close I can feel his breath on the back of my neck, but he doesn't close the distance. I stifle a shiver and ignore the heat pooling in my stomach.

"I've got it, Mia." He takes the fabric from my hands, our fingers grazing. This time, the small touch is like fireworks skating up my arm. Even though not a single other part of us touches, every one of my nerve endings comes to life. His arms cage me between them, and I fight the urge to sink back into his embrace. I tilt my head to look at him and instantly meet his intense gaze. His hair has the perfect bed head look, which has me thinking about him in bed. *Naked chest, hand dipping under his sheet, stroking.* I swallow hard and face forward.

River shifts closer, his chest barely grazing my back, and his mouth drops to my ear. "Are you going to ask me today?"

*Fuck.* Heat floods my core, and I know for a fact my panties are wet. This time, I don't fight it and let myself fall into him, basking in his warmth. God knows I want to, but I needed that liquid courage last night to take the next step. Something to take off the edge of the million worries that come along with them. If I ask River, what would happen to Alex? Would he move out of the room, would he stop talking to me? My chest twinges at the thought. Even though we'll go back to not seeing each other when we leave, I don't want to miss a single minute with them. Even if it means I combust from horniness.

David's shouting something at us, but the buzzing in my head blocks out his words.

I take several deep breaths, and River's cedar-and-leather scent mixes with Alex's from his hoodie, which does absolutely nothing to calm my racing thoughts. River's heartbeat pounds against my back, and his ragged breaths undermine the collected mask he presents to the world.

David shouts again, and his words pierce the fog. "Get ready to let go. We're putting in hot air now."

I squint against the rising sun as a rainbow of hot-air balloons ascend into the sky. Bursts of colors and patterns soar rapidly, filling up every inch of my view. In the sun's light, they seem to have an inner glow, as if ignited by its warmth.

"Breathe, Mia." River's chest vibrates against me, and I inhale sharply. Tingling excitement dances under my skin, and I turn toward him with a beaming smile.

His gaze takes me in, and a slow smile takes over his face. I hold my breath for an entirely new reason. River almost never smiles, but when he does, he's beautiful. All his hard edges are softened, giving him an almost playfulness. It makes me want to earn that smile every day. We stay there, breathing in each other's air, before he gestures to our group climbing into the basket.

Alex wraps his arm around River's waist. "Come on, Kitten. Let's get you up in the air."

If I wasn't already staring at him, I would've missed the faint hint of a blush that tinges River's neck. I tilt my head, watching them. There's always been a heavy, palpable connection between the three of us, but maybe there's more to explore.

Alex lets go of River and bends down, throwing me over his shoulder and pulling a high-pitched laugh from me. "Put me down."

I beat him with my fist, but he just chuckles. "Kitten's got claws."

He sets me down a few feet from the basket and fixes my hoodie, which lifted from being tossed over.

I place both hands on my hips and say, "I'm not your Kitten."

"What would you rather me call you, Sweetheart?" His grin brings out his dimples, and my insides turn to goo. River and Alex are polar opposites. One quiet and dominant and the other playful and open. Somehow, that just makes them both more attractive.

I swallow hard, liking the sound of that entirely too much. "Mia's fine."

"Mia," River says from behind me in a dark, quiet tone, and my nerves come alive. *Great...not even my name is safe.* He gestures toward the basket, which is when I realize everyone's staring at us, already inside.

"Shit. Sorry." I ignore the flush across my cheeks, and my eyes dance everywhere other than the people in front of us.

Alex gets in first, extending his hand to help me to the basket door. I step over the one-foot ledge, and he immediately pulls my back into his chest, placing his chin on my head.

"What do you think you're doing?" I ask.

His arms band around my stomach, holding me closer. "There's not much room in here."

The wicker-like woven plastic creaks as River, Alex, and I cram into the small space. The basket feels tight with our five bodies packed in like sardines. I run my hand along the edge. There are four thick ropes attaching the fabric overhead to metal O-rings connected to the basket. Each one has a red knot at its end for security.

I should pull away, say some kind of smart-ass comment and break free. But I don't want to. Especially when River steps to our side, his arm grazing mine.

I ignore the tingles dancing along my arm and look around. There's a small older lady who must be in her seventies who looks between me and the guys and winks at me.

Screw it. I rest my head on Alex's shoulder, letting myself relax for the first time in months.

"Everyone ready?" David calls out. "Hold on tight." He pulls on a lever hanging from the center of the balloon, and fire shoots up with a deafening roar. The basket shakes as we lift into the air, and I freeze suddenly, not at all sure about this.

Alex drops his mouth against the curve of my neck, drawing all my attention. "We've got you."

We.

The world below us gets smaller and smaller as we ascend until cars look like toys and the fields all blur into one.

"Look up," Alex murmurs against my skin.

I lift my gaze and gasp. Mountains flank both sides of us. They're dotted with patches of green trees and open areas planted with row upon row of grapevines. The sky turns pink, then red, and my eyes widen as the sun crests over the ridge, bathing everything in a soft amber glow. "It's beautiful."

"Yes, it is," River says, but he's facing me.

# CHAPTER 12
## RIVER

IT'S clear the second Mia stiffens that something's changed. She'd been relaxed, leaning against Alex, eyes wide on our surroundings. My gaze flicks to Alex, and he gives me a short nod before burying his chin into Mia's throat. She freezes before melting against him.

I watch as his hands burrow into the pouch of her hoodie, and his arms tighten around her. He's always touched her like she was already his, and it used to drive me crazy. It took no time after she disappeared to realize what a fucking idiot I was. I swore if she ever came back into our lives, I'd make her see that things could be different.

I can't keep my attention off the two of them. It doesn't matter that we're a thousand feet in the air, and I'm sure the view around me is immaculate. The only thing I want to see is how they are together. I watch the muscle in Alex's jaw work, and the tendons in his neck pull taut when she looks back at him with a smile, green eyes round with wonder.

They flash to mine, and I step in closer until she has to tilt her head all the way back to keep her gaze on mine. A shiver runs through her, and I smile. Between me catching her with her vibe and her listening in last night, it's clear our girl is getting desperate for a release.

"Cold?" I press into their side, giving a quick glance to Alex, making sure it's okay, but all his attention is on her. She shifts so she's sandwiched between us.

"A little." Her voice is strained, and if we weren't so close, I wouldn't have heard it. She swallows hard and fixes her gaze on the horizon while Alex's and mine never leave her.

"So, Kitten. What have you been up to the last three years?"

"Study, work, sleep, repeat." She sounds tired just talking about it, and I have an overwhelming need to take some of the load off her shoulders.

"How about the two of you? Big-time NHL players. Is it all you thought it would be?" she asks, a bit stiff, but it's a start.

"Could be better," I say, and her gaze snaps to mine before looking over the horizon.

"What, not exciting enough for you?" Her tone has a slight edge to it, and I tilt my head.

"A bit lonely, to be honest."

She huffs out a laugh. "Yeah, right. I've seen your Instagram. The two of you are always out."

Alex squeezes her harder. "Just because we were out doesn't mean it wasn't hollow. You never know when someone is genuinely interested in you or just your proximity to fame."

She stiffens, biting her cheek. She didn't like something he said. Then she shakes it off and asks me, "How are your parents? Farm still doing okay?"

I shrug. I don't talk to them much. Leaving home at fifteen to live with a billet family put a rift between us. "Fine. With the land prices going up, they're thinking about selling it and settling down."

"I always liked picturing you on the farm. Throwing hay bales and riding horses like you're a cast member of *Yellowstone*."

"You picture me, eh? What else am I doing?" My voice is a low rumble, and a hum travels through my chest as goosebumps cover her neck.

She clears her throat. "Yeah, cleaning up manure must have sucked."

I laugh, and both Alex and Mia watch me with matching smiles.

"Well, you can keep dreaming  because I have no plans of ever doing that again. Plus, we grew corn. No horses, hay, or manure involved."

I grew up a farm kid, but my skill on the ice had me moving out young. The AAA team from a nearby city scouted me, and the rest is history.

"How about you? Parents still royal dicks?" Mia asks Alex with more concern than I'm sure she intended.

"You know how it is. Some might say they're

right about sports not being as good as academic success." His shoulders tense.

She twists to look at him and says plainly, "*And* those people would be idiots."

A smile curls his lips. "Fuck 'em, right?"

She nods. "Right."

David calls over the wind, "We're descending. Brace for landing."

My grip tightens over them both, and I plant my feet just in time for the bottom of the basket to reach the ground. The entire thing shakes, shifting our weight, and Mia face-plants into my chest with a groan.

I stroke my thumb over her cheekbone. "Careful."

She makes a small squeak-like sound and steps back from both of us. "That was fun."

I step around, not liking the space she's created, and cup the side of her jaw, pressing upward so she's forced to meet my gaze. "Good. I'm glad you liked it."

Her mouth's open, chest rising and falling with her rapid breaths. I lean in until my nose just barely grazes hers, and she shifts closer, her breaths fanning over my lips.

"Everyone off, one at a time. Watch your step." David breaks the moment. Mia huffs out a breath and skirts around me to be the first one off.

"That was fucking hot." Alex smirks at me before winking and following after her.

I let out a deep breath, praying that I know what the fuck I'm doing.

We get back into the car without a word. The seats aren't quite wide enough for the three of us, and her legs are raised. It looks uncomfortable. I lift her up, closing the space between Alex and me, and set her on my lap sideways. Her ass is in my lap, and Alex turns toward us, connecting her back to his chest. His hand flies up to her arm to steady her.

She shivers between us, goose bumps visible over her collar, and she shifts her weight. I swallow hard when her hooded eyes meet mine.

"Andre. Step out for a minute. We need a moment alone with our girl," I say, not bothering to look up.

Mia's eyes flash, mouth dropping open.

The driver gets out immediately, shutting the door behind him.

"What's wrong?" I ask her, keeping my voice low and my mouth against her ear.

"N-nothing," she stutters, and I move in closer, adjusting her on my lap. Her eyes round when she feels my hard cock against her.

I grip her calf furthest from my chest and drop it onto the floor, leaving the other one tucked to my side, spreading her legs wide.

Alex groans, and his hand splays over her sternum. "Your heart's going crazy."

She nods, and her mouth opens, but no words come out.

I grip her jaw and lean into them. "Ask me now."

"What?" Her eyebrow lifts in question.

"Last night, you wanted me. Ask me to make you come right here. Let us show you what we can give you." My voice is rough, laced with a command. I know she listened to me last night. Just like I know she's been going crazy all morning.

Her gaze flicks from Alex's dark one to mine. "We're in a car," she whispers.

"Mia, I want you." I gesture to Alex. "*We* want you. For the rest of the weekend, we want you to just enjoy yourself. You've been working too hard."

"For the rest of the weekend?" she asks, barely above a whisper. I can practically see her brain working through the offer.

Alex's brows pull together, and his jaw locks. I know he wants to say something, but we both know there's no point.

"Until you leave. Let us take care of you, Love. Can you do that?"

Her throat moves with her swallow, and her eyes are wide on mine before a slow smile curls her lips. "Yeah, I can do that—"

I press my lips to hers, groaning deep in my throat. I'd been waiting years for this. She opens immediately, and I don't waste time filling her with my tongue, tasting sweetness as I explore her mouth.

She moans and digs her fingers into my hair, holding me in place.

"Fuck," Alex hisses and dips his hand under her sweatshirt, pulling up to reveal bare skin. She shivers again when his hand draws circles against her heated stomach.

I pull away, loving the way she tries to follow me.

Alex runs his nose along her jaw, and she twists until their mouths graze each other's. Her fingers tighten in my hair when he deepens the kiss, pulling needy sounds from her. He murmurs between breaths, "I knew you'd taste so fucking good—so soft—perfect-fucking-mouth—"

She responds to his words by rocking her hips and grinding her ass into my hard cock. I hiss out a breath and grip the sides of her hips, guiding her exactly how I want.

She arches, mouth never leaving Alex's when my thumbs stroke up her thighs until they brush her apex. The fabric's already soaked through, and I fight back the urge to pull them off and see her glistening pussy.

She jerks, and her head falls back, her moan breaking free.

I trail my thumb over the center seam of her leggings, barely grazing the fabric. "That's what you want?"

She nods vigorously, hips lifting into my palm.

"Mia, you agree to our terms? You're ours for the weekend."

She grows still, and I can see her hesitance take over. There's a battle behind her eyes as she struggles with the decision.

I pushed her too far. Before I can back off, Alex cuts in.

"Maybe she needs a taste. Something to show what she's in for."

My gaze narrows on hers. "Want that? You want to come right here between us?"

She nods.

"Ask me. Tell me what you need." I insist.

"Make me come."

Alex groans, his fingers tightening around her waist. I meet his gaze. "You heard her. Make her come."

"*Fuck.*" His head drops into the crook of her neck.

"Slide your hand under her pants but above her underwear," I direct him, and my cock grows painfully hard.

Alex's throat bobs with his swallow before he does as he's told.

Mia squirms when his hand cups her core, visible through her tight leggings.

"Good. Tell me how she feels."

She whimpers, and her legs pull together. I grip them to keep them open.

Alex sucks in a breath. "She's so hot." He must move because her ass squirms on my lap. "And soft."

Fuck yes. "Pull her panties to the side and trace her seam."

Alex bites his lower lip. "Fuck, she's so wet."

Mia's eyes roll back, and small pants escape her lips.

"Eyes on me, Love."

They snap to mine.

"Alex is going to fuck you with his fingers until you soak through your pants and come all over his hand. You want that, don't you?"

"Yes," she breathes out.

Alex doesn't waste time, and they're both sucking in air. My hand twitches with the need to squeeze my dick, but this is about her. *About them.*

She has to understand that we're doing this together. That she doesn't need to choose between Alex and me.

Alex's hips rock against empty air, and his jaw clenches with the need for pressure. I grip Mia's thighs harder to prevent myself from reaching over. Besides a few heated looks, he hasn't shown he's open to exploring, and now isn't the time to push it.

Mia begins to squirm between us, wide green eyes on mine. I wait until small moans escape her mouth. I press down on Alex's hand, grinding it into her clit.

It takes seconds before she's coming undone between us, hips rocking, mouth open with a silent cry. She collapses back, body limp between us and a ghost of a smile on her lips.

I lean in close. "Better?"

Her eyes slit open, and her smile grows. "Perfect."

Alex's heated gaze meets mine, and then he raises his fingers to his mouth and sucks her taste off them. His eyes roll back, and he groans deep in his throat. "Fuck me."

Fuck me is right. My fingers curl, and the tendons strain in my neck as I fight the urge to lick the last of her flavor off his fingers. He gives me a knowing smirk, and I fucking hate the bastard as much as I want him.

The man is killing me, and he doesn't even know it.

Life has a sick fucking sense of humor, making me want to fuck the shit out of my straight best friend. My eyes travel over Mia's blissed-out face. Best *friends*. Preferably together.

I need to calm the fuck down. I open the door a few inches and tell the driver we're ready to go. It's a twenty-minute drive before the car pulls to a stop, and I set Mia's legs on the ground, getting out first before helping her. She leans against me like she can't support her own weight, and I wrap an arm around her waist.

Alex climbs out his own side, his hands dropping to adjust his cock before turning back to us with a smile. "What do you think, Kitten? Do you want more?"

"Yes...no...maybe." Her gaze heats before she freezes, and fear flashes in her eyes. I grit my jaw, not liking that look.

I kiss her temple. "Answer tomorrow. Enjoy tonight with the girls."

She nods and steps away from me and keeps going until she's around the corner and out of our sight.

"We better not have fucked that up." Alex lets out a long breath. "You know what you're doing, right?"

"I never know with her. I didn't think she'd run the last time." This isn't just sex for me, but it's a start, all I had to do was convince her we're worth it.

# CHAPTER 13
## MIA

THE SECOND I got out of the car, I ran from Alex and River. I've spent the rest of the day hiding at Sidney's. She took one look at me and kicked Jax out to hang with the boys.

Even after I locked myself in her villa for the last eight hours, eating and watching reality tv she hasn't asked any questions, but I can tell it's killing her. She's brought up Alex and River a few times, feeling me out, but I've miraculously been able to divert the conversation.

I can tell the curiosity is finally getting the best of her, and she's just about to press when there's a knock on the door.

Sidney lets a beaming Piper in, and relief floods me, knowing she's going to have to drop it for the rest of the night.

Tonight's all about Piper. The wedding's tomorrow, which means all the girls are having a sleepover here.

"Where have you two been?" Piper collapses on the couch beside me. Her hair's pulled up in a messy bun, and she's wearing a simple sundress.

"This one's been hiding and won't tell me why," Sidney says from the door, where she's waiting for the others to arrive.

Piper squeals and turns toward me. "What happened?" She looks entirely too excited.

"Nothing." My phone buzzes, saving the day. I bend over to grab it from my bag, but any sense of relief disappears the second I check it. Another unknown number. This time, three texts back to back.

**Unknown: Where the hell are you?**

**Unknown: Don't fucking ignore me Mia.**

**Unknown: I swear to God if you're fucking around.**

I hit delete before I can finish reading the last message, a shudder running down my spine, and slide my cell into Do Not Disturb mode. There's no way I'm letting him ruin tonight.

"Who was that?" Piper's watching me, head tilted to the side. She's entirely too observant.

I put on my best fake smile and lie through my teeth. "Scam. You know how it is—"

Misty and Shana walk in together, the latter holding a giant bottle of rum. "Who's ready for tonight?"

I huff out a laugh. "Isn't getting wasted the night before the wedding a bad idea?"

"Well, considering the guys are already well on

their way, I'd say it's pretty normal," Shana says, taking the chair across from me.

The living room of Sidney's villa is twice the size of ours, even though we have one more person staying with us. The space is dominated by a long sofa of pale blue linen upholstery with two club chairs to its left, currently occupied by Shana and Misty.

Sidney grabs the bottle and heads to the small kitchenette area to prepare drinks.

"How was hot-air ballooning?" Piper asks, and my cheeks heat.

I clear my throat, suddenly thick. "Good. Pretty spectacular."

She bites back a smile. "I bet. I ran into River and Alex after. They were both looking a little flush. Hot up there?"

"Um. No, not really." By the gleam in her eyes, I realize I really should've just lied.

Misty leans forward, a smirk crossing her lips. "So are you going to tell us about it?"

"It's pretty slow. Balloon just floats around."

The girls laugh, and Misty presses. "You want to tell us what has you blushing like a freaking tomato?"

"Nope."

"Not fair." She pouts, then gives me a wink. "You've got both eligible players staying with you. The least you can do is give us the deets if you aren't going to share."

I have to remind myself Misty is actually pretty

cool to stop the jealousy from taking over. "Nothing to share."

"Leave her alone, guys." Sidney comes from behind me and hands me a fruity cocktail. I take a deep drink, sending her a thank-you with my eyes.

She just smirks. "Plus, she'll spill once she's ready."

Not liking where that's going, I redirect the conversation. "So what's the plan?"

Shana's the first to answer. "Drinking games."

I groan, knowing I'm totally screwed.

It takes less than an hour for me to feel tipsy and to sway a bit where I sit. Somehow, in the hours I'd spent here, we'd forgotten to eat. The rest of the girls aren't any better off than I am, giggling the entire time. We played beer pong, where Piper beat us all soundly, which left her the only one remotely sober. Apparently, it's not the type of game you play with someone who grew up with all guys.

Sidney throws back the rest of her drink. "Let's play never have I ever." Her eyes meet mine before moving to Piper's.

"No way." Piper sits on the couch on my left and Sidney on the right. I'm squished between them, reminding me a little too much of my earlier car ride. I clear my throat.

Shana laughs and leans over her knees. "Piper played with Lucas once and accidently admitted no guy had managed to get her off. He then proceeded to do it. Repeatedly."

Piper turns bright red, and Sidney laughs. "Yeah, this is happening."

"Never have I ever kissed anyone in this room," Misty adds with a smirk, clearly knowing something.

Both Shana and Piper drink. I raise my brow, and Piper shrugs. "What? I was experimenting."

"Worked out for me." Shana blows a kiss her way.

Shana cracks her neck and looks at me. "Never have I ever fucked one of my guy friends."

I'm the only one not to drink, and I'm suddenly grateful that my last shred of willpower held out.

Sidney squints at me. "You're telling me you never, with either of those boys?"

I shake my head. "Nope."

She collapses back into her chair as if I just dropped something that altered her known reality. "I'm not going to lie, I'm kinda disappointed. I thought you were hooking up."

Piper smirks. "You and everyone else."

Misty leans forward. "Never have I ever gotten off in a public place."

Piper, Sidney, and I all drink.

Misty squeals. "Details now!"

"Not the way it works," Piper quickly adds.

Misty's quick. "Never have I ever gotten off at a restaurant."

Piper groans and takes a drink.

"Never have I ever gotten off in the same place as anyone here," Shana adds next.

Piper drinks, and Sidney scrunches up her face before taking another sip. "We weren't nearby."

Both my brows raise. "Wait? Was it me?"

She flushes bright pink.

"Where?"

"Offside behind the speakers," Sidney replies.

"You're my hero." Misty beams.

We look at Piper, and she holds one finger up as she chugs her drink for courage. "Under the table at Brewhouse with everyone there. Pretty sure River knew."

"Oh my God." Misty laughs.

Piper shoots her a look. "You've gotten off entirely too easy, Misty. Never have I ever had sex on the player bus."

Misty glares and takes a drink.

All of us cheer.

Piper leans in closer. "Never have I ever wanted to have a threesome with Alex and River."

Their eyes are on me. "Not freaking fair." I take a deep gulp, finishing off my drink. It hits my head, and I sway in my seat.

"I don't know. Seems fair to me." Piper smirks.

Sidney drops her voice, tone turning serious. "Why did you ghost them before?"

I huff out a laugh, thinking about that night. My chest tightens, remembering how everything clicked into place. "River got jealous. Ended up punching Alex before anything could really get started. I decided it was better for everyone to just go my separate way."

"And that worked?" Shana asks.

"It did until this weekend. Now I don't know what's happening."

"What does that mean?"

"They...they made a proposal..." They all lean forward, and I know I'm not getting out of this. "They want to fool around for the rest of the trip."

Misty makes a high-pitched squeal. "Like all together?"

I think back to the car. "Yeah, I think so."

"And do you want that?" Sidney asks. She sounds hesitant. She, of all people, knows how hard it was for me to walk away the first time.

My gut twists. "I don't know. Yes?"

"Show of hands. Who thinks Mia should have nasty, dirty sex with Alex and River while in Napa?" Misty looks entirely too eager.

Their hands lift immediately.

"What's it to you, Misty?" I ask and smile, knowing their teasing is in good fun. I'm lucky to have friends like this in my life.

She points at Shana, Sidney, and Piper. "These three are in long-term, committed relationships, and I'm single as fuck. You're the only person I can live vicariously through, and honestly, who turns down a threesome with two gorgeous men?"

I choke on a laugh. "I'll think about it."

———

I sip my coffee, feeling the warmth radiating through my hands as I wait for Piper's final touches.

I'm grateful and relieved that the wedding isn't until two in the afternoon.

The bottle of rum Shana had brought over last night was nearly empty by the time we'd all fallen asleep. Even with the two Advil I took, I still feel like someone's trying to escape my skull from the inside.

I probably would've slept past lunch if it wasn't for the three cheerful women who showed up at eleven with roller bags full of beauty products.

Just over two hours later and we're all primped and shined, waiting on Piper's final touches. She'd gone into the bathroom so we wouldn't be able to see until she was completely ready, and the anticipation is killing me.

The door creaks open, and the esthetician who'd been helping Piper steps out.

She beams at us. "She's ready."

Piper steps out from where she's hiding, and my mouth drops open. She's stunning in a pearlescent satin dress cut in a classic silhouette. It's tight around her waist and fans out below her hips, giving her an almost princess-like quality.

She looks down at herself and back at us. "So what do you think?"

Misty claps her hands together. "Lucas is going to die."

# CHAPTER 14
## ALEX

THE VENUE IS a large barn that sits in the middle of a vineyard. Just by looking at it, I can tell it's being used exclusively for special events. The exterior is made out of a warm wood with black accents that give it a modern edge. I'm not big into architecture, but I can definitely get behind this style.

Jax, River, myself, and a nervous-looking Lucas pulled up less than fifteen minutes ago.

River steps up beside me. "How did you manage to fuck that up?"

I cock a brow at him, turning away from where Jax was talking to Lucas, who is now hopping from foot to foot on the spot.

"What are you going on abo—" My words are cut off when River's knuckles skim my jaw as he straightens my collar. A little zing of electricity shoots through me, and my breath hitches in my chest. His gaze is focused where he adjusts my tie how he wants it, despite the fact that I know it was already perfect. My skin heats under the gentle brush of his fingers, and I swallow hard when River gives the knot a tight tug.

It feels like time stands still, even though it's over in a minute, and he's turning away from me, not meeting my gaze.

Gravel crunches under car tires outside, and we all look back toward the door.

"Shit," Lucas says and makes a hasty escape out the back door toward where he's supposed to be set up next to the altar. Pretty sure Piper would kill him if he saw her before he's supposed to.

The girls walk in, Sidney leading the way. She goes straight to Jax, who lets out a low whistle.

Mia walks in next, and I swear my heart stops. She's wearing the exact same champagne-color dress as the other girls, but she makes it look a million times better. Her blonde hair's down, styled with waves like you'd see in an old movie and pulled over her left shoulder. It exposes the long, smooth column of her neck, and suddenly, my mouth waters with the need to taste her there.

Her makeup's simple, perfectly accentuating her features with long lashes and cherry-red lips. Intrusive thoughts of those lips around my cock have me fighting against the hard-on threatening to take over.

"Fuck," River whispers beside me, like the word fell out unintentionally.

"Yup." My thoughts exactly.

My feet are already moving before my head catches up, and I cup the exposed side of her neck, tipping her head back. "You are fucking gorgeous, Kitten."

Her cheeks pinken, and her gaze roams over my face, then travels down my navy blue suit. "You don't look too bad yourself."

I see Piper's mom and dad step inside from the corner of my eye, but I can't look away from Mia. After three long years of waiting, it's hard to believe she's standing here in front of me. She's everything I've ever wanted, and I'm not sure I can ever explain to her why she's so important. Not without laying myself bare at the mercy of her approval.

Piper's mom claps to get our attention. "Okay, it's time to pair off. Jax with Sidney. Alex and Mia. Misty, you're with Shana."

My hand drops to Mia's waist, tugging her closer to me.

"Mia," River says, only a foot from us. "No matter how much I want to be the one to walk you down the aisle"—I catch the hidden meaning to River's words, and by the way Mia's lips fall open, so does she— "I've got to officiate this wedding." His eyes roam over where my hand clutches her waist. "You two look good together."

I clear my suddenly dry throat. "Thanks, man."

The hint of a grin curves his lips before he replies, "You owe me."

I nod. I really fucking do.

River walks away and out the back door. Mia huffs beside me, and I chuckle. "Don't worry. I guarantee he's still thinking about the way that dress hugs your curves. I know I can't stop."

"You are nothing but trouble." Her gaze doesn't meet mine, but a small smile pulls at her lips. I wrap her fingers in the crook of my elbow and stare down at her, tracing the delicate lines of her collarbone when the music starts playing. "Shall we?"

Her fingers tighten their hold. "I bet Lucas cries."

I laugh. "I guarantee it."

I guide her down the aisle toward the altar decorated with white flowers set against the mountainside backdrop. It pains me to let her go to take her place as a bridesmaid. I already know I'll be counting down the seconds until I can have her next to me tonight. There's only a handful of people here. Lucas's and Piper's parents and some other extended family I don't recognize sit in the chairs facing us.

The wedding march music starts, and the back double doors open, revealing Piper. Her eyes are bright, and I follow them to where Lucas is standing. Mia was right. Tears track down his face, and his smile wobbles as his soon-to-be wife walks toward him.

The second Piper's within touching distance, Lucas has her pulled against his chest, his mouth taking over hers in a long, slow kiss.

We all laugh, but they don't stop until River clears his throat. "Ready?"

Lucas pulls away slowly, but not before stealing another kiss. He doesn't let go of her hand even when he faces the altar.

"Ladies and gentlemen, family, and friends, we gather here today to celebrate and witness the union of Piper and Lucas. As we come together on this momentous occasion, let us take a moment to appreciate the profound love and commitment that has brought them to this day."

River starts the ceremony, but my attention is pulled across the aisle to where Mia stands, eyes glued on the couple. Her cheeks are bloomed pink, and her eyes are glossy as she watches her friends.

"I, Lucas Knight, take Piper Adams…"

Mia swipes a stray tear with her knuckles and shares a look with an equally affected Sidney before her gaze lands on me.

"I, Piper Adams, take Lucas Knight…"

The world goes quiet as River says the words that tie the couple together, but my brain twists it as I'm frozen in place. For the briefest of seconds, I can imagine she's the one standing across from me.

"I now pronounce you man and wife. You may kiss the bride. Again."

Cheers erupt, and Mia's attention pulls away from me as she wraps Misty in an excited hug. I'm still glued on the spot when Jax slaps a hand on my shoulder in a half hug. He's grinning at me. "Treat her right, or Sidney will kill you."

I choke. "That obvious, huh?"

He laughs, letting his arm drop. "So fucking obvious." He looks toward where River approaches Mia and gestures toward them. "Is that going to be a problem?"

I shake my head, warmth flooding my chest. "Not this time."

I follow River and Mia back into the barn. It's decorated in white and gold decorations. Flowers, cards, and God knows what else. Looks pretty though.

I can't look away from where her dress slides down her back and molds to the curve of her ass. I fist my hand to prevent myself from closing the distance and smacking it just to watch it bounce. One day, I promise myself.

There's a long rectangular table with place settings on each side. Lucas and Piper sit in the middle, their heads dipped toward each other, and Jax and Sidney sit across from them. River sits on Jax's left, guiding Mia to the spot beside him. One of Piper's guests goes to sit beside her, and I step up uncomfortably close, raising one eyebrow. Not a fucking chance, buddy. "That's my seat."

He swallows hard and takes a step back. "Sorry about that. My mistake."

Mia's smirking at me when I sit next to her. "Was that really necessary?"

"Yes." I reach under the table and wrap my fingers just above her knees. The slippery satin fabric is warm under my touch. Her gaze darts to mine, but she doesn't move away, and I take it as permission to keep my hand there. I run my thumb in an arch, loving the way she presses into my touch.

River settles his arm behind her and cups the

back of her neck beneath her hair. Her eyes darken when they meet his, and he says, "Comfortable?"

She nods in reply. Fuck, I love when she's speechless.

The girls are all wearing matching smirks as they look at us from across the table, and Mia's cheeks turn cherry red, but she doesn't move.

I eat my food with one hand, never letting go of her thigh. My fingers have shifted up a few inches, and she squirms when I tighten them.

Piper gets up with an easy smile and gives Mia a cheeky wink before walking to the area that's cleared off for a dance floor. We watch as the newlyweds twirl around for their first dance, the lights dimming low. After a few minutes, the parents join, followed by Sidney and Jax.

I lower my mouth to just above her ear. "May I please have this dance?"

Her gaze darts to me, then River. He nods and removes his hand from her. A flash of excitement takes over Mia's face, and she smiles. I lead her onto the dance floor and pull her into my chest. Her eyes widen on mine when I grip her hip, spreading my fingers to coast over the top of her ass and tug her closer.

"What are you doing?" she breathes.

"Helping you decide. I want you tonight. I want every second with you until you get on that plane."

She runs her tongue over her red lips, and I can feel her heart pounding. She wants this as badly as I do. I close the distance between us and run my nose along the curve of her neck, breathing in her sweet scent and marveling at the goose bumps that follow my path. I nip her ear, and she shivers. "Stop thinking. Just let go."

She turns her head, mouth grazing mine, and I can feel her breath on my lips when she says, "Okay."

Fuck. I'm about to close the distance between us when rough fingers graze mine over Mia's hip.

River's gaze is pitch-black when it meets mine, and a muscle ticks in his jaw. "Sorry to interrupt. You look so good I couldn't resist."

This is the second time in our friendship he's interrupted me kissing Mia, but unlike last time, I don't mind. We have bigger plans for tonight. It's just up to Mia to decide.

I lay it all out for her again, keeping my voice low so only the two of them can hear me. "Did you think about what we asked you yesterday?" Her eyes meet mine, and she bites her lip, nodding. I smile internally. River will break her out of her shyness soon enough. "Let me be crystal clear. For the rest of this trip, River and I will do unbelievably indecent things to you. We want you ready and willing, screaming our names as we each take turns fucking your sweet little pussy."

She sucks in a sharp inhale and looks around, making sure no one heard. Her green eyes are nearly black with wide pupils, and her chest rises and falls with her rapid breaths as my words sink in.

"Do you want that?" River asks, voice rough.

I wait for her response. If she says she doesn't want this, I'll let her go no matter how badly I want her.

"I want to be yours for the rest of the trip."

"Good fucking girl," River growls.

"Let's go back to the room." My voice is raw and low, but she hears me over the music.

Mia slowly opens her eyes. "Please."

Such a simple word has me nearly coming in my pants.

## CHAPTER 15
## MIA

BEFORE WE LEAVE, I wrap Piper in a fierce hug. "Congratulations, girl. I'm so happy for you."

She squeezes me back just as hard. "Calling it a night?"

"Is that okay?" I ask, not wanting to insult her by heading out too early.

Piper scans my face, no doubt still flushed, before checking out the guys, and a slow smile curves her lips. "I fully support this. You know that, right?"

I roll my lips between my teeth and fight against the cheesy grin that threatens to escape. Piper's been close friends with River and Alex since she lived with them her freshman year. Which just makes her easy acceptance that much more calming.

"You don't think it's crazy?"

"Honestly?" She raises a brow. "I think you deserve a wild weekend. Let someone take care of you for a bit."

I channel the girl I was back in school. At some

point, during my relationship with Jason, I'd let her go and let him mess with my head. "I want this."

"I bet you do." Piper winks and gives me a gentle shove in the direction of the door. "Go have fun. I want all the details tomorrow."

"You're going on your honeymoon tomorrow." I'm glad for the excuse.

Her gaze darts to Lucas, who's chatting with Jax, and her eyes soften. "As soon as I get back, we'll do a FaceTime with Sidney."

"Yup. Of course." Which means I have two weeks to think of a way to get out of spilling everything to her.

I turn and spot Alex and River standing near the door, both watching me. Alex rolls his neck, his cocky smile missing, and he locks his hands behind him. He looks like he's working hard not to come after me, and warmth fills my chest, knowing that this is purely my decision. Which is good, because I'm way out of my comfort zone.

I step forward, making my way toward them, and marvel as Alex's mouth transforms into a grin the closer I get.

I'm so focused on him that River's low voice has my head snapping his way. His brows are pulled together, and his gaze darts between Alex and me. "I understand if you want to go with just him. This doesn't have to be an all-or-nothing deal."

Alex stiffens and makes a quiet sound of disapproval, but River's attention never leaves me. He gnaws on his cheek, and a muscle ticks there. The look of insecurity has my chest caving.

"I want you. Both of you."

He lets out a deep breath, then entwines our fingers, and the corners of his lips curve the way I like. "Perfect."

———

River sits in the front passenger seat of the taxi, which is a good thing because I don't think I can take a repeat of yesterday's car ride. Being pressed between them while dancing already has my heart beating out of my chest and my thighs rubbing together. Anticipation mixed with fear—no, not fear...nervousness— has me shifting in my seat. The idea of walking into our villa and just standing there awkwardly, not knowing how to start, has me on edge.

This is a first for me, and I've done a *lot*.

A shiver runs down my back when Alex's thumb skims my neck. He's been playing with a strand of my hair since we sat down. I'm not sure he even knows he's doing it.

The car's quiet except for the low-playing radio during the fifteen-minute drive to the resort. In that time, I've managed to work myself up to the point my breath comes out in shallow pants, so focused on the swirl of thoughts pummeling me I don't notice we've stopped and River's opened my door.

He leans in so our heads are level. "Breathe, Mia.

You are in control of what happens tonight." He cups my neck, running his thumb along my cheekbone. "Repeat it back."

I take a deep breath, well aware that he's the one actually in control right now, but I like not having to think for a change. He wouldn't push past anything I didn't want to do. Even if that meant going to sleep alone. Lucky for both of us, I'm not going to let that happen.

"I'm in control."

He nods and trails his fingers down my neck, over my shoulder, continuing his path until his fingers wrap around mine and guide me out. River has never talked much, but the way his dark eyes pierce mine leaves no room for interpretation.

Alex steps up to our side and smiles, soothing my nerves. "Let's go, Kitten."

He follows close behind us as River leads the way through the paths toward the villa. Unlike the first night, I don't notice our surroundings. Instead, all my focus is on the warmth of Alex's hand pressed against my lower back and the tingle rolling up my arm each time River grazes his thumb over my palm.

By the time we enter the villa, I'm a walking puddle.

Before I can worry about how this is going to go, River steps up behind me and places a soft kiss below my ear. "Relax, Love. We've got you."

# CHAPTER 16
## ALEX

RIVER PLACES a soft kiss below Mia's ear, and she drops her head back against his shoulder. Her chin tilts, mouth open with her shallow breaths. I search my thoughts, but there's no jealousy. Only need.

I grasp her hip, and she moans when I press my lips into hers. River's hand wraps her jaw, coaxing her to open for me. We groan when my tongue delves into her mouth. She tastes so fucking good I can't stop myself from bucking into her.

She sucks my tongue deeper in response, and I'm completely lost to her.

"You taste so fucking good." I kiss her again before pulling back and twisting her chin to face River. "Taste her."

Mia's fingers dig into River's collar, pulling him closer against her back at the same time as she tugs my hair. He groans and captures her lips. I watch his tongue slip into her mouth, stroking hers in a dirty, needy kiss, and my cock twitches against her thigh. *Fuck. Why is that so hot?*

I capture her exposed neck, sucking hard enough to leave my mark, and press my knee between her thighs. She writhes between us, rocking her clit against me, searching for the much-needed pressure. She cries out in frustration as her dress blocks direct contact, and I smile into her neck, lifting the fabric of her dress above her hips, but instead of my knee, I cup her core with my hand. Her hips lift, and her body shakes in my grasp.

"That's it, Kitten," I murmur against her shoulder and grind my palm down against her clit, listening to the soft sounds she makes to guide my tempo. Her words lose all meaning, and pride fills me when her mouth opens with a silent cry as her orgasm washes over her.

She goes limp, and I tighten my grip to hold her in place before meeting River's hooded gaze over her shoulder. *We're really fucking doing this.*

I curl my fingers into her silky dress and slowly lift it above her head. Mia raises her arms automatically, still in a fog from her orgasm. She makes an adorable humming sound, and I catch her in a quick kiss the moment the fabric clears her face before leaning back to get a look at her but not releasing my grasp.

*Holy shit.* I inhale at the sight of her standing in just a thin black thong. Her nipples are a dusty rose color, and they stand in hard peaks. My mouth waters, and I capture one, unable to stop myself. I suck and swirl my tongue, and she cries out, fingers digging in and tugging at my hair.

"You like that, Love?" River asks, watching over her shoulder, fingers grazing her sides. She trembles and nods her head. So fucking responsive.

River points at the club chair in the corner and tells me, "Take off your shirt, sit, and don't let go of the chair arms."

Fuck, my cock aches as I do what he demands, doing my best to ignore just how much I like it.

I separate from them and take a seat, the leather cool against my heated back. Mia's eyes are hot on my chest, and her tongue sneaks out, wetting her bottom lip, still swollen from our kiss.

I clench my fist into the chair arms. I want to grab her, but there's something so fucking delicious about River being the one in control.

He ushers her closer to where I'm sitting and presses a hand between her shoulders, guiding her to bend at the waist. "Put your hands on his quads, above his knees."

The way he has her positioned, she has to tilt forward to reach, and it causes her to be off-balance. I groan when her fingers dig into my thighs as she holds herself steady. Her crisp green eyes lock onto mine, and we both struggle to breathe. I've never been so hard in my life, waiting for what happens next.

Her eyes close when River runs his hand from her shoulder blades down her spine and cups her ass. "Have you ever been spanked, Mia?"

Her eyes snap open, and a shiver runs through her. Fucking Christ.

"Y…Yes."

He lifts his hand, and she shifts, following him. "I'm going to spank you now."

"Yes." The word comes out as a plea, and she moans when his palm comes down with a sharp snap.

He soothes the sting with slow circles before slipping her underwear off, leaving her naked between us. "I'm going to spank you five more times. Look at him, Mia."

My dick twitches and leaks in my pants. Her eyes meet mine as her grasp tightens, nails digging into my thighs until I'm sure she's broken the skin.

"I want you to count after each one. Can you do that for me, Love?" River asks, and Mia rapidly nods her head.

River spanks her again, and her eyes close, mouth dropping open.

"Eyes on me, Kitten." Her pupils dilate, taking over her irises, and a pink flush crawls up her neck. Oh, I fucking like this.

"*One,*" she counts. Anticipation thickens the air between us, and even though it's impossible, I swear I can feel what she does. We breathe in unison, waiting for the next slap.

"*Two.*" This time, her eyes don't leave mine, and I have to grip the chair arms harder. Being so close to her when she's undone like this but not able to touch her is driving me wild. I have no doubt that River knows exactly what he's doing to me.

"*Three. Four.*" With each crack, she settles further into me, and her gaze softens, almost zoned out.

River runs his hand between her thighs. "Fuck, Mia. You're making a mess for us."

He brings his fingers to my mouth, and I don't hesitate to open for him. My eyes roll back when he pushes down on my tongue, opening my mouth wider, and slides deeper. The sweet taste of Mia mixes with a burst of salt from River's fingers and I groan deep in my throat, licking every last drop.

That should make me pause, but I've never been this turned on in my life.

Mia's taste, her sounds. The fucking feel of her nails cutting into me.

River removes his fingers from my mouth, spanking her one last time, and I can barely make out her saying *five*. Then, he stabilizes her with a hand on her hip and delicately rubs circles along her red-hot skin until she catches her breath.

I stroke her jaw, and it takes several moments for her eyes to clear. "Feel good, Kitten?"

"Yes." She nods, still a little out of it.

"Do you want to keep going?" I ask.

"Yes." Her voice comes out strong, and I smile. Fuck, I love her feistiness.

"Good. Take out his cock and wrap him in your fist." River commands.

*Fuck*, the low demanding words pulls a groan

from me that switches to something guttural when she undoes my pants in jerky, hurried movements and curls her fingers around my cock. I nearly come. With only one hand stabilizing her, she tilts to the side, and I grab her arm, holding her in place. I take several deep breaths, regaining some semblance of control.

River gently gathers her hair in his fist and drops so that his mouth is level with her ear. "You want to taste him, don't you, Love?"

"Please."

Mia's hand grips my cock, and I hiss through my teeth. "*Fuck.*"

Her eyes are hot on mine, and the seductive grin curving her lip as she lowers herself is my fucking undoing. My balls tighten when she licks the precum from the slit of my dick before taking me further into her mouth. She can barely take me in.

River runs his thumb over her hollowed cheek, relaxing the muscles there. "Breathe, Mia. Take a little more." She lowers another inch, taking my cock deeper, and I try to keep my shit together as River praises her. "There you go. That's it. You're doing so well."

She works me up and down, needy sounds escaping her, and takes me deeper each time.

"You look beautiful with your mouth full, Mia." River's words sink into me, and my eyes roll back.

My cock swells, and I clench my muscles as a ripple of pleasure shudders through me. I try to warn her. "Fuck. I'm coming."

She goes impossibly deeper, swallowing around

my head as I shoot into the back of her throat. My orgasm is so long and so intense I'm barely able to hold her upright, and she has to place her other hand back on my thigh.

She grins at me, and pride flashes in her eyes.

I run my thumb over her bottom lip, wiping the remnants of my cum. "Proud of yourself?"

She sucks it into her mouth, the pull going straight to my cock, and hums. "Mmhmm."

Jesus. I'm already half-hard again. "Good. You should be."

I kiss her, not giving a single fuck that she tastes like me, and she rests her arms on my chest. She curls her fingers through the back of my hair and deepens the kiss.

Mia squeals, body jerking, and I spot River kneeling behind her. He grips both sides of her ass, pulling her apart and buries his face into her pussy.

I hold her squirming body in place. She drops her forehead to mine and squeezes her eyes closed as shivers ripple through her body.

This time, none of us say anything, just letting the indecent sounds of River devouring her and Mia's incoherent sounds as she writhes hard, grinding back into River's face, fill the room. Fuck, she's going to come. I crave being a part of it, so I reach between us and draw circles over her clit. She moans deeper, and her movements turn frantic. She's so close. River's wet, hot tongue runs over my fingers, and I hiss through my teeth.

It's then I realize how close his face is to my cock, and I can hardly breathe.

Mia's body shakes, her fingers digging into my scalp as she comes, and I capture her cry with my mouth.

River stands, lifting Mia into his arms, and heads toward the bed.

# CHAPTER 17
# RIVER

I STRIP the bed back and lay Mia down, giving her a minute. My heart pounds against my chest so hard it threatens to shatter ribs. What the fuck was I thinking licking his fingers like that? *I wasn't thinking, that's what happened.* Mia's moans, mixed with Alex's and her sweet taste, had me fucking mindless. Before I could think better of it, I had my tongue over his fingers as he made her come.

The only saving grace was he didn't pull away. Maybe he didn't even realize it.

I'm bi, but Alex isn't, and I had no fucking right to touch him. *Fuck.*

I glance up at him, expecting to see his eyes narrowed, but he makes his way closer with a dopey smile. It does something to me to know that I put them both into this state.

It's addicting, and we aren't done yet.

I watch Mia's eyes widen when Alex strips down, then climbs into bed beside her. He rolls her beneath him, rising to his knees and sitting on his ankles with her thighs wrapped around his hips.

I lean forward and kiss her, licking the seam of her lips until she opens for me and tastes herself on my tongue then deepen the kiss until we're both searching for air.

I search her gaze to see if she's worn-out for the night, but I'm met with hooded eyes and pupils blown wide with anticipation. Her fingers dig into my hair, pulling me back to her, and I give her what she wants before pulling back.

"Are you on birth control?" She nods. "Good. I want to see Alex fuck you."

"Jesus," Alex groans, and his hips grind into her.

She tugs him closer so she can rub against his cock in response.

"You are a dream come true, you know that, Kitten?" Alex grips her thighs, pulling them even closer and lining his cock up, flashing her a cocky grin. His words break apart as he thrusts inside her, and her back bows off the bed. I adjust my position so I can see where they connect and grind my teeth as I watch his cock thrust into her. He's thick and veiny, and he's making her moan with each one of his strokes. She's practically gushing around him, soaking his balls as she takes him in. Fuck, she has a pretty pussy, stretched around him like that.

I rub my hand over my cock, still covered by my black slacks. There's something indecent about standing over the two of them fully dressed while they're both bare for me to see.

"Come here." Mia eyes my hand as I stroke myself slowly, glancing up. "Your turn."

Fuck me. The muscles in my thighs tighten, and I move to the head of the bed. Her mouth parts, and Alex's rhythm quickens as he looks between us.

"Off now," she commands, and I can't help but smirk.

"You're the boss now?"

"River, if you don't get your cock out and in my mouth in the next five seconds, I'm going to wrinkle all your shirts."

Alex snorts but doesn't stop.

I don't give a single shit right now, but she's too adorable to deny. Mia licks her lips when I unclasp my belt and unzip my pants, pushing them down just far enough that my cock falls heavy in my hand.

She sucks in a breath when she sees I'm not wearing boxers and reaches out with a greedy hand. I capture her wrist to prevent her touch. It's like fucking torture, but I'll come before I get in her mouth if she touches me.

Alex adjusts her so her head barely hangs off the edge of the bed, perfectly lined up with my cock. She takes me deep instantly, and I collapse forward, bracing a hand on Alex's back to keep myself up. She's a quick fucking study and shows none of the hesitance she had with Alex.

She sucks, licks, hums, and I fight every second from losing control.

Alex grunts, and I shift my gaze to him. His eyes are focused on her mouth taking me in. He's matching his pace with her, cheeks bright, and his mouth is hung open in the shape of an O. He doesn't notice me staring, and he doesn't look away.

Mia grazes her teeth along my cock, breaking any control I had left. I jerk forward, hitting the back of her throat until she gags.

Alex's eyes roll back, and then his gaze returns to where Mia and I are connected. She looks up at me, tears streaming down her eyes. I go to pull away, but she grabs my belt loop and pulls me forward until I slam into the back of her throat. I dig my free hand into her hair and start fucking her mouth.

Tingling starts in my lower back and tightens in my balls as the pressure from my orgasm grows. I swallow hard. I'm too fucking close.

"Alex, make her come," I command him and don't bother looking at how he does it, too captivated by the ways she moans around my cock as her release rolls over her, tugging me with her.

I pump into her with my never-ending release, then collapse to my knees and drop my forehead to hers. Alex groans with his own orgasm and falls to her other side.

I place a soft kiss to her temple, then head to the bathroom and wet a cloth. When I get back to them, I hand her an open bottle of water. "Drink this."

She takes several drinks then puts it on the table. "Thanks, my throat's sore." She says it with so much mischief and playfulness it pulls a groan from my chest. I love her like this.

Her smirk drops when I spread her legs. They

tremble in my hand as I carefully clean her before tossing the cloth toward the bathroom floor.

"Make room for me."

Alex groans, already half-asleep, and shifts them both closer to the other side. I strip down and climb in. It takes a bit to find a comfortable position. I lie on my back, Mia's head in the crook of my shoulder, leg slung over mine, with Alex wrapped around her back. I pull the sheets over us, still too hot for the comforter.

Mia trails her fingers along my chest and places a soft kiss above my heart.

She buries her face and stiffens in a way that has my nerves on end. Alex looks up, noticing the change in her too. Her words are muffled against my chest. "Have you done this before? Shared a girl?"

Fuck. Alex's head drops back on the pillow, regret immediately registering on his face.

I run my fingers under her jaw, encouraging her to meet my gaze, and answer honestly. "Yes. Does that bother you?"

Her brows pull together. "A little."

Alex kisses her nape. "Trust me, Kitten. Nothing we've ever done has come anywhere close to what we just did."

Her body softens, and I push a strand of her hair behind her ear.

The knowledge that this is the only night we'll have together feels like a cruel twist of fate. A deep ache builds between my ribs. How can I possibly let her go? "Stay another night."

"My flight's already booked." There's a sadness in her voice, like this hurts her just as much as it does me, and I'm a sick fucking man because I'm happy about it.

"We'll pay to switch your flight." Alex raises onto his elbow and leans over her, kissing her deeply. He doesn't break off until they're both breathless.

She swallows hard, her eyes darting between his and mine. I can see all the worries crashing against each other.

"Just one more night." I run my nose along hers and take a deep, shuddering breath. "Please, Mia. Just one more."

"Okay... One more." Her words come out almost pained, and Alex wraps his arm tighter around her middle.

I lie there, listening to their breathing grow heavy and settle with sleep while thoughts bombard me. What the hell am I thinking? How could this weekend ever be enough?

Of either of them.

# CHAPTER 18
## ALEX

MIA STIRS BESIDE ME, slowly climbing out of sleep. A warm smile curves her lips when her crisp green eyes meet mine.

She cups a hand over her mouth. "Morning."

I raise a brow and pull it away. "Don't hide from me, Kitten."

She turns her chin into the pillow and groans. "Morning breath."

I climb over her, caging her in with my arms, and drop my weight, sinking her into the mattress. She laughs and tries to squirm out from under me, but I catch both of her hands and suck on her bottom lip.

She freezes, then melts when I stroke my tongue inside her mouth. It's a gentle, tender kiss. Nothing like the hurried need from last night. I'm savoring every sip of her.

She nips my bottom lip, and I pull back, matching her smile with my own.

"I can't breathe." she groans, and I roll onto my

back, pulling her with me so that she is still tucked in my arm. "Better?"

"Mmhmm." She scans the empty bed, then raises a brow at me.

"He went to get coffee."

I don't want to tell her that when River woke up this morning, he took one look at her, and the muscle in his jaw ticked as he stroked her hair behind her ear. He watched her for several minutes, not knowing I was watching him. He looked almost tortured, like somehow he had exactly what he wanted and everything he didn't.

"I could get used to this," River says from the doorway. He steps into the room, closing the door behind him, and leans against the wall with the tray of coffees in his hands. He looks so relaxed, black t-shirt, with low-slung shorts and his perfectly styled hair a mess from her fingers running through it. I don't think I've ever seen him like this.

River's eyes follow her legs dangling over my waist, and they darken as they trace the smooth skin leading to the center of her thighs.

He smirks as he brings his coffee to his lips and says, "You better get up. Everybody's waiting for you."

"Oh my God." Mia stiffens and pushes up on her palms, flying off the bed.

My lips curve, and I smile as I watch her frantically run through the room, searching through her suitcase to grab something to wear. She throws on this adorable pink sundress but doesn't even think to put anything else underneath it. I drop my feet to the floor, grabbing behind her knees and leading her toward me. She tries to wiggle away, but I run my palm from her calf up the back of her thigh and grasp her ass. "How about you dress like this every day?"

"I'll remember that when I get home." She bats my hands away, ignoring my growl, and heads toward the door, smiling up at River as he passes her a coffee.

Her cheeks flush pink as she takes him in, and he watches her with intense eyes.

"Morning," she says.

"Morning, Love." River cups the back of her neck and tugs her up on her toes, placing a kiss between her brows. "You better hurry. The girls are asking about you."

My gaze trails Mia as she rushes out the door before meeting River's hot gaze. His eyes dart away, and he studies the scenery out the back windows.

I'm sitting on the bed with my feet planted on the floor, completely naked, and something feels off. River must think so, too, because he clears his throat and nods toward the door before heading out.

I lick my lips, which still taste like Mia, and pull on shorts and a loose white T-shirt before following them out.

By the time I get to the lobby, everybody's there— Jax and Sidney, Piper and Lucas, and Misty and Shana. Their luggage is stacked in piles at the front door, waiting for the bellmen to take them to their car.

I watch Mia talk with Piper. She's all smiles and warm and happy. A gentle hum vibrates my chest. It's such a stark contrast from how she looked a few days ago. The delicate skin under her eyes had been tinged purple from lack of sleep, and she had a nervous skittishness about her. All of that's replaced with a bright easiness. She practically cackles at something Sidney and Piper say, and it tightens something in my chest.

"So, you want to talk about it?" Jax grins at me as he grips my shoulder and gives it a squeeze.

"Talk about what?" I raise a brow, not ready to talk about this weekend. Not ready to assess how much I fucked up.

"Don't look at me like that. You know this was all a part of Sidney and Piper's plan, right?"

I give him a side-eye look. "You told me you had nothing to do with this." I huff out a laugh, pinch my nose, and look toward the sky. "I'm not sure if I should thank you or punch you."

Jax's brows pull down in the middle as he looks at me with concern. "It's just the weekend?"

"Yeah." He's right—it's just a weekend, but it's not what I want. It's not what I ever wanted.

"So how did you convince her to stay an extra day?" Jax smirks

I can feel heat climbing my neck. "A lady never kisses and tells."

Jax laughs before his gaze turns serious. "She looks better, you know. Whatever you guys are doing, it's helping."

A mixture of pride and dread fills my chest because it is working. I can see it in the way she smiles with her whole face. In the way she stands straighter and how relaxed she is when she talks to Sidney and hugs her goodbye. I want to make her feel like this all the time. I want to be the one that she depends on. That's what makes this being the last day so hard.

I pat Jax's back. "Just take care of her. I know you and Sidney already do, but look out for her for me. Alright? Make sure she's okay."

Jax nods, looking way too serious. "I've got her."

Mia walks up to us, giving Jax a warm hug, and then stands to my side.

He looks back and forth between us and grins. "So tell me, Mia, what convinced you to stay another night?"

She rolls her eyes, her cheeks a pretty hue of pink. "I'll see you at home, Jaxy."

He laughs at the sound of Piper's childhood nickname and rubs his knuckles against the top of her head.

The pinch of jealousy surprises me, not because I think he's hitting on her; anybody with eyes can see he is a goner for Sidney. It's his easiness with her, the familiarness. The fact that I know after tomorrow, she'll be gone from my life again, and she'll still be in his. I swallow hard and grab the back of my neck. I'm being an asshole.

"See you at home." Jax shoves her shoulder lightly. "Don't do anything I wouldn't do."

I wrap my arms around her middle, pulling her back to my chest. I rest my chin on her head as we watch them leave.

River comes up to us and tilts his head as he takes us in. "We got to hit the gym, but I scheduled you a massage for the afternoon."

She makes an almost squeal-like sound of excitement, then clears her throat. "You didn't have to do that."

"No, I didn't have to do that, but I wanted to."

We walk her to the spa, and I kiss her temple before she leaves. I glance up at River, suddenly furious he's making me work out and miss out on time with her.

He smirks. "Trust me, she needs a break for what I have planned later."

# CHAPTER 19
## MIA

"HOW WAS YOUR MASSAGE?" an attendant asks warmly the second I step out of the treatment room. I take the small glass of water she holds out to me and smile.

"So good." And it really had been. The bed was heated, she tucked pillows under my knees and ankles, relieving all pressure, and she gave one hell of a head massage. Between that, the body scrub, and the facial, I've never been this relaxed.

"I'm happy to hear that. Mr. Davis has opted for the package that includes full-day access to the rest of the facility."

There's a tug on my chest, pulling me toward the guys. I've already been away from them for hours, and it feels like a waste to not go back. I glance at the large wood door, curious about what's on the other side. If it's anything like the rest of the spa, it's probably amazing. River wouldn't have booked it if he didn't want me to go in, right?

Maybe I can convince the guys to get a pedicure or something. I bite back a smile at the image of River with painted toes. "Yes, thank you."

She pushes open the door, and my mouth falls open. The walls are covered in deep blue-gray mosaic tiles that glimmer in the low amber light, and the ceiling is paneled in low-hung cedar planks, making the entire space feel like a warm hug.

There are a few other people lounging in what can only be described as oversized beanbags, snuggled into their soft seats with their robes pulled around them. I don't think I've ever seen a more appealing place to nap.

We turn a corner, and the lights are dimmer here, giving it a cave-like presence. There are three pools the size of a parking stall, side by side and dimly lit with underwater lights.

The attendant gestures to the first one. "This is our contrast hydrotherapy section. First is a cold plunge pool that's kept at a crisp forty-five degrees. You climb in, submerge for a few seconds before getting out. Then you have a hot pool and finally a relaxing hydrotherapy pool. You're meant to alternate between the cold and hot. It increases your circulation."

A couple leisurely relaxes in the last one, their backs leaning against sunken lounge chairs.

I'm not sure about the plunge pool, but I'm definitely trying the bubbles.

I silently follow, my gaze focusing on a large gold

abstract painting of a naked woman, and nearly walk right into her. "Shit. Sorry."

She gives me a warm smile, and I make a mental note to make sure she gets a tip.

"Here you'll find our steam room." She points to a large glass door. The door beside it opens, and the sounds of water fill the space. "And this is our rain shower room."

I take a quick peek and spot rivulets pouring from the ceiling, covering the entire space. *Stunning.*

"We suggest you start in the steam room before rinsing off in this one prior to making your way to the pools. You can hang your robe just here."

"Thank you very much." Why am I so freaking awkward? I hang my robe next to two others, leaving me in my swimsuit, and step into the room, my lungs instantly filling with the damp air. I blink to focus, but the steam is so thick I can't make out the benches lining the walls until I nearly trip into them.

I climb over the first level, choosing instead to sit on the middle step, and rest my shoulder blades against the top one before tipping my head back and taking several breaths. The air is scented with cedar and leather. I instantly wish River was here. The wooden seat is hot against my thighs, and I shift until they get used to it.

With my eyes closed, my senses narrow in on the sound of shifting fabric from across the space. I lift my head and strain my eyes, but even though I know someone's there, I can't see anything through the white vapor.

I jolt upward when the person—who I didn't even know was there—shifts beside me, lining their thigh to mine. I start to lose my balance, tipping forward, and brace my hands in front of me. I cringe, sure I'm going to hit the ground, but strong arms wrap around my middle and haul me back before I land.

"Careful, Mia," River breathes against my ear, and my skin breaks out in goosebumps despite the heat. The man has a way of saying my name that turns it into something indecent.

My heart is still pounding from being startled, then nearly crashes as I hiss, "What are you doing?"

I expect him to answer. He should answer. It would be normal to answer, but quiet as always, River lets go of me and lifts himself to the bench above me, dropping his knees to either side of my head. Any irritation I felt moments ago instantly vanishes. I turn toward him, confused, but he cups the nape of my neck and directs me forward.

I suck in a breath. The move feels like a command, reinforced when he tightens his grip once before letting go. My fingers dig into the cedar planks on either side of me in an attempt to keep still.

River's palms settle on my shoulders and tug me until my back arches and my chest lifts into the air before his fingers shift lower. He covers every inch of my skin painfully slowly, taking time to outline my collarbone before lowering further. His palms are like lava against my already heated skin. By the time his fingertips graze the cup of my bikini, my entire body feels like he lit a fire within.

I take a long, slow breath as he dips under the fabric, sweeping back and forth just below the edge. My nipples harden until they tingle with the need for his touch. All of my attention is focused on where he caresses the sensitive curve of my breasts. My chest aches, and my head blurs, almost fuzzy with anticipation.

"Breathe." River nips my ear, and his hands back off, drawing a whimper from my mouth. I hold my breath, and my eyes shoot across to where the other person in the room's located, but I still can't make anything out.

"Will you breathe, or will I have to stop?" I feel his words more than hear them. His mouth grazing the shell of my ear. I nod and take several deep breaths, pausing before letting them out.

"Good girl." His gravelly praise goes straight to my core. Before I can inhale again, he pushes the cups of my bikini to the side, leaving me exposed. Cupping my breasts, he pushes them together and ever so slightly squeezes.

I arch into his touch and press back between his thighs, loving his groan when the hard length of his cock presses against my shoulder. I shift, and he squeezes my breasts again, this time just shy of painful, making his command clear.

I want to turn around and take him into my mouth. Drive him out of his mind for once, but I want what he wants to give me more.

He circles his thumbs around my nipples until they're painfully hard. The way this man has me coming apart with just his hands... Time is drawn out until every molecule of my being is focused on his touch. I'm about to beg, not caring we aren't alone, when River pinches my nipples between his thumbs and forefingers, shooting an electric current straight to my clit. I buck my hips, drawing in a sharp gasp.

The door opens, and I stiffen, realizing my top is completely missing.

"About fucking time," River says as the new person steps closer.

Alex comes into view less than two feet from my face and rests his palms on my legs. His thumbs stroke the inside of my thighs. He's close enough now I can make out his hooded eyes roaming over where River's rolling my nipples. His gaze meets mine. His lips shift, revealing a smile that's more primal than flirtatious. "Look at you, Kitten."

River cups my breasts, holding them out for Alex. He leans forward and sucks my nipple into his mouth. *Shit.* Alex swirls his tongue, soothing the tender peak.

I should be mortified that we're doing this in public. Wetness soaks my thighs at the idea of being caught with their hands on me, driving me out of my mind with their touch.

I release the bench, digging my hands into Alex's hair and holding him against me. A low chuckle rumbles through his chest before he releases my nipple.

River runs his palms down my arms, collaring my wrists between his fingers. He slowly tightens his grip until I release my grasp of Alex's hair. I whimper when he places my hands back on the bench, making it clear that I'm not allowed to touch. I stiffen and go to move away when he kisses the back of my nape, just below my hairline. The motion is so unexpectedly tender that I freeze.

He trails kisses along my neck before sucking the bottom of my ear between his teeth. "Do you want to continue?"

No. Yes. *Please.* My brain short-circuits between them. But no one touches me, waiting for my answer. I take several calming breaths. "Yes."

River wraps his hand around my throat and tilts my head back until I meet his black gaze towering above me. Even upside down, he looks like Lucifer, here to claim my soul. "That's our good girl."

Alex's mouth descends on my other nipple, and my hips tilt, searching for friction.

A masculine sound that's between a groan and a cough comes from the other side of the room too far to see through the steam. Sparks of heat dance in my lower stomach, everything's more intense knowing the stranger's getting off listening to us.

The hand around my throat tightens, and the world grows small. River's gaze hasn't left mine as he slowly tightens his grasp until my chest burns, then releases. By the time Alex is kissing down my stomach and pulling off my swimsuit bottoms, I've forgotten about anyone else.

River releases his hold completely before lifting me and taking my place on the bench. He quickly settles my back against his chest, hooking my legs on the outside of his thighs. He spreads his knees wide, exposing me to Alex's hot gaze.

Alex groans as he takes me in. His eyes dart to mine, and what can only be called a sinister grin curves his mouth. He leans in, capturing my lips in a kiss that leaves us both panting. "So fucking perfect."

He stands, stepping back, and the air shifting reminds me that I'm nearly naked, stretched, and exposed, but my brain shuts off the second Alex drops to his knees.

He runs his nose along my seam, breathing me in before flattening his tongue against my clit. I jerk, and my knees pull inward, only to be met with River holding them further apart.

I grip the bench, unsure if I'm allowed to touch them yet, and my arms tremble with the force required to keep them in place. I breathe out a sigh of relief when River lifts my hands up and behind me to wrap around the back of his neck. I give a sharp tug of his hair, and his stiff cock bucks into my ass. So I do it again.

His hands are back on my breasts, fingers abusing my nipples while Alex licks me from entrance to clit until I'm squirming between them, barely able to breathe with how taut I'm pulled.

I roll my hips, desperately needing more. I grind back into River while rocking forward, but nothing will touch the ache.

My teeth clench together, air rushing out my nose, biting back my moan when Alex slides two fingers into me. He sucks hard on my clit, and tension radiates out into my back, my limbs, my spine. I just need *one more* thrust.

Alex and River pull back from me, and I can't stop my cry at the loss of being so fucking close. A frustrated tear tracks down my cheek, and River catches it with his thumb before thrusting it into my mouth.

He presses my tongue down and grips my jaw, holding me in place.

Alex's breaths pant over my core as I shake between them, simultaneously hating and loving this.

Alex guides more fingers into me, working them back and forth while sucking on my clit until my world goes white. I tighten around him before my orgasm detonates, sending shards of pleasure through me. I moan loudly around River's thumb, completely lost to their touch, and revel in the feel of them.

There's a muffled, distinctly male groan from across from us. Alex smiles and presses a kiss into my stomach. I should feel disgusted, but not a single thing feels wrong about this moment. Whoever it is gets up and escapes the steam room, the open door letting in some much-needed cool air.

"I'll be right back." Alex leaves behind the stranger and comes back with a robe. He makes quick work of finishing removing my bathing suit top, and wrapping the robe around me.

Unable to stand on my own, River's arm bands around my middle as he kisses my temple. "Let's get you cleaned up."

# CHAPTER 20
# MIA

THE RAIN SHOWER room is just as nice as I thought it would be, with its cool slate floors and deep blue subway tiles.

River cradles me to his chest, my legs wrapped around his waist and his hands buried under my thighs. I tuck my face into the curve between his neck and shoulder. I'm too exhausted to even consider holding up my own weight.

Alex takes his time, dragging a cloth lightly between my shoulder blades, drifting over my hips before trailing down my leg and capturing my foot. He chuckles when I jerk away from being tickled and starts on my other side. A soft moan forms on my lips when Alex gently kneads the muscles in my back. I let myself go limp and relax into them as they take care of me.

The water pouring from the ceiling is cool on my heated, slick skin, but the constant contact from the men has warmth radiating from inside of me.

Alex massages shampoo into my hair, followed by conditioner and I hum in the back of my throat, leaning back into his touch.

River shifts one arm, banding around my waist to keep me from tipping back.

I'm overcome with the feeling of being cherished, and tears sting my eyes, knowing that this is the last day.

River sets me down on shaky legs, only letting go of my waist so Alex can thread my arms through my robe and tie a knot over my navel.

The walk back to the villa is a blur. I spend the entire time tucked into Alex's shoulder, barely looking at my surroundings.

When we get inside, he directs me to the bed, and I crawl on top of it, allowing him to pull the covers over me. I can vaguely hear River's voice speaking on the phone, but my eyes are heavy, and sleep slowly pulls me under.

Alex whispers against my temple. "Sleep, Kitten. We'll wake you up when the food's here."

———

Muffled sounds pull me out of my sleep, and the sharp click of the door shutting has me sitting up, a yawn stretching my mouth.

River sets a tray of food in the center of the bed and shifts it further away when I reach for a grape, earning a glare from me. The soft smile on his lips has my breath hitching.

Alex steals my attention as he climbs up near the pillow beside me, crosses his legs, and grins. "We figured you'd be hungry…and you need your energy up for tonight."

"Uh-huh. And what's happening tonight?" I raise a brow, already feeling my skin grow hot.

Alex leans in, kissing my breath away before pulling back and winking at me. "Whatever you want, Kitten."

River pushes a strand of my hair behind my ear. "We forget about tomorrow and just enjoy each other." His voice is raw and low, and it pulls at my heart. There's something so wrong about this not lasting, but I refuse to let those feelings affect this moment and steal it from me.

The mattress compresses when River sits on my right so that I'm between them, and he sorts through the charcuterie board. He takes his time making a small sandwich-like tower with a cracker, salami, and cheese before handing it to me.

I bite into it and moan in the back of my throat. It's all melted cheesy goodness.

"Good," I say to an entirely too pleased River.

"What, you aren't going to make me one?" Alex teases River, but his mouth snaps shut when River already has one ready for him.

A slight blush tinges Alex's cheeks, and he speaks before I can ask him about it. "Tell us about your charity. What happens next?"

The buzz of excitement travels through me, and I tell them all about it before anxiety takes over. "Now

I just need to figure out exactly how to get more donors. Misty had a few ideas on how to run the social media campaign, and we're going to work on it for the next few weeks. Then, I guess, just hope like hell it works."

"It'll work." River feeds me a grape, and my mouth bursts with sweet and sour.

Alex pulls me into his arms so my back is against his chest and runs his nose along my neck, casting my skin in goose bumps.

River looks pensive, then sets the tray on the nightstand. "What was the class you forgot about and ended up having to study for the final for thirty-six hours straight?"

"Ethics…You had to remember that?"

"I remember everything." River hands me another grape, and I bite into it before I can say something stupid. "I remember that you had the second-highest score and that Charles guy was furious about it. Tried to rat you out to the teacher."

My brows pinch together. "Oh yeah…Whatever happened to him?"

"We had a nice chat on why it's stupid to tattle on your friends." Alex smirks, stealing the grape River tries to hand me, and pops it into his mouth.

"Then there's the time you hustled half the hockey team playing pool," River says, and there's something settling in his confidence in me. He slides my robe off my shoulders, and his lips follow its path, placing open-mouth kisses along the newly exposed skin.

"You need to trust yourself. You've got this," River whispers before dipping his tongue into the hollow above my collarbone, and my mind blanks out.

Alex slides my robe down the rest of the way before discarding it over the side of the bed. He kisses the nape of my neck as River stands and strips out of his clothes, revealing his thick cock. I swallow hard.

He kneels back on the bed and leans over me, bracing a hand on the bed. He strokes his thumb over my cheekbone before cradling my neck, pulling my forehead to his.

His movements are slow and measured, like he has infinite time to explore me. His hands trace every curve of my body as if he's memorizing it, trailing his thumbs over my breasts and across my nipples, circling my navel, leaving goose bumps wherever his touch lingers.

I meet his hooded gaze and tilt my chin up to brush my lips over his.

I lick the seam of his mouth and let out a long, low moan as he takes control of the kiss. I shudder when he cups me between my thighs. His fingers move in slow, lazy circles, and I break our kiss to bite down on my lip to keep from crying out.

"Please," I say against the side of his throat.

"Please what?" River rasps, curving his palm and circling my entrance before pulling away.

I make a low, almost pained sound at the loss of his touch.

"Kitten, you better answer him." Alex exhales and touches his fingers to the curve of my hip where it meets my waist. He drags his fingertips along my rib cage, drawing my attention and brushing a kiss on the nape of my neck. Nipping playfully, he shifts down under the covers to lie behind me and guides me down beside him.

River follows, pinning me between them.

Their hearts beat faster with every single touch. Each pulse vibrates where we're smashed together.

"Touch me," I reply and close my eyes as warm hands graze my skin.

I forget who they belong to and squirm between them, shifting my hips, searching for more. They touch everywhere, massaging the tension from my muscles, leaving me pliant between strong hands. My nipples pebble under callused fingers while nails rake my flesh and tongues tease my skin. Soft fingers roam over my hips, and every nerve sparks to life, following their path as they dip between my thighs and sink deep inside.

My back arches at the connection, my eyes snapping open to see River's hand press into me.

"Holy shit," I breathe.

My heart pounds in my chest, and I rake my hands into River's hair, dropping my head back to rest on Alex.

Alex's fingertips roll over my nipple before pinching the tip hard enough to draw a sharp cry from me, then caress down my stomach to rub my clit between his two fingers.

Their pace is agonizingly slow. My breathing quickens, my heart pounds in my chest, and my skin's alive with tingling sensations as the pleasure spreads from my toes to every corner of my body. My thighs tremble, and I feel the warmth of an orgasm beginning to build deep within me.

River bites down on my jaw and kisses up to my ear. "Come for us, Love, so I can finally *fuck* you."

The thought of him sinking deep inside me has wave after wave of intense pleasure shattering me apart. They'd been building the orgasm so slowly that the fierceness of the release has my eyes rolling back, my body trembling between them.

They let me come down for several seconds before River places his strong hands around my leg and delicately hoists it over his hip. His eyes are filled with anticipation as the tip of his erection teases my entrance, generating a spark between us that sends shivers up my spine. In one fluid motion, he pushes himself inside me, filling me completely.

I knew he was big, but he fills me so thoroughly that the feeling of pressure is almost more than I can take.

Alex kisses along my shoulder blades as River slowly strokes inside me, letting me adjust to his size.

I feel cherished, cared for, loved—

I tense at the thought, and River pinches my nipples, drawing a squeak from my mouth.

"Stop thinking," he says and bites my lower lip.

I let my mind go blank and lose myself to them.

His strokes grow quicker until he is pounding inside of me, hitting that perfect spot.

A loud moan escapes from my lips as another orgasm builds inside of me. The pleasure is too much, and I clench around him again, making him groan against my mouth.

Alex returns his hand to my center, massaging my clit in tight circles, driving the pressure upward.

River growls low in his throat, his hips bucking into me with his release, triggering me over the edge with him.

Just as I start to catch my breath, I feel him carefully slide out, only to feel Alex notch his cock against me.

"You ready for me, Kitten?" Alex's hot breath skates over my ear as he nips the lobe, and I press down on him, enveloping his cock in my slick heat.

A satisfied grunt rumbles up from his chest. I want to purr. We both groan as he fills me completely. A spasm rocks through me as the crown of his cock bumps my G-spot. We pause, savoring the moment.

River lays his forehead against mine, nuzzling and kissing me tenderly. His hand holds my thigh high on his hip, locking me in place while his friend thrusts into me from behind. I reach behind me and thread my fingers into Alex's hair, holding on for dear life as every muscle in my body tightens, and another wave of pleasure erupts from deep within me. Alex thrusts a few more times, and then his grip tightens as he finds his own release.

"That was incredible," I say between breaths.

River smiles softly, his brows creasing slightly as he looks at me tenderly. "You're incredible," he murmurs back.

My chest tightens, knowing there's no coming back from this.

# CHAPTER 21
## RIVER

THE CLOCK READS SIX FORTY-FIVE. There are fifteen minutes before our alarm's set to go off, and with each change of the numbers, my chest tightens a little more.

Mia's leaving this morning, and no matter how tempting it is to ask her to stay longer, I know it wouldn't be fair to her. She has her internship and charity to get back to. I'll be damned before I'm responsible for the dark purple creeping back beneath her eyes.

Instead, I watch the clock like it's personally to blame for us running out of time.

Mia's back expands against my chest with each of her breaths. She's burrowed her face against Alex's chest, and he's buried his hand in her hair. If it wasn't for the way she held my fingers locked over her sternum, entwined in hers, I might have thought they were their own couple.

I knew from the beginning this was temporary.

She lives in Ottawa, and we're in Boston. Hell, even if we could manage it, there's no guarantee she'd want that. It's one thing to have a weekend fling. It's a whole other thing to get involved with two NHL players. The media coverage alone would be enough to bury someone.

She's amazing and selfless, and there'd be no doubt if she decided we're worth it. She'd put up with whatever bullshit came with that. But I can't do that to her. Not when she's already stressed-out. Not when she's already giving all of herself.

There's no part of me that wants to make her life harder.

Alex shifts, and his grip tightens on her like he's afraid she'll disappear, even in his sleep. I tuck a strand of her hair behind her ear, and a sharp pain pierces below my ribs when she turns into my palm.

A quick glance at the clock tells me there are less than five minutes left, and I nuzzle the curve of her neck, breathing in her lavender vanilla scent for the last time.

For a few days, I had everything I wanted, and it might kill me to let it go.

———

Mia doesn't look away from the rain-streaked window as we head toward the San Francisco airport. She's been quiet for the almost two-hour drive. Alex and I don't fly out until tonight, but we insisted on traveling with her. If it gives me another two hours, I'll take it.

The resort offered a chauffeured car service to the airport, and we chose a large Mercedes SUV so we could all fit in the back. Alex sits directly behind her. He's pulled a few strands of her hair over the top of her seat and plays with them mindlessly. His unfocused gaze is straight ahead, lost in thought.

Mia shifts, and I fight the urge to turn her to face me. She looks calm while it feels like my body is roiling inside me. Every mile is a mile closer to saying goodbye. Forever...I can't process that thought, so I let it slip from my mind to keep me up later.

Was she this collected back when she ghosted us in university? I understand what happened. I know it was my fault for being a jealous asshole. Hell, I'm surprised Alex still speaks to me.

I never thought it was easy for her. She's just selfless by nature. Was I wrong? An uncomfortable churning fills my gut at the idea that none of this mattered to her.

Is this easy for her? Because I think it might kill me.

Words bubble up in my chest. I want to demand she acknowledge that this is something more, even if it was just a few days. Her cool demeanor is killing me.

She sniffs and turns further away from me as the blood drains from me. I'm such a fucking asshole. If I thought her indifference was bad, this is a million times worse.

I reach out and catch her jaw with my knuckle, directing her to face me, but she shakes off my touch and raises a hand to wipe under her eye.

"Mia, look at me," I say with a hint of too much command, but I need to see her.

The green of her irises is brilliant against her red-rimmed lids. She gives me a watery smile. "I'm sorry." She sniffs and rubs her face. "I'm being silly."

She looks so unsure of herself, and the flush of embarrassment takes over her cheeks. How can she possibly not know how we feel about her? "I'm going to miss you, Mia. You know that, right?"

Her shoulders raise, and I fucking hate the insecure look that crosses her face.

Alex leans over the seat and kisses her temple. "Hey, Kitten. Where's your claws?"

She rolls her eyes. "How long is it going to take to convince you to not call me that?"

He grins with his dimples in full view. "Forever."

A soft chuckle tumbles from her lips, and I'm overwhelmed with gratitude for him. I've never been good at levity. Always a little too serious. Intense.

But that's where Alex levels me out, and within seconds, her tears have dried, and there's a small smile curving her lips. Fucking magic.

———

We pull up to the drop-off zone of the airport entirely too soon. It's like the seconds melted away without feeling them. I pull her small carry-on from the trunk and hold on to the handle as she tries to take it from me. Fuck.

She gives it a little tug, and I know I have to let it go, but I just grip it harder.

Alex slides up beside me and puts his hand on my upper back. He rubs it back and forth over my shoulder blades, and the tension leaves my muscles. I let go of her bag and shove my hands in my pockets to stop myself from doing anything stupid. The thought of kidnapping isn't out of the realm of my fantasies.

She pulls it toward her, the drizzle of rain dampening her hair as she stares up at us with round, glassy eyes. "So that was fun, right?"

Her tone doesn't match her words, and I have to take a deep breath before speaking. "Right."

A shiver visibly runs through her, and Alex reaches behind his head, pulling off his deep blue hoodie in one move, and drops it over her head. The heavy fabric engulfs her to mid-thigh. He adjusts the strings near her neck, fiddling with them longer than necessary, and says, "Don't want you catching a cold."

She digs her hands into the center pouch, and her shoulders rise. "I won't be able to return it."

Alex runs his thumb over her cheek before dropping his hands to his sides and giving her a cocky smile. "Keep it. I'll get it back the next time I see you."

"Oh yeah? When's that?" she asks, and her eyes shine.

Alex's smile grows, and he chuckles. "When we come up there and kick Jax's ass in a few months."

"You wish." She laughs, but it breaks at the end.

Alex wraps her in a bear hug, pulling her off her feet, and kisses her slowly for several moments before returning her to the ground. I'm so fucking jealous because I know I can't handle doing the same.

She looks at me from where she stands, Alex's arm wrapped around her shoulder. "What, no hug goodbye?"

Fuck. I want to so badly, but I dig my hands further into my pockets and shake my head. "You're going to be late."

She flinches, and her chin trembles at my brush-off, and I lose all restraint, pulling her into my arms and smashing my mouth to hers. She folds into me instantly, grasping my shirt and tugging me closer. I deepen the kiss, tasting Alex's mint gum, and groan. All thoughts of what's right to do or sane dissolve; all I care about is staying in this moment.

She's the one to pull away. Her fingers play with the top button of my pressed white oxford shirt. "At least we had the weekend."

Alex's face crumples before he hides it in the curve of her neck. He takes an audible breath before letting it out and backing up, giving us both a wide smile that doesn't reach his eyes. "We'll always have Napa."

It's such a cliché thing to say, but it breaks some of the tension. Both of us step away from her as she takes a few steps toward the airport entrance before glancing back. "Always have Napa."

This weekend had been a dream, a bubble of time where we could forget the real world and just be together. But now, reality is crashing back in. Mia's eyes meet mine, and I see the pain there, the same pain no doubt visible in mine. It's like we're both treading water, trying to keep our heads above the surface but knowing that eventually, we'll drown.

"I'll text you both when I land," she says, her voice barely above a whisper.

I just nod, unable to speak, afraid my voice will betray me, that she will hear the desperation in my words.

Alex chimes in. "Dirty text, I hope."

"You're disgusting." She huffs. "Just for that, you'll have to wait for River to tell you when I land."

"Oh, come on," Alex says playfully.

She laughs before she gives us a final, sad smile and then turns to walk away, her carry-on bag rolling behind her.

She disappears into the airport, her small figure swallowed by the throngs of people, and I feel like a part of me is being ripped away.

It takes everything in me not to chase after her. I channel that energy and punch the departure sign to my right. Blood drips from the split in my knuckles, but it doesn't matter. I need the pain as a distraction.

Alex grips my shoulders. "Come on. Let's go get wasted."

That's an absolutely perfect idea.

We stumble into the nearest bar and find a booth hidden in the back. The low lighting, combined with the smell of alcohol, hit me in the face like a brick. I don't even bother with the menu and just order a whiskey neat. Alex orders four shots of tequila and places them in front of each of us.

He throws back his shot and slams the glass on the table. "Fuck, that was intense."

I nod in agreement and take a sip of my drink. "It's fucked."

Alex leans back in the booth, his eyes unfocused as he traces the rim of his shot glass. "It feels like getting hit by a train."

"Yeah," I say, finishing my whiskey and gesturing for another.

We just let the best thing that ever happened to us walk away. *Again.*

# CHAPTER 22
# MIA

I PULL Alex's hoodie over my head, grabbing fistfuls of its softness to comfort myself. I know I'm overreacting. It was just one weekend with two guys I hadn't seen in years. But it felt like more: the way they looked at me, the things we talked about, the hours we spent together spread across their bed.

It's always felt like more with those two. I still can't wrap my head around how everything can click into place so perfectly while simultaneously not working out at all. First, I was in university with them fighting, and now, I don't even know what could've happened. Like, are throuples a thing? Would they go for that?

Is it even worth thinking about when neither of them even brought it up? Not to mention, we live in different *countries*. Can't forget that.

My chin wobbles, and I turn into the curved plastic window, angling my face away from the passenger beside me.

The condensation from my breath fogs up the surface, obscuring my view until I wipe it away with my sleeve, which now clings wetly to my arm.

There are another two hours left of this flight, and I'm going to let myself cry the entire time because when I land, I need to get serious about work and Prosthetics For Kids again. I already took more time off than I'd planned for. More time than I could afford, but I don't regret it. How could I?

A hand lands gently on my shoulder, and I turn to look at the older woman beside me. She asks with a soft, lilting accent that I can't quite place. "Are you okay?"

I sniff and do my best to smile. "I'm fine."

She raises a brow. "Not to be nosey, but you don't look fine, Honey. Chocolate?"

I take the foil-wrapped chocolate from her and pop it into my mouth. I hum when it melts, instantly flooding my tastebuds.

"Nothing a little chocolate can't fix," the woman says cheerily. "I'm Shirley, by the way."

"Mia. Nice to meet you.

"You too, dear. Now, why don't you tell me what's got you all worked up?"

I freeze. "Oh no. I'm fine."

"You can just cut that out now. I've been around entirely too long to fall for that one."

Shit. I drop my hood to my shoulders and shrug. "I don't know where to start."

"Start where it hurts."

I inhale slowly and let it out. It all hurts. "I fell for my two best friends back in university."

"Hmm. How did that go?" There's no hint of judgment in her voice; instead, it's somehow soothing, encouraging.

I laugh. "Not great. Alex tried to kiss me, and River punched him."

"Well, that will do it. But that's not what's bothering you now?"

I puff out my cheeks and sigh. "No. No, this is a whole other screwup. I kind of ghosted them back then."

"Ghosted?" Her brows pull together.

"Oh, sorry. I stopped talking to them or seeing them. We call it ghosting because, poof, you're gone."

"I like it. I'm going to use that. So, what happened to bring this back up? Did you run into one of them with their family?"

Pain radiates in my chest as I realize that's a very real future possibility. I swallow hard and smile, processing how I'm now going to explain to this stranger that I slept with two guys? Am I really doing this? "I went to a mutual friend's wedding, and they were both there."

She nods along, not interrupting me.

"And, well… Ikindasleptwithbothofthem."

"I'm sorry, what was that?"

"I slept with both of them."

"Good for you, Honey." She practically beams at me. "I always wanted to do that. Two guys at one time. Really missed out on my chance when I was young."

I can feel my cheeks growing redder by the second.

"Was it good?" she asks curiously.

I'm not sure I can blush any harder. "Yeah…yes…it was good."

"So tell me. Why are you crying?"

Dammit. I was hoping we wouldn't circle back to that. "It was only for the weekend."

"And you want it to be more than that?"

I shrug because the answer is yes…yes, I very much want it to be more, but that's not happening. "It's complicated. They live in Boston, and I'm in Ottawa."

She shrugs as she says simply, "Then uncomplicate it."

*Just uncomplicate it.* If only it were that simple. If things had been different, if the universe had conspired in our favor, then maybe it wouldn't have been so complicated after all…

———

It's night by the time I roll into my apartment's dimly lit parking lot. Exhaustion takes over, and I drag my bag behind me as I mindlessly make my way toward the elevator and hit the button for the fifth floor. The building's at least thirty years old, with a musky scent that's permanently embedded itself into the walls and carpet.

I lean my back against the scratched vinyl wood panel wall and close my eyes. I can't wait to get into my apartment, change into some comfy pajamas, and crawl into bed. My phone buzzes.

**Alex: Hello?**

**Alex: M.I.A. you're missing in action. Don't make me fly out there.**

**River: Your flight landed almost an hour ago.**

Group chat status.

A message chimes in outside of the group.

**Sidney: Please text Alex you're home so he leaves us alone.**

I flip back to the guys.

**Me: Home safe.**

**Alex: Where? I don't see you.**

I ignore the tightening in my chest and type out my reply.

**Me: Funny…**

**River: How was your flight?**

**Me: Fine. No delays which is a miracle.**

**River: You're in your apartment?**

The elevator hits my floor, and I'm just about to hit Send on a message confirming I'm at home when the doors open and I spot Jason leaning on the wall beside my door. He's been acting increasingly erratic as time goes on, and him showing up here's a bad freaking sign.

"What are you doing here?" I step back, but the elevator doors are closed behind me.

He lifts from the wall and straightens. "Your

schedule's pretty easy to find at the hospital. Says you were gone all weekend."

"Why do you care?" Unease starts to settle in my bones. That's a level of creepy I'd like to avoid.

"You haven't texted me back."

I'm entirely too tired for this right now. "That's because there's nothing left for us to talk about."

"The hell there isn't. We're good together. You know that," he snaps, and his words slur at the end. He's drunk. I fold my arms over themselves, remembering how he'd manhandled me the last time he drank.

My body tenses out of instinct, and alarm bells sound in my head. You always hear about exes snapping and going psycho, and there's something way off base about him showing up like this.

I keep my voice soft. *Deescalate.* "You're the one that broke it off."

"Yeah, because I thought you needed a reminder that you can't ignore me."

*I'm ignoring you fine now.* Rage builds in my chest, but I bite back my words, acutely aware we're alone. "I told you I wasn't ignoring you. I just have a lot on my plate—"

"Yeah, your internship and your *charity*." He practically spit the last words, and my nose scrunches in revulsion. What the hell was I thinking dating this guy? He continues. "I told you I would take care of you. You didn't need that job, plus you're not even getting anything from the charity you spend *all* of your free time on."

I breathe in slowly, trying to keep my heart rate steady. "You could have done it with me, you know? If you'd been willing to go to an event, maybe you wouldn't have felt like you were stuck at home. You know I needed help."

"Help you? With what? Your pointless charity that's only managed to help a few kids? You are delusional if you think this is taking off. Look at the time you put into it. What do you have to show for it? Nothing!"

I flinch, and the back of my eyes burn as his words hit their mark. "Just stop. We're not together anymore. Why are you doing this?"

He stalks closer, leaving only two feet between us, and sneers down at me. "You know what I think? I think you're doing this for the clout. I think you want to be able to go around all high above everyone and say how you helped the *needy* children."

"They aren't needy!" A spark of anger burns through my self-preservation. "I have the opportunity to make people's lives better. What's *wrong* with you?"

"Nothing, Love," he says, and I wince. It somehow sounds slimy when Jason says it. He takes another step. "I love you. Come home."

"We. Are. Not. Together." I grip the handle of my bag in both hands, prepared to swing it at him if he comes any closer.

He scans me, and his eyes narrow. "What are you wearing?"

"What?" The question is so out of nowhere that I look down. Oh shit.

"Whose hoodie is that?" His voice is low, sharp, angry. He grabs my arm hard, and a pained cry breaks free.

"It's...it doesn't matter." Fear alights my nerves, and I try to shift back. My shoulder blades connect with the elevator door. My heart skips frantically. I'm trapped.

He uses his hold on me to shake me. "Where the fuck were you? Were you out there fucking someone else?"

"You're hurting me." My mouth freezes open, and his eyes widen.

"You were. You are such a selfish little slut," he hisses at me. "That wasn't very smart. You wouldn't want me talking with the board, would you?"

I swallow back the bile threatening to climb my throat. His dad sits on the hospital's board of directors, and he has more influence than he should. It's not the first time he's tried to use it against me.

"Hey, buddy. Get your hands off of her." My head whips toward the new masculine voice, and my breath comes out in a whoosh. Mark. I've never been so grateful to see my neighbor.

He glances toward me. "You okay?"

I swallow. "Yeah, fine."

Mark's brows pull up, and he tilts his head toward Jason. "This guy bothering you?"

*Yes.* "He's my ex. And yeah, he is."

"Mia." Jason sounds shocked. I have no idea how he can be this delusional.

I push off the door and skirt around Jason, not turning my back to him as I make my way to my apartment. "It's late. I think you should go."

"We're not done talking," he says through clenched teeth.

"I think you are." Mark steps fully out of his apartment, revealing his full size. He's over six feet tall and twice as wide as Jason's wiry frame. He's so warm and friendly I've always thought of him like a teddy bear, but right now, all tatted up and giant, he's scary as shit.

Jason must think so, too, because he raises both hands in front of him in a placating motion. "You're right. It's late. I'll talk to you later." He hits the button for the elevator, and the doors open within seconds.

"Answer your texts next time, Mia," he shoots over his shoulder as he steps inside.

"Are you going to be okay handling him?" Mark asks the second the doors close.

I rub my palm over my face. What if I said no? "He was just drunk. I'll talk to him, and I'm sure it'll sort itself out. If not, I have a friend I can stay with."

Jax will definitely get arrested if I have to explain why I want to move in there. "I'm fine. Thanks though. Just tired."

"You need anything, just knock."

"Will do. Thanks again. Seriously, you really helped me out."

I shut the door behind me, lock it, then collapse against it, sliding my back down the wood until my ass connects with the floor. Crookshanks meows and weaves around my legs, purring loudly. I stroke his hair and take deep breaths until the adrenaline dissipates enough for me to breathe normally.

My phone vibrates nonstop in my pocket, and I click Accept. River's face fills my screen, and he scans me back and forth before his eyes meet mine. "Are you alright?"

How the hell did he know?

"Yeah, of course, why wouldn't I be?" My voice cracks at the end, and the back of my eyes burns.

His brows pull together. "You're not alright. What happened?"

He sounds so genuinely concerned I nearly crumble right there. I wish I could rewind time. Crawl back into bed between them and just forget about everything else.

"What happened?" Alex shoves his way into frame, and his smile drops when he looks at me. "Mia?" He sounds entirely too serious to be my funloving Alex.

"It's fine. I'm just being silly, really. Nothing happened. He wasn't even that close."

"Who wasn't that close," River growls low in his throat.

"Um." Both men watch me through the phone and wait for my answer. "My ex. He...ah...he was at my apartment, wondering why I hadn't been answering his texts... He was...he was drunk and scared me a little, but it's not a big deal. Like I said, I was just being silly, overreacting."

"Mia. Listen to me. First, I want you to check that you locked your door." River's voice is a steady command, and I get up and confirm it's latched.

"It's locked."

"Good. Now, I want you to go sit on the couch." His tone is gentle, like he's talking to a frightened animal.

I sink into the rough fabric of my sofa and pull my legs up. I flick on the light beside me and look at the two men still filling my screen. "Okay." I try to change the subject. "What are you up to?"

River lets out a breath. "You're trembling."

What? I look at my hand holding my phone, and sure enough, it's vibrating in the air. I give them a wan smile. "Okay, so maybe I was a little freaked-out." I punctuate it with a fake laugh, but neither of them matches it. "But I swear, it's fine. He didn't even stay long. I'm just tired from the trip."

"Want me to call Jax?" Alex asks.

"No," I say too sharply and clear my throat. "The last thing I need is this blowing out of proportion. My ex was drunk. He came to talk, but it's late. I was alone and uncomfortable. Nothing happened. I'm fine."

Alex scans my face, and a menacing grin curls his lip. "Want me to talk to him?"

I bark out a laugh, and my tension drains with it. "You'd scare the crap out of him."

"That's kinda the point, Kitten." He winks.

I chuckle. I just can't with him. "Wait. How did you know something happened?"

"You didn't answer." River's gaze bores into mine like he's searching for secrets.

"Answer?"

"Check your phone."

I flip through my texts, and there are at least twenty messages growing in concern. I make a note to message Sidney, who they clearly contacted to tell her I'm fine. The last message mentions if I don't pick up, they're calling the police.

"You guys sure know how to freak out." I force a laugh.

"I hate that we're not there," River responds, ignoring my comment completely.

My eyes snap to his, and I swallow. I hate it too. "It's fine. I promise. I'm just tired."

"Promise to call us if you're not?" Alex asks, and he looks so unsure for a moment that I want to tell him I need him. But what good would that do?

"I promise. But I'm good. Really. You guys have a good night."

"Goodnight," they reply in unison, and I click off the call. It takes another ten minutes for me to assure Sidney that Jax doesn't have to come here before I lift Crookshanks in my arms. Heading to my bedroom, I climb in and let exhaustion take me under.

# CHAPTER 23
## ALEX

I DUCK JUST in time to dodge River's fist. It's so close it grazes my ear, and I have to dance back on my feet.

Moisture drips from my forehead and lands on my bare chest as I watch his hand close in preparation for another round. The musty smell of sweat coats the Bruins' fitness room, filling my nostrils. I can taste it in the back of my throat, and my arms are beginning to feel the strain of blocking punch after punch. His brows furrow, and he grits his teeth—if I don't do something quick, I'm not going to make it out of here.

"Why did I agree to this again?" I ask as River comes at me again. "Oh yeah, I remember now. I'm taking one for the team because you've been a pent-up ass since we got back two weeks ago."

River stalks in closer, and his lips pull into a sneer. "Keep talking. I dare you."

"Fuck, I miss her too," I say, exasperated. "You aren't the only one fucking going through it."

His eyes widen, and I take advantage of his momentary distraction to sweep his legs from under him. He lands hard on his back with a thud. We'd silently agreed not to mention Mia since we watched her disappear into the airport. It was an asshole move to do it while sparring, but fuck, he's been a beast this morning.

I drop down onto him, throwing my leg over his side before he can get up, and straddle his hips to keep him in place. He struggles against me, but I grip his shoulders, slamming them down. He hisses out a breath, and I lean forward until my face is directly above his. "You need to fucking relax, man."

His intense black eyes meet mine, and fire ignites inside me, suddenly all too aware of our position. My hips pin his to the mat, and there's no mistaking his rock-hard length against mine. I bite back a groan when I involuntarily rock forward as heat ties a knot in my gut.

River takes advantage of my distraction and flips us over so I'm underneath him, looking up. His pupils are blown wide, and his gaze searches mine. I feel the heat emanating from his body as he looms over me, his powerful presence commanding my attention.

My heart pounds in my chest, sending my pulse rushing in my ears.

What the fuck is happening?

Why aren't I pushing him off?

"Fuck, Alex." River's fingers dig into my shoulder, and his thumb presses into the base of my neck. "You're not ready for this."

He springs up, leaving me panting on the floor, and walks to the corner of the ring. I struggle to process what just happened. My chest is so tight I'm struggling to breathe, and my cock is painfully hard. *Fuck me.*

A white towel sails through the air, dropping onto my chest, and I can't help but shift my gaze upward to River. His wide shoulders twitch with tension as he vigorously rubs his face and hair with the cloth, every muscle in his back and arms flexing and moving gracefully. I swallow hard, unable to look away, trailing my tongue over my lips, and the taste of salt fills my mouth.

The gym doors crash open, and one of the team's assistant coaches steps through. "Hey, Coach Sutherland wants to see you. Both of you."

A thrill travels through my chest. There's been rumors of me becoming the captain, and I haven't had it in me to hope. I understood why they gave the title to Lucas in university, but I fucking wanted it then. I still want it now. Thank God they traded Sidney's dad after one season—that guy was a complete dick.

"Get up. Can't keep Coach waiting." River reaches down to me, his hand held out between us. For the first time since I've known him, his gaze is to the side of my head, not meeting mine. There's a pink flush up his neck and over his cheeks. I can't tell if it's from the workout or whatever just happened between us.

"Do you think it'll be good news?"

He yanks me to my feet, and a hint of a smile curves his lips. "Fuck knows we could use some."

River's shoulders are relaxed as he strides out of the gym. Any of the awkwardness that was between us is now gone, almost like nothing happened. *Don't be a fucking idiot, Alex. Nothing did happen. Bodies naturally react. Can't fucking help it.*

Great, now I'm the one with pent-up energy. I wish Mia was here so I could fuck her against the wall, letting her whimpers and moans clear my mind.

"Hurry up." River calls from the door he holds open for me, and I shake myself out of it.

"Yeah, buddy. I'm coming." I jog out, pulling my shirt on as I head for the coach's office.

———

As soon as I walk into the room, I know something's off. Damon Everette, the team owner, sits at one end of the small conference table with crossed arms. Misty's on his right, gaze laser focused on the thin folder that lies open between them.

Fuck me. The glimmer of hope he's here to bestow the captaincy disintegrates the second he glares up at me. I hit on his niece *one time*, not knowing who she was, and the man has never let it go. How was I supposed to know she was off-limits? Plus, I didn't even fucking sleep with her. I haven't told him that—it's always been too much fun seeing him get pissed—but there's nothing fun about what's about to go down.

"Sit." His voice is flat, neutral, but there's no missing the command.

I plop down instantly across from Misty, and River takes the spot on my left. I take a brief moment to look her over. As the head social media manager for the team, I've seen her at work a few times, but I'm always amazed by the outfits she comes up with. Today, her hair is pulled into a multicolored twist bun thing, and she's wearing a sunshine-yellow dress. It's just too fucking bad none of that sunshine glow is showing on her face.

"Alex, do you know why I called you in?" Coach asks from the far end of the table. His tone is nothing like I'd hoped. *Where's the congratulatory pat on the back and take a seat, son.*

I swallow hard. "Not sure, Coach. Congratulations on being the player of the year?"

Damon's eyes narrow at my remark. Fuck, why can't I keep my mouth shut. He steeples his fingers in front of him. "I suggest you drop the cocky act if you want to get through this."

I feel River tense beside me. He leans forward as if he's putting himself between me and the owner. I feel the heat emanating from River's body as he looms over me, his powerful presence commanding my attention. I can almost feel its intensity radiating off him.

Misty clears her throat, cutting through the thick air, and all eyes turn to her. "I think what Damon was trying to say—"

*Damon?* They're on a first-name basis?

"—is that the Bruins are going in a different direction this year. In the past, it's all been about the game, but with how things are progressing with social media, fans want to see their players on and off the ice."

"I've got an Instagram," I say.

The owner huffs out a breath, but Misty keeps going before he can say anything.

"That's sorta the problem. Your Instagram is basically you partying and surrounded by girls. Our rebrand is all about the team being family friendly and community focused. Right now, you don't fit that." She glances my way, and there's a hint of disparagement written in her gaze.

Heat crawls up my neck. They're calling me out, and they aren't wrong. Well, they weren't wrong. Whether Mia's here or not, I won't be going back to that lifestyle. Not after I've seen what I really want. There's just one thing I don't understand. "Why's River here?"

"That was my idea," Coach interjects. "I need you to understand how serious this is. We're cutting someone this year, and—" He glances at Damon, who nods. Coach winces as he delivers the blow. "—we won't think twice about cutting you."

"What the actual fuck? And what's your plan? Get River to babysit me?"

Damon's voice is cold when it cuts through the room. "You've given us zero reason to believe you'll get your act together without someone keeping you in check. You're an asset we don't want to lose. River here has proven himself to be responsible. We're putting him in charge."

The muscles in my back spasm, and my jaw clenches shut. I don't want to be River's responsibility.

"That's not the only reason." Misty gives me a weak smile, then faces River. "A part of this is you being more public-facing. It's one thing to have a clean image. It's another to be seen as approachable and friendly. It's not just you helping Alex. It's both of you balancing each other out."

River stays completely silent, but he seems to relax beside me.

"So what's the plan? There must be one," I ask the room.

"I've got an idea that I'm just getting the finishing touches on. I'm confident you'll both be happy to participate." Misty's smile is genuine. I tilt my head, trying to figure out her hidden meaning. "I've already run it by Damon. I've also been working remotely with Dr. Mia Brooks and Piper Knight. There's still a few things that need to be worked out. Once we're ready, I'll set up a meeting to go over the details."

My heart slams against my chest as I take in her

words, and I bite my lip against my grin. No reason to let the bosses know just how much I want this now.

Coach Sutherland drops his palms to the table with a loud smack. "We're counting on both of you to make this work."

"We've got it." I put my hand on River's shoulder, and the muscles twitch at my touch. "Don't have to worry about anything."

Damon turns to River. "Is that right? You've been quiet."

River's shoulder tightens. "Yes, sir."

"He's always quiet. Don't worry. I'll get him to loosen up a bit," I butt in, wanting to get the fuck out of here before we screw this up, and pull River toward the exit. The second the door closes behind me, I can't stop the grin from taking over my face. I've been racking my brain, trying to think of a possible reason to see Mia again, and Misty just dropped it in my lap.

River steps closer so the tips of his shoes brush mine, and a hint of a smile plays on his lips. His eyes glint with amusement and something else that I can't name as his face nears mine. A warmth spreads through me, and my heart rate triples with anticipation. He's so close that I can feel the heat emanating from his body and smell the mint on his breath.

"You as desperate to see her as I am?" he asks, his voice deep and low.

I nod slowly, looking deep into his eyes, searching

for any detail that would tell me more about what he's feeling.

The corner of River's mouth quirks upward. "What are we going to do about it?"

A mischievous grin pulls at my mouth. "Whatever it takes."

# CHAPTER 24
# RIVER

ME: **How are you?**
Erase the message to Mia and start again.
**Me: I miss you.**
Erase.
**Me: I lied. I don't want it to be just one
weekend.**
Erase.
**Me: I need you.**
The elevator dings, and I step off unsteadily, my
heart pounding. The emptiness in my stomach
mirrors the hollowness in my chest, and I shove my
phone into my pocket, another message unsent.

How could I let her walk away like that? She's
worth more than any fucking career, and if it wasn't
for Alex, I'd already be in Ottawa right now.

Then there's what happened in the gym today. I
can still feel Alex's hard cock rubbing against mine.
The way he looked up at me with his hooded eyes
had me nearly coming undone. It was my last vestige

of sanity. The knowledge that it would cost me more than I could afford is what had me hauling myself off him.

Alex's apartment door is closed. He'd gone to Lucas's place after our shitty-ass meeting with Coach.

I unlock my door across the hall and step in. My place is all modern lines and masculine finishes. I'd told the designer I wanted it to be clean but moody. Somewhere I could sink into after a brutal game.

I pick up the semi-full decanter of bourbon on the sideboard and pour two fingers into a glass tumbler before making my way to the living room. Sunlight floods through the floor-to-ceiling windows, spilling onto the black leather couch.

Collapsing on my sofa, I take a deep drink from my glass and flip on ESPN. Alex's smiling face immediately fills the screen. He's got the perfect balance of cocky and playful that the cameras eat the fuck up.

I cannot believe Damon Everette's getting on Alex's case about his image. As if we don't know this has nothing to do with building a wholesome image and everything to do with Alex nearly hooking up with Everette's niece.

It took all my willpower not to round the table and tell him exactly what I thought about his bullshit.

I've always been protective of Alex, but something snapped into place in Napa, and now, that boy is mine. No one fucks with what's mine.

Napa gave me a taste of everything I'd ever wanted. Alex, Mia and me. The family I've always craved but never had. At fifteen, moving out to play AAA hockey felt like a dream come true, but I didn't understand then I was giving up my parents for my career.

That I'd never experience that sense of belonging again. They say your team is your family, but with the ever-present possibility of being traded, it never quite fills the void created by my decision over a decade ago.

My parents thought they'd still see me, but with the high demand of hockey and the endless travel schedule, the distance grew between us until it felt easier to stay apart.

Mia and Alex are different. I'd do anything to have them both in my life. They threatened to trade Alex, not knowing I'd be gone with him. I don't give a single fuck about the game compared to him.

He's my only true family, and now I need a plan to get Mia back. Because life will never be whole without her.

She completes Alex and me. I have no doubts he feels the same way about her as I do.

Now we just need to figure out how to bridge the gap between us in Boston and her in Ottawa to prove we're in this for real.

That we'll do what it takes to make it work. However, before we do anything drastic, we need to know our girl is ready. Because she is ours, even if she hasn't admitted it yet.

# CHAPTER 25
# MIA

"WHY DON'T SCIENTISTS TRUST ATOMS?"

I smile at Carl as I check his vitals. He's an elderly man with pure white hair and big bushy brows that crinkle as he asks his umpteenth dad joke. He came into the hospital this morning with chest pains. After some tests, we decided to keep him overnight. "I don't know. Why?"

"Because they make up everything." He winks and steals a laugh from me. "Finally. I was starting to get worried you'd never smile," Carl says, tone light but concerned.

I tense, my stethoscope hovering in the air above his chest. I thought I'd been good at pretending. Pretending that none of it mattered. It was just a weekend, and my chest doesn't ache, and it's definitely not hard to breathe. Clearly, I'm bad at it.

"What are you talking about? I smile all the time."

His brows pull together. "You smile, but it doesn't reach your eyes," he says softly.

Shit.

"Don't worry. A few more of your jokes will have me fixed right up." I look away and put the round diaphragm to his chest and listen to his lungs. Strong. Good.

He grins. "I told my wife she was drawing her eyebrows too high. She seemed surprised."

A chuckle bubbles from my throat. Absolutely ludicrous, but it dissolves when I see Carl's face.

His eyes are glassy as he stares at the wall. "She sort of looked like you. A few inches shorter, but my Elsie had your hair."

My chest tightens painfully, and I ask quietly, "When did you lose her?"

He sniffs and shakes his head like he's shaking off the memory. "Long time ago now. Cancer. You know how it is."

Unfortunately, I do know how it is. It's an all too common reality here. "I'm sorry for your loss."

"Enough of that now. Old man, remember? I've lived a good life."

I nod. It's clear he doesn't want to talk about it more, so I plaster on my best smile, hoping it reaches my eyes. "Everything looks good. I'll be back in an hour—try not to get into trouble while I'm gone."

He raises a white brow playfully. "No chance I'm getting out of here today?"

"Not a single one." I'm still shaking my head when I shut Mr. Neman's door.

I finish punching his notes into the system when someone whistles behind me.

"You're good to take your lunch. I've got your rounds," Kristie says as she walks up to me. Her light brown skin is mottled with freckles, and she has this endless source of joy that keeps her humming, no matter how many patients we have or how few hours of sleep she gets. When everyone else is walking around like the night of the living dead, she's practically bouncy with energy.

I'm normally in the pediatric unit, but it's pretty common for us to be flipped around for rounds. Even though working with kids is my goal, I'm not at the stage of picking my specialty yet. Which means I work wherever they need me. Soon though, I'm hoping to earn my spot.

I walk quickly to the locker room, scanning my work badge for access. In no time, I'm slipping a light sweatshirt over my purple scrubs and grabbing my bag. A quick glance at my phone shows a few texts from an unknown number, which I immediately delete, and another one from Sidney, letting me know she's almost there.

"You heading out?" a nurse I'm not overly familiar with asks from the door, noting that I'm fully changed.

"Taking an extended lunch break."

"Fair enough. Come find me when you get back. I've got a patient I think will interest you." She smiles and holds the door open for me to leave. Curiosity bites at me, but she's already down the opposite hall before I can ask my questions.

———

Sidney picked a small sandwich shop around the corner from the hospital to meet up. It's renowned for its bread, and the sweet aroma of freshly baked sourdough wafts through the air, making my mouth water.

I spot Sidney, and she gives me a wave from one of the patio bistro tables. She's dressed in an over-sized blue cardigan, and her deep brown hair is pulled back into a bun. She still looks sun-kissed from our trip, making her olive-toned skin bronze.

She holds up a white paper bag. "I grabbed you your usual. Hope that's okay."

I collapse beside her, then unceremoniously unwrap and take a giant bite of my turkey-and-cran-berry sandwich. I mumble, "You're a freaking godsend."

She grins at me. "Good to see you feeling better."

My chest constricts, and I ignore the sharp pain. I'd been less than great the two weeks since Napa, but I thought I at least hid it from her. Turns out, I'm completely shit at it. "How'd you know?"

"I'm pretty sure you've taken every possible shift available. I literally had to threaten you to meet me here."

"That was cruel, by the way." She'd threatened to have the hockey team show up to my work and sing to me. Fucking sing! I was ninety-eight percent sure she was full of it, but that two percent was enough to get me here.

"So you *are* feeling better though, right?" she prods gently.

Lying isn't an option with my best friend, so I simply shrug before responding truthfully. "I'm not sure 'better' is the right word when I wasn't supposed to be upset in the first place."

She places her sandwich on top of it's bag. "I think it's pretty natural to be upset with your history."

Both my brows shoot up. "You're the one that convinced me that one weekend was a good idea to begin with."

"Do you regret it?" She raises one perfectly arched brow.

I take another bite and give myself a second. Do I regret it? Thoughts of firm hands and ravenous kisses fill my head. "No. It was pretty spectacular. It just hurts, you know? The three of us have always been the case of the right people at the wrong time."

A weight presses down on my shoulders, and I put down my sandwich, no longer hungry.

Sidney watches me, and then, to my relief, she switches the subject to her and Jax's plans for the last two weeks before he has to report back to the Ottawa Senators. They're going to the Maritimes to do some whale watching and head up the Cabot Trail. She's pretty excited about her Newfoundland iceberg spotting, clam digging in New Brunswick, and Prince Edward Island.

Sidney smiles sheepishly. "I'm rambling. But seriously, Anne of Green Gables? Totally stoked." Her brows pull together. "You going to be okay while we're gone?"

I drum my fingers on the table and roll my eyes. "Yes, Sidney. I'm all grown up and able to take care of myself for two whole weeks."

"Don't give me that sass. We both know you'll miss me." She gives me a cocky grin that she definitely picked up from Jax.

My phone beeps, and I check the time. "Shit. Got to go." We both stand, and I pull her in for a bear hug, holding her for an extra second before letting go. "Thanks for lunch, and have fun on your trip. Don't worry about me."

"I always worry about you. Just promise you'll call if you need anything."

I huff out a laugh. "What could I possibly need?"

She places her hands on her hips, and I give in, promising, "I'll bug you every night if I have to."

———

My heart sinks, and my chest tightens with dread as I round the corner and see Jason standing in front of the back door to the hospital that I always use, blocking my path. There's a deep crease between his eyes, and a muscle ticks in his jaw.

"You scared me." I take a slow breath to steady

myself. It's daytime. People are around. Unpleasant, but not unsafe. "I don't have time for this right now."

"You fucking slut." Jason closes the ten feet between us, and I stumble back. "This is what you were doing? Whoring around?"

He holds up his phone, and there's a picture of Sidney and Jax by the pool. In the background, I can just make out Alex with his arms around me from behind and River's face close to mine. You'd have to really be looking to spot us. "Where did you get that?"

"It's posted to your friend's Instagram," Jason sneers. "I told you not to fuck with me. You think you can go around making me look like a fool? You don't have time? We'll see about that."

"Jason, you need to understand. We're over, we've been over. Please, just let it go." The back door opens, and I don't hesitate to run. He's a spoiled nepotism baby who's never been told no in his life, and I don't trust what he's willing to do next.

I make quick work of stuffing my things into my locker and make my way back to the unit.

"You're back!" Kristie's smile drops the second she sees me. "What happened?"

"Just Jason being his typical delusional self." I play it off, not wanting to get into it, but she doesn't let it go.

"If he's bothering you, we should call security." Kristie grabs the phone off the wall, and I place my hand on her arm to still her.

"Seriously, he just surprised me."

"Girl, we've been working together for months." Placing her hands on her hips, she stares me down. "Just tell me."

I run my tongue along my top teeth, trying to think of a way to get out of this, but give up when she quirks her right brow. "He's being weird. Like, he's been an ass since we split, but he showed up at my apartment drunk the other night."

Her mouth drops open. "Holy shit."

"Yup. He was out there waiting for me to get back from lunch too. I guess he found some photos of me and some other guys while in Napa, and he's pissed."

"Okay, I totally need more details on the whole 'other guys' thing, but seriously, Jason's getting creepy as hell. You need to report him. At least security can keep an eye out for him."

I mull my words over in my head before telling her, "Remember when I told you he helped me with the connections to get this internship?"

"Yeah." Kristie's tone has lost some of its pep.

"Well, his dad's on the hospital board. There's literally nothing security can do."

I hate knowing that this isn't uncommon. That countless women have been in the same position I am now.

"That's totally messed up."

I nod. "Nothing like a psycho ex to mess up your day."

# CHAPTER 26
# ALEX

JAX: You two still moping?

Alex: Shouldn't you be clam diving?

Jax: I'm not touching that one.

Alex: Come on.

River: Sidney will kill you and we'll all watch

Lucas: *popcorn emoji*

Jax: Have you spoken with Mia?

Alex: What is this, some kind of intervention?

River: Drop it.

Lucas: You're kidding me right? Do you have amnesia? Don't you remember all those chats we had where you lined me up?

River: You mean the ones where I told you not to be an idiot when it came to Piper? I was right.

Jax: Practically clairvoyant. It was nearly impossible to see those two were meant to be.

Alex: Watching you two make fools of yourselves was my favorite part of university.

Lucas: Gotta say, I'm enjoying you two doing it now.

Alex: What's that supposed to mean?

Jax: He means Piper and Sidney practically teed you up when they put you three in the same room and you still struck out.

Alex: Not sure if I should be annoyed or kiss them.

Alex: Definitely kiss.

Jax: Nice knowing you. Lucas, you got this?

Lucas: Already on my way.

Alex: Kidding. Kidding. Jesus.

River: Did Sidney say anything about Mia that I need to know about?

Jax: Sid checked in on her. Says she's been upset. She's not talking about it though.

Lucas: WTF. What did you two fuckers do?

Alex: Well, I'm pretty sure I fell in love with her so I'm not sure how we're to blame.

Jax: Please tell me you didn't tell her that?

Alex: Of course not.

Alex: River stopped me.

River: She's skittish.

Lucas: Jax, maybe have her over to your place and send over an update?

Jax: Can't. Clam diving, remember?

Lucas: How are we friends?

Jax: Come on, man. Don't be like that. I know you love me.

Alex: Are we getting all cuddly? Because I'm totally down.

River: Text me if Sidney doesn't get in touch with her.

Lucas: What are you going to do?

Alex: Call a friend from the Senators and have him check in on her.

River: Call her... Make the call, Alex.

Alex: Or... Hear me out. We fly there.

Jax: This is going to be so much fun.

River: We live in different countries.

Jax: Aware. Figure it the fuck out.

Lucas: Seriously guys. Learn from our mistakes.

Alex: So you admit you fucked it up!

Lucas: Repeatedly. But look who's married now.

Jax: How many times are you going to mention that?

Lucas: You're jealous because Sidney hasn't said yes yet.

Jax: Fuck off.

Alex: Maybe clam diving will change her mind.

Jax: I'm going to kick your ass so hard when we play you next.

Lucas: Good fucking luck with that, Jaxy. You go after my forwards, I'll take you out.

Alex: No need to be hostile gentlemen. It's just a game.

River: Since when?

Lucas: Alright fuckers. I'm getting back to my wife. Jax go have fun staring at icebergs. And the two of you better have figured something out the next time I see you.

# CHAPTER 27
# MIA

EMAIL:
*From: hr@ottawaregional.on.ca*
*Subject: mandatory alignment meeting*

*Dear Dr. Brooks*

*Your presence is required at a meeting scheduled by HR at 10 am in room 3028. The meeting addresses matters related to your current position. Your timely presence is required. If you have any concerns, please contact us.*

*Best regards,*
*Olivia Masters*
*HR Administrator*
*Ottawa Regional Hospital*

My chest tightens as I stop in the hospital lobby and scan the email for the third time. *Required. Mandatory.*

I make my way to the third floor, and my stomach lurches as I try to make sense of it all—what's an alignment meeting, and why do I have to be there?

I drag my feet down the hall, desperately wanting to turn around but knowing I can't. Room 3028 comes into view with only a minute to spare. There's a woman standing in the doorway, wearing a navy satin shirt tucked into sleek black pants. Her face is expressionless as she says, "Dr. Brooks, please take a seat. I'm Olivia Masters, one of the HR administrators here at the hospital."

My boss's silhouette looms in the corner of the sparsely decorated conference room, intentionally avoiding eye contact with me. I shuffle over to the oval table in the center and cautiously lower myself into my seat, facing him.

Olivia takes a seat, straightens the papers in front of her, and lifts them up, tapping the bottom of the pile on the table.

"Dr. Brooks," she says, her voice clipped and professional, "Do you know why we've asked you here today?"

My heart pounds in my chest. A creeping suspicion crawls up my neck, but I push it away. It's only been three days since I saw Jason. There's no way he could have gotten me fired that quickly. Right?

"Not really…no." My voice comes out as a whisper.

"The hospital is downsizing our intern program," Olivia continues, unfazed by my distress. "You will be let go immediately and will be transferred your remaining payment, as well as two weeks' severance."

My mind races as I struggle to process what's happening.

"What?" I breathe, staring at her in disbelief. I turn to my boss, hoping for some kind of explanation or support. But he winces and looks away.

"You're firing me?"

The weight of Olivia's words sinks in with a sickening thud.

She shifts her posture and lifts her chin. I'm sure this isn't the first time she's laid someone off. "Not fired. We're simply realigning our organizational structure. Routine protocol."

Routine my ass. "How many people are getting let go?"

Olivia leans back in her chair and gives me a plain smile. "Dr. Brooks, if you keep getting upset, I'll be forced to call security."

Air hisses through my teeth as I try to take a calming breath. "I'm sorry. How many interns will be let go?"

She meets my gaze. "One."

There's no way this is a coincidence. Jason can't do that? There are laws or something. What the hell had he even said to his dad to get him to pull strings like this? *Screw this.* "You can't do that. I've had nothing but great feedback. Isn't that right, Eric?"

My boss presses his lips together, and there's a clear look of pity across his face.

"Dr. Brooks. The hospital has experienced a wave

of regulated pain medicine thefts since you started with us. Someone has brought forth suspicions of your involvement. You should consider yourself lucky we're laying you off. The only reason you aren't being arrested right now, is because our internal investigation didn't provide sufficient proof of your involvement. But, Dr. Brooks, whether we have proof  enough to charge you or not, your accuser left no room for doubt." Disgust breaks through her professional mask. It's clear she'd rather have charged me anyway.

Shock crashes through me as her words hit home. They think I stole from the hospital? A mix of hurt and embarrassment swirls in my gut as I try to work through what's happening. It's so far-fetched that I can't even process it. She said someone stepped forward, but who would do that?

The second the thought registers in my brain, I know exactly who caused this. Fucking Jason. My stomach sinks, and nausea climbs the back of my throat. He's been stealing from the hospital, and now he's pinning it on me. That psycho could've gotten me arrested!

I want to push her, force her to admit it was him. At least then I can fight this. I can pull my bank statements or whatever they need to see it had nothing to do with me. But that's the reason they're laying me off and not firing me, isn't it? Because then I don't get a chance to fight back. I'm hit with a wave of helplessness, knowing that without proof, it's his word against mine.

"Please sign here." Olivia slides the paper across the table, and I have to fight back tears as I sign the document.

*I'm going to kill that asshole.*

I walk out of the room on autopilot, not processing what's happening around me. There's a man dressed in a security uniform waiting outside the door, and he holds out a small cardboard box of my belongings.

"I got Dr. Kristie to double-check your locker for any loose items." He gives me an empathetic smile, but I can't concentrate on his words. My mind is too preoccupied with my own thoughts.

The security guard leads me through the building, and I can feel all eyes on me. Everyone is already starting to make assumptions as to why I've been asked to leave my residency. Out of all the guesses, none could possibly come close to the truth.

I keep my head down and my gaze locked onto the floor as I wander through the many halls for the last time. When I'd first stepped foot within this building, I was brimming with enthusiasm and eagerness; now, it feels like those walls are crumbling around me.

I push the thought down and let my mind go blank. If I go down that path, I won't make it out of here without crying. I push through the front door and wince when I leave the shadow of the building and move into the harsh sunlight.

"Do you have a ride home, Dr. Brooks?" I glance

back at the security guard. He's standing just inside the doors.

"I've got my car, no worries." I barely have the words out when the automatic doors click shut behind him, and I have to blink back tears. Not here. With my luck, Jason's lurking somewhere, watching this whole thing.

"Hey."

I spin and spot Kristie standing with her back close to a tall brick column that's hiding her from view.

The second our gazes meet, I can't stop the tears from streaming down my face.

"What the hell happened?" She wraps me in a hug, arms squeezing around my sides, and I let the box full of my belongings fall to the ground.

"They think I was stealing from the hospital." My words wobble as I force them out.

"What the actual fuck?" Kristie hisses, and the corner of my lip twitches.

If everything wasn't going to shit, her uncharacteristic swearing would be funny. I take several deep breaths, needing to get my shit together. "I think it was Jason. Now he's trying to pin this on me."

"Okay," she says calmly in her best patient voice. "You have options. We can make an appointment with the board and tell them that."

"There's no way they'll listen to me if I don't have proof. It's not like I can go in there and be like, my ex, who just happens to be one of your sons, is a creepy dickwad who's probably trying to frame me for his own crime. Please give me my job back," I say, and then my own words slap me in the face.

Oh my God. I'm never getting this job back.

I try and fail to suck back a sob.

"Listen to me, Mia. I'll ask around. Someone's got to know something. That bastard is not getting away with this. We'll string him up by his balls, and then you can come back and be my work bestie."

I bark out a laugh, some of the weight lifting from my shoulders. "I owe you."

She gives me a mischievous grin. "Not for this, girl. This is going to be fun."

———

My mind's blank as I drive home from the hospital. The sky is a perfect blue, and the sun shines brightly, but it all feels muted. Like someone turned down the volume on life itself. I pull into my parking spot, shut off the engine, and sit there for a few moments, gathering enough courage to go inside my apartment.

When I finally open the door, Crookshanks meows at me and rubs against my legs until I pick him up. He purrs in my arms as dread slowly rises inside me like a tide.

I drop to my couch and bury my face in his soft fur. The reality of how screwed I am crashes over me like a wave. It will be nearly impossible to find another internship in Ottawa, and even if I could, it wouldn't compare to the one I just lost. An overwhelming sense of helplessness sinks into me, and I hug my cat to my chest, taking several breaths before reaching for my phone.

I click to Sidney's contact, knowing she'd want to know about this, but freeze. She'd cancel her trip if she knew, and I can't do that to them. Instead, I send a quick text to the men I've been desperate to talk to.

**Me: How have you been?**

I watch my phone as the moments tick by, and anxiety starts to tighten my shoulders. What if they don't answer? What if I'm crossing the line by reaching out to them when it was all supposed to be a short-term thing?

Bubbles form on the screen, and I can't look away.

**Alex: Where have you been, Kitten? Missed you.**

**River: Mia, are you okay?**

I sniff. How does he always know?

**Me: Of course I'm fine. Just checking in.**

**Alex: Why do we think she's not fine?**

**River: Because she hasn't texted in nearly three weeks.**

Shit.

**Alex: You okay, Kitten? Need me to kick some-one's ass?**

I have to stop myself from typing out just how badly I want that. Knowing them, they'd be on the next flight out here, always ready for a fight. Except we aren't in university anymore, and they're more likely to end up in jail than anything else. Talk about making headline news. Two famous NHL players beat up a local billionaire's son for their thief girlfriend.

**Me: You two keep this up, I won't text you for another three weeks.**

**Alex: Woah now. Don't be hasty. Just worried about you. Have you spoken with Misty recently? She mentioned you the other day.**

Now I feel bad for not returning her call. I'd been so caught up with my own problems I hadn't been working with her like we planned.

**Me: Things have been hectic. I'll call her back.**

**River: How have you been?**

Bad. Horrible. Lonely.

**Me: Busy. You?**

**River: Busy.**

This conversation's going nowhere. I don't even know why I started it. That's a lie. I wanted to tell them everything and just collapse into them. I wanted River to say he'd take care of it while Alex made me laugh. But that's not who we are to each other.

Several minutes pass in silence before my phone vibrates.

**Alex: Please don't be a stranger. Don't make me wait another three weeks to hear from you.**

My eyes sting for a whole new reason.

**Me: Okay.**

**River: You promise?**

**Me: Promise.**

# CHAPTER 28
# MIA

MY PHONE RINGS on the end table beside my sofa for the millionth time, and I flip it over, facing it down. I've been hiding in my apartment, only leaving to stock up on ice cream since Olivia called me into that conference room and ruined my life.

I know it's Sidney, who somehow used her Spidey senses to find out I'd been let go and is now freaking out on vacation. I swear that girl has more connections than Beyoncé.

If I answer that phone, I know she'll be full of understanding and *ideas*. That's who she is. She's a solver. But I just want to lie here and wallow in self-pity. Is that really that bad?

Anger sears my veins, thinking about my dick-head of a controlling bastard ex. I can't believe I fell for all the shit he used to say. He loves me. *Bleh*. I can't even blame being distracted in medical school because even then, a little voice in the back of my head was telling me there was something off about him. By the time we graduated, it just made sense for me to follow him to Ottawa. It was easy, especially with Sidney and Jax living here. Well, it was supposed to be easy. I was supposed to have *the boyfriend, the friends, the career.*

Now I'm careerless, all because my psycho of an ex is a spoiled rotten brat that's never been told no and has completely screwed up my life.

I can't believe he got me fired!

On top of all of that, I haven't gone a single second without thinking about Alex and River.

At first, I tried to brush it off as a need for sexual release, but I've never been good at lying to myself. There's a rightness when I'm with them, and that little voice inside my head screams to stay. To never let them go.

Knowing it can't happen just makes everything worse. I keep telling myself that time will ease the ache in my chest, but if anything, I feel a constant tug to be near them. Which is a total bitch because that's not happening.

Texting them had turned out to be a new level of torture I'm not sure I'd survive again. And yet, I've had to force my masochistic self not to reach out.

I pull my blanket higher on my lap, covering my teddy-bear-print flannel pajamas I've been wearing for three days straight—*Why do I need to shower anyway? No one's going to see me*—and scoop a spoonful of chocolate chip cookie dough ice cream into my mouth, letting the sugary goodness numb my brain.

Nope, I don't want solutions. Not for another solid week, at least.

I have enough money for two months' rent, which should be just enough time for a good sulk before I have to go scrounge for another job. Only the rich have the luxury of being jobless; the rest of us would be out on the streets. An increasingly sinister thought dawns on me: *Was this Jason's plan all along?*

Memories of what he said to me outside the hospital have the hair on the back of my neck standing up. *"You don't have time? We'll see about that."*

He likes me helpless and dependent. The terrifying feeling of powerlessness paralyzes me. So, instead of thinking about any of it, I cuddle further into the couch cushion and swallow a spoonful of creamy goodness.

My phone vibrates again, and I switch it to Do Not Disturb without looking at who it is. Can't a girl just eat a few pints of ice cream while crying about her lost job while simultaneously planning on how to get away with murder? Actually, once my pity party's over, I'll definitely recruit the girls with that. Nothing says friendship better than figuring out how to hide a body. The last mafia book I read highly implied hungry pigs are the way to go.

Ice cream tub in one hand and remote in the other, I flip through Netflix mindlessly. I haven't watched more than thirty seconds of a show for the last hour.

Crookshanks licks one of his orange paws, staring

at me from across the room, where he's perched on one of the cardboard boxes I haven't gotten around to unpacking. If I didn't know better, I'd swear he has judgment written across his face. Sometimes he seems just a little too smart to be a cat, but then he'd lick his orange furry butt, and I'd snap out of it.

My spoon hits the bottom of my container, and I get up, leaving it on the coffee table with the others on my way to get a new one. I pad the five feet to my kitchen and open the white plastic freezer door that still has marker stains all over from the previous tenant and groan when all that's left is a bag of peas.

A loud bang on the door has me snapping out of my daze and a prickle of unease crawling up my neck.

"Mia, let me in," Jason says. He sounds cocky, like he already knows I don't have a choice. *Screw that.*

I cross my arms over my chest. "Go away, Jason."

"Mia, we both know you're opening this door eventually. No need to be stubborn."

The audacity. "Why would I do that?"

"Because you know I'm your best shot to get your internship back." There's a chuckle in his voice that makes me grind my teeth.

"You think I don't know you're the reason I was let go?" My hands squeeze around my upper arms as I hold myself tighter. Something feels off, and a creeping sense that I'm not safe settles around me.

"Come on," he croons, and I fight back a shudder. "Don't be like that. All you have to do is come back to me, and it'll all work itself out." There's a soft thud on the wall beside the door, and I can almost picture him leaning against it.

Delusional, controlling, narcissistic prick.

"Just leave."

"Stop pretending you don't want this. The *hard to get* act was fun at first, but knock it the fuck off," he yells through the door, punctuating his words with a pounding fist. "Open this fucking door, Mia, or I'll break it down."

I swallow hard, my nails digging into the back of my arms hard enough to bruise through my sleep shirt. He wouldn't break in here, would he? Fear laces my veins because Jason doesn't live in a world with consequences. He's spent his whole life with daddy's money getting him anything he wanted. He probably thinks he's impervious to being arrested, and God knows money rules the world.

There's a loud bang against my door, and it rattles on its hinges. It happens again, and I have to fight against freezing.

I inhale deeply and try to hide the shaking in my voice as I say in a soothing tone, "Okay, I'll let you in. Just give me a minute."

"Hurry the fuck up," he replies, but some of the urgency has dissipated.

Not for me though. I rush and grab my phone, dialing 911. At this point, I don't even care if he gets charged. I just need him to leave.

My thumb hovers over the button when a familiar voice growls, "Get the fuck away from her."

*River.* River is here.

# CHAPTER 29
# RIVER

RED TAKES over my gaze when my eyes land on the cocky asshole banging on Mia's door. There's no doubt in my mind I'm looking at her slimy ex-boyfriend.

What I don't understand is what the fuck he's doing here. Sidney called this morning telling us we needed to check on Mia, that it had been days since she'd answered her calls. I had to fight back the sickening twist in my gut when she didn't answer my messages either.

Sidney and Jax are stuck on their holiday in the Maritimes, and the earliest flight they can get out is tomorrow night. I didn't hesitate to call up my buddy and pull in the favor he owed me to borrow his private plane.

I'd been an anxious mess the entire hour-and-a-half flight, but nothing prepared me for the pure rage I'd feel toward this sniveling piece of shit.

Alex, always the first to react, has him pinned to

the wall by his collar, his face going red with the lack of oxygen.

The asshole smirks and sneers. "Do it. I fucking dare you. I'll have your ass in jail so fast, and a pretty boy like you won't like it there." He looks Alex up and down, and even from his pinned position, he smiles. "Or maybe you would like it."

Alex pulls her ex toward him, then slams him back into the wall. The asshole grunts with the impact, and his head falls forward. Now Alex is the one with a devilish smile.

"There's no one out here who will corroborate your story. From what I can tell, you showed up here already beaten. Isn't that right, River?"

The darkness in Alex's tone has a shiver running down my spine. I have no intention of stopping him from killing this guy. I have to stop the strong urge to do it myself.

I close the distance between us and dig my fingers into the asshole's hair, slamming the back of his head into the wall with a sickening crunch.

"You have no idea how badly you fucked up thinking no one cares for her. She's all that matters to us, and you're about to learn exactly what that means." I move to do it again.

"Stop!" Mia looks panicked as she tries to pry herself between us. "You need to stop. Jason will report it. Neither of you can afford assault charges."

Of course his name is Jason.

Alex's eyes narrow on the asshole. "I'm not sure about that. Sounds worth it."

"Please." Mia's voice is actually begging, and I drop her ex immediately. I never want to hear that sound again. Not when it's laced with fear.

Alex tightens his grip, jerking Jason once more before letting his feet hit the floor.

He straightens his collar, trying his best to look unaffected, but all it does is highlight how much his hands shake. "Wait 'til my—"

"Father hears about this?" I let a vicious smile cut my face. "You're not the only one who knows people."

Mia tucks herself into my side, and I wrap my arm around her, running my fingers up and down her skin. I can feel the tension leaving her as she sinks further into me.

"Are you going to let him talk to me like that?" Jason snaps at Mia.

"Shut the fuck up." Alex lunges at him, and the asshole barely dodges to the left.

Mia stiffens before disengaging from my side, taking a step toward him, her chin lifts and there's a spark to her that has me tuned into every move she makes. She looks fierce with her shoulders back and her head held high. Then she goes and gives him a *go fuck yourself* grin, and I've never seen anything hotter.

"Look, Jason. Your dad's not here right now to back you up. They look like they want to kick your ass. So let me be perfectly clear. You are deluding yourself if you think I could ever want you back. You were a mistake from the get-go, and you dumping me was the best gift you ever gave me. Don't come by, don't call me. Don't even think about me. Because I sure as shit won't be thinking about you."

His face flushes red and turns an almost purple color. I don't like the way he's looking at her. Like he's going to put her in her place as soon as he gets her alone. It's not fucking happening.

"You'll regret this, Mia." Her ex goes to move around us to get to the elevator, bringing him within reaching distance of Mia, but Alex blocks his way.

"I highly suggest you back the fuck up," Alex growls. He's glaring down at him, chest heaving with the pent-up desire to kick this guy's ass.

The asshole swallows hard and stumbles back before fleeing out the emergency stair exit.

I watch Jason until the door closes behind him with a bang, and I take several calming breaths, pushing down the rage threatening to bubble over, then look at her. My anger evaporates, turning into concern when Mia's ragged inhale fills the air.

I spin her to face me, and my stomach drops at the naked fear written over her face. I close the distance between us and tuck her into my chest, resting my head on her shoulder. The scent of lavender fills my nose with every breath. She's shaking so much it's vibrating through me, and I tighten my hold even more. "You're okay, Mia."

"I know. I know I'm being stupid, but he... I thought he was going to get through my door. I thought..." She presses her face into me, mumbling. "I wouldn't have been able to fight him off."

"We've got you, Kitten." Alex is behind her the second she gets the words out and rests his forehead against the crown of her head. He's visibly shaking, and I close my hand around his bicep, rubbing a circle with my thumb.

"You good?"

Alex's eyes meet mine, and he gives me a barely there nod before closing them.

Mia's hands fist my shirt, and I want to lift her jaw and kiss her until we're the only things she thinks about, but I don't. I don't know where we stand—everything we've talked about ended the second she got on the plane.

Instead, I kiss her temple and lean back, keeping one hand around her waist, and wipe away the wetness under her eye. "You need to put in a report."

She lets out a sardonic laugh. "What good is that going to do? His dad controls everything. When you're that rich, you can do whatever you want."

Alex nudges his nose in her hair and takes a deep breath. "How rich?"

"Put it this way. Oprah looks up to him. He's the CEO of Pharmacorp."

"Damn," Alex says.

"Yup." Her shoulders shake with her laugh. "I sure can pick them."

He grabs her hand and spins her to face him with a goofy grin on his face. "Yeah, I think you're getting better at it though."

"I...ah..." She stutters her words, and I take pity on her.

"If you aren't reporting him, then you aren't staying here."

She grips the back of her neck. "I can stay at Sidney's. I have her spare key... wait."

She backs up, looking between us, both her brows up near her hairline. "What are you doing here?"

It's a testimony to how terrified she is that it took her so long to clue in. "Sidney called us. Said you haven't been returning her calls. The rest is just luck."

"I'm sorry about your internship, Kitten. I know how hard you worked for that."

She sniffs and glares at the door her ex had fled through. Sidney explained it was that asshole who cost her her job, and I want to kill him all over again.

"Truth is, we're lucky we showed up when we did." A tremor crawls down my spine, knowing how different this could have ended. "Which is why I think you should come back to Boston with us."

She huffs out a laugh. "Funny."

But she stills when we don't respond, realizing Alex and I are dead serious. I didn't need to ask him, knowing he feels the same.

"I can't just *go* to Boston on a whim."

"Why not?"

"I have work—" Her face crumples, and she sucks in a breath. "I can't just pack up and move."

"Sure you can, Kitten. Plus, Piper and Misty will be there."

That seems to cheer her up a bit. Misty mentioned working with her on the Prosthetic For Kids charity before.

I stroke my thumb over her cheek. "It'll be good to get your mind off things. Fresh start."

She mouths *fresh start* but still looks unsure.

Pressure builds under my ribs that feels dangerously close to desperation. "You don't have to stay forever. Just until you get your feet back under you."

Her brows pinch together. "I can't afford to live there."

Alex squeezes her shoulder. "Don't worry about that. We know a player who's got an empty place. Never uses it."

"Um, no. I can't do that."

Alex grins. "Mia, he's a multimillionaire. I assure you it'll be fine."

I can see the cogs moving in her head as she processes everything. "Just until I get things figured out. Then I'm coming back to Ottawa."

Alex whips her into the air and spins them in a circle, drawing a laugh from her. I swallow hard, watching them. He always was able to make her laugh.

He sets her down, and she's breathless when she says, "When do we leave?"

"Tonight," I reply.

"Pretty sure it's too late to get tickets for tonight."

Alex tips his head to the side and gives her a soft smile. "Good thing we have a private plane."

Her eyes go wide as saucers, and her mouth drops open.

"Don't worry, we borrowed it," he adds, and she seems to relax at that. First person not to be impressed by our money. Not that I expected anything different from her.

We enter her apartment, and the first thing I notice is that it's small. Really small. It's a studio, and the only thing separating the living room from her bedroom is a wood slat privacy screen.

I have to fight off the unease that she's been living here. I'm sure she wouldn't be pleased with that kind of possessive bullshit. I glance over at Alex, who's looking at the place with the same distaste as I am. Neither of us likes that she's been living here. Not when we'd be able to give her so much more.

She may not have been ours for the past few years, but that doesn't change anything.

A loud meowing comes from a giant orange cat as it winds its way around Alex's feet. Alex reaches down to pick it up while Mia simultaneously gasps.

"No! He'll scratch—" Her mouth snaps shut, then falls open as the cat purrs in his arms, rubbing his face against Alex's chin.

"Huh." She tilts her head. "He normally tries to claw anyone who goes near him besides me."

Alex gives her a cheeky grin. "Your cat likes me."

She rolls her eyes. "Don't let it go to your head."

"What can I say? Your pussy likes me." Alex says with a grin.

She turns bright red and I choke on a laugh.

Alex puts the cat down, who doesn't look happy about it, and claps his hands. "Alright. Let's get packing."

"Yeah, there's just a small problem."

I raise a brow. "What's that?"

She looks around her studio apartment. "I can't just leave all this here."

"Have you paid your rent until the end of the month?"

"Yeah, but what am I thinking? I've got bills. I need to find a new job. I can't just get up and leave."

"Why?" I deadpan.

"What do you mean why? This is my *life*."

"Is it? Seems like your asshole ex has been downsizing your life since you left him."

She gapes at me but doesn't deny it.

I tilt my head. "What are the chances of you getting another internship in Ottawa?"

"Next to none, okay? Are you happy? Does my patheticness get you off or something?"

"You are not and have never been pathetic," I growl. "And there's nothing about this that makes me happy. So tell me what you want, and we'll make it happen."

Tears pool in her eyes. "I just need time…to figure everything out."

"Let us help you with that, Kitten." Alex crosses the room and brushes a loose strand of hair behind her ear. "Come stay. We'll pack up here so you've got the essentials, and you've got a bit of time before you need to let your apartment go. Who knows, maybe you'll get a lead on a new internship by then." He gives her a shy smile, and her expression softens. "But until you do, let us take care of you."

She looks between us, then straightens. "Fine, but only until I get back on my feet."

"We can work with that." I nod, trying not to show the rush of happiness bubbling up my chest. "Now tell us everything about your asshole ex. Start from the beginning and don't leave anything out."

————

It took less than two hours to get her packed and loaded into the plane. Turns out, she hadn't unpacked all of her things since moving out of her shared apartment with her ex.

As we packed, she answered our prying questions about Jason. Where did they meet? *Med school.* How long were they together? *One Year.* Was he always a complete psycho? *Probably?*

The more she told us, the angrier we got. She explained how he'd started off sweet, feigning interest in everything she did. Love bombing the shit out of her.

He'd been so meticulous with his manipulation she hadn't realized he was slowly chipping away her confidence the entire time they were together. Working hard to make her feel small, so he could control everything she did. Making her feel like doing something she loved somehow made her selfish.

Anger builds in my chest, and I take a breath through gritted teeth.

Guys like him know what they're doing. They pull out every technique, gaslighting their partners until they don't trust themselves to know what's real or not. But that asshole fucked up when he broke up with her. He thought she'd come crawling back. Instead, Mia used that moment of separation and slammed a door between them.

Alex was the one to ask what I was too afraid to. He'd asked her as gently as possible if Jason had ever been physical against her. She looked timid when she answered that he'd grabbed her arm a little too hard and shook her around a bit when he got drunk, but other than that, he was all words.

A string of cusses had flown from Alex's mouth and my mind had gone red with rage. Every fiber in my being screaming to kill that bastard.

I halt my thoughts. I have to stop thinking about it, or I'll lose my fucking mind.

I distract myself with the sight of her tucked into Alex's side. She'd been exhausted by the time we made it to the airport, and I'm not surprised she passed out before takeoff. Alex wrapped an arm around her shoulder, and she fell asleep on his chest.

Crookshanks kneads his paws into my thighs, his sharp claws puncturing holes in my deep gray pants.

"Hey, now. Those are expensive." I lift the orange furball and hold him in my arms. He immediately rubs his head into me, an act so much like Mia that it has a soft, warm glow filling my stomach. "You aren't so bad, are you?"

The cat meows as if he knows what I'm saying before closing its eyes.

Mia mumbles in her sleep, and Alex unconsciously pulls her closer. The sight of the two of them has my chest growing uncomfortably tight. The two people I need most in the world, and at least for now, we're together.

# CHAPTER 30
# MIA

THE SCENT of leather and cedar wraps around me. I bury my face in my pillow, humming in the back of my throat as my body relaxes deeper into the comfy mattress...River.

I shift, grazing my fingers over the blanket, and freeze. Where my bedding is made of cheap box-store sheets, the thread count so low the fabric's just shy of abrasive, the ones wrapped around me are smooth as silk.

Memories of River leading me into his room last night filter through my grogginess. He'd insisted on me taking his bed until they'd arranged everything with his friend's apartment that I'll be staying in. Whose apartment? I know they said there's no rent, but I have to pay something.

Last night, they made perfect sense, and this morning, it's like a whirlwind in my head. I told them about Jason showing up and how I suspect he'd framed me for his own theft. If they weren't so eager to get me on that plane, I'm pretty sure they'd have hunted him down.

This has all happened so fast my mind can't keep up with it.

I sigh out a breath, giving up trying. I peel my eyes open and blink against the soft light filtering through the shades.

River's room is exactly how I'd expect. It's cast in muted tones of silvery gray and deep navy blue silk bedding. It's all smooth lines, no clutter, but with luxurious fabrics warming up the space. It's somehow both minimal enough to feel standoffish while simultaneously being comfy enough, cocooned in layers of satin, to feel like I belong here. Total River vibes.

I roll over and kick my feet off the side of the bed. There's a tall mirror propped against the wall that reflects my image back at me. Jesus. My hand flies to my hair, piled messily on top of my head, so greasy it could be mistaken as wet. The fact that I can't remember the last time I washed it is not a good sign.

At least I'm wearing one of my cuter sleep sets with a lavender button-up long-sleeve shirt and matching shorts. Alex searching through my suitcase and choosing my outfit was quite the experience. I definitely thought he'd go for one of my thin strap mid-thigh sleep dresses and was pleasantly surprised when he'd held out this monochrome set.

A soft knock raps on the door.

"Come in," I croak and take a sip of the water that

someone left on the nightstand. It's cool on my tongue, so it's been placed there recently. I'm not sure how I feel about them being here while I'm asleep, but I can't say I hate it.

"Hey, Kitten. I thought I heard you moving around in here." Alex leans against the doorframe, resting his head on the hardwood as his gaze travels over me. He has legit reasons to think I'm gross right now, but his eyes soften, and his lips tilt in a smile. "You're cute, all ruffled like that."

Meanwhile, there's nothing cute about the man standing in front of me. He's already dressed in a pair of straight-leg jeans that hug his thighs and a white T-shirt that's stretched slightly over his chest. Fuck, he looks good.

I swallow hard, and his eyes darken on mine. For a second, we're back in Napa, me crying out his name while he makes me come apart.

River stops at the doorway. "Good morning, Mia. Breakfast is almost ready. Why don't you take a shower, and we can eat together."

I stiffen at River's stilted, almost formal tone. None of the low, soothing bass from the night before.

I can practically feel the boundary he's setting between us, and I'm suddenly not sure of anything.

Alex raises a brow at him, no doubt clueing in to the same vibe I am.

I stand, swallowing down my questions. "Okay. Just need to find my stuff."

"We put your toiletries in the bathroom, and your

suitcase is on the chair by the window." River gestures to them, then walks out of the room.

My chest squeezes. It's not that I thought things would be like they were in Napa. Did I even want that? I'd be kidding myself if I said there isn't a part of me that desperately wanted to lose myself in how they make me feel. But after Jason, the pressure to get more funding for the charity, compounded by losing my job...maybe River's right to keep a little distance between us. That doesn't stop my chest from aching.

I need time to sort through everything, to figure out what I want, and that's if they even want to continue. After all, the deal was one weekend only.

———

I twist the towel in my hair and bundle it on top of my head. It feels good to be clean after days of my self-inflicted pity party. Nothing like your ex threatening to break down your door to put life into perspective. A shudder runs through me, and I step out of the bathroom, following the sweet scent of fresh-brewed coffee to the kitchen.

Like his bedroom, River's condo is all sleek lines, but the deeper color palette gives the entire space a moodier feeling that fights off the space feeling too cold.

Light pours through the floor-to-ceiling windows on my right, highlighting the two men working in the kitchen with their backs to me.

I take a second to admire River in his crisp, fitted

oxford that pulls along his back. My throat tightens as his muscles shift under the thin fabric when he flips something in the frying pan.

"You didn't drown, I see. Feel better?" Alex says, giving me a knowing grin.

Heat floods my cheeks at being caught practically salivating over his friend. "Ah...yeah...good."

Alex's gaze travels over my tight black leggings, and he bites the corner of his lips when he recognizes the hoodie he lent me. This would be the perfect time to give it back, but I have no plans to. From the way his eyes darken and how he leans over, gripping the counter, I'd say he's happy to let me keep it.

"Your breakfast is ready." River slides a plate across the island, and I sit on one of the stools. My mouth waters. The scent of basil and melted feta fills my nose, mixed with the salt from crisp bacon.

My gaze darts between the guys. "You just had this in your fridge?"

"Riv went to the market this morning. Figured we'd pick you up a few things for your new place."

Warmth floods my chest, and I take my first bite before I can overthink how thoughtful that is. I moan the second the food hits my tongue, and River leans back and props his elbows on the counter, facing me with dark eyes.

Alex grins. "You keep making sounds like that, I'll cook every meal for you."

I tilt my head to the side. "Come to think of it, what are you doing here?"

Alex places a hand to his chest. "You wound me,

woman. I'm helping move us."

Okay, that makes sense...

"Wait? What do you mean *us*?"

"Well, I'm moving in here, and you'll be taking my place across the hall."

My fork clatters on my plate. "I thought you said you had a friend."

Alex points his thumb at his chest. "Friend."

"You can't do that. I can't force you to live together. I'll figure something else out," I say as I go to stand, but River moves fast and places both hands on the island counter.

"We can, and we are. After the shit that went down last night with that asshole, do you really think we'd put you up just anywhere?"

"He won't follow me here."

River's face grows serious. "Are you sure about that? Did you know three women are killed every single day by their intimate partners? Every. Single. Day. He may be a regular asshole and not a complete psycho, but do you really want to risk it? Because I don't."

Fear lances my veins, and my eyes burn because I never thought I'd be in this position, and I fucking hate how helpless I feel.

"We can still report him," Alex adds.

I shake my head, knowing just how pointless that would be. Even without his father's influence, this kind of thing is never taken seriously until it's already too late. "So you're really okay with moving in here and me taking your place?"

"Kitten, I'm more than okay with it. Not going to lie, my initial thought was for you just to move in with one of us, but we thought you'd be more comfortable with your own space. Were we right?"

A tiny part of me is disappointed, but the more rational part knows I need a clear head to get my feet under me. "So you say it's next door?"

River eyes my near full plate. "Finish your breakfast, and we'll take you over there."

I take another delicious bite but quickly spot something out of place. "You're not eating?"

"We ate a few hours ago. Thought you'd like to sleep in."

I try not to let the idea of them cooking breakfast together for me go straight to my head. After all, River still hasn't warmed up, even after his display of protectiveness.

I take a deep drink of my coffee before addressing the elephant in the room. "So what happens between us?" My voice shakes. I'm not sure how I want them to answer; either way scares the crap out of me.

Alex rubs a hand against my spine, and I relax into it. "Nothing has to happen. We can figure whatever this is or isn't out slowly. There's no rush. We aren't going anywhere."

It's like the pressure I've been holding inside me releases, and I take a deep breath. I had no idea how much I needed to hear that.

Alex kisses the top of my head. "Come see your new place. We've been working on it all morning."

# CHAPTER 31
# RIVER

I RUN my hand through my hair, pulling at the ends the second my apartment door clicks closed behind me. We'd spent the last half hour helping Mia get settled, and every second of it felt like absolute torture.

From the moment she woke up, I wanted to go through all the reasons the three of us should be together. But I fucking know the last thing she needs is some asshole guy pressuring her into something she's not sure about. Not after everything that happened with her ex.

Moving her to Boston was already a huge over-reach on my part, but I couldn't stand the idea of leaving her there. Not when I knew I could do something about it.

Knowing I need to give her space to make her own decisions doesn't mean I'm happy about it. My muscles ache from the force it took to keep myself together.

It took all my fucking willpower not to pin her to that bed and make her come so many times she doesn't know which way is up or down.

Until she's as addicted to me as I am to her.

# CHAPTER 32
# MIA

"LOOKS like you're all settled in," Alex says, standing just inside my apartment door. He's close to me but not touching. Instead, his hands are buried in his pockets.

"You didn't have to do this, you know?"

"Kitten, the proper response is *thank you*. Maybe throw in some adoration. A little *how will I ever repay you?*"

A laugh bursts from my chest, and he grins mischievously. The last twenty-four hours have been rough, but he's all fun and playful with a large spoonful of sexy as fuck. I shouldn't be able to laugh. Not after getting fired, being terrified I was about to be attacked, then leaving my life behind to come here.

But here I am, cheeks burning from the pinch of my grin. That's Alex though. It's like a freaking superpower.

"I'll make sure to remember that the next time I move into some guy's house."

He groans and stalks toward me, his eyes hot on mine. "Not funny, Kitten."

I dance away from his attempt to grab me and smile impossibly wider. "You've always been so easy to tease."

"Maybe I'm done teasing. Maybe…"

A thrill shoots down my spine. "Maybe what?"

Alex looks at the ceiling, taking several deep breaths before letting out an exasperated sigh. "Fucking River." He rubs the back of his neck, shaking his head like he can't believe what he's about to say. "Nothing. We'll talk about it another day."

I raise a brow. I'm too unsure of my own feelings to push, and maybe that's exactly why he stopped.

"Okay then. Thank you."

His grin shows off his dimple. "My pleasure to have you, Kitten."

My skin heats, and there's a tug in my stomach to move close. If his first talent is hockey, and his second is making me laugh, then his third is the ability to make a simple sentence dirty.

He rubs his hand on the top of my head like you would a child, effectively breaking the moment. He's already walking out the door when he calls back. "Don't be a stranger. I hear your neighbors are superhot."

"You are so corny."

"You love it." He winks, and then he's gone.

And I'm left standing in my new entry. I kick off

my shoes before exploring. I'd been so focused on the guys I hadn't processed how huge this place is.

It's a similar layout to River's, but the windows face the west instead of the east, and the vibe is completely different.

River's place has a crisp, modern aesthetic with clean lines and neutral colors, while Alex's place is the epitome of relaxed comfort. Warm-toned wood cabinetry runs along the walls with built-in shelves that are filled with books. In the center of the room, an enormous L-shaped sectional takes up almost the entire side, its luxurious cushions beckoning me to sit down. A giant flat-screen television, equipped with surround-sound speakers, hangs on the wall, and an Xbox controller lies carelessly on the floor. An involuntary smile creeps onto my face as I think of Alex and River still playing video games like they did in college.

The place has notes of sweet coconut with salty undertones, and I can't stop myself from collapsing into the leather cushions to take a second to process everything.

I'm living in Alex Grayson's apartment while he lives next door with River Davis.

A giggle bubbles up my throat at how ridiculous it all is.

There's a sharp knock against the wooden door, and I snap to face it. My heart pounds against my chest when it happens again. I freeze in place, every muscle on high alert.

"Mia Brooks. Open this door right now!" Piper

shouts, and a wave of relief washes over me as my body relaxes. I stumble toward the door and swing it open to find Piper standing there with her hands balled into fists, her face red with anger. She pulls me into a breath-stealing embrace and whispers, "Are you okay? How could he do something like this? Why didn't you tell us?" As she goes to pull away, a fire lights up her eyes, and she growls through clenched teeth, "I'm going to kill him."

"Get in line," says a muffled voice that sounds distinctly like Sidney.

Piper holds up her phone, and I bite my lips as Sidney glares at me through the glass. She looks like a concerned mom whose teenager came home after curfew. She takes a few visible breaths before asking, "Are you okay?"

"Yeah, I'm good."

"Don't *I'm good* me," she shouts. "Your ex got you fired, then attempted to break into your home."

"I wouldn't go that far. He banged on the door." I do my best to brush it off.

"Were you afraid he'd break in?" She searches my gaze, seeing the answer there. "Just as bad. It's okay to be upset about this, Mia. We're here for you."

It's like a dam breaks in my chest. I'd been holding myself together with the thought that I was overreacting, nothing happened, but with those quick words from her, the weight of the fear I felt hit my shoulders.

My eyes burn, and I sniff. "I didn't think it would

get this bad. I should've told you then he could have—"

Sidney's voice is low and serious. "Listen to me, Mia, and listen well. None of this is your fault. Do I wish you'd told me he was escalating? Yes, but don't think for a second you're to blame for this. Now, tell us what happened."

"Okay, but I'm going to need a drink for this." I walk into the kitchen, open the fridge, and have to do a double take. River's filled it with an impressive array of fresh produce, lunch meats, and snacks. There are tomatoes of all shapes and sizes, squash interspersed among kale leaves, lunchmeat piled high between bright orange baby carrots, and my favorite cheese slices tucked neatly in the corner. A warm hum fills my chest, thinking about him going out to get all this. I push a jug of milk to the side and smile when my fingers land on the cool metal cans.

I take the seat beside Piper and pass her a can of hard apple cider. She's propped her phone on the coffee table so we can both see Sidney, who is looking at me with one raised brow. I explain everything that's happened, their eyes growing wider with each revelation from Jason being at my apartment when I got home from Napa, him waiting at the hospital, getting me fired, and finally showing up at my place.

"Okay, so we're agreed he has to die, right?" Sidney says, completely serious.

I choke on my drink. "You're in politics. You can't talk like that."

"It's only a problem if we get caught, and I've

watched enough true crime to get this done," Piper adds helpfully.

Can't deny I've thought about it. I'd love to have the control over him he's been using against me, but the reality is, the only thing I can do is stay away from him.

"Yeah…well…I'd settle for getting him nailed for stealing painkillers." I take a long drink.

"Do you really think he did it? He has a lot of money," Piper asks.

I put my cider down and rub my temples. "There's a lot of things I thought I knew about him that don't make any sense anymore. And yes, I think he used me as a fall guy to cover up whatever he was up to."

"So we just need to prove it," Sidney says, face filling the phone screen.

I rub one hand over my face. "Easier said than done."

"We just need someone on the inside," Sidney adds coaxingly.

The corner of my lip tilts up as an image of Kristie's fierce smile comes to mind. "I've got someone. She's another doctor on the unit, and I trust her."

Sidney smirks. "Good because once we get a lead, I know a guy who can look into stuff like this."

Piper and I both raise a brow at her, and I say, "What do you mean 'know a guy.' You sound like you're in the mafia."

"How do you think we dig up dirt on our opponents? Everyone has a guy in politics."

A laugh escapes me, tumbling from my chest. It feels good to talk to them about it. And I know I should've told them right away. It just sucks so freaking bad.

I wipe away a traitorous tear and try to hide my face. "He ruined everything."

Sidney's eyes grow glossy. "We'll figure it out. Jax and I are flying in tomorrow."

I shake my head. "You don't have to cut your trip short."

Piper laughs, speaking to Sidney. "I'm honestly surprised you aren't already here."

"If flights weren't so stupid from the Maritimes, I would be. Tomorrow, we'll send the guys off to hang out, then we'll come up with a plan. Everything will feel better when we nail down a plan to ruin that asshole."

A smirk curves my lips, and I hold up my drink. "Cheers to that."

## CHAPTER 33
# MIA

THE SKY IS a deep orangey red. The sun has already started its descent when Piper gives me another concerned glance before heading out. By her worried looks when she thought I wasn't paying attention, I got the distinct impression Sidney had tasked her with looking after me.

I'm not sure how I got so lucky to have the friends I do, but they're the only reason I'm keeping my shit together.

It's not until the door clicks shut behind her that unease settles in my bones.

I sigh heavily and make my way over to the cabinets. I grab the long-stem glass from the shelf and the bottle of chilled white wine I recognize from Napa and pour the golden liquid an inch from the brim. I gulp down half, savoring the bitter burn at the back of my throat before refilling it.

My life's become an absolute dumpster fire, and without Piper here to distract me, my mind quickly

dissolves into a panicked mess of worst-case scenar-
ios. I'm never going to get another internship. Jason
will find me wherever I go and make some kind of
sick game of controlling my life. I'm not naive
enough to think this is anything else. He doesn't
actually care about me. He's mad that I'm not doing
what he wants, and now he's going to prove to me he
has all the power.

The worst of it is he *does*. I'm jobless and terrified,
exactly how he wants me. The one thing he didn't
account for was two protective NHL stars coming to
my rescue. I'm not going to sit here and pretend
that's not what happened. They scared off the
monster and whisked me away to an enchanted
castle.

I'm so freaking grateful for it. For once, I'll put
my need for independence aside for the feeling of
safety. Because that's exactly what I feel when they're
close. Like nothing can touch me. That they won't
let it.

Warmth coils in my stomach, and I push it down.
I need to get a grip on myself and relax.

I walk through my bedroom, which is just shy of
the size of my entire apartment back in Ottawa, and
make my way into the bathroom.

I run my hand along the smooth coolness of the
Carrara marble tile wall, watching as the light
bounces off its mix of grays and blacks, highlighting
its warm caramel veining. I take in the beauty of the
vanity with its double sinks framed by a deep wood
that warms the room. Then there is the centerpiece of

this grand bathroom: a standalone bath that looks out onto a floor-to-ceiling window that's just slightly tinted so no one can see me from outside, but I can still experience the stunning view. The entire thing looks like it belongs in a *House & Home* magazine.

I twist the tap and wait for the water to turn warm before putting the stopper in the bath. There's an assortment of bottles in an open shelf tucked into the wall on the right, and I sort through them. Shampoo, conditioner, bodywash… My hand stills on the one that says body oil, and I imagine thick, callused hands kneading my muscles. A shiver rolls down my back, and I return the small glass bottle to its home, grabbing instead one of the scented bath bombs from a small basket on the bottom of the shelf.

I toss it into the nearly full tub and watch it fizz as it creates a mass of orange bubbles that smell like creamsicle. I hum as I inhale deeply before pulling my shirt over my head and divesting the rest of my clothes in a small pile on the textured stone floor. The tub is so big I have to sit on the side and swing my leg over. I let out a hiss when my toes breach the surface of the water but don't stop descending. I want it hot. I want it to burn into my muscles and loosen their constant ache.

By the time I sink back fully, I've adjusted to the temperature and moan as my back contacts the curve of porcelain. Whoever said money can't buy happiness was a freaking idiot.

With every breath, I relax more until my mind drifts to the two men I've been trying to avoid thinking about. When I woke up this morning, surrounded by River's scent, there was nowhere else I wanted to be, but then he'd spoken to me in his odd formal tone, and a sickening rock dropped in my stomach.

It's like he built a wall between us, and it wasn't until we sat together that the smallest of things gave him away. When I set my fork down, he frowned until I started eating again. His eyes darkened as they took me in, and I damn near melted at the slight flush on his cheeks.

I close my eyes, and images of the two of them touching me, hands roaming hungrily over my skin, like they'd die if they didn't feel every inch. My fingers inch over my stomach at the thought of being pinned between the two of them, and I lower them slowly, inch by inch, between my thighs.

I can almost trick myself into believing it's Alex's fingers dipping over my slippery core, and I moan as he presses two inside me, stroking at a torturously slow rhythm. My breath hitches, and my nipples tighten as I imagine their mouths descending on them, scraping the peaks with their teeth until my hips buck.

I press my palm against my clit and grind down like River did, causing me to let out a small cry. My hips rock, and the water splashes around me as I imagine him digging his hand into Alex's hair, pulling him off my nipple with a loud pop. My orgasm hits me like a tidal wave as their mouths collide, and they let out simultaneous moans.

It takes several seconds for the image to fade and for my breathing to return to a normal pace. Where the hell did that come from?

My phone vibrates on the ledge, and I nearly jump out of my skin. I grab my towel and take my time to wipe my hands before swiping it open.

**Alex: How's it going, Kitten.**

My cheeks flame, and I have to take several deep breaths. He doesn't know what just happened. He doesn't know I came to the thought of him making out with his best friend. It's just a coincidence.

**Me: Fine.**

Thank God I didn't have to say it out loud, or my voice would have cracked for sure.

**River: Fine? Do you need something?**

**Alex: Fine or FINE?**

**Me: I'm good.**

**Me. Just relaxing.**

**River: What did you do today?**

**Me: Piper came over. Pretty sure Sidney asked her to babysit me.**

**River: Good.**

I roll my eyes.

**Alex: Want us to come over?**

I stiffen and rub my thighs together because the truth is, my body definitely likes that idea. I groan because I know I'm not ready for that.

**Me: No. Just getting out of the bath, then I'll be going to sleep.**

**Alex. Jesus Christ, Mia. You can't say stuff like that. Are you trying to kill me?**

I laugh, even as my core clenches.

**Me: Calm down before I stop talking to you.**

**River: Don't be mean, Mia. You know he can't help it.**

Shit. I was playing with fire, but recklessness has taken me over.

**Me: How about you? Can you help it?**

There are several long beats before his reply comes through.

**River: Not when it comes to you.**

**River: Good night, Mia. Sweet dreams.**

I squeal and dunk myself under the warm bathwater, letting it wash over me as I hold my breath, basking in the bubbles of excitement popping in my chest. The way Alex and River treat me is like an addiction that I can't get enough of. There's a connection between us that's so much deeper than I'm ready to admit. Not when there's still a chance this will all disappear again.

After graduating, leaving them had been absolutely devastating. No matter how many times I told myself it was the right thing to do, I still reached for my phone.

I used school and work to numb those feelings, burying them deep down, but being here with them makes it impossible to ignore. They chip away at any excuse I put between us, and for the first time since medical school, I don't want to go back to my internship. I don't think I'll survive leaving them again. They owned a part of me then, and they still own it now.

# CHAPTER 34
# ALEX

"TWO MORE. MOVE IT," Coach's voice booms over the ice.

My quads burn with the buildup of lactic acid as I do my thirtieth consecutive lap. I hiss in deep breaths, fighting my body's response to hyperventilate. I take the corner around the back of the net with sharp crossovers.

You'd think playing hockey since I could walk would make the transition back from summer easier, but it fucking doesn't. During our off-season, River and I focus on muscle training instead of endurance, building up the additional strength without having to fight against the constant cardio.

It's a fucking sound plan that's kept us on the first line year after year, but man does it suck the first few weeks back.

My legs grow heavy, and my speed dissipates against my will. River's right behind me, shouting for me to move my ass. He may not talk much in public, but he has no problem telling me what to do on the rink, or in bed for that matter. Images of him directing me on how to touch Mia take over my head, and I miss a step, nearly taking myself out.

"What the hell is wrong with you?" River comes up beside me.

*You, asshole.*

"Fuck off." I pant out the words.

"You two stop giving each other fuck-me eyes and get moving." Lucas passes me on my left, and I groan.

River looks away the second my eyes meet his, and I get the distinct feeling he'd been watching me. He's facing forward, eyes anywhere else, but I don't miss the hint of pink crawling up his neck. My dick twitches in my cup, and I drop back a few paces. I need to get my shit together.

A whistle pierces the air. "Alright, boys. Hit the shower."

Fuck me. I brace myself on my knees, taking in heaving breaths, and glide on my skates toward the bench. That's going to fucking hurt later. I wonder if I can convince Mia to rub it better. I groan.

A glove smacks into the back of my helmet, and one of the new trades gestures for me to move out of the way. "Wake up, buddy."

*Shit.* I scramble through the gate in the boards and head down the hall toward our locker room.

Before I can make it, a young reporter steps forward. "Hey, Alex. Got a minute for a few quick questions? Need to get a start on the season soundbites."

I glance to where the rest of the guys disappear down the hall and internally groan. No, I don't want to do an interview, but I know it would make Coach happy, so I plaster on a smile. "Of course. What do you have for me?"

She asks the standard questions. How was my summer? How are my legs feeling? Do I think we stand a chance at the cup this year? All easy answers until she turns the question personal. "There's been a lot of chatter going around about how no one sees you out on the town anymore. Has *the* Alex Grayson finally settled down?"

My stomach dips and curls because I want to be able to scream yes from the rooftops. Yes, I've settled down because I'm head over fucking heels for a girl and have no plans of ever changing that. But I can't say any of that because the girl in question isn't even mine, even though I'm sure the fuck hers.

River steps up beside me and speaks for me. "We've been keeping our head down and getting ready for the season. You know how it is."

The reporter looks disappointed she didn't get the answer she obviously wanted, but I can't turn myself away from Riv. I've always been the one to field all the questions, and here he is, stepping in to protect me. Something twitches hard in my chest, and I don't look away from his back as he heads down the hall.

"...Good game next week." I turn to face the

reporter, just now clueing in to the fact that she's still talking.

"Thanks. Ah, have a good one." I don't look back as I head toward the dressing room.

The Bruins train at the Warrior Ice Arena, and it's mint as fuck. Contrary to popular belief, we don't practice where we play; instead, we spend ninety percent of our time in our training facility. There are multiple arenas here, making it easy to split us into different groups.

I make my way to my locker, sit on the hardwood bench, snap off my helmet, and dump the entire contents of my water bottle on my head. I groan as the ice-cold liquid cools me down.

Lucas chuckles from across the room. "You looked rough out there."

"How are you so fast? You're a fucking defense-man," I bark out.

"Just means I'm faster than you going forward and backward, man." He balls up a piece of tape and shoots it in a perfect arc, landing in the garbage. "Don't beat yourself up about it, man. No one expects you to be faster than me."

"If you don't cut that shit out, I'll tell your girl, and she'll kick your ass for me." I wink and barely duck the ball of tape he throws at my head.

"Good luck with that. How's your girl doing? Or are you still pretending she's not yours?" Lucas asks, and his eyes dart between River and me.

River tenses beside me, and I push down on his thigh, holding him in place. He might be the most rational out of all of us, but there's nothing rational about him when it comes to her. The room's chatter grows eerily silent as the tension grows thick between them.

"She's not with either of us. Her asshole ex just tried to break into her place, for fuck's sake," River growls, and Lucas puts his hands up.

"You're right. Fuck, I'm sorry, man. You know she and I are good, and Piper fucking loves her. She going to be okay?"

"Yes." River clips out his reply. "We'll take care of her."

Lucas gets up and walks over to us, leaning close so only we can hear. "I'm telling you this because when I was being a complete dipshit with Piper, you tried to tell me. That girl is perfect for you. Both of you. Don't fuck it up."

I let my head drop back against my locker. Like any of it is that simple.

I rip the rest of my gear off and grab my stuff to head to the shower.

"Don't bother. We've got an hour in the gym."

My head whips around to River. "I didn't hear the coach say that!"

He shuts his locker and folds his arms across his chest. "'Cause he didn't. I'm saying it."

"Fuck, man. We're supposed to lay off now that the season's starting."

"Get your shit." He turns and walks out the door, as if it's a given I'd follow.

I groan and grab my shit, proving the fucker

right. This is going to be brutal.

———

A bead of sweat trails down my bare chest, and my back sticks to the leather bench as I lower the weights behind my head.

"Five. You've got three more in you." River's voice is a low rumble that sets my nerves on edge. He stands behind me, so close the fabric of his shorts skim the bench. I can smell the sharp tang of salt with each inhale. He's spotting for me, and his hands hover below mine, ready to catch the weights if I fail the set.

There's a distant sound of clanging metal, but the world is muffled, like we're in our own little bubble. Exercise always makes me tune in to my body, to narrow down on each movement, but this is different. This is like the world paused, and all there is, is River and me, inches away from each other.

My arms drop an inch, and his fingertips graze my knuckles, sending an electric shock up the back of my arms. I swallow hard. My heart thuds in my chest, the tempo ringing in my ears, and I try to focus on the steel ceiling and not on River's sweat-soaked hair. If I shift my gaze a millimeter back, I'll be able to see the firm lines of his abs and the dusting of black hair that runs down their center and tucks into the band of his gray gym shorts. My gaze moves there instinctively, and I catch the hard bulge outlined beneath the thin fabric. I lose concentration, and my arms drop. I swallow hard, getting my shit together. Slowly, I continue to lower the weight until my arms are extended back parallel to my head and then bring them up above my face.

"Good. That's six."

I ignore the way River's voice reels in my attention, and I push through the intense burn in my arms. Exercise is all about precision. Control. Which is exactly why I need to get my head on straight before I fuck my shit up.

"Seven. There you go. Give me one more," River says encouragingly, and a minuscule shiver trails down my neck. Fuck, why do I like that so much?

I drop my arms back again, even though they ache like crazy. My muscles twitch, and my arms shake at the bottom of my rep as I struggle to bring them back up. The burn shifts into a ripping sensation, and I tense, allowing my back to bow off the bench. *Fuck.*

Hands so hot they practically sear my skin grab my arms just above my elbows. "I've got you."

He supports my arms, instantly curing the pain, but the only thing my mind registers is him. It's like every fucking molecule of my being is focused on his touch. His callused fingers scrape my skin, leaving me feeling raw. I'm coated in sweat, and his hands glide, creating a deliciously wicked sensation as he changes his grip to support my elbows.

The motion allows him to take off the weight, and my eyes meet his. He's looking down, and where I expected a raised eyebrow for dropping a rep that should've been easy, he's watching me. His mouth is open, and his chest rises and falls in small pants. His black eyes dance between mine, trying to find whatever he's looking for. Sweat pools at the top of his lip, and I groan when his pink tongue comes out to lick it off.

His expression goes blank, and he adjusts to help me up. "I'm sorry. I pushed you too hard."

"It's fine." I grab a cloth off the floor beside the bench and wipe the sweat from my face. My heart is still beating a fucking mile a minute, and I use the fabric to help hide the reaction while I take a few calming breaths.

"How's your arm? Did you tear anything? We can pick you up some ice on the way out." River's practically rambling, and I drop my cloth to look at him.

Why did he sound like he cares so fucking much? Like he felt responsible for the outcome and guilty about how it went. People tear muscles lifting weights every day, but it wouldn't have been his fault. So why is he so intent on checking to make sure I'm okay, and why do I like it so much?

# CHAPTER 35
# MIA

"I'M glad to hear you're enjoying your time in Boston." Gerard's, my sponsor from AstroCore, voice comes through my phone. I'm in the apartment lobby with my cell tucked into my ear as I pace in a ten-foot-long oval. The rubber soles of my shoes squeak on the gleaming marble floor with each step.

I'd been on my way out to visit Piper's clinic when Gerard unexpectedly called. He wants an update on where I'm at with my funding ideas for Prosthetics For Kids, and I just manage to distract him from asking too many questions by going on about how cool the city is.

"Yeah, it's pretty great here. You should check it out sometime," I say, voice a little too high, filling any gaps in our conversation that could open up room for inquiry. I just need to get through this freaking call without letting him know I don't have anything new for him.

"I'll actually be in town this week. I'll have my

administrator set up a meeting. I'm looking forward to hearing what you've come up with."

*What?* "Ah...okay."

"That will give you a few days to get your information in order. See you then," Gerard says, and then the phone goes dead. I swear that man has a thing against saying goodbye.

The truth is, I'm not any more ready than I'd been the last time we spoke, and suddenly, all the time I've wasted curls in my stomach. I take a deep inhale, trying to get my breathing in hand. I need to do something... I can't meet him...not until I have some kind of way to stall Gerard...until I have an actual plan.

**Piper: Still coming?**

I rub my palm down my face and shake the feeling of dread off me. There is nothing I can do to fix this right this second.

**Me: Yup *smiley face* On my way.**

———

Piper was quick to inform me that driving isn't really a thing in downtown Boston. That not only is traffic ridiculous, but it takes a small miracle to find parking. Luckily, the clinic she works at is only a fifteen-minute walk from my place...Alex's place...River's place...whatever.

I take a deep pull from my metal cup I'd filled with ice water. It's early fall, and there's a cool breeze, but the sun is still pounding down on me.

I follow the directions app on my phone and halt when I turn the corner and spot the clinic. It's painted Pepto pink with large flower designs in deep greens and purples up the entire brick side. It looks bright and welcoming. The perfect spot for kids to come in the first hard months after surgery. There's a rack on the side with several bikes lined up, some of which have special modifications that help make them adapted for someone who's lost a limb.

There's a chime of a bell as the glass front door opens, and Piper grins at me, her golden-blonde hair wrapping around her shoulders. She's wearing seafoam-green scrubs and bright pink Crocs. "About time you made it. I thought I might have to send an SOS to one of the guys."

My mouth pops open. "You wouldn't."

"Oh yeah I would. Are you forgetting what *just* happened?"

"You should've seen the fuss Alex and River put up when I said I'd be walking here." They'd stopped by this morning before heading to practice and tried to insist I take an Uber as if that's not a total waste of money. I heard them murmuring about skipping practice before I pushed them out of the door. Over-protective oafs. Not going to lie though, it was a little cute the way they fussed over it, and they didn't actually do anything stupid like attempt to forbid me from walking. Probably because they know I'd kill them if they tried.

Piper laughs. "I'm honestly surprised one of them didn't iTag you."

"They wouldn't."

"Wouldn't they?"

Shit. "I'll talk to them."

Piper nods. "Oh yeah, definitely have that talk. I suggest Find My Phone as an alternative."

I cock my head. "Please tell me Lucas stalks you."

She shrugs. "I like it."

"Of course you do." I roll my eyes, ignoring the hum of interest under my skin, wondering what it must feel like to know you're someone's entire world. "Alright, enough of that. Show me this place."

Piper claps her hands and beams. "Oh my God, you're going to love it." She leads me into the brightly lit entry with a shiny white desk. There's a young girl sitting there with a warm smile, and I give her a little wave.

"Reception. We try not to make them wait too long out here, but we've got toys and games. Sometimes kids need quiet when they come in, so we also have a sensory area around the corner with headphones and beanbags that swallow them whole."

"Smart." I nod, my eyes wide as I take everything in. She's so connected to all the things that I want to be.

Piper grins and swings the glass door at the back open. "Here's the good part."

My mouth drops open when I step in. Unlike the sterile atmosphere of a hospital or normal rehab center, this place is designed with kids in mind. Just like the exterior, the walls are painted in bright colors, but instead of flowers, there is a giant rainbow that arches over the entire back wall.

The beams and equipment are all equally bright. I can't stop the smile from curling my lips. "This place is amazing."

"Piper. Is this your friend visiting from Ottawa?" A black woman with twisted back hair wearing bright fuchsia scrubs comes up to stand beside us.

"Yes. Dr. Jones, this is Dr. Mia Brooks, the girl I've been telling you about. I thought she'd like seeing this place."

"Piper here has told me all about your charity. If there's any way I can help, please let me know." Her voice is smooth and friendly, and there's a warm twinkle in her eyes. I'm not surprised she's chosen to work with kids. She has such an easiness about her.

I shrug, trying not to make a big deal of it. "I'm giving it my best shot."

"From what Piper's said, you've done a fantastic job already."

I shoot my treacherous friend a look. She knows how precarious my funding is, so I would not say *a fantastic* job. "I'm still working on some things, but I'm hopeful."

Hopeful is probably not the right word, but at least I'm not a defeatist yet.

"How's your internship going? I assume by your choice in extracurricular, you want to specialize in the field of pediatrics?"

I swallow hard and clench my back teeth as I blink away the sting in my eyes. "That's the goal.

Unfortunately, the hospital I was at had to downsize my position, so I'm currently without an internship."

"Is that so?" Dr. Jones glances at Piper with one raised brow, and my friend nods at her enthusiastically. "I don't have a spot open at the hospital, but I'd love to have you work here until we can find you one."

The world tips, and I almost let out a giddy laugh. "Really?"

Her smile grows, showing off perfectly straight white teeth. "Really, really. I can rush the forms for an H-1B visa. With the doctor shortage, they're pushing them through. Can you start next week?"

I shout, "Yes!" then lower my voice. "I mean, yes, I would love to."

"That's settled. Piper, go ahead and show her around."

She walks me toward the back room, where there's a kid of about fourteen walking on a treadmill. He has a prosthetic that goes all the way up to his thigh that's decorated with different illustrated designs.

"Pretty cool, right?" The boy's wearing a smirk. "Custom design. All *One Piece* and *Demon Slayer*."

I mouth *Demon Slayer*, not quite sure how to respond to that.

"Robbie, this is Dr. Brooks. She's new here," Piper chimes in. She gestures to the prosthetic. "He's here to make sure it fits. The designs are all anime. Don't you know that's the cool thing now?"

"Always *been* cool. *One Piece* is like one of the OG

animes. It's basically a masterpiece." He's quick to respond with that air of correctness only teens have. His stride is easy, and it's clear he's had his prosthetic for years.

He seems so genuinely interested that I can't help but say, "I'll check it out."

"Shit, really?" His eyes are wide on me, completely ignoring Piper correcting his language.

I shrug. "Sure, but it better be as good as you say it is, or we're going to have a chat."

"Oh, don't worry, it is."

"So how's the leg, Robbie?" Piper asks.

He hits stop on the treadmill, backing off and giving his leg a shake. "Nub's fine. It's a good fit."

Piper bends down and checks the rim where it connects to his leg. "Why don't you tell Dr. Brooks about yourself?" I like that Piper didn't just give me the rundown for Robbie in front of him, like a doctor would in the hospital, instead making him a part of the conversation. I'll definitely keep that in mind for the future when I'm working here. Holy shit! I'm going to work here.

"Ran over by a car when I was six. Had to get the ol' choperoo. The rest is brutal history."

I roll back on my heels, pretty sure he's testing me. "Okay…but what about you? What grade are you in? How old are you? Play any sports?"

"Do I look like I play sports?"

I tilt my head, giving him a once-over. Sure, his leg's amputated, but he's got a decent amount of muscle on him. "Yeah…you do."

He lets out a laugh. "You're alright, Dr. Brooks. I row. I tried a few other sports, but I'm pretty good at it."

Piper lifts to stand and rolls her eyes. "By pretty good, he means his team has won on the national level."

"No shit?" I say without thought.

"Oh, Doctor swore." He winks in a way that reminds me so much of Jax it's not even funny. "Don't worry. I've got you. Anyway. Time's up. Good to go, Piper?"

He calls her by her first name, and suddenly, being called Doctor seems so stuffy, no matter how long it took me to earn it.

"All clear. Come back in a week, and we'll check it again."

"Next time you're here, call me Mia," I add lamely.

"Sure thing, Doc."

When he's gone, Piper knocks her shoulder against mine. "Well, look at you already fitting in. Robbie there doesn't like anyone, and here you are charming him on your first day."

Warmth shimmers in my chest. "I had to be good at something. Now, finish giving me the tour."

# CHAPTER 36
# MIA

PIPER TAKES me to a small pub located between the clinic and my place. Sidney and Misty are meeting us here for an impromptu celebration.

Never in a million years did I think I would land a job when Piper asked me to visit her. I glance her way. She's talking to Lucas, giving him an update on what's up. Her hair's whipping wildly around her when we turn the corner, and a chill settles in my bones.

Piper covers her phone, trying to protect it from the wind. "Okay, love you." Pause. "Yes, I'll text you when I'm ready." Pause. Her cheeks flush bright pink, and her eyes flutter. "Lucas Knight, you'll pay for that later."

I can hear his laugh through the phone before she hangs up.

We're here. She stops in front of an old brick building with a large red sign with Lucky's written in red letters outlined in white. It has black-framed windows that are divided by square panes. Looking through, I can see the place has red leather booths, wood tables, and an old-world vibe to it.

The bitter smell of Guinness fills the air, burning the back of my nose, and mixes with the salty smell of greasy fries.

There are a few guys tucked into one of the corner booths, all wearing perfectly tailored suits, with their hair styled a little too perfectly. They're like a knockoff imitation of River, who looks like he was made for his crisp oxfords and wool pants, whereas these guys look like they're playing dress-up.

River's hair falling into his dark eyes flashes through my thoughts, and I shake it off. I can't let myself go down that road, or I'll be thinking of them all night.

"Mia, Piper!" Sidney stands from a table at the other end of the bar and waves us over. Misty sits beside her, munching on what looks like mozzarella sticks. She gives me a wide smile and looks freaking adorable with her shoulder-length hair pulled up in bright purple space buns.

"You didn't have to come," I say and wrap Sidney in my arms. She'd caught the first flight out to Boston the second she knew I was here.

She raises a brow. "You should've told me."

I settle in beside her. "I didn't want to ruin your vacation."

"Are you kidding me? The icebergs aren't going anywhere."

"Actually, I hear we're losing one hundred billion metric tons of ice every year," Misty chimes in.

I huff out a laugh and raise a brow at Sidney.

"See? Perfectly reasonable not to ruin your last chance to see the icebergs."

She narrows her eyes at me before rolling them. "Whatever. You should've told me you lost your job."

I scrunch up my nose. "I know. I just didn't know what to say. Like, how do you tell someone your ex got you fired?"

"Sidney, Piper, my asshole of an ex went crying to his dad, and the dickwad got me fired. Easy peasy," Piper adds.

I laugh. "I'll remember that for next time."

"Oh no. There's never going to be a next time. I'm honestly astonished that Alex and River let him walk away." Sidney's smile is devious.

My shoulders droop. "They didn't want to."

"Hell, Mia. I don't want them to. Should've broken an arm or a finger at least," Misty adds helpfully.

My whole body vibrates with my laugh. "Noted."

"Any news from your doctor friend?" Sidney asks.

"I got a text from her saying nothing yet, but she thinks she may have a lead."

Sidney grins. "Can't wait to bring that fucker down."

Misty takes a long drink of her tall beer and asks, "Okay, now that we have that out of the way. Spill."

"Spill what?" I know what, but I'm not going to divulge what went down in Napa.

"Come on, you've all got these hockey stars. How am I supposed to live vicariously through you if you don't give me any details?"

"Don't you work with them now? Why don't you pick one up?" *Just not Alex or River.*

She drops her head forward dramatically. "I can't date them now that I work there. There are rules and all that."

"That sucks."

"It sure does. Which is why you're going to spill."

"There's nothing to tell. We hooked up for the weekend, and then I went back to Ottawa."

"Okay, so what happens now that you're living with them?" Sidney asks entirely too innocently, and Misty squeals.

"Relax. We aren't living together."

Piper snorts. "No, she's just living in Alex's place across from River. Totally not living together. That five-foot hall makes all the difference."

"So you're living with Alex?" Misty raises a brow.

"No. Alex moved in with River."

"To be a fly on their wall," she hums.

"What do you mean?"

"Honey, if they weren't stealing looks at you, they were stealing looks at each other."

I check myself, and there's no jealousy there. Instead, something warm and happy buzzes in my chest. I'm still lost in my thoughts when Piper cuts in.

"What are your plans with them?"

How can I explain that I want everything, but I'm terrified of what that'll mean? My world just imploded, and I don't think I can handle anything else. On top of that, I'm already dangerously close to falling hard, if it's not already too late.

"It's complicated. We're friends."

"Just friends? No benefits?" Sidney asks.

I gnaw on the side of my mouth. "Just friends."

"Well, that should be a crime. What I'd give to have a guy look at me like that, let alone two." Misty pouts.

"Oh yeah, and how is that?" I ask.

"Like they want to eat you," Misty adds while wiggling her eyebrows suggestively.

My cheeks flame hot because I definitely remember all the ways they did just that. I clear my throat and take a sip from my glass as they all giggle.

The waiter drops off our drinks, and Piper lifts hers in the air. "Alright, Misty. Leave her alone. We're here to celebrate!"

She explains how her boss loved me and how she knew she would and how there's a really good chance her boss will be able to get me an internship.

"Don't go that far."

"It's okay to get your hopes up. I know things have been hard, but good things are coming your way."

"How's Prosthetics For Kids? Did you figure anything out?" Sidney asks.

I groan and drop my head on the table. "No. Gerard called this morning. He's in town and wants to *meet* to go over my plans. Everything I think of relies on pure luck to take off. Why did I think I could create viral content?"

Misty sits forward, a gleam in her eyes. "Tell me your ideas."

She sounds so genuinely excited that I spill everything I've been thinking about.

"So I'm like ninety-nine percent certain the only way this is going to work is if I start a trend. Which is like catching lightning in a bottle, so I've spent the last few months looking up every successful trend that raised money and how they did it," I say, and all three girls nod encouragingly. I swallow. "It looks like there's a few very key elements. It has to be cheap, easy to duplicate, give them a sense of pride, and freaking funny. Oh! And there's got to be a way that they'll keep going, or it'll be done in a day, even if it does catch on."

"Holy shit. I'm assuming you have something in mind," Sidney says, taking a bite of her nachos, and just manages to catch the gooey cheese melting off the side.

"Why do you say that?"

"Because you always have something. Let's hear them. Maybe you can even let me help for once."

I laugh. "I let you help."

"When?" she deadpans.

I scrunch up my nose. "Fine. Okay, I was thinking of a challenge. Something uncomfortable that you can dare your buddies to do. Something that's funny enough that you'll want to be dared to do it too." I bite my lip, then let it out and wince. "I was thinking people could challenge each other to dump a bucket of ice water on their head. So they say I will donate this amount of money and dump the water. Then they challenge their friends." I close my eyes. "Stupid, right?"

Misty smirks. "No, Mia, that is anything but stupid. That's freaking gold, and I know exactly how we're going to make that happen."

———

Lucas drops me off in front of my apartment, and I hurry inside to get away from the crisp wind. It dropped several degrees in the hours I'd spent with the girls, and the outfit I'd worn out is no longer enough to cut the chill.

I stumble over my feet as I step onto the polished marble floors and sway to the side, only to be caught by strong hands. A scream builds in my throat, but it's cut off.

"Easy there, Kitten. Didn't mean to scare you,"

Alex says, wrapping his arms around me from behind and dropping his forehead on my shoulder.

"Were you waiting for me?"

"Lucas called before you guys left, thought it was best to walk you up from now on."

"From now on?" I ask incredulously.

He chuckles, and his warm breath tickles my neck, sending shivers running down my back. "Just let us be overprotective for a little while, before you ruin all our fun."

I roll my eyes, and the motion makes the world tilt a little. Maybe I'm a little more tipsy than I thought. "Fine, but only until it's not cute anymore."

Alex runs his nose up my neck, and his lips brush the back of my ears. "Oh, it's cute now, is it? You like having two hockey players thinking about you day and night? 'Cause, Kitten, we fucking are."

I melt back into him, loving the sound of that and trying my best to ignore the way my thoughts swirl in my head, making the room fuzzy. I spin in his arms and grin at him. "I got a job today."

He smiles right back. "I heard. Proud of you. Although, it looks like you celebrated without me."

"Too slow." It's meant to be playful, but he's so close it comes out breathy. "Take me upstairs."

Alex's eyes darken on mine. "Are you sure?"

"Yes."

He entwines our fingers, says good night to the bellman, and leads me onto the elevator. As soon as the doors close, he spins me so my back presses against the mirrored wall and buries his face in my hair. Everywhere I look, there's a reflection of us, and nothing has ever looked so perfect. Before I can kiss him, the doors open. He groans and huffs out a breath. "Can't catch a break."

"Come on." I lead him to my apartment and bite my lip as he looms over me.

He leans his head forward, and his lips brush my temple, my cheeks, and drift over my jaw. A low rumble rolls from his chest. "Fuck, I missed you."

Heat floods my stomach and travels lower. "I missed you too."

He growls into my neck and digs his fingers into the back of my hair, tugging my head back before shifting to look down at me with ravenous eyes. "You are so fucking perfect, Kitten."

I grin, then smile, and then my smile turns into a giggle, and then I'm laughing until my cheeks hurt.

"Fuck. Are you drunk? Please, for the love of God, tell me you aren't."

I grin up at him and tilt my head to the side, holding my thumb and pointer finger close together. "A little drunk. Not too drunk though. Not too drunk to kiss you."

He groans and drops his forehead against mine. "Who did I hurt in a past life to deserve this? I'm not touching you until you're sober and begging me for it."

I scoff. "Beg."

His voice drops to a low croon, and I can feel my thighs grow wet. "Don't you remember? You begged for us so well."

"Holy shit."

His lips skim mine, and I stay perfectly still, unwilling to risk stopping him, but he blows out a breath and rests his chin on top of my head.

"You're going to be the death of me, you know that, right?"

# CHAPTER 37
# RIVER

"HEY, WAIT UP!" Misty cheerfully calls out from behind us.

Alex and I turn, spotting the pixie-like girl skipping toward us.

Alex lifts his chin in a nod. "What's up?"

"So, I was out with Mia last night."

Fuck, I don't need any reminders from last night. I'd heard Alex and Mia coming down the hall; then, seeing him press her against her door had me shoving my hand down my pants. Which I then had to whip out because Alex was opening up the door without even kissing her. I'd asked him what the hell happened, but he just collapsed on the couch, pulled a pillow over his face, and screamed into it.

"That rough, eh?" I asked, and he just groaned.

"So fucking rough."

"Earth to River?" Misty waves in my face, and I snap out of it.

"Do you need something?"

She and Alex tilt their heads, and a slow smile curls on her lips. "I'd kill to know what has you so distracted, but you're going to want to pay attention because we're talking about your girl."

I lean closer and wait for her to continue. I've been called intimidating, but nothing seems to faze this girl.

"Do you plan to help Mia with her charity?" she asks.

Alex raises a brow like he can't believe she asked. "Yeah. I'm not sure you know this, but of course we will."

"No. I know you *would* help. But are you willing to help, help? In an official capacity?"

"Yeah?" he replies.

"Okay!" She claps her hands together. "She wants to do this amazing challenge, which is honestly pretty brilliant. She just needs a tiny boost, and you can give her that."

Mia may not know it yet, but I'd give her anything she asked for. I don't think I'm capable of saying no. "She know what you're up to?"

"Kinda. She knows I've got some ideas but that I'm still working them out. You know?" Misty talks a mile a minute, and her voice raises in pitch with each word.

Alex nods and grins at her. "Alright then. Don't leave us hanging. What does our girl need?"

"She needs spokespeople for her charity. She's got this wicked idea to do an ice water challenge, and she needs someone with a big enough social presence to do it. I figure we can start with you and River, then hopefully rope some other players in. Plus, this is exactly what Damon's looking for."

"What, like stick your head in ice water?"

"Something like that."

"Oh, Lucas would be down for that." Alex grins.

Misty raises a brow. "What's with that smile?"

"What do you mean?" Alex sounds anything but innocent.

"Anyway. Will you help?"

"We'll help," I say, but then I look at her seriously. "You know Alex and I can do this on our own, but we can't involve the team without permission from Damon Everette."

"Oh, I know." Misty's brows pull together, and for the first time, she looks something other than happy. "Don't worry. I know exactly what I'll do about him."

———

I climb into the passenger side of Alex's Audi R8. We're lucky we can leave our things here because there's no way our gear will fit in this car. It's sleek, black, and so fucking fast. Alex always had a thing for living a little closer to the edge.

Alex drops his head to rest on the seat. "Do you think she's alright?"

"Mia?" I tense. "Did something else happen last night?"

"No. Honestly, it's not fair that she's still that hot

when she's drunk. Like, at least go cross-eyed or something."

I bite back a laugh. "I don't think she would let that asshole get the best of her, but that doesn't mean she's okay. She's doing that thing where she pretends everything is fine when it clearly is fucking not."

"You sure we can't kill him?"

I grit my teeth, wishing I was someone other than a hockey player for the first time in my life. "Pretty fucking sure."

He huffs. "So what are we going to do?"

"We're going to take care of our girl. Starting with dinner."

————

I knock on Mia's door, and my chest clenches when I hear her thin voice. "Who is it?"

"It's us, Love."

There's a rustling sound, and then the doors swing open and she's standing there like she has no idea how fucking beautiful she is. Mia's wearing these fucking tiny sleep shorts that have...ducks on them and a thin white tank top.

My jaw snaps shut when I realize it's dropped open, and I hold up the bag of Chinese food we'd grabbed on our way here. "You hungry?"

She looks ruffled, her hair twisted up with a pencil, a chaos of loose strands framing her face. The setting sun illuminates her from behind, giving her an almost ethereal look that feels perfectly fitting.

"You got me food?" she asks.

I look around her and see the floor is covered in a sea of multicolored sticky notes, and there are highlighters and pens everywhere. It looks like she's been in some kind of mad scientist zone for a while. "When's the last time you ate?"

She looks away. "Um…I ate."

I gently hold her chin between my finger and thumb, tilting her head up so she meets my eyes. "Don't lie to me, Mia."

"Okay, I had some cheese slices a few hours ago. I'm fine."

Alex squeezes by me, wraps his arms around her waist, and hauls her into his chest. "Kitten, eat with us, please?" He looks at her with sad, round eyes, and she caves.

"Okay, but then you have to go. I've almost got it figured out."

"Figured what out, Love?" I divide the food onto a few plates and bring them to the living area, passing one to her and the other to Alex before going back for my own.

"The main financial backer for Prosthetics For Kids is coming to town this week and wants to go over my plans for the charity." She takes a bite and hums in the back of her throat. I have to adjust my spot on the chair across from them.

Once she clears half her plate, I ask, "How can we help?"

"You really want to help?"

How can she not know? "I always want to help."

She lets out a long breath, and her shoulders relax a little. I want to go over there and pull her into my arms, but I stay where I am, knowing that's not what she needs from us right now. Now, she needs our support.

She looks over the stickies and opens and closes her mouth a few times before giving us a sheepish smile. "I'm not exactly sure where to start."

Alex nudges his shoulder into hers and grabs her plate before standing. "Misty told us a bit about your idea today. Ice water. Nice."

I gesture toward the array of sticky notes. "Why don't you tell us what you're working through."

# CHAPTER 38
# MIA

BOTH GUYS ARE LOOKING at me with eager eyes, like they're honestly interested in what I'm doing. Not once had Jason cared about any of this, and here they are acting like it's no big deal to want to help. I ignore the slight stinging in the back of my eyes. If I pay attention to it too much, I may start crying, and how mortifying would that be?

"Really?" I ask them. We've moved into the living area, Alex taking the spot next to me on the couch, and River's sitting cross-legged on the floor, flicking through my notes.

Alex lays his head in my lap and smiles up at me. "Really, really, Kitten." He tucks a loose strand of my hair behind my ear. "Show us what that smart brain of yours is working on."

"Alright...hmmm... Okay. So Misty told you about the concept, but now I'm trying to figure out how to raise money off of it. It's one thing to get something to trend; it's a whole other to get people to give up their hard-earned money."

"So what's your plan?" Alex's fingers trail over my jaw, and I fight back a shiver.

"I'm going to make them feel good about it. I'm going to make it so that when they donate, they get to brag about it. People like to show off when they've done something good."

River looks up from the pages in his hands. "How are you going to do that?"

"Well, first, there's the challenge itself. You've got to state your donation before you can challenge the next person. So bragging rights and all that, but I want to go further than that, and that's how we got..." I gesture over my mess with both hands. "... here. I thought, well, maybe we could offer different tiers? Like if you donate this much, you've sponsored one prosthetic, or a different tier could be sponsoring a kid through certain ages. I don't know. It's just an idea."

"You're fucking brilliant, Kitten."

I shrug and can feel my cheeks growing hot. "It's not like I'm coming up with anything new. I'm just trying to rework it a bit."

River leans forward so his elbows are on his knees, and his forearms are loose between his legs. He's done that thing I love, where he rolls up his sleeves, and I have to force myself to breathe.

"Mia, you're smart, and unique, and determined. Don't for a second doubt it. You've done so much already, and now it's just that last push. We're all

RULES OF OUR OWN 293

here to help, but don't forget you're the one making this happen."

I can't stop my eyes from burning this time, and I blink back the tears. "What if it doesn't work?"

"Then *we* try something else." River says it so simply, in his perfectly confident tone, that I can't help but believe him. It's like a massive weight lifted from my shoulder.

"Just like that?"

"Just like that, Kitten. Now, what sticky note should we start with first?"

I take a deep breath. "The thing that's causing me the most problems right now is I can't afford a web designer, and for any of this to work, I'm going to need a working website. I was thinking about using Kickstarter, but I checked it out, and it's not quite right. Unfortunately, the few YouTube videos I've watched haven't magically made me into a coder."

River grabs the bright yellow sticky note. "I'll handle that."

"What do you mean you'll handle it?" I gasp.

"Exactly what I said. I'll get it done. What's next?"

I sit silently for several seconds, realizing just how much I needed someone to take some of this load off of me. To not ask me a bunch of questions on how they were going to do it, but to just wave a magic wand and get it done. A smile curves my lips as I picture River holding a fairy wand, waving my problems away.

Alex winds my hair around his finger. "What's next?"

"Well, Misty's going to help me set up an event, but I need someone to host it. Someone who's not afraid to talk on camera and who's charismatic."

"Kitten, you could've just asked. You didn't need to go through the trouble of describing me."

My mouth falls open. The *audacity*. "You're too cocky for your own good."

"I don't remember you complaining about me being cocky before."

"Come to think of it, it could've been bigger—" I squeal as his fingers dig into my sides, sending ticklish shivers through me. "Stop. Stop!"

"Not until you take it back."

I'm gasping for breath between my laughs. "I take it back."

Sometime during his torture session, he'd positioned himself over me on the couch. He lowers down until his mouth is so close to mine I can feel each breath before he reaches for the floor, pulls up the pink sticky, and sits back. "This one's mine."

I roll over, wiping the drool from my mouth, and blink open my eyes. I'm in my room, safely tucked under the covers. I have fuzzy memories of being lifted into strong arms and gentle lips on my forehead. I close my eyes, trying to relive that moment, but it's gone, like a dream you can't remember.

I grab my phone, scrolling through social media for a few minutes before pulling myself out of bed to face the day.

The sun is illuminating the apartment in bright, warm tones that wash away the shadows. It's nine, so I still have five hours before I have to meet Gerard, and the nerves are already settling in.

There's a plate covered in tinfoil on the counter with a sweet scent wafting off it. I slowly roll back the foil and uncover blueberry pancakes.

There's a note beside it.

*I know you plan on skipping breakfast, but I want you to eat every last bite. Can you do that for me, Mia?*
*-River*

*P.S. Syrup and whipped cream are in the fridge*

Heat pools in my lower stomach, and I cough, my throat suddenly dry, even as my mouth waters. What is that man doing to me?

I make my way around the island and open the steel double doors. Syrup and whipped cream aren't the only things in there. There's also cut-up melon and strawberries. It's starting to become abundantly clear that River has a thing about feeding me.

I toss a few strawberries over my pancakes, then drench them in maple syrup and moan when the sweet goodness hits my tongue.

My eyes roll back as I take another bite, and I imagine the two of them making these this morning.

There's something extra sweet, knowing they must have done it at River's to not wake me up.

Warmth fills my chest, and my breath comes out tight. I don't need a single second more to know I need the two of them. To know that, whatever it is between us, we have to try. I'm done being scared because the idea of not trying is too hard to bear. I just need to get through this meeting, and then I'll tell them. It might blow up in my face, but so be it. They're worth it. Even if it's just a few more moments basking in their attention, I'll take it.

Because no matter how much I want to deny it, I'm in love with them.

# CHAPTER 39
## ALEX

JAX: Sidney said you and River are helping Mia out with her charity.

Alex: Incorrect. WE are all helping.

Lucas: Oh yeah? What's in it for me?

Alex: I don't even need to answer that. I already know Piper's told you about it. And she's all the encouragement you need.

Lucas: Are you saying I'm whipped?

Jax: Are you saying we aren't?

Lucas: No. Just checking.

River: The deal is, we do whatever Mia asks. She was stressed as shit yesterday.

Jax: Uh huh and we're the whipped ones.

River: I would be fucking lucky to be whipped by that girl.

Alex: I'm blushing just reading that.

Jax: I know what you meant, but buddy that visual.

**River: Stop picturing my girl, Jax. Or I'll tell Sidney.**

**Jax: Relax. I was totally picturing you and Alex.**

I choke on my water.

**Lucas: I swear, I look away from my phone for two seconds and this is the shit you're talking about?**

**Jax: Meet up for dinner?**

**River: Not tonight. Mia's got a meeting with Astrocorp and we're taking her.**

**Lucas: Does she know that?**

**Alex: She's about to. Bye boys.**

I throw on a plain black hoodie and a pair of white Adidas before leaving my room. River's already waiting for me by the door, and my steps slow as I take him in. He's wearing a crisp black dress shirt and black dress pants, making him look more like a member of the mafia than a hockey player, and fuck is it doing something to me. His shirt is pulled taut across his broad shoulders, and I can see the ridges of his muscles move as he takes his time uncuffing and rolling his sleeve to his elbow, exposing his muscular forearms lined with thick veins. My cock swells against my zipper, and I swallow hard, trying to ignore the fact that I'm reacting like his arms are literal porn.

Since our little workout, my curiosity has switched to something *more*. Something I want to explore. I just don't want to fuck up our friendship to do it.

By the time my gaze makes its way to his face,

he's already looking at me with his piercing black eyes. His chest is rising and falling faster with each breath, and there's a tinge of a pink flush crawling up his neck.

The hint of vulnerability vanishes, and it's replaced with a controlled dominance that practically pulses in the air.

*Fuck me.* My cock stiffens and beads at the tip from the way he's looking at me. I try to give him one of my cocky smiles, but it falters when he raises his hand and runs his thumb along his bottom lip. A shiver tingles down my spine, and I swallow against my dry mouth.

"Ready?" River's voice is a low rumble.

"What?" I rasp.

"Are you ready to go get Mia?" He's looking at me with a knowing gleam in his eyes but doesn't mention how fucking dazed I am.

"Yeah, let's go get our girl." I clear my throat, passing him through the door, and head across the hall.

Like the smart girl she is, Mia asks *who's there* before she answers. She swings it open and gives us a warm smile. She's pulled her hair up and out of her face in a simple twist, leaving the smooth column of her neck exposed. I follow its descent over her collarbone, half-hidden under the collar of her sleek navy dress that hugs her curves and brushes the top of her knees. My mouth waters as my gaze travels down her long, toned legs and catches on her black patent leather heels. My blood heats as I drink in every detail. Everything about her looks perfectly in place, and all I can think about is taking it all apart.

"Hi." Her cheeks pinken, and she bites the corner of her lip. "Thanks for breakfast."

I reach for her, gripping her hip and tugging her closer to me. "Anything for you, Kitten. You ready to go?"

She pulls away from me, tilting her head to the side, and her brows pull together. "Actually, I'm about to head out. I've got that Astrocorp funding meeting."

I hop up on the counter and grab an apple from the bowl, taking a bite. Her eyes follow the motion as my teeth sink into its red flesh. I swallow and give her a wink. "We know. We're taking you."

"Oh, I can just grab an Uber. No big deal." The way she's wringing her hands in front of her and the tenseness of her shoulders contradicts her words. Her lips are red from biting on them, and she's moving in jerky movements, like a skittish animal. I can practically feel the nervousness coming off her.

I glance at River to tell him to *do something*, but he's already approaching her.

He steps up to her, and she has to tilt her head all the way back. She swallows hard as he grazes his fingers down her cheek and along her neck. "I know you could. But we want to take you."

She nods slowly in the same fucking daze he put me under not even two minutes ago. "Yeah, okay."

He rests his palm on the back of her neck, and she visibly melts into his side. I'm good at making her laugh, but River does something special. He knows how to make you feel like he has you. He'd take care of it.

*He makes you feel safe.*

Our first game on the ice for the Bruins, I'd been absolutely scared shitless. He'd caught me throwing up in the back, half leaned over a garbage can. He'd grabbed my neck, like he's holding Mia's now, and pulled me to my feet. I swear to God I surrendered control to him and just believed him when he said we'd fucking kill it out there, that he'd take care of me. And he did, like I knew he would, tossing me a beauty of a pass and landing me a goal in my first game. Practically unheard of. The fucking news went crazy, and people were shouting about me being the next Crosby, but I knew different. I knew it was him who made it happen and would keep making it happen.

"You alright, Alex? You look a bit lost," Mia asks. She's already grabbed her jacket, and River's helping her shrug it on.

I shake myself out of my thoughts, jumping off the counter, and walk up to her, dropping my lips so they brush against her temple, fucking eating up the way she shivers. "Perfect. Let's go get you that funding, eh?"

Her breath catches in her throat, and her teeth sink into her bottom lip before she whispers, "Then what?"

I cup the side of her neck and lift her jaw with my thumb until she looks at me. "Then we celebrate."

# CHAPTER 40
# MIA

GERARD LEANS FORWARD in his chair, a thoughtful expression etched on his face as he clasps his hands together like a tent. I can't help but take notice of the opulence that surrounds me—from the dark granite floors and walls to the framed prints and bonsai tree, plus the spectacular harbor view outside the floor-to-ceiling windows that illuminate Gerard's silver-flecked hair. He's dressed in an impressive three-piece suit, but there's something about this man that radiates kindness rather than power.

"Do you think this will work?" he asks.

I feel my anxiety begin to melt away as I speak, confident in my abilities as I explain my ideas in detail. Gerard attentively listens to every word, not breaking eye contact except to take notes.

Something within me changed between yesterday and today—I'm confident this project will be successful and express it with no hesitation. "Yes, sir.

I have it all set up—just need one more month, and I promise you'll have everything you've asked for."

Gerard raises an eyebrow at my boldness. "I told you no more extensions."

I feel my body tense up like a coiled spring as I try, and fail, to swallow the golf-ball-sized lump that lodges itself stubbornly in my throat. "I know, and I know why you said that, but the PR manager for the Bruins asked for time to get everything ready on her side. Don't worry. I already have buy-ins from several of the players."

My stomach flutters at the thought of the boys last night, their eyes locked on mine as I spoke about my ideas. Their genuine interest was like a balm to my nerves, soothing away any doubts or fears I had been harboring. It was a complete contrast to what I had grown used to with Jason. He didn't care what I did on his best days and actively discouraged me on his worst. The absolute confidence that Alex and River have in me caught me off guard, almost knocking the wind out of me.

When they look at me, it isn't just with interest but with a deep-rooted belief that I can do anything, be anyone I want to be. They don't try to hold me back or stick me in a box; instead, they go out of their way to show support for my every endeavor. My heart squeezes with a warmth that creeps up from my chest because they're quickly becoming an essential part of my life that I will never be able to give up.

Gerard's hands land on his desk, and he stands.

"Alright, Dr. Brooks. You have your extra month." He raises one eyebrow. "Don't waste it."

I can't help the giddiness bubbling inside me, and it's practically spilling over by the time I exit the elevator into the lobby. Alex and River are talking to each other, and they both look up at the same time. A smile takes over Alex's face, showing off his dimples, but it's the grin on River's that does me under.

I don't stop running until I crash into them, holding them both in the world's most awkward hug. "I did it. I'm getting the extension, and he thinks it's a good idea," I say between raspy breaths.

Alex kisses the top of my head. "Of course he does, Kitten. It is a fantastic idea. It's a fucking brilliant idea."

The thrill of my meeting mixes with the warmth of their heady scents, and suddenly, all my adrenaline turns into something hot and aching. I turn and rest my head back on Alex's shoulder when he wraps his arms around me from behind, and I stare up at River.

He cups my jaw, sliding his long fingers around my neck, and strokes my cheekbone with his thumb. He presses his lips to mine, taking my mouth in a soft kiss. "I'm so proud of you, Love. I knew you had this. Now, let us take you home and show you just how good you've been."

My breath hitches, and Alex's chuckle rumbles against my back. River leans down until his mouth is beside my ear. "I want to take you home and fuck that pretty little cunt of yours and show you how proud we are. Will you do that, Love? Will you let us show you how good we can be together?"

I'm burning from the inside, and I can't hear the world around us. All I can see, hear, and feel is them, and I so desperately want what they're offering. "Please."

# CHAPTER 41
## MIA

ALEX SLOWLY CROWDS me until my back hits the elevator wall. His tongue slides over the uneven edge of his teeth as he takes me in with his hooded gaze. Gone is the playful guy who makes me laugh, and I'm suddenly faced with the power he wields on the ice.

"I've been dying to kiss you, Kitten. I'm pretty sure I haven't been completely soft since the last time I had you pressed against these mirrors." His breath smells like mint as he shifts closer, and his knee slides between my legs. "Is that what you want?" His lips graze over mine in a featherlight touch, lighting up the nerves all over my body.

"This isn't a part of our deal," I say shakily. I glance at River where he's leaning against the other wall, watching Alex's hands curve around my hips.

His dark eyes meet mine. "There's no more deals, Love. There's just us."

Alex runs his nose along mine and rests our heads

together. "So tell me, Kitten. Do you want me to kiss you?"

I lift onto my toes, grip his shirt in both hands, and close the distance between our mouths, a sense of power filling my veins when he growls deep in his throat and his hips buck into me.

Alex devours me, not pulling away until my lungs burn for air. He reaches behind me, dragging the zipper of my dress down, and groans as it slips over my shoulders. His mouth is hot on the exposed sensitive skin, and he leaves a trail of wet open-mouth kisses, a stream of words tumbling from him—*fuck...so good, Kitten*. The smooth edge of his tongue dips into the hollow just above my collarbone, and my head tip back, connecting with the mirror. His nearly incoherent words vibrate against my skin, sending a trail of goose bumps down my arms. "—*fucking—I missed this—so fucking good.*"

Alex's left hand slips beneath the hem of my dress, the fabric caressing my skin as he slowly drags it up my leg. His nails scrape a slow path up my thigh, the heat radiating from his touch intensifying until I moan and arch into him. He hums in the back of his throat and grazes his knuckle over my lace panties.

Alex grips my chin firmly with his free hand and directs it toward River. "Look at him, Kitten. Show him how desperate you are for us."

I swallow hard and swivel my head toward River. He's hovering closer than I expected, our torsos almost touching as he bends in and seizes my mouth with his own.

River's kiss is hungry and seductive. Like it's full of a million dirty promises he's just waiting to show me, and I'm so ready for him to. I clasp the front of his shirt and tug him closer.

Alex's teeth bruise the spot just under my ear, and I reach between us, attempting to push down his shorts. I suddenly can't wait another second to feel them both bare against me.

*In me.*

Making me scream their name and owning every little piece of me that I will gladly give them.

But we're wearing way too many clothes. Alex chuckles, gripping my wrist and pinning it by my ear. "As much as it pains me to say it, we're a little too well-known to get caught fucking our girl in the elevator."

He nips my jaw and pushes off. I hate the chill from the cold air immediately replacing him.

River hits a button on the elevator, and it jerks. I have no idea when they even stopped it. He wraps his arm around my lower waist, tugging my back to his chest, and rests his mouth on my shoulder, his hot breaths branding me through the thin silk.

I close my eyes as my senses reach out for both of them. If there was any chance of stopping before, it's nonexistent now. There's a ding, and the doors slide open.

River places a kiss just below my ear. "Your place or ours?"

I glance at Alex, who's standing in the doorway, keeping it open, and answer, "Yours."

There's a low, pleased rumble from River's chest that travels through my back.

My voice is cut off from saying anything else by Alex lifting me off my feet and tossing me over his shoulder like I weigh nothing.

He carries me into their apartment but doesn't move toward the bedroom like I expect— instead, he heads toward the dining room. His arm bands around the back of my thigh as he slowly slides me down his chest, every inch of me coming alive as it comes in contact with him until he sets me on my toes.

I reach for him, but he catches my hand, kissing my palm. "Just a second, Kitten."

The displeased sound that escapes the back of my throat just makes him smile wider. Then he steps to stand a few feet back with River.

I drop my hands to my sides, ignoring the anxious pull at my chest. I'm not sure exactly what I thought was going to happen when we got in here— something along the lines of all-encompassing ravishment—but I definitely didn't expect them to put this distance between us. I shift my feet from side to side, and unable to wait another second in silence —*I hate it*—I say, "What are you doing?"

"Take off your dress, Mia. Let us see you," River commands in a low, throaty voice that sends tingles down my stomach and swirls low between my thighs.

Any doubt I was feeling a second ago vanishes, and I reach behind me, pulling my zipper the rest of the way down. I take my time, slipping the fabric over my shoulder, basking in the way their eyes devour every inch of newly revealed skin. There's a heady power in controlling their attention, and I use every ounce of it. River's fist clenches at his side, and his teeth sink into his bottom lip when the navy fabric catches on the peak of my breast, halting its path down.

"You're fucking killing me, Kitten," Alex groans, drawing a slow, devious smile from me. Because I know exactly what I'm doing.

"Is this what you want?" I gently tug the fabric, and it pools low around my waist, exposing my navy lace bra. It has straps that crisscross like ropes around my ribs, and by the way River stumbles forward, he *really* likes it.

Their chests heave with each breath, and I can make out their hard lengths through their pants. I swallow, remembering how they felt in my hands, *my mouth.*

I push the dress down, letting it fall to the floor. My panties match my bra, sheer fabric with criss-crossing ribbons over top. I smirk when their eyes descend to the edge of my thigh-high tights.

Alex groans, biting his fist, and meets my gaze. "I don't deserve you, but Kitten, I don't fucking care. I want you anyway."

I let out a high-pitched squeak when he closes the distance between us and drops to his knees.

"I've been thinking about eating this pussy for weeks."

He buries his nose between the apex of my thighs and runs his tongue along my clit over my panties. I tremble, my legs giving out, and Alex catches me behind my thighs, lifting me onto the table without removing his mouth from where he's tracing my core with his tongue.

I fall back, my forearms bent at my side, and my legs dangle over the table as Alex looks at me with molten eyes. His finger trails under the strap of my underwear, and he places a kiss on each hip bone. "I'm sorry. I promise to buy you a new pair."

He snaps the fabric before I even know what's happening, but I don't have time to think about the loss because his tongue dives into my core. "Fuck, Kitten. I didn't think—I didn't think I'd get to taste you again—so good—so fucking good—"

"Oh my Go...oh my...oh my God," I cry out.

He swirls his tongue around my clit before delving it back in. I reach out blindly, and River steps into my touch.

My fingers splay over bare skin, and my eyes snap open. He's stripped down to his black boxers, providing me with the perfect view. He looks like he's carved from stone—years of playing hockey and working out have definitely been good to him.

"Like what you see, Mia?" River asks, leaning down so that his lips brush mine when he speaks.

Alex shifts, licking from my ass to my clit, and I arch off the table. "Yes."

River pushes a strand of hair behind my ear that's escaped from its tight bun. "You going to do what we tell you to?"

There's something different, more, in what he's asking. This is a whole new level of play for me.

Alex pauses, and my whole body revolts against the loss.

"Yes."

His mouth is back on my clit, and I can feel liquid drip over my ass. That's how wet I am.

River runs his thumb over my bottom lip, then pushes it into my mouth. I instantly suck on it, twirling my tongue over the grooved pad as his taste floods my senses.

"Perfect, Mia. Just like that," River says and starts to thrust it deeper into my mouth at the same rhythm Alex sucks my clit. He pulls it out, and I move to catch it again. He drags it along my bottom teeth, keeping my jaw open. "You like having something in your mouth, don't you?"

I nod, not daring to talk.

River steps back and meets Alex's blaring eyes. There's a silent conversation before Alex shifts my entire body so my head's at the edge of the table. My mouth goes dry, then pools with saliva as River pushes down his boxers and grasps his hard length in his hand. Jesus. I thought I imagined how big he is.

He shifts forward and taps the heavy tip of his cock against my lips. "Open."

I instantly comply, and I'm rewarded when he

pushes the head between my teeth. I moan as my mouth fills with the musky tang of precum, and my thighs tighten on Alex's head.

He pries them open. "Oh, our girl likes that."

Before I can hum my agreement River thrusts his cock into the back of my throat, and I gag around it. He backs off slowly before pushing in further. *Holy shit.* I swallow rapidly and moan when he slips down my throat. He pulls all the way out and wipes the tears streaking down my face. "You're doing so good, Love. I'm going to fuck your pretty mouth."

My body clenches, and Alex chuckles. He switches from devouring me to sliding my clit between two fingers in slow, steady movements as if he knows I need time to adjust.

I meet River's stormy black eyes. The truth is I don't know how much I can take, but I know I want to give it to him. Give everything to them.

I nod, and a slow, pleased smile curves his lips.

"That's my good girl."

He notches his cock against my lips, and this time, I take him in fully on his first thrust. He groans and digs his fist into my hair, dislodging the pins holding it in place. He starts slow, pulling out and thrusting back in, a litany of breathless encourage- ment guiding me. *"There you go—just like that—there —fuck—God, right there."* I swirl my tongue over his tip and moan as he bucks deeper.

Alex's fingers are replaced with his mouth, and he delves two of them inside my core. I moan and gag around River's cock as the sensation takes me over.

My hips rock, and I dig my hand into Alex's hair, yanking him harder against me. He moans and adds another finger, stretching me impossibly wider. I fuck myself on his fingers as River pounds into my mouth.

A coiled ache builds between my thighs, pulsing with each thrust, and I writhe in their touch, needing more. Alex's teeth graze my clit, and he scissors his fingers, hitting the soft spot on my inner wall. River pulls back before my teeth can clench down as I grind through wave after wave of my orgasm.

My body is motionless as I slowly come down, basking in the feeling of their hands stroking over my sensitive skin. Up my thigh, down my chest, between my breasts.

I gaze up at River. He's fisting his cock, stroking himself in long, unhurried movements.

My brows pinch together. "You didn't come."

He laughs, and the sound sends a thrill through me. "We are nowhere near done."

Alex spreads my legs, drawing my attention. He's stripped naked, but I don't get a good look because he bends over me and takes my mouth with his own. His tongue swirls against mine, and a deep, low groan vibrates his chest.

My eyes pop open to meet him. There's a pink flush over his cheeks. My mouth is still steeped with River's musky taste, and I hold Alex's gaze and stick out my tongue, guiding it deeper into his mouth. His hips buck against me, his hard cock rubbing against my pubic bone as he sucks the taste off me.

He pulls back, and worry pulls at his brows. I shake my head and nip at his bottom lip, smiling against him. Whatever is going on between him and River, I'm here for it.

Alex meets my smile. "You ready?"

For what? I don't care. I know whatever they're planning is going to feel amazing. "Yes."

He chuckles, grasping my hips and flipping me facedown on the table so that my ass is in the air, hanging off the end. I struggle to balance on the tips of my toes, and Alex palms my hip, steadying me. He rubs his cock in circles through my wetness before slowly entering me. My eyes roll back as I try to adjust to his size. He strokes my back and hums his approval. *"Fuck, Kitten. You feel so good—so fucking tight—"*

River moves somewhere I can't see, but Alex pins me with a hard thrust when I try to look. "Patience, Kitten. You're going to like this."

My eyes shut, and my core clenches in anticipation. Alex lets out a low, pained groan. "Fuck, if you keep that up, I'm so not going to make it."

His unhurried and steady pace is driving me freaking insane. Alex holds me in place, making it impossible to set the rhythm myself and torturing the ever-loving shit out of me. In…one…two…three. Out…one…two…three. I need more, and I need it right *now.*

I try to push back, chasing his cock as it retreats. I let out a sharp cry when a slap lands on my ass, sending a stinging tingle between my thighs. I groan low in the back of my throat, nerves sparking.

"You like that, Mia? Do you like being spanked?" River asks as he approaches the table.

"Y...yes." I've only done a few times before, but I'm definitely into it. I wonder if I shift my hips back just a little more if I can get Alex to do it again.

Alex chuckles and leans forward, the weight of his chest against my back, and his hips press mine into the edge of the table, holding me in place. He places a kiss between my shoulder blades before he straightens himself but doesn't let me budge.

"Mia?" River strokes a damp strand of my hair back from my face and crouches so I don't have to strain my neck to look at him from where my head is turned to the side against the table. I suck in a breath when his gaze meets mine. His eyes are hooded pools of black lust.

"I got you something. I'll admit it was wishful thinking on my part, but now that we have you laid out here, I'm so fucking happy I did," River says and holds a small steel object in his hand. It's thick like an egg, but one end is pointier, and the other has a crystal-encrusted circular disk.

My eyes flash wide when I realize what it is. "Holy shit. Is that a buttplug?"

He twirls the object, his large hands making it appear small. "Have you ever used one before?"

I shake my head, breath caught in my throat.

He moves it to my back, and I can feel the cool

metal on my spine, and it sends a shiver straight to my core. "Do you trust me?"

Am I really doing this? Apprehension, maybe even fear, tightens my chest, and my fingers curl into my palm. I search River's gaze. It's calm, open. Whatever we do next would be up to me. "What if I don't like it?"

Alex's palm rubs a small circle on the side of my hip. "Then we stop. We'll only ever do things you like, okay?"

I swallow hard. "Yeah, okay."

River kisses my temple and whispers in my ear. "Good, Love. So fucking perfect."

A shiver rolls through me at his praise, and I suddenly want to do anything he asks. He moves back, and I lose sight of him, not that it matters because every ounce of concentration I have is focused on River trailing the toy in a languid path down my back. I clench when he reaches my tailbone and pauses. He sets the small object there, forcing me to stay perfectly still so as not to drop it. If there's a book on the most horrendous torture techniques, I'm sure this is in it.

What feels like Alex's hands knead into the sides of my ass, relaxing the muscles. The second the tension leaves my body, he pulls them apart and lets out a low groan. "Fuck, Kitten. You are so pretty."

His words ease some of my anxiety at being displayed like this.

The toy is removed from my back and replaced by River's kiss. "We're going to get started. Tell me to stop at any point you're uncomfortable. You're going to feel stretched, but it shouldn't hurt."

I nod and place my forehead to the table, my arms curling into my sides instinctually. My mouth drops open when a tickle of warm liquid is poured down my crack, followed by River's touch. He starts by rubbing a smooth path from my tailbone over my hole, where he splits his fingers to circle where Alex's cock is deep in my pussy before pulling back. Alex makes an almost pained sound, but he doesn't move. Instead, we're frozen as River works us over. The motion is soothing in its slowness, and the muscles in my back start to relax until I'm melted on the table.

The pad of his finger circles my tight hole, and it's not until I push back toward him that he breaches the rim. "Holy shit. Holy shit."

River hums and moves until he's knuckle-deep. He gives me a moment to adjust, pushing in and out several times before adding another finger and pressing back in. A low moan is pulled from my throat as the pressure builds. It's almost too much, and I have no idea how I'm going to take the toy.

Alex stays perfectly still, cock still buried deep inside me as River leisurely strokes me until I release my breath.

"Good, you're doing so fucking good, Love." River removes his fingers, but my whine of disapproval is cut short when his tongue flattens over my asshole. I jerk hard, no doubt bruising the crap out of my hip bones.

River just hums and does it again. My eyes roll back at the smooth slide of the sensation.

"Feel good, Kitten?" Alex's thumbs stroke my skin before pulling my cheeks apart further.

"You have no idea," I say through clenched teeth.

Alex's hips buck into me, and he lets out a guttural groan. I have a moment to wonder if he wants to try before the steel tip of the toy is pressed to my entrance. My jaw locks, and I tighten against the invasion.

"Relax your muscles, Love. Breathe."

I take a deep breath, and my eyes roll back in my head when the cool steel breaches my hole, and the constant pressure grows as it moves deeper.

"That's it, Love. There you go. You're doing so well." River's encouragement, mixed with the added pressure, has me pushing toward the edge of another orgasm. When it's fully seated, he gives my ass a little tap and groans. "You're beautiful. Taking his cock with my toy in your ass. Soon, you'll be ready to take us both."

My pussy clenches hard, drawing a groan from Alex, who bucks into me. The sensation of fullness doubles now that he's moving within. My body trembles as the sensation rises, tightening my tendons as an unbearable ache builds in my core. My breath catches as I'm edging toward release.

Alex pulls out, and I scream, my orgasm stolen from me. He just laughs and kisses my spine before flipping me over and sinking right back in. My back arches off the table as the pressure rises again with each stroke.

River kisses me, his tongue stroking in time with Alex, and his fingers dig into my hair. I don't think I've ever felt more attuned with my body, more alive than I do right now. River moves back and nips my bottom lip with a rumble of a laugh when I chase after him. I'm quickly settled when he licks the edge of my jaw, down my neck, and leaves a bruising path to my nipple.

# CHAPTER 42
# ALEX

FUCK. My eyes roll back when Mia clenches around my cock. The butt plug makes her twice as tight. I have to bite down against my impending orgasm. There's no way I'm going before we give her another one.

My vision's trained on where River's flat tongue travels the underside of her breast over its peak. It swirls around her rose-colored nipple, and her hips rock into mine. My skin feels like it's on fire as I watch his spit drip from his lips and land on her pale skin, flushed pink before he sucks it into his mouth.

Mia pulses around me, and I groan. River's hot stare snaps to mine, pulling me under.

My breath catches in my throat when he sucks her harder, cheeks hollowing out without releasing our stare. I can feel it all the way to my cock, and my thrusts start to grow erratic. A steady stream of nonsense tumbles from my lips. "Fuck me—so tight —so good—"

River pulls back, his tongue swirling around her nipple, a line of spit from his lips to her peak. A sudden overwhelming need to lick it up tightens my balls, and before I can stop myself, my tongue is millimeters from his, circling her same nipple. Mia tenses before digging her fist into my hair almost painfully, holding me in place.

Whatever's happening, she's not trying to stop it.

My breath comes out hot, and all my nerves are alight. River's gone completely still, his tongue still pressed into her nipple. I don't dare look up at him when I graze his tongue with mine. He groans in his throat, his body tensing, but he doesn't move, as if he's letting me control what happens next. His tongue is soft, wet, and I want more. I run mine along his, this time letting it linger, and River's control snaps.

He yanks my head back, sucks my tongue into his mouth, and my eyes roll in my head. *Fuck.* My hips snap against Mia, and I can feel her tighten around me as she chases her own orgasm. My balls are impossibly tight, and my dick pulses with every thrust. I'm so fucking close.

Mia cries out at the same time River's tongue fills my mouth, burying itself before pulling out. I'm trembling with how close I am. River sucks on my tongue like I know he would my cock, and the world detonates around me. My release comes out so fucking hard my vision goes white. River lets go of my hair, and I drop my head to Mia's chest bone as tremors rack through me. That was the best orgasm of my fucking life.

I turn my gaze to River's. He's looking at me with an unsure gaze and a blush across his cheeks. He looks so much more vulnerable than I've ever seen him, and I bite my lip with a smile, letting him see just how much I enjoyed it.

His eyes darken, and a slow, wicked smile pulls at his lips. I'm in way over my fucking head, and I love it.

My cock slides out of Mia, the oversensitive tip landing heavily against my thigh. I have to brace both hands on either side of her to keep myself up. Her green eyes are hazy, and she's wearing a soft, loopy smile.

I lean over her as she raises onto her elbows to meet me, and I take her mouth in a languid kiss. "You okay? Feel good?"

Her smile brightens. "Are you kidding me? It's all downhill from now because there's no way you're topping that."

River laughs and brushes her hair off her face. "That's cute, Babe. So fucking cute." He kisses her temple, and I take a step back, giving them room. River glances my way. "My room."

"Okay, Boss," I respond without thinking, but the way his eyes darken and his throat bobs with his swallow has my dick twitching. *He fucking liked that.* I smirk at him playfully, and there's a faint tinge of pink over his cheek. I like him like this, unguarded.

River scoops Mia in his arms, and she tucks her

face into his chest. With hockey, I'm pretty used to walking around naked with other guys, but I can't stop my eyes from dropping to River's hard cock. He's thick, with veins running up his length, and the head is an almost angry red. My tongue slips over my bottom lip as a bead of precum catches the light. Fuck. I shake my head, doing my best to knock myself out of it.

Mia's beautiful, splayed out on the bed. Her chest and neck are flushed a pretty rose shade, and her hair is spread around her head like a halo. Fucking angelic.

River steps between her thighs and grasps her ankles, pushing her knees up until her feet are by her ass. I can just make out the shape of the butt plug still in place and the remains of my smeared orgasm.

"We should get her cleaned up," I say and head toward the bathroom.

"I plan on it." River's voice is darker, hungrier than I expect, and instead of following me to grab a towel, I watch as he drops between her legs, resting her thighs over his shoulders and taking a long, slow lick.

"Too sensitive." Mia squeals and nearly shoots off the bed, but River clamps down on her thighs, pinning her in place. He doesn't look away from her pussy when he says, "I've got you, Mia. I'll go slow."

She looks at him for a moment before lying flat. River hums his approval and lifts her slightly so he can reach his tongue lower. My dick grows entirely too fucking hard for someone who just had the best orgasm of their life as I realize he's licking my cum from her pussy, cleaning off every inch of her. River's hips rock forward, looking for pressure, but he keeps himself up, denying himself the friction.

Mia's legs shake and quiver. She moves in almost brittle movements as he takes her higher and higher. It's not long before she's gripping his hair, pulling him harder against her clit, holding his face down until I'm not sure he can even breathe, and I'm positive he doesn't fucking care.

I run my palm over the length of my cock, stroking from root to tip, squeezing the head before repeating the action at the sound of Mia's desperate cries. River's got her near the peak; her voice has turned indecipherable.

River rips his head away, and she sits up, eyes flashing with anger.

"What. The. Actual. Fuck. River." She takes a panting breath between each word, and she looks like she's contemplating killing him.

He just looks at her warmly and pulls her into his chest. He has to band an arm around her waist to keep her secure. He smirks as she mumbles threats against his neck and a word that sounds distinctly like *torture.*

"If you come again, you'll be done, and I still have plans for you," he says in a plain, matter-of-fact way. Whatever's happening, we're playing River's game. I wonder how he would handle it if the roles were reversed. The thought sends a thrill through me, and my cock twitches in my hand. River catches sight of the motion and jerks his head toward the bed. "Lay down on your back."

I make quick work of getting on the bed, shifting up so that my head's on a pillow. River lifts Mia like she weighs nothing and gently guides her down to straddle me. Her mouth drops open on a moan, and her head drops back as she slowly sinks onto my cock.

My hips thrust up the second her walls close around me. "So fucking tight, Kitten."

She hums and wiggles to seat me fully into her.

"Lean into him, Love," River says, gently guiding her down with a palm on her back until her chest is flush with mine.

The second he removes the toy from her ass, I know exactly what's coming next, and I nearly nut right then. I grit my teeth and breathe through my nose to keep my shit together. He's got a bottle of lube in his hand I didn't see him pick up, and then he drizzles it over her ass.

"What?" Mia flinches against me, and I run my hand up and down her side in a soothing motion.

"This is going to feel good, Kitten. Promise."

I can tell when he's notched against her ass because she stiffens in my arms.

River leans in and places a kiss on her spine in the same place I did earlier. "We've got you, Babe." She loosens, and he enters her slowly, in shallow thrusts that go deeper with each one. The space grows impossibly tighter as he stretches her.

River meets my gaze and mouths, "You good?"

I nod yes because I'm way fucking better than good.

He lowers so his mouth is on her shoulder and whispers in her ear, "There you go, Love. Breathe. You're taking us so well."

Her fingers thread into my hair, and she holds on to me as he rocks. By the time he's fully in, we're all dripping with sweat.

I take heaving breaths, my head so fucking cloudy with pleasure that I'm overwhelmed.

Then River pulls out and thrusts back into her, and all three of us groan. What was overwhelming a second ago is nothing compared to now.

With each of his thrusts, I can feel the drag of his cock against mine. "*Fuck.*"

"You feel so fucking good," River says, but instead of speaking to Mia, his eyes are on mine. My legs tremble, and I'm quaking all over, completely at his mercy.

River pulls nearly all the way out and sinks back in.

I feel everything. Mia clenching. River thrusting like he's fucking us both.

My hips snap up into her, meeting River's pounding rhythm, and she moans, her walls pulsing around my cock.

I grasp her hands, entwining our fingers on either side of my head, and capture her mouth in a messy, needy kiss.

River leans over and wraps his hands around Mia's and my combined wrists, and his movements become ragged. The control he's been holding on to breaks apart as he sinks his teeth into Mia's shoulder.

She shudders out her orgasm, clenching so hard around us she pulls us both with her until I'm emptying myself into her pussy, and River's filling her ass.

We collapse, River pulling out slowly then lifting Mia off of me so that she's nestled between us on the bed. We're all silent, completely motionless for several minutes, before River leans forward, kisses the bite mark on her shoulder, and rolls out of bed.

He comes back from the bathroom with two wet cloths, tossing me one, then proceeds to gently clean Mia, taking care with her sensitive pussy.

He disposes of both cloths in the hamper before crawling back into the bed and pulling the sheet over all three of us.

She buries her nose into my chest, and River curls around her back.

"We're going...to...morning." She's so tired her words come out broken around her yawn, and she's already drifting to sleep before she's finished the sentence.

I stroke her hair back, lulling her deeper into dreams. Once I'm sure she's completely out, I look up at River, whose eyes are already on me, searching my face.

I swallow hard. I don't think I've ever felt so vulnerable. "Do you think she'll be okay that we kissed?"

His eyes go blank, like a shutter dropped, hiding his emotions. "Are you okay with it?"

I lick my lips. *Screw it.* "Yeah. I liked it."

A slow, sexy-as-fuck smile pulls at his lips, and his eyes go from dull to striking in their intensity. He reaches a hand toward my cheek, but I pull back, not ready for that. He watches me for a second before releasing a breath. "Mia will be fine with it. Pretty sure she wasn't surprised."

His words are hilarious, considering I'd been surprised as fuck. Or maybe not. Maybe it's been building this whole time? "You think?"

River nods, and his confidence is calming. "Mia's just like that. She's perfect for us. Always was. We were the problem."

# CHAPTER 43
# MIA

SOFT LIPS PRESS against my temple, drawing me slowly from sleep, and my eyes blink open. River's sitting on the edge of the bed, leaning over me with a soft, boyish smile. They're becoming less and less rare, and it sends warmth flooding through my chest.

"Morning." I bite the corner of my lip.

River's hair is all over the place, some strands pushed back, others dusting the corner of his eyes. "Morning, Love." He guides a strand of my hair behind my ear, and my skin tingles under his touch. "I'm going to make us some breakfast."

I go to sit up, but Alex's arm tightens around my middle, and he mumbles into the curve of my neck. "Five more minutes."

A bubble of laughter builds in my chest, but it's cut short when he places an open-mouth kiss on my shoulder, his tongue running along the edge.

"Hmmm...taste good, Kitten."

I stiffen. "Shit! Crookshanks!"

"Don't worry, I checked on him last night. He's all set," River says and stands before walking out of the room.

"See? All he wants—" Alex places barely there kisses up the curve to my ear. "—is to take care of you."

I tilt my head to give him better access. "And you."

He freezes behind me, and several seconds pass before he speaks again. "I kissed River."

"I know, I was there. And?"

I can't see his face from this position, but I can almost feel his hesitation. "It...made me come."

"Why is that so fucking hot?" I hum and turn in his arms. I'm immediately accosted by the sight of his naked chest.

"Hot? Hey, Kitten. Eyes up here."

My gaze snaps to his. He still looks so uncertain that my heart aches. "Sorry."

Alex searches my eyes. "You're not mad?"

"Mad? Why would I be mad?" The sight of River's tongue stroking into Alex's mouth will be permanently imprinted on my brain. The moment felt right, almost meant to be.

"Well, jealous?" Alex clarifies.

I go completely still, ice freezing my lungs. "Why? Are you saying that you guys want your own space?" I take a deep breath, struggling to get the next part out. " I can do that."

His brows shoot up. "No, of course not."

"Asshole. Don't scare me like that—"

He cuts me off, kissing me long and deep until my fingers curl in his hair. "We're in this together. All three of us, right?"

"Yeah." My voice comes out as a rasp. "I say have some fun. Explore, see if anything sparks in you."

He nods, then runs a finger down the bridge of my nose and smiles. "River said you'd be cool about this."

"Did he?"

"Said you knew."

"I've known about how he looks at you."

His eyes widen. "What does that mean?"

"Oh no. You two have to figure that out."

Alex makes a playful growl sound, pulling me over his chest and kissing me hard. Once we're both panting, he pulls back. "So we're good?"

"Are you good?" I ask. "Does it turn you on to know that River wants you?"

"Yes."

"Then we're good."

He nods, his eyes focused on the ceiling, and I can practically see the wheels turning in his head.

I run my thumb along his jaw and tilt it down. "Hey. Just remember, this doesn't mean anything *has* to happen. Hell, you might just like the idea of it. Feel it out. Go at your own pace. There's no pressure, however this goes. It's okay to be unsure. There's no one making you label anything. Trust River. He'll help you figure it out."

Alex rests his nose against mine. "Thank you."

"For what?"

"Everything."

# CHAPTER 44
# MIA

A HUM of excitement lives under my skin as I get ready for my first shift at the clinic. The last twenty-four hours have been a whirlwind of highs. First, Gerard loved my idea, then...I can feel the blush traveling up my neck. Then I'd had the best sex of my freaking life. I can't even think about it without growing wet.

I sit on the bed, pulling on my socks. I've decided to wear my bright green scrubs, figuring the kids will love it. Sure, I want to get an internship and be able to work as a doctor, but I'm no less excited about starting at the clinic. If anything, it's its own form of training.

My phone rings, and I grab it from the end table, surprised to see Gerard's number pop up on the screen.

I quickly answer it. "Good morning."

"Morning." He sounds serious, and I stiffen. Did

something change? Is he cutting my funding? "Mia, something was brought to my attention by security."

My brows pull together, not knowing where this is coming from. It's not like I left there and did anything crazy... I freeze, remembering exactly what I did.

"There's video footage of you with what appears to be Alex Grayson and River Davis. As they both play for the Bruins, I have to tell you I'm concerned."

A flicker of anger travels up my stomach. "I'll be honest with you, Gerard. I'm not exactly sure that's an issue."

He huffs out a breath like he's going to explain something to a child, and my teeth clench. It's not like I'm in a position to argue with him.

"You are starting a children-based charity, and a part of something like that is being completely above board. It's unprofessional to date someone who is actively involved with Prosthetics For Kids. You chose to make the players the headliners of your project and the media will spin you dating one as conflict of interest.." He clears his throat, and his tone is full of understanding. "I know it's not what you want to hear, but if you're going to keep the Astrocorp funding, we'll be insisting on a no fraternizing with players rule. Everything must be completely professional. Do you understand?"

I swallow hard, tears burning the back of my eyes. "I understand. It won't be a problem."

Just saying the words feels like I'm shoving a knife through my sternum.

"I'm trusting you, Mia."

"Of course. I know how important this is. I won't let you down." I'm barely able to keep the tremble from my voice. Thank God he didn't video call, or he'd see the tears track down my cheeks.

"Good. Then I look forward to seeing you succeed," he says, then lets me go.

I'm frozen on the bed, fist buried into my pants. I can't do this.

"Hey, you ready, Kitten?" Alex walks into the room, and my face crumbles. I can't hold back from crying.

"Holy shit. What happened?" He's kneeling in front of me, thumbs running along my jaw, and it's so comforting I sob harder. How can I possibly give this up?

"River, get in here!" Alex shouts between whispering encouragement. "Everything's going to be okay. Just tell me what's wrong, and I'll fix it. Please, Mia. You're scaring me."

Alex climbs into the bed behind me, and River takes his place, kneeling between my thighs. His callused fingers grip my jaw, and he tilts it up to look at him. "Look at me, Love."

I stare at the second button on his shirt. It blurs with the force of my tears.

"Mia. Look. At. Me," River commands, and my eyes snap to his. There's concern written across his features as he searches my face. His brows pull together. "What happened?"

My mouth wobbles. I don't want to tell him. I

don't want to see their faces. I don't want this to be our reality.

Frustration begins to build, burning below my navel. "Gerard called. Apparently, security saw us kissing in the lobby, and Astrocorp finds our relationship..." We hadn't even called it that yet, and I'm already losing. I inhale and continue. "They're implementing a no fraternizing with the players rule, or they'll pull funding."

Alex's arms band around my middle, and he takes a raspy breath.

River's Adam's apple travels with his swallow, and he clenches his teeth several times before he asks, "Do you want to break things off?"

There is the barest hint of pain, but he covers it well. River's always looking out for me, even now.

"No. I don't," I answer completely honestly, and I can feel Alex's exhale on the back of my neck, and he collapses against me.

"Thank fucking God," he says, lips brushing my nape.

Even River's lips are tipped up in a smile.

"I'm not sure how that solves anything," I say.

River brushes a loose strand of my hair behind my ear. "All that matters is you want this. Everything else we can figure out. Astrocorp doesn't agree with our relationship. Then they don't need to know. Do you want to be with us?"

I'm so tired of feeling helpless, like other people hold the power to control my life. Not River and

Alex. They've always let me decide. "So, a secret? And you're okay with that?"

Alex's lips trail up my neck, and his breath fans over my ear. "Oh, I'll be your dirty little secret, Kitten."

"Fuck, that's hot," River says just before his mouth meets mine. I open for him immediately, and he deepens the kiss until my heart beats frantically in my chest, and a loud moan escapes my lips.

He backs off, nipping at my bottom lip before sucking it into his mouth, kissing the sting away. "Fuck Astrocorp. You're ours."

A shiver runs through me at his words. They're way more possessive than anything we've declared, and warmth builds in my stomach at the idea they may feel the same.

Soon, I'll take the risk and tell them they're all I've ever needed.

An alarm goes off on my phone. "Oh. My. God. I'm going to be late."

I completely forgot about my first day. Piper is going to kill me.

River shakes his head. "Car's already out front. One day, you'll believe me. We've got you."

———

They managed to get me to the clinic with thirty seconds to spare. My heart's still racing from everything that happened this morning.

Piper comes through the back doors, and the big

smile she's wearing drops from her face. "What happened?"

"I look that bad, huh?"

"Worse. Now, spill."

"You know Gerard? Well, he saw Alex, River, and I kiss, and apparently, Astrocorp has a no fraternizing rule."

Piper puts her hands on her hips. "Brand-new rule, I'm sure."

"You got it."

She looks me over. "So you're pretty deep with them, hmm?"

I nod, not bothering to hide it.

"What are you going to do?"

"The guys want to keep it a secret."

"And what do you want to do?"

"I don't want to give them up, but I also can't just give up on Prosthetics For Kids."

"So, what's the problem, then? Are the guys giving you a hard time about keeping it low-key?"

"No, not at all."

Piper shrugs. "Sounds like you have it sorted. But Mia, there's going to come a time that all this will have to come out." Then she grins. "Let's hope you don't need their funding by then."

I smile because that's exactly my plan.

# CHAPTER 45
## ALEX

ME: **When will you be home?**

**Kitten: Half hour.**

**Me: Perfect, we'll order dinner.**

**Kitten: What are the chances I can get some nuggets and fries?**

**Me: For you? Chances are very good. See you in a bit. Miss you already.**

Bubbles appear and disappear on the screen, and my grip tightens. I'm not exactly sure where we stand after last night, but I have to push the boundaries because if she feels half of what I feel for her, I'll marry her tomorrow.

**Kitten: Miss you too. See you in a bit.**

I bite the side of my lip, smiling at my phone as her words flutter in my chest.

"What's got you smiling like that?" River asks from across the living room, and I swallow hard when I spot him. Jesus fucking Christ. He's wet from his shower, drops of water falling from his pushed-back hair. I follow a rivulet where it lands on his collarbone and have to bite back a groan when it reaches his nipple. Fuck me.

As if the little drop of water knows exactly what it's doing, it continues its path down the center of River's abs and disappears beneath the low-slung white towel wrapped around his hips.

My cock pulses painfully hard against my zipper. How the fuck have I been ignoring this for years when my attraction is all-consuming now? One kiss was all it took to throw my world off its axis. Now, all that seems to matter is the two of them. My tongue wets my bottom lip as I follow another drip.

"Like what you see?" River says, his voice low and gravelly.

"Yes," I rasp.

River groans and takes a step closer.

Alarm bells go off in my head and panic sets in. I have no idea what I'm fucking doing here. What if we start something and it all goes to shit? I take a step back. River freezes, and he looks away. There's a muscle ticking in his cheek, and his knuckles whiten where he grips his towel.

"Did you ask Mia what she wants for dinner?" His voice is devoid of all emotion, and it makes me irrationally mad. How can he be so collected when I'm coming apart?

I smirk, knowing this will kill him. "She wants nuggets and fries."

"She's lucky she's cute."

"So cute."

"Okay, get in the shower—you fucking reek after practice—and I'll Uber Eats." River says it, but there's nothing in his expression that makes me think he's disgusted by my smell. I pass him, letting my fingers graze his hand at his side, and a shiver visibly travels through him. Satisfied that he wants me, I take his advice and head to the bathroom.

There's a shower attached to my room, but I go to his instead. I leave the door cracked open. If I'm pushing boundaries today, I'm going all out. The water is already warm from River's shower, and the room quickly fills with steam.

I strip out of my clothes, leaving them in a pile on the tile floor, and climb under the steaming water. I duck my head under the stream, supporting both hands against the wall, and let it pound down on my shoulders. I need a moment to get my head in gear and figure out what I actually want from this.

I close my eyes, and I'm assaulted by memories of last night.

*River notching his cock against Mia's mouth and how she opened for him. She looked so pretty with her cheeks hollowed out, taking him deeper. I couldn't look away from where his cock disappeared, and she moaned around him.*

My mouth waters, and my dick's already stiff in my hand. I squeeze the tip before grabbing the bodywash from the ledge and covering my palm to help it slide. The earthy smell of cedar fills my nose, and I grip the base of my dick hard.

*River's tongue swirling around her nipple, spit dripping from it over her hard peak.*

"River," I growl out and buck into my fist, stroking as I picture what happened next.

*I'd been overcome with the fucking need to lick it off her, and the second my tongue touched River's where it soaked her breast, my body came alive. He'd been hesitant at first, but a dam broke, and then his fingers were buried in my hair, and his tongue was fucking my mouth.*

I stroke myself hard, breathing in the smell of him like he's here, and squeeze the tip with each ascent before thrusting it down.

*My hips matched the rhythm River set, and I fucked Mia just as hard. Everything in the universe shifted in that moment, like a missing piece finally clicked in place, and I came deep inside her while River sucked my tongue like he would my cock.*

"*Fuck*...River," I cry out, and cum spurts from me, covering the shower wall. I collapse against it, taking heaping lungfuls of air. There's one thing I know for certain, and it's that I want to do it again.

It takes several minutes before I can get my heart rate under control enough to climb out of the shower after scrubbing my body and hair. I feel dizzy from my orgasm, but I have no room for embarrassment because it was that hot.

I wrap a towel around my hips and step out of the room. River's waiting for me. His eyes are blown wide until they're black pools of pure lust—he'd heard me fuck my fist, calling out his name. My thoughts go blank when his mouth lands on mine, hot and commanding, and I open for him, diving my tongue against his. A growl rumbles in his chest, and his fingers yank at my hair until it hurts, sending pleasure straight to my dick.

I bury my hands into his hair, needing him closer, and delve my tongue into his mouth. I hum deep in my throat. He tastes like brandy, and it goes straight to my head. *Fuck.*

River slams my back against the wall, closing any gap between us. My towel hits the floor, and my skin turns to fire naked against him.

River's shirt is unbuttoned. I push it off his shoulders and run my fingers up his bare chest. My cock presses against the rough fabric of his pants, and I can feel his hard ridge against mine. I rock into him, and he bites my neck, a groan pouring out of him.

"Fuck, Alex." He nips my jaw, and a shudder bolts down my chest, going straight to my hard length, and precum leaks from the tip.

He grips my hip, holding me in place, and rocks his cock against mine without mercy. Holy shit, I can totally come from just this. My hips struggle against his grip, searching for the friction I desperately need.

River nips my collarbone hard and lowers further.

"*Fuck me,*" I grind out through my teeth.

He chuckles, his breath over my peck. "I plan on it."

"Jesus fucking Christ. You're killing me."

He hums in the back of his throat, and then his mouth is hot on my nipple. My balls tingle and tighten, and my head lands on the wall with a thud. His tongue swirls around my nipple, exactly like he did to Mia, and I hiss in a breath when he grazes it with his teeth.

"You like that?" River asks, and all I can do is breathe out.

"Again."

He smirks against my pec, and then his teeth scrape my nipple harder this time. A moan is ripped from my throat. I need to touch him, right fucking now. I reach between us, but just as my hand wraps around his cock, he pulls away.

All my muscles tighten, and panic fills my veins, but then he drops to his knees.

# CHAPTER 46
# RIVER

ALEX'S COCK bobs less than an inch in front of my lips. It's dripping with precum, and my mouth waters to lick it up. I check in with him. "You good?"

He's pressed against the wall, hands fisted at his sides, chest heaving.

"Y…ye…yes." he croaks, and without hesitation, I swirl my tongue around his tip, savoring his salty, musky taste.

"Fuck," Alex says, his cock twitching. I can see how hard he's straining to stay still, and I can't fucking have that.

I wrap my lips over him, sucking until he hits the back of my throat before swallowing. Alex lets out a pained whimper, hips shifting, and I pull back slowly, taking care to stroke the vein under his head, then deep-throat him again.

His hand drops hesitantly to my hair, and I continue to suck him vigorously, cupping his balls in my palm.

"Holy…shit…River." Alex's hips come off the wall, hand gripping my hair, thrusting himself deeper, and I take all of him.

The door opens, and he tries to pull back, but I refuse to let him go. I see Mia leaning against the wall from my peripheral vision, and she's grinning at us, eyes filled with pure lust. I knew our girl would like this.

"Mia, come here," Alex asks, voice strained.

"No. I want to watch," she says in a soft purr, and her hand disappears under her waistband.

Fuck, that's hot. I swirl my tongue, circling Alex's throbbing length, and suck him deep, pulling his attention back to where it belongs. *On me.*

My cock begs me to stroke it, and I tear my pants open, gripping the base before moving at the same pace as my mouth. Alex holds my head steady, fisting my hair, and fucks my mouth uncontrollably. I take everything he has, moaning and humming around him. He groans, chasing his release, each thrust growing more desperate.

I jerk myself harder with each stroke, and my balls grow tight with my building release. I desperately need him to come over the edge with me.

Still caressing his balls, I reach my middle finger back to press against the rim of his ass.

He convulses, legs trembling, and grips my shoulder to support himself. "*Fuck—fuck—fuck.*"

A groan vibrates through my chest, and my dick grows painfully hard. I slowly circle him, adding the smallest hint of pressure, and take him as deep as I can. His thrusts become erratic, a guttural growl rips from his chest, and my orgasm detonates as I eagerly swallow down his pulsing release.

I keep his cock in my mouth, cleaning him off as he grows soft until he's twitching against my touch.

"Fuck, *River*." He's watching me with wide eyes filled with wonder. I kiss his hip bone tenderly, not looking away, rising to kiss over the ridges of his abs and taking my time flattening my tongue over his nipple. He tastes like salt and sex, and it's fucking with my head.

I stand fully so we're face-to-face and search his eyes. This close, they're a warm brown with a gold rim around the center, making them look like they're shining from within. I brush my thumb over the three freckles on his left cheekbone. Alex swallows hard, and warmth fills my chest when he leans into my touch. He closes his eyes when I run my thumb across his jaw and press down on his chin, urging him to open for me.

"Look at me."

His eyes flash, and his pupils are blown wide.

I sink my tongue into his mouth, caressing it across his, forcing him to taste what I did to him. The kiss turns hard, frantic, and our teeth clash together when I dig my fingers into his hair and tug his head back. He grips my hips, pulling me closer, and groans deep in his throat.

I drop my forehead, run my nose along his, and breathe in his sweet coconut scent. Our lips graze with each inhale, and I cup his neck, holding his face gently in my hands, thumbs brushing along his temples.

"Let me take care of you."

He trembles in my touch, not ready to answer me.

My chest constricts. Each beat of my heart desperately needs this to be more to him than a new experience.

I lower my mouth, taking his in a slow, delicate kiss before pulling away. He leans forward, chasing my mouth, and I grin.

"Good boy."

# CHAPTER 47
# MIA

THERE'S a happy fluttering under my ribs, and my lips curl up in the corner as I watch the guys. River gently brushes his thumb across Alex's cheek as they look at each other with excited anticipation mixed with a healthy dose of awe.

I relax against the opposite wall, eyes hooded from my own orgasm, marveling at the two of them. There's a rightness in the air, like puzzle pieces perfectly clicking into place.

A knock on the door pulls me away from the vulnerable scene in front of me, and I hurry to get it before it interrupts them.

I grab the paper bags full of food from the delivery guy, glad that he's already been paid and tipped through the service. Funds were low before, but they're seriously low now. I'm going to need to make a decision about my apartment back in Ottawa soon, but that also means I'll be moving out of here.

The thought sours my stomach. It wouldn't be horrible to drag it out a little longer. *Right?*

I rip open the seals and pull out the thin cardboard boxes, spreading them over the counter.

River comes up behind me and wraps me in a side hug, kissing my temple. "It's a true sign of just what I feel about you that I'm letting this crap into my place."

A swirl of giddiness bubbles up my chest. "Not a fan of nuggets?"

"I'm a fan of you." He kisses my jaw before letting me go and grabbing his own meal. Both he and Alex ordered double-stacked burgers and large fries.

"Thanks, Kitten." Alex takes a large bite of his, humming in the back of his throat. He's still flushed a pretty shade of pink, and I can't help but smirk at him. He's had quite the night.

"I didn't do anything."

He holds up his burger. "Riv hasn't let me have one of these in years. Fuck, good thing you're here. He might finally loosen up."

"Anything for you, Baby," River says over his shoulder while heading toward the living area and sprawling on the sofa. He kicks his long legs over the coffee table and flicks on a hockey game, completely oblivious to the way Alex and I gawk at him.

Alex widens his eyes at me before a wide smile takes over his face. "Come here."

I don't waste time entering his space and play with the ends of his hair above his nape.

His eyes search mine. "We good?"

I lift on my toes and place a soft kiss on his lips. "More than."

He drops his forehead to mine. "Fuck." He breathes in. "How are you so perfect?"

"Looking at my track record, I'd say I'm an entirely flawed person. Seriously, I've been barely getting by. Nothing perfect about me."

He growls low in his throat. "I'm going to fucking kill Jason for making you feel less than. And I'll spend the rest of my life proving just how wrong you are."

"I get the feeling it's pointless to argue about this."

"So fucking pointless, Kitten." He kisses my forehead.

"How's Kristie's information hunt going?" River calls out.

"Good. She sent some stuff over to Sidney's guy, but we're still waiting."

"I can't fucking wait." Alex rubs his hands together in excitement, then proceeds to grab my nuggets, following River into the living room and taking the spot next to him.

I go to sit in one of the chairs, but Alex pulls me onto his lap and runs his fingers absent-mindedly over my thigh. Both guys are absorbed in the game, and there's something peaceful about the three of us just chilling together. No sex, no tension, just being near each other. I pop a nugget into my mouth. I could get used to this.

The players fly across the ice, but the play is suddenly called to a stop. "What happened?"

"Icing," River answers matter-of-factly, like I'd have any idea what that means. He slowly turns to me. "Do you not know what icing is, Love?"

"Um...should I?"

Alex's chest rumbles beneath me. "This is a fucking travesty."

The guys spend the next twenty minutes explaining what's happening. It's not my first time watching hockey, but it's definitely the first time I've gotten excited about learning the game.

"So what positions do you play?"

Alex scoffs, offended that I don't already know. Like, I kinda know, but I want them to explain it anyway. "We're both forwards. I'm center, and Riv here is my right winger."

"So you score all the points?"

"That's right, Kitten. We score all the points."

Before I know it, the game switches to the intermission show. There are four *experts* talking, and River mutes it. "Fucking, idiots."

Apparently, these two feel the same as Jax about their opinions. I go to climb off Alex's lap to toss out my garbage, but he holds me in place.

River takes it from me. "I got it."

"Thanks." I settle against Alex, giving up any attempt to argue, and just let them take care of me.

"You're coming to our game tomorrow, right?" Alex asks, and I twist in his lap to face him.

"You want me to?"

He raises a brow. "If I could force you to go to every game, you'd be there."

"Okay." I shrug.

"I'll get you one of my jerseys."

"The fuck you will." River sits beside us, closer than he was before. "If we start that shit now, it'll be a never-ending battle. I'll get you a jersey that says Brooks. I'd wear it too if I wouldn't get in shit."

I roll my eyes. "Oh yeah, you'd wear my last name? Puh-lease. I know how you guys get about your names."

River's jaw clenches. "The fact that you even asked that pisses me off."

"Can we just talk about the fact we haven't played doctor yet? Feels like a missed opportunity," Alex chimes in, breaking the moment.

I huff out a laugh. "I'm not that kind of doctor."

"That's fine. I'm happy to pretend." A thrill shoots through me, suddenly imagining exactly what that could entail, and Alex grins, both of his dimples on full display.

I search for a change of subject. "Okay, so now that you're both big hockey stars, what's the next goal? What do you have planned for the future?"

Alex stiffens slightly beneath me, and I shift back to see him fully.

"I want to be captain."

"That's awesome. Do you think you have a shot this year?"

He tilts his head to the side. "Yeah, so long as I don't fuck things up."

"You're not going to fuck things up. And even if you do, you don't need to prove anything to your parents anyway," River growls out.

My head snaps between them. "What do you mean *prove*?"

Alex exhales a slow breath. "I'm a grown man, and this is so fucking stupid, but it's the last step. What else can I do to impress them?"

"Wait. You're telling me your parents aren't *already* impressed by what you've accomplished?"

He leans in close and rests his head on my shoulder so I can't see him. I hate it.

"Well, they sorta are, but not in the way they're proud of my brother." He whispers it, and it's so low I wouldn't have been able to make it out if he wasn't inches from my ear.

I stiffen, rage coiling in my gut at the fucking audacity of these people.

"I knew they didn't come to your games back in school, but Alex, if they aren't amazed by you, they're idiots. You're smart. Caring. You take the time to know people. You are so much more than just a hockey player. So what if they have doctorates? It basically means they're extremely knowledgeable about a very specific thing. If they think that makes them better than you, that just shows you how stupid they really are."

"I know."

I grab his chin and force him to face me. "I'm serious, Alex. Don't let them make you feel otherwise. I'm so proud of you both."

My phone vibrates in my pocket, and I pull it out, expecting a call from Sidney now that she's gone back home. Dread drops in my stomach at the unknown number. Before I can swipe it away, Alex grabs it from me.

"Sorry, Mia can't get to the phone right now. This is her boyfriend speaking. Can I take a message?" He drops the phone on the table. "Ooops, he hung up."

"Boyfriend, huh?" I ask.

"Yup." He twirls me so I'm straddling him. "I only have one goal this year."

"What's that?"

"You."

# CHAPTER 48
# ALEX

THE ROAR of the crowd envelops me as I skate onto the ice, and my heart pounds in time with the rhythm of the game. There's an electric energy in the air, and I can feel it coursing through my veins, driving me forward. The ice is smooth beneath my skates, and the chill in the air is invigorating. It's fucking go time.

River lines up to my right on the circle and gives me a firm nod. I know he's got my back out here.

I steal a quick glance up at the stands, where our girl's sitting. She's wearing the jersey Riv got her. It's a little too big, but it fits her perfectly in all the right ways. She looks good in black and gold, but she'd look even better without it. Her smile is radiant as she waves at us, and I can't help but grin back. I fucking love having her here.

The puck drops, and I'm in the zone, focused on the game. The opposing team is tough, but I've got River by my side, and we're ready to take them on.

The puck flies from end to end, and every time it comes my way, I'm determined to make something happen. I skate hard, dodging checks and weaving through the defense, trying to set up the perfect play.

As the minutes tick by, I can feel the energy in the arena build. We're tied with seconds left in the game. The crowd is hungry for a goal, and we're determined to give it to them. I catch another glimpse of her in the stands, her eyes locked on me, and it fuels my determination even more.

Then, it happens. River shouts at me from across the ice and sends me a beauty of a pass. I grab it, taking off like a rocket down the ice. I can hear the crowd's anticipation, their collective breath held as I break away from the defense. The goalie is the only thing standing between me and the net, and I can't let him stop me.

With every stride, I can feel the wind in my face and the ice beneath my skates. I can hear the thud of my heartbeat in my ears, and it drives me forward. The goalie comes out to challenge me, but I have a plan. I deke left, then right, and just as he sprawls to make the save, I slide the puck past him and into the back of the net.

The arena erupts in a deafening roar, the sound washing over me like a tidal wave of pure exhilaration. My gaze locks on Mia's, and she's grinning right back at me. Her eyes widen seconds before a weight crashes into me, and River hauls me into the air.

He's fucking grinning at me when he says, "Well fucking done, Baby."

The nickname shoots straight to my dick, and I swallow hard. "Thanks, Boss."

"Fuck, I can't wait to get the two of you home." His voice comes out raspy, and he takes a few seconds too long to put me down. He grabs the back of my helmet and gives it a shake. "Coach wants to have a talk before we head out. Let's get this over with."

I glance up at Mia, pulling off my helmet, and mouth, "See you at home."

She nods and follows Piper, who I hadn't even realized was here, out of the aisle. Fuck, I'm so gone.

———

My phone lights up where it sits on the wooden bench. I finish pulling my suit jacket on and grab it.

**Jax: Looking good out there boys.**

**Lucas: Well one of us was.**

He'd already left the locker room, changing quickly to meet up with Piper.

**Me: You wish you looked half as pretty.**

I glance up at River, and he just shakes his head at me, not bothering to participate in the chat.

**Jax: You looked distracted out there Alex. Did I see Mia on the jumbotron?**

**Me: Not sure. Wasn't looking. Had a game to play. It's called concentration. You should try it.**

**Lucas: The amount of times I caught you looking over at her is laughable.**

Jax: As if you don't do the exact same thing. Fucking miracle the coach doesn't bench you three.

Me: Speaking of coach. We've got a meeting.

Jax: Good luck. Don't get traded.

Me: Fuck you.

Jax: Maybe later.

River: You can fuck right the fuck off with that.

Heat crawls up the back of my neck, and I raise my gaze to his. His eyes burrow into mine, and I swallow hard. There's an intensity there, something different. Edged. I tilt my head to the side. Is he fucking jealous?

We walk into the coach's office and immediately freeze, spotting Damon Everette. Coach looks at us, then at the owner. "I'll leave you to it."

My muscles tense. Nothing good is coming from this. River's hand lands on the small of my back, gently guiding me into the room. It's hidden from Damon's sight, but that doesn't make it any less comforting.

"I thought I told you to keep your shit clean, Grayson." Damon's glaring at me, and I fight back the urge to attack back.

"I have been, sir."

"Oh, by fucking around with the charity girl? You think that'll go over well when it comes out?"

Rage floods through me, fire prickling under my skin, but it's River who loses it first.

"I don't care who you are. The next time you say shit about Mia, you're fucking done."

Damon looks between River and me. He cocks his

head as if realizing something, and his shoulders slump. "This will ruin her career."

Fuck me. It would hurt less if he stabbed me.

"Leave it. We'll take care of her," River says, tone an icy crisp.

Damon sucks on his front teeth. "You better. I won't have players on my team fuck with other people's lives."

"Don't worry. She's ours." With that, River leaves, and I follow after him. Fuck, I liked the sound of that. Not mine. *Ours.*

The second I'm out of the room, River's backing me into another one. His eyes are hard on mine. "This could fuck with your career. Are you sure about this?"

"Dead."

"Right answer." His lips land on mine, taking every fucking thought with them.

# CHAPTER 49
## RIVER

"WHEN PROSTHETICS FOR KIDS came to us with this opportunity, how could we say no?" Alex answers the news reporter, the bright sun shining off his blonde hair. It's surprisingly warm for a fall day in Boston, the grass in Lucas's backyard still a vibrant green.

Alex's wearing his signature confident smile he uses for the press. For a Canadian, he's nailed the stereotypical All-American look. The reporter's looking at him a little too interestedly for what they're talking about. Luckily, Mia's too pumped to notice.

Today's the big day, and we're here to do whatever we can to support her. Last night, she was a walking stress ball. Even her cat kept his distance.

I could practically feel the electricity crackling off her as she ran through the list of things she needed for the event to be successful. She's been killing herself for weeks preparing, and I know it's going to be better than she expects. But there's no telling her that. You'd think she winged it for how little confidence she has in herself.

There's a compressed oval in my carpet from where she paced for hours. It took Alex lifting her off her feet and collapsing on the couch to keep her still. He worked his strong hands into the tight muscles of her back while I kneaded the bottom of her soles.

She'd passed out between us, exhausted from the stress.

"What made you start this charity?" the reporter asks Mia.

Alex tilts his head toward Mia as she answers more questions. Only the people closest to us would spot the change in him. The way his smile softens and his eyes crinkle while he watches her.

Mia's completely oblivious to it all. She's gripping her hands behind her back so tight her palms turn pink, and she's abusing her poor bottom lip.

A small boy, face painted in red and black with white spiderweb details, comes barreling down Lucas's lawn toward me, two girls with rainbow-painted masks following a few feet behind. His below-the-knee prosthetic doesn't slow him down, and I barely dodge out of the way before they crash into me.

Smiling, I grab two white buckets from the porch and walk them to where everything's set up. There's a camera placed directly in front of the few chairs we'd laid out. There are towels and coolers a few feet away. We'd gotten here first thing this morning, and from the smile on Mia's face, it's totally worth it.

Mia wants the Center-Ice challenge to feel accessible to everyone, so she skipped all the fancy decorations and opted for a simple setup in Lucas's backyard. She's done an amazing job with this event, and the crazy thing is, I don't think she even realizes it. She's so focused outward that she never takes the time to look at her own accomplishments.

The entire team is here to show their support. With them are their wives and kids, making for the perfect amount of chaos.

I've never wanted kids, but that doesn't mean I don't like them. I glance toward where Mia's wrapping up her interview. I think I'd give her anything she wants.

"You're staring." Lucas dumps several bags of ice on the ground and rips into one, a knowing look in his eyes.

"Problem?" I ask, not bothering to look away from where Alex is now ushering her toward us. I don't give a single fuck if anyone notices my obsession with them. Hell, if it wouldn't mess things up for Mia, I'd be screaming it from the rooftops.

"Nah, just wondering when you're going to do something about it." Lucas tips the bag over the bucket, and the ice splashes water everywhere.

"I *am* doing something. We're just keeping it private."

Lucas huffs out a breath. "How long do you think that'll last?"

I peel my gaze away from Mia and raise one brow. "As long as she needs it to."

"So, what gives? Mia doesn't want to go official?" Lucas looks sympathetic; he'd been a complete dick to Piper, then had to work his ass off to get her back.

"Her financial backer threatened to remove funding for the charity if she's caught fraternizing with a player." I bite out the words and have to fight off the low growl forming in my chest. I understand Gerard's point, but I'm not happy about it. "Something about this being family-friendly and giving the wrong impression."

"The fuck?" Lucas says a little too loudly and gives an apologetic smile to the people around us. "Sorry."

I roll my neck, and it cracks with the motion. "My thoughts exactly, but this is important to her, so it's important to us."

"Yeah, but how long will the secrecy last?"

"As long as she needs it to," I answer plainly. Secret, public, all that matters is she's with us.

He eyes me. "Fuck, you've got it bad."

"Never said I didn't."

Mia and Alex make their way to us. She's shifting on her feet, her nerves practically radiating off her. It's killing me not to pull her into my arms and give her all the reassurance she needs. Instead, I clench my fist at my side and lock my thigh muscles in place.

Lucas smiles at me, his white teeth flashing. "Go time."

I approach Mia. "Everything looks great."

She spins toward me. Her lip is raw and red from where she's been gnawing on it. I desperately want to soothe it with my tongue. Say *fuck everything else* and kiss her right here. The only thing stopping me is knowing how important all of this is to her. I'd never fuck this up for her.

She gestures to the buckets and chairs we'd just set up. "Thanks for doing all of this. You didn't need to haul all this stuff out here yourself."

I shake my head and get closer than I should, meeting her eyes. "You don't have to be selfless with me. I want you to be needy. I want you to wake up and know that I've got you. That you can lean on me."

She inhales through her teeth and nods before a slow smile curls her lips. "Okay, go get wet."

Alex is the first to volunteer. He steps directly in front of the camera, his smile turning cocky as he reaches back with one hand and hauls his white T-shirt over his head. My mouth waters when he stands tall, showcasing his defined muscles. The reporter's eyes darken on him, and the look on her face practically screams *fuck me*.

Mia stiffens, a low, growl-like sound escaping her, and I can't fight back my smile. I lean over her shoulder, careful not to touch her.

"So fucking cute, Love."

She bristles. "Like it doesn't piss you off too."

"It would," I admit, "if I didn't know how obsessed he is with you."

She turns to face me. "With us. Don't forget you."

My gut twists, and I can feel heat climbing up my neck. "I don't know what's happening there."

"Well, it's a good thing I can see it just fine." She refocuses on the scene in front of her.

Alex sits in a green plastic chair, and Lucas stands behind him with a bucket loaded with ice water. We all thought Mia should do the honors, but she insisted it would be more impactful if we kicked it off with the players. I didn't bother fighting her on it, not when I could tell it made her uncomfortable to be front and center. It had been on one of her sticky notes, and Alex was more than happy to take that off her plate.

He speaks directly to the camera as if he'd been born for the spotlight. "Hey, I'm Alex Grayson. I play forward for the Boston Bruins, and I pledge fifty thousand dollars to the Prosthetics For Kids charity."

Mia gasps beside me.

The second the words leave his mouth, Lucas dumps the contents over Alex's head. He jumps up, letting out an undignified squeal, earning a laugh from the entire crowd. Alex being Alex eats it up, then snaps back into character. "I challenge River Davis to participate in the Center-Ice Challenge."

Mia looks at me hesitantly. I don't know what more I can do to convince her I'm all in.

I'd worn shorts and a T-shirt, my usual attire not appropriate for this event, and in a move Alex would be proud of, I take my shirt off one-handed and copy what Alex said. "River Davis, starting forward for the Boston Bruins, and I pledge one hundred thousand to the Center-Ice Challenge."

Mia stumbles back, and I laugh just as Alex dumps freezing cold water over my head. I thought ice baths were bad, but this has me snapping up from my chair and shaking it off like a dog fresh from the river. I bite back my curse, knowing Misty would kill me. "I challenge Jax Ryder to participate in the Center-Ice Challenge."

"Cut. Back in five." The reporter gives us a wave, letting us know they've switched over to the news crew at Jax and Sidney's.

Sidney wanted to be here, but Mia insisted she needed her to be in Canada. Help make it kick off internationally.

I rub my towel over my head, drying off from the freezing water.

"Are you crazy!" Mia hisses through her teeth.

"Not normally. No."

"A hundred grand! *A hundred grand!*" She searches my face, smile wide but arms crossed over her chest like she can't decide how to feel about it.

"Mia, I would have donated a million if I didn't think it would deter the other players. And I still plan on it in the background."

Her mouth drops open, and she's shaking her head. "But—"

"No buts, Love. Good luck convincing Alex not to do the same."

The news crew set up a computer so they can watch what's happening in Ottawa, and Jax's smiling face fills the screen. He's all scruffy hair and dimples as he pledges an obscene donation, Sidney beaming behind him.

Sidney does the honors of dumping water over his head, and he shakes it off, soaking her with the spray. He grabs Sidney around the waist, hauling her into his side, before grinning at the camera and challenging another Bruins player like we'd planned.

The reporter whistles impressively. "Live in one."

Alex prowls toward Mia from behind, and she shrieks when he lifts her off the ground. "Your turn."

"Wait, no." Mia wiggles, trying to break his hold. People watch them, and we're lucky we have the cover of being longtime friends. "I can't afford to pledge what you're all pledging!"

"Pledge a hundred K," Alex says while walking toward the chairs.

"I don't have a hundred K. Put me down," Mia grinds out.

Alex complies, sliding her to her feet. "Pledge one hundred K, Kitten." He gives her a Cheshire cat grin. "It's for charity, remember?"

Mia opens her mouth to argue, but she's cut off by the reporter counting down. She looks between us with wide, pleading eyes, and I shrug. Too late to get out of it now.

The reporter holds out the microphone, and Mia swallows hard. "Dr. Mia Brooks, founder of the Prosthetics For Kids charity." She looks back at us, then says, "And I pledge...I pledge..." She takes a deep breath before continuing. "One hundred thousand dollars towards the Center-Ice Challenge."

Piper dumps the water over Mia's head. The pale green dress she's wearing clings to her, showing off every detail of her curves, and my cock's instantly hard. I'm not the only one who notices—several players from our team notice her with heated gazes, and I have to breathe through my growing jealousy. This girl's going to kill me.

Mia challenges Lucas, and Misty tosses her a towel. She wraps it around her shoulder, and some of the tension loosens in my back. Unfortunately, she stays on the other side of the chairs, watching as player after player pledges and challenges the next.

It's another forty minutes before it's over, and I'm already closing the distance between me and my girl, Alex following close behind.

Misty wraps her in a giant bear hug before holding up a clipboard. "You just raised two million dollars." Her voice raises with each word, and she's bouncing on her feet.

Tears form in the corner of Mia's eyes, and Piper does what I desperately want to do but can't because I'm a secret and wraps her arms around her.

I've never been so jealous in my life.

# CHAPTER 50
## ALEX

MIA'S practically vibrating with excitement by the time we get back to the apartment. She dances and twirls on bare feet the entire way up the elevator, her shoes soaked from the challenge. Piper gave her spare clothes to change into, and it pisses me off that I couldn't just wrap her in mine.

When River grabbed my black hoodie and pulled it over his head, something fucking primal tore at my chest. Seeing him wearing my clothes, out in fucking public, had my dick hardening in my shorts. I'd caught him raising the collar and smelling my scent, and it took every ounce of my willpower not to slam him into a wall and claim him right there.

I'm done playing around. This isn't some kind of sexual exploration. This is *real* for me.

River heads to his room, presumably to change.

My gaze follows him until Mia wraps her arms around me in the kitchen and raises onto her toes, mouth brushing mine. I don't waste time deepening the kiss, tugging her hips against mine.

She pulls back, a soft smile playing on her lips. "Thank you."

My brows pull together. "For what?"

"For the donations, for the help, for being your usual charming self and convincing everyone to join in."

I shake my head. "You can't thank me for this."

"Of course I can."

"Not unless you thank yourself first."

She huffs out a breath and rolls her eyes.

"I'm serious, Mia. Give yourself credit."

She stares at the wall behind me. "Of course I did things. I've done a lot of things."

"That was pathetic, Love," River cuts in, joining us.

He trails his mouth along her neck from behind and nips at her ear. She shivers in my arms in response. The atmosphere grows heavy, like a thick veil encasing us. He meets my gaze and darts out his tongue, running it along her jaw.

"Fuck." I lean in and suck his tongue into my mouth, pride filling my chest at his deep groan. Mia rocks her hips in response, and I press my knee between her thighs to give her something to rub on.

River takes over the kiss, hand digging into my hair and holding me in place as he explores my mouth.

I bite his lower lip, and he gives me a devious grin I've never seen before, and it sends blood rushing to my already hard cock. I buck into Mia, and she grinds down on my thigh, writhing between us.

"I need more," Mia pleads, and it's my fucking undoing. I haul her over my shoulder, not waiting for River as I walk to his room and drop her on the bed. She sits up, raising her arms for me as I strip her dress off, growling when she's naked underneath.

"Fucking Christ, Kitten. You're lucky I didn't know about this before, or everyone would know our secret 'cause I would've had you spread out on their porch." I strip out of my clothes, loving the way her gaze devours my naked body, and she wets her bottom lip.

I guide her shoulders to the bed and climb on top of her, knees on either side until I'm straddling her chest, her breath panting on my cock.

"I'm going to fuck this pretty mouth for keeping this from me." I tweak her nipple, and she attempts to arch her back, but I've got her pinned down.

River kicks off his pants, leaving him bare before leaning over and kissing a trail up her inner thigh. I smirk as she strains to move but can't beneath me.

I wait until his mouth is hovering over her core, then lean forward, gripping the headboard in one hand and the back of her head in the other, and thrust into her waiting mouth.

Her eyes roll back, and she moans around my cock.

"Like that, Kitten?"

She nods the best she can.

I grip her hair tighter and pull back before slamming into her throat. She gags around me, and I pull back to give her a chance to breathe before doing it again. Like the good girl she is, it only takes her a second to adjust to me, and I start to fuck her in earnest. Her wet mouth coating my cock, tongue swirling over its tip, and her throat swallowing around my length makes me lose control and pound into her. Tears stream down her cheeks, and I clench my quads, holding myself back.

"Fuck, Kitten, I'm sorry."

She shakes her head no, buries her nails into my ass, and forces my hips forward, taking me deep into her throat.

River groans behind me. "Fuck, she's practically gushing. Do it again."

I rock forward, and she takes every thrust. "Bite it."

Her eyes flash wide, and I grip her hair tighter. "I said bite it."

"Fuuuck." I hiss through my teeth as pain turns into intense pleasure, and I fill her mouth with my cum, pulling out slightly so it drips down her chin. Her eyes are closed, mouth open in a cry, and she trembles beneath me as River forces her orgasm out of her.

I lift higher on my knees, removing any remaining weight from Mia, and rest my head against my forearm draped over the headboard.

The post-orgasm bliss has my head spinning, and it's everything I can do not to collapse.

A warm, callused hand trails up my spine, and my skin erupts in goose bumps. River caresses two hands up and down my back while I catch my breath. I close my eyes, zoning in on the feel of his fingers grazing over my hip bones and grasping the joint between my hips and legs.

"Ready?" he asks.

*For what?* River tightens his grip and drags me backward on my knees in one hard yank, leaving me folding over and resting my forehead on Mia's stomach with my ass in the air. River doesn't let go, and my heart beats erratically in my chest. I feel completely exposed. I shift my weight to the side, ready to flip over, but River stops me with a hard slap to my ass.

Fuck, it burns. I go rigid, my face hidden in Mia's soft stomach while she plays with my hair. River rubs soft circles with his palm, soothing the sting. It takes me several moments before I can lift my head.

Mia gives me a mischievous smile, knowing exactly how that feels, and I twist to look at River. He's looking at my ass with such fucking heat, like he's never been so turned on, and my nerves start to settle.

*I can do this with him. I want to do this with him.*

"Okay?" River asks.

I nod, and he searches my face and must decide I'm telling the truth.

He pushes my head down into Mia's navel. "You're going to like this, Baby."

The nickname sends tingles up my spine, and I

nearly come off the bed when his tongue flattens on my hole. "Fuck, Jesus Christ, River."

He turns it into a point and circles the rim, and I groan into Mia, fingers digging into her side. It feels fucking amazing. Nerve endings I didn't know existed send tingles down my hamstrings. Like sin and ecstasy mixed into one.

He takes his time licking and swirling until I'm shifting my hips back, searching for more. His teeth sink into my ass, and he growls around it before pulling back, drawing a pained sound from my chest.

"Mia, come here," River commands, and she grins at me before scrambling to him.

Her smaller hand runs along the side of my ass, and she grazes her nails over the sensitive flesh. I'm breathing into the mattress, half-embarrassed, half-undone, when River says, "Lay your tongue flat."

Mia licks my hole, and my fingers dig into the sheets. "*Fuck, Kitten—that—*" She does it again. "*—feels—so—fucking—good.*"

I can't shut the fuck up as she works me over with her tongue, following River's directions exactly. He's playing us like puppets, and my dick's leaking all over the place because of it.

Mia lifts her head, and cool air hits my skin. My teeth clench when River's hands grip my ass cheeks and pull them apart.

I can feel him loom over me, and then he spits, and the warm liquid drips between my cheeks. "Holy fucking shit—holy-fucking-shit, River."

He cups my balls, giving them a firm tug before

trailing his fingers upward, covering my crack with his spit slowly back and forth.

By the time he circles my rim, I'm shaking with the need for him to push into me. He presses firmly, and I lock up.

He goes back to circling. "Breathe."

Mia trails her fingers up my side and rakes them lightly through my hair. She's standing behind me next to River, but I can't lift my head to look at her. I take a deep, shuddering breath.

"Good, that's it."

His finger breaches my hole, and my eyes roll back in my head. He doesn't go further, just barely entering before he pulls away.

"More." I rock back. "River—*please.*"

He pulls his hand away, and I growl into the mattress. *Fuck him.*

I go to get up, but he presses his hand firmly between my shoulder blades and holds me in place. There's a plastic click sound, and then he's drizzling lube down my crack.

River rubs his palm over my ass, and it's still tender from his slap. I bet there's a fucking bruise. "This requires lube. Always."

I nod, forehead down, arms bent beside my head.

He trails one finger down my crack, then buries himself up to the knuckle.

I grunt through clenched teeth at the foreign invasion, and River stays still while I adjust. I relax into the bed, and River inches back steadily before gliding in. This time, it doesn't feel foreign. It feels right. So fucking right.

I rock my hips, taking more of him, and River pulls out again. I'm going to fucking kill him.

Two fingers are at my entrance, and my mouth drops open as he enters me. Twice as full, my body takes its time adjusting to him.

"River?"

"I've got you."

I nod, unable to speak again.

He adjusts his fingers, grazing a spot that has a delicious pressure shooting up my spine. I cry out, and River pushes down on it, turning my cry into a moan.

"There it is." He massages my prostate in measured movements. It's more intense than anything I've ever done, and I'm frozen in place.

"Mia, put your hand here," River says, and her delicate fingers touch just below his. He pulls out and instantly guides two of her fingers in.

She's smaller, and I rock back, wanting more pressure. River chuckles, spanking my ass in the same spot as before, sending shards of pleasure to my weeping fucking dick.

I go to grab it, and he growls. "Touch it and this ends."

Breathing through the frustration, I resist snapping at him. Barely. *I'm fucking dying here.*

I grip the sheet in my fist by my head and don't move.

River rubs careful circles over my red cheek, then

moves his hand to Mia's. This time, he pushes in over hers, my ass burns with the stretch, and every muscle in my body locks up. My chest tightens as he adjusts her finger, compressing the air from my lungs.

"Just here. You feel it?" River's coaching her in low tones, and the second she hits my prostate, I buck into her.

"That's it," he says to her like I'm not even here. I twist my head so I can see them; they're just at the corner of my vision. River's wrapped around Mia's back where she stands at the edge of the bed between my knees.

His fingers roll and pinch at her nipple as she buries her fingers into me. My dick pulses. The bed's soaked from my dripping cock.

"You got it?" River's voice is a low rumble.

"Yeah," she replies, voice raspy.

He's gone for a moment before returning to her side. He runs something smooth and round down the length of my back, then between my thighs. It takes me a second to realize it's a fucking dildo.

Mia pulls out, and River applies pressure with the head of the toy but doesn't enter.

Shivers run along my spine as I get used to the feeling of something so big pressing against me.

River shifts to the side so I can see him. He holds up a toy that's not quite a dildo. It's blue and round but thinner than I thought. It's curved downward, and my mouth waters, knowing the exact spot it'll hit.

"Okay?" River asks, and it's so casual, like we can

stop right now and he'd be completely fine. My chest warms, knowing he's giving me control on purpose.

"I'm nervous as shit," I manage to grind out.

His gaze pierces mine, dead fucking serious. "Say stop and it's over. You don't have to do anything you don't want to."

"What will it be like?"

"Pressure but no pain," Mia answers, having recently experienced something similar.

"Alright."

"I need more than an alright, Baby," River says, and my balls tighten at that fucking nickname.

"Please."

He hums in the back of his throat, and the lubed toy is pressing into my ass.

The stretch burns, but it's more of an ache, and Mia's right that there's this all-encompassing pressure. River takes his time sliding it in and out. Soon, I'm moving with him, taking more.

"You got this, Love?" River asks her, and they shift behind me. River comes into view beside my head, but he must have passed the toy to Mia because it hits my prostate, and I'm lost to it.

River grabs the back of my hair, tugging. "Up."

It's pure command, and I raise up on my palms, grunting as it pushes the toy deeper. Mia pauses, the length still buried inside of me, waiting for River's cue.

Kneeling on the bed, he shifts so that his heavy cock is inches away from my face.

He paints my lips with his tip and growls, "This

mouth's mine, Baby."

I'm so fucking hungry for him I open, and he thrusts forward, his taste bursting in my mouth. I hollow my cheeks, sucking hard, and take him deeper until I gag. I groan, running my tongue along the thick veins below the head of his dick, basking in the weight of his cock between my lips.

I nearly bite him when Mia starts to work in and out of me, and they fuck me from both ends. I'm helpless, in fucking heaven and hell all wrapped in one.

"Your mouth is perfect, Baby."

I preen under his praise and take him deeper.

He pulls back, and I chase after him.

"You're a fucking tease," I bite out.

"You have no idea," he says low and dark.

He's disappeared behind me, and the toy is removed. They don't touch me. I feel so fucking empty, desperate. Like I'd do anything to have that delicious pressure back.

Mia moves to the head of the bed, sitting down with spread legs so I can see her glistening pussy. Fuck, she looks delicious.

"I want to watch." She smirks, fingers sliding down her abdomen and dipping between her thighs, back arching with the touch.

My eyes roll back, and I groan low in my throat, desperately needing to be touched. I look back at River, whose gaze is heated on Mia, and growl. "Whatever the hell you're doing, just please do it, now."

River grips my hips and flips me onto my back, knocking the wind out of me. He guides me up the bed so Mia's knee is inches from me and crawls over me as his mouth captures mine, tongue thrusting in deep.

It's like a brand, a fucking claim.

He drops his forehead to mine, his breaths panting against me, and shifts his hips. The head of his cock notches against my hole, and my eyes fly open.

What I'm not prepared for is how soft River looks. There's no hint of the dominance that he'd been a second ago. He looks vulnerable and open as he searches my face. I lift up and take his mouth in a slow, deep kiss, taking my time to explore every corner. I pull back, leaving my lips touching his as I say, "I want this."

"Fuck," River groans and drops his head into the curve between my neck and shoulder. His entire body's shaking, and I realize just how much control he's using to take this slow for me. "I'll go slow."

"Just fuck me."

Mia moans, and River lifts his head, a sheepish grin on his face. My chest constricts. He is fucking beautiful when he smiles. He pins my hands beside my head, then threads our fingers together, his grip tightening as he enters me.

His dark eyes never leave mine as he gently pushes further. He's way fucking bigger than the toy, and the stretch has the air catching in my chest. He goes deeper before backing off and doing it again.

My lungs burn I'm so tense.

River drops his mouth to my ear. "That's it. Breathe, Baby. You're doing so well. Just a little more."

I inhale, my muscles relaxing, and he seats himself fully into me. I'm a fucking raw nerve, lost to the feel of him. Chest gliding against chest, fingers laced with mine, and his soft pants against my ear as he works himself in and out of me. My cock's pinned between us, but the friction isn't enough.

"River," I rasp.

"I've got you." He lifts onto his forearms and angles his hips, making minuscule adjustments.

A groan rips from my chest when he hits the sensitive spot inside me and fucks it harder. "So good. Fuck—Riv—so fucking good—"

He chuckles, head above mine, black hair wet and hanging in his eyes. "I've always loved it when you run your mouth." He punctuates the sentence with a firm thrust that has me clenching around him.

Mia shifts lower, her gaze full of heat as she takes us in. River grabs her chin and pulls her into a kiss while continuing his relentless pounding.

He pulls out of me, leaving a hollow ache in his wake, and stands at the foot of the bed before his fingers grip my calves, and he yanks me down the sheets until his dick's pressed against my ass. He circles it a few times before going all the way back in and stopping. In this position, he feels fucking huge, like he's taking up every millimeter of space.

"Get on top of him, Love."

Mia grins and climbs over me, her blonde hair cascading around her. She straddles me and sits back, taking my cock all at once. My vision blurs, and I groan through my teeth as her pussy clenches around me while River fills my ass.

The sensations are overwhelming, like everything is too much and not enough. River wraps Mia's hair around his fist and tugs her up so that her back's against his chest. She's fucking stunning, head thrown back against his shoulder. His fingers twist, pinch, and pull at her nipples as she fucks herself on my cock.

"Fuck, Kitten. I'm going to come."

"I'm close. So close," she says, and it comes out as a plea. Her nails dig into my abdomen as she takes more.

River's thrusts grow uneven, his pants loud in the room. He slides his hand between her thighs where she's soaking me. I can feel his fingers around my cock as he gathers her wetness before bringing it over her clit.

"Y-yes. Fuck, yes!" Mia bounces harder, less controlled, and River fucks me deep. I dig my fingers into her thighs, gripping her as she helps River build my orgasm until it's prickling under my skin, begging me for release.

River bites Mia's shoulder, fingers still massaging her clit, and I can feel her pulse around me with her orgasm. He bands one arm around her waist, holding her in place, and I slam into her from below.

"Come with my cock buried in you," River

demands and rocks hard, cock deeper, motions rougher as he fucks me. His movements grow jerky, hot liquid coating my ass, and my balls tighten painfully before filling Mia as I shatter between them. I take deep, raspy breaths as Mia collapses on my chest and jerk when River pulls out of me.

His gaze rakes over us, lip pinched between his teeth and a satisfied flush over his cheeks. His eyes are hooded when he meets mine. "You take us so well, Baby."

I swallow hard as a shiver runs through me. Jesus Christ.

While River heads to the bathroom, I adjust Mia and myself so she's on my right side, head tucked into my chest.

River comes back and runs a wet cloth between her legs, gentle with his touch, before grabbing another one and doing the same to me. It feels intimate, personal.

He wraps himself behind me—one arm under my head and the other hand drawing circles on Mia's hip —then places a sickeningly soft kiss on the back of my neck.

I close my eyes, heart beating out of control as it all hits me at once.

I'm in love with them, and if this world does anything for me, if I've done anything right, if I'm judged and found to deserve them, I fucking hope they love me back, because they're all I'll ever need.

# CHAPTER 51
# MIA

"ALRIGHT, HOW DOES THAT FEEL?" I ask Ethan, who's sitting on the red chair in front of me, twisting his leg right and left, checking out his new prosthetic. This one's a metallic gray, designed to look like carbon fiber, and it replaces his dark red Spider-Man one he's grown out of.

He sets the new foot down, applying pressure. "Feels okay."

"Go ahead and walk around a bit, and we can adjust it if needed." I don't offer to help him up. Ethan's always pushed for his independence.

He stands and walks around the room, then jogs a bit before turning back to me. "You did good, Doc."

I smile wide. "Of course. Did you expect anything less?"

"Oh, there were definitely doubts in the beginning. Remember when you held the band upside down?" He's been coming in the last few weeks to get fitted and run some basic physicals. We've grown close. He's constantly throwing the kind of jokes only near teenagers can pull off.

The little punk's been growing on me.

"Whatever you say. Take a seat over there so Dr. Jones can clear you out."

Ethan gives me a sharp salute and heads to the other side of the room. His strides are even, and I give myself a small pat on the back for my fitting job.

Piper skips over to me, a wide smile taking over her face as her gaze follows Ethan. "Looking good. You're fitting right in."

She looks cute in lime-green scrubs and her golden hair pulled up in a high ponytail.

Pride fills my chest. This job means more to me than anything I've worked on in the past. It's as close as I'm going to get to being back on the pediatric unit until I land a new internship. Whenever that is.

"How are the guys?" Piper asks, and I can feel my cheeks heat as memories of last night fill my brain. I've never done anything like that. Hell, I've never even considered it, but something tells me River can convince me to do anything he wants. Not that I didn't love it, because I absolutely did. Probably the hottest night of my life.

She laughs, pulling me out of my thoughts. "That good, huh?"

I don't even bother to lie, knowing what I was thinking is written all over my face. "You have no idea."

"Both of them?"

"Yup." I pop the *P*.

She squeals, clapping her hands together. "I freaking knew it."

"Think it's been a long time coming."

"So...are things serious now?"

My heart clenches, and it feels like butterflies are trying to fly out of my chest. It's a mixture of anxious excitement, not knowing exactly where we're heading. "I freaking hope so. Nothing's official."

She bumps her shoulder against mine. "I see the way those guys look at you. They'll treat you well, and Mia." Her brows pull together. "You deserve it."

Dr. Jones walks up to us. "Am I interrupting something?"

I choke on my own spit and cough. "Nope. Nothing."

She quirks a brow, clearly not believing me. "I want to talk to you in my office. Do you have time?"

I check my watch, more to give me a second to internally freak out. Ethan was my last patient today. "All free."

"Perfect."

I follow after her, glancing back at a smiling Piper. She gives me two thumbs up. I'm glad she's confident—the last time I was called into an office, it didn't go so well for me.

Dr. Jones's office is painted a soft pastel purple and is furnished with soft chairs and a crisp white desk. She sits behind it and pulls out a folder.

I swallow hard as I take the seat across from her

and wipe my palms on my pants where she can't see it.

"Have you been liking it here?" she asks.

I'm already nodding. "Loving it."

"You've seemed to settle in well."

My pulse is rushing in my ears, unsure if she's pumping me up or letting me down easy. I lose control of my nerves, and my words tumble out. "Dr. Jones, if I'm doing anything wrong, just let me know, and I'll fix it."

She chuckles and shakes her head. "I didn't call you in here to fire you. I called you in here because an internship position opened up beneath me, and I want you to join my team."

My mouth drops open, and I replay her words over and over in my head just to make sure I heard her right. "You want me." I point at my chest. "To intern for you."

She smiles. "Yes, Mia. I would love to take you on as my intern."

I clasp my hands together, barely able to contain my excitement. I got an internship. I got an internship in Boston.

I realize I've been silent way too long. "Oh my God. Thank you."

"Of course, the hospital will be contacting you with your shifts. But I'm hoping you'll still pick up days here at the clinic."

It never crossed my mind not to. "I'll be here."

"There's a fundraiser gala coming up for the hospital. I expect you to be there."

Somehow, that makes it feel even more real. An overwhelming excitement bubbles through me, and I wring my fingers together to stop myself from hugging her. This woman has just changed my whole life for the better, and she's just standing there like it's no big deal.

"This means so much to me," I say, trying to force all of my feelings into the statement.

"You earned it. Go on, get out of here. Your shift's over." She gestures toward the door and dismisses me.

I'm not five feet out of her door before Piper wraps me in a tight hug, pulling my feet off the ground.

I look at her, eyes wide. "You knew?"

"Only today."

"How on earth did you keep it a secret?"

"It freaking killed me, and thank God it's over." She beams at me. "You got an internship."

Reality slams into me. "I have an internship."

"Is that you?" Our receptionist holds her phone for me to see, and my mouth drops open. I take it from her, holding it closer to my face, not believing what I'm seeing. The picture captures the exact moment Lucas poured ice water over Alex. The banner taking up the top says, "Viral trend called the Center-Ice Challenge is sweeping the country."

I hand her phone back and scramble for my own, pulling up the first social app I see and punching in #centericechallenge. I scroll through post after post of regular people challenging each other.

I pull up the website River figured out, and I suck in a gasp, eyes burning. The donations counter is ticking up in real time.

It's already raised over a million dollars. My head buzzes, and my vision blurs. This is going to work.

# CHAPTER 52

# RIVER

ALEX: **Lucky bastard.**

**Me: You can always join us.**

**Alex: Tempting.**

**Alex: I think it's better if you guys do this alone.**

**Alex: You can practice tying me up later.**

Fuck. Images of Alex, trussed up, completely under my control, flood my head, and I have to suppress my groan. I reach down and adjust my hardening cock.

**Me: You're going to pay for that.**

**Alex: Looking forward to it. *winky face.* **

I tuck my phone into the back pocket of my wool pants. I'd dressed in all black for tonight's activities. I inhale and exhale slowly, shaking off my thoughts. This is not the place to be turned on.

I push open the door to the PlayfulMotion clinic.

"Can I help you?" a woman asks from behind the front desk, her fingers never leaving the keyboard.

I straighten the buttons on my sleeve. "I'm here to pick up Doctor Mia Brooks."

She looks up and smiles at me. "You must be River. Just right through those doors, Honey."

I push through the doors and scan the clinic. It's painted in bright colors and decorated with kids in mind.

I spot Mia in the back. She's kneeling in front of a girl who can't be more than five years old. The little girl's grinning at Mia as she helps her with some kind of arm brace. I'm frozen in place watching her work. At how she's lit from within as she speaks with the kid.

I can't make out what she's saying, but whatever it is has the little girl giggling.

"You gonna ask her out?" a boy asks from where he's sitting on a giant beanbag chair that practically swallows him. He side-eyes me. "Scared or something?"

I look at him and note the way he seems to be judging me. "Something like that."

"Why do you look so terrified? I'm the one who's about to get his leg chopped off."

I gape at him, unable to form words.

He bursts into laughter and holds up his leg. "Just kidding. Already did."

"Ethan. Stop picking on him," Mia says, laughter filling her voice.

"Come on, Doc. Couldn't let him pick you up without at least testing him."

Mia smiles. "Did he pass?"

"We'll see."

Tough crowd.

"Just let me grab my stuff." She disappears into the back room, leaving me with Ethan.

He's watching me with a raised brow.

"Would you feel better if I told you I love her?"

He smirks. "Who doesn't?"

As Mia enters the room, my eyes are drawn to the way her deep purple dress flows effortlessly around her curves, stopping just above her knees. The soft fabric of her dress sways with each step she takes, and I catch myself holding my breath in admiration. She's let her hair down, and the pale blonde strands tumble around her shoulders. My heart races as she approaches me.

The air seems to hum as I take in the sight of her, feeling like time has stopped for this moment.

We head out to my Range Rover I parked illegally in front of the clinic, and I hold the door out for her. When she climbs in, I lean in, kiss her cheek, and buckle her seat belt.

She rolls her eyes at me, but I can't fucking help it. I'm addicted to doing things for her.

Mia's smiling at me when I take the spot beside her. She's practically vibrating with excitement, and I can't stop myself from smirking back. "You're happy tonight."

Her smile grows impossibly bigger, and my chest squeezes tight. Fuck, she's stunning.

She wrings her hands in front of her, and I reach out, steadying them. "Tell me."

"Dr. Jones offered me an internship!" Mia's voice pitches higher until the last vowel is practically a squeal.

Emotions slam into me. Pride, elation, excitement all come at once. No one deserves it more than this girl. "Congratulations, Love."

"It's not just an internship. It's specifically under her. So I'll be working in the pediatrics department. I can't freaking believe it. Oh my God."

She's talking a mile a minute, and I have to give her all of my attention just to keep up. Her joy is contagious, and soon, my cheeks hurt from smiling. My girl's happy, and that makes me happy. I cup her neck and rub my thumb over her cheek. "You're amazing, Mia. I'm so proud of you."

Tears form at the corner of her eyes, but the smile never leaves her face. "I can't believe it's happening."

"I never doubted it." I'm not lying—there was never any chance she wasn't landing a new internship. She was made for this. She's practically glowing right now, but nothing can top the way I feel knowing she's not leaving. She has an internship in Boston. *Boston.*

I pull her toward me and capture her mouth in a deep kiss until my lungs scream for air. *Move in with me.* The words hover at the edges of my teeth, but I bite them back, not wanting to ruin this moment. I'd give absolutely anything to keep her this happy.

Her cheeks are flushed, and her chest rises and falls with her breaths when we break apart. "So, where are we going?"

My mind is momentarily blank before memories of what I have planned for tonight come crashing back. "I have a Shibari exam I need a partner for."

Her eyes flash wide. "You mean like, tying people up?"

"Yeah, Love, like tying *you* up."

———

I pull around an old brick building that blends in with the surroundings so well you'd never know what happens inside. The only giveaway is the dark tint on all the windows, preventing anyone from looking in.

I park the SUV and glance over at Mia. Her teeth are gnawing on her bottom lip, and I gently run my thumb over it, freeing it from the abuse.

"We don't have to go in."

Her movements are jerky, almost skittish. "I'm okay. I want to go."

I lean in closer and wrap my hand above her knee where the hem of her dress has ridden up. "If at any point you aren't comfortable, we'll leave. You can tell me."

She nods, but she's looking away.

I want to push her against her boundaries, but I'd never purposefully cross them. "Love, look at me."

Her gaze snaps to mine, and my chest hums. She's such a good listener.

Entwining my fingers to stop myself from dragging her into my lap, I say, "We're going to have safe words for this."

Her mouth drops open. "Do we need them?"

"Yes." I don't leave room for debate. "Green for go, yellow for slow down, and red for stop. Repeat it back."

Her brows pull together, and for a second, I think she's going to balk at this. Which would be really fucking unfortunate because we aren't going any further until we get this laid out. "Mia," I warn.

There's a small gleam in her eyes like she knows I'm going crazy. "Green for go, yellow for slow down, and red for stop."

I run my thumb along her jaw and wrap my fingers around the back of her neck. "Promise me you'll use your safe words if you're uncomfortable."

"I promise."

I kiss her deeply, tucking a strand of loose hair behind her ear, and whisper, "You're such a good girl."

---

I ring the doorbell at the back entrance. Mia's hand is hot in mine, and I give it a reassuring squeeze just before Violet opens the door.

"Mr. Davis. It's good to see you," she says and holds out her hand. She's in her mid to late fifties, and it only manages to make her even more regal. Her black hair is twisted up into a sleek updo, her lips are painted a deep red, and her extra-high heels put her only a few inches shorter than me.

"It hasn't been that long." I take her hand in a soft shake without letting Mia go. She's already looking at the older woman with narrowed eyes and clenched teeth. I stroke my thumb along her forearm.

"It's been a few weeks," Madame says and turns to lead the way into the building.

The second the older woman's back is turned, Mia stiffens and tries to pull her hand away. I tug her to my side and whisper in her ear, "It's fucking adorable that you're jealous, but you have no reason to be. She's the teacher. Nothing more."

The tension drains from her, and she buries her face in my chest, mumbling, "I don't know what's wrong with me."

I kiss her temple. "Nothing. I like it."

We walk down the dark hall. It's painted in a nearly black maroon color. Mia's eyes go round as she takes it all in. "Is this a sex club?"

I chuckle. "No, just classes."

She's silent, eyes wide as she lets me lead her forward. We enter the training room, and she gasps. I try to see it the way she does.

There are hooks attached to the ceiling with thick ropes hanging down, all deep red against the black walls. The lights are dimmed, only bright enough for us to see. She's blinking against the dark, teeth gnawing on her bottom lip, trying to take it all in.

"I'm Violet, and you must be Dr. Brooks." She

holds out her hand, and Mia reluctantly lets go of mine and shakes it.

Mia's head tilts to the side. "How do you know my name?"

"When Mr. Davis called to tell me after years of training here he was bringing his first partner to class, I admit I pummeled him with questions." Violet smiles gently.

Mia smiles at that and looks at me from the corner of her eye. "First person."

"*Only* person."

# CHAPTER 53
# MIA

AS HIS WORDS wash over me, I feel a warmth in my chest and a wave of relief that he hasn't come here with someone else.

The room's dimly lit, but I can still make out the surrounding details. The mirror in front of me bounces off the one behind us for an almost panoramic view. A surge of anticipation shoots through me. Despite my unease, there's something deeply exciting—and slightly terrifying—about being in this moment.

I'm *really* doing this.

River runs a knuckle over my cheek, caressing me gently, and smiles down at me. "I've got you."

I instantly relax, all the tension leaving my shoulders because there's no doubt in my mind that this man will take care of me. That I can trust him to make this good for me.

I nod. "I know you do."

The side of his mouth curls in a playful grin. "I may have practiced a few knots on Alex's wrists."

I choke on a laugh. "How did he not know?"

He shrugs. "He wasn't ready."

Lifting a brow, I ask, "He's ready now though?"

River nods, a flush of pink over his cheeks, and his voice comes out raspy. "Yeah, he is."

I look around, spotting Violet sitting in a black chair ten feet away. My palms grow sweaty, and I wipe them on my dress. "What happens now?"

She gestures toward River. "Mr. Davis has been training in the art of Shibari for over a year now. He's practiced several rope patterns using one of our body forms designed for this purpose. He requested the space to be able to perform the knots on you with me as a safety check since this will be the first time with a live participant. River will lead you throughout. Just pretend I'm not here."

My breaths are shallow, my muscles tingling in anticipation as I take the first steps toward River. Time seems to stand still, and all sound fades away as our eyes connect.

"Do you want to continue?" he asks, so casually I feel confident he'd be completely fine if we left, but the last thing on my mind is leaving. I want to know what it feels like to have this man take complete control over me.

"I want to stay," I rasp, and he gives me a dark smile that makes a million promises that I know he'll keep. Warmth pools in my lower stomach, and I rub my thighs together against the growing ache.

"Perfect, Love." River's voice drops to a deep, rumbly command that has shivers running up my spine. "Color?"

My body buzzes with anticipation. "Green."

"That's my girl," he says and walks behind me, lifting my hair off my neck. He kneads his fingers, massaging my head, and a soft gasp escapes me. He combs through my hair in slow, deliberate motions, carefully untangling the ends.

"That's nice," I hum, unable to look away from his intense dark eyes looking back at me in the mirror. My skin feels electric as his fingertips graze the sensitive spot behind my ear. His tall frame looms behind me, and I feel my heart flutter in response. He leans closer, as if to make sure he has my full attention, and wraps my hair around his fist, placing a gentle kiss against the nape of my neck.

"Your hair needs to be up to continue," he explains calmly.

I check my wrists for the tie I had at work, but I must have left it there. Shit. I go to tell him, but my mouth drops open when he pulls a small elastic from his pocket.

He parts my hair in neat sections, and my heart skips when he starts french braiding from the tops. A shiver travels down my neck as his nail grazes me when he lifts a new section. He speaks low, close to my ear. "It's to protect your hair from getting twisted in the ropes."

He sounds so matter-of-fact, but a quick glance in

the mirror shows his eyes are hooded and his chest is rising rapidly.

The action is so intimate my chest squeezes. "Where did you learn how to do this?"

He gives me a lazy smile that goes straight to my core. "YouTube."

An unlikely image of him practicing braids on Alex has a laugh bubbling from my throat. He gives a firm tug on my hair, and I inhale sharply, focusing my attention back on River.

River takes care of wrapping an elastic around the end and tucks it under itself. He cups the back of my neck, giving it a light squeeze. His fingers trail along my shoulder and collarbone, keeping even pressure as he steps around to face me. "This technique uses three ropes. You'll feel pressure, but it shouldn't pinch."

There's motion in the corner, and I spot Violet. I forgot about her. I swallow hard, fingers grazing the hem of my dress. There's a hum under my skin, but for the first time tonight, it's not comfortable.

River uncurls my fingers and holds my palms in his hands before wrapping them around my back. "Fold them behind you and cup your opposite elbow." His tone drips with dominance, sending heat to my core, and I comply.

"I don't have to be naked?" I ask.

"Not this time," he says, his voice full of future promises, and I wet my lips.

"Okay," I breathe out, cupping my elbows behind me.

River grabs three ropes from a nearby table. They're made of twisted red fiber, and if I had to guess, I'd say it's a half inch thick. He slowly trails the end down my neck and follows the neckline of my dress. The baby-soft fabric sends tingles where it touches, and I struggle to inhale. I thought it would be rough, some kind of coarse material, but this is almost luscious in how it feels against my sensitive skin.

"Color?" River checks in.

"Green!" I say a little too excitedly, and it pulls a chuckle from River.

"Good, Love." He rounds behind me and meets my stare in the mirror's reflection, then reaches forward, banding the rope a few inches below my shoulders. He's folded it in half so it's double stacked and lays it flat against my chest. His rough fingers graze the exposed skin above my neckline as he straightens it, then ties it in a knot behind me.

"Watch in the mirror. See how good you stand still for me." River drags a finger underneath, checking the tension, and heat floods my core at his gentleness. It's tight enough to feel snug but not to the point that it restricts my breathing.

I look at the mirror but can't look away from him. River looks like the devil himself, dressed in all black. Strands of his hair fall in front of his eyes, shading them from me, and I twitch to brush them out of the way. My mouth waters, watching his muscles shift in his forearms as he ties me up.

The next step is a matching red band of ropes just

above my elbows, this one pulling a little tighter, forcing my arms back. His knot cinches me in place until I feel a gentle bite against my skin, and I sink into the loss of control. I'm trussed up, immobile, and a thrill runs through me at being completely at his mercy.

River steps around me, fingers grazing my hip, before tilting my chin up and running another rope over my lips, causing my mouth to drop open before he trails it down my neck. The nerves come alive at his touch, and goose bumps follow in its wake. He wraps the rope around my arms and chest in a complicated pattern, forming a perfect harness that ties in the front.

River steps back, eyes blown wide, and a growl rumbles in his throat. "You look so fucking good tied up."

Liquid pools between my thighs at his praise.

"You're being so fucking good. My perfect girl." He hooks a glossy black carabiner on the ropes banding my chest and threads a thicker strand through it before attaching it to the ceiling. He gives it a light tug, and the pulley system lifts me onto my toes before he lets me down.

Anticipation flashes through me, but he doesn't lift me back up, instead turning toward the teacher and gesturing her over. "Ready."

Violet takes her time, checking each knot, running her fingers underneath to check the tightness before stepping back and smiling. "Perfect."

River cups my cheek. "Yes, she is."

"Alright, don't forget to lock up on your way out," Violet says, then slides out the door, leaving us alone.

"Where's she going?" I ask, still looking at where the door shut moments ago.

He's closer now, breath hot on my lips. "I rented the space for the night."

Heat and shock course through me. "Holy crap. How much was that?"

A sly grin pulls at the corner of his mouth. "Enough."

He pulls effortlessly on the rope attached to the ceiling and raises my body so that only my toes barely touch the ground. The sudden sensation of being weightless makes me tingle with exhilaration.

I expected it to feel uncomfortable, but the intricate pattern he's created disburses my weight, eliminating any pressure points, allowing me to rest against his holds.

River's serious as he double-checks his work, then looks at me.

There's a fire burning from below my navel, traveling through my limbs and pulsing in my core. I need him to touch me, and I need it right now. "Green. So freaking green."

His mouth meets mine in a leisurely kiss like he has all the time in the world and I'm not hanging, soaking through my panties. He's not going to be hurried. He's in complete control.

"Please, River," I beg, and his eyes flash.

"I love it when you beg. Say it again."

"Please," I keen, and he groans in response.

"That's my girl." He drops to his knees and drags his callused hands up the outside of my thighs, pushing my dress up with them. He buries his nose against my clit and takes a deep breath through the thin fabric before humming in his throat.

His intense gaze meets mine as he tucks the hem of my dress under the bottom rope, leaving me bare from the waist down, in nothing but my black lace panties.

"*Fuck, Love,*" he growls, and a shiver rolls through me as he starts to come apart. He snaps my underwear at the seams, ignoring my sound of protest, then flattens his tongue over my clit, circling the sensitive spot before speaking against me. "You taste so fucking good."

I moan as he slides his hands up my thighs and gently lifts my right leg, draping it over his shoulder. His tongue darts in and out of my depths with slow thrusts, exploring every inch before settling on my clit and teasing it with circles and flicks. With each touch of his tongue, I shudder until I'm nothing but a bundle of nerves begging for more. "I'm close. So close."

River sinks a finger into me, and I immediately clench around him, but it's not enough. "More... River...please."

He slides out, adding a second finger, then scissors them, hitting the sensitive spot on my front wall. I hiss through my teeth, my orgasm building with each thrust. Incoherent sounds escape my mouth, a mix of pleading and desperation.

He bites my clit, and sparks skate under my skin, lighting me up. The mix of pain and pleasure sends me hurtling over the edge of my release.

I sag in the ropes, head falling forward, unable to hold myself steady.

River stands, immediately lowering me to my feet, and unwraps me in controlled, practiced motions. When the last rope is released, he rubs his hands up and down my arms, helping return the circulation. "You did so well, Love."

I sway, and he holds me steady with one hand around my back. He drops his forehead on mine. His chest heaves, and his uneven breaths brush against my mouth. "How are you?"

I give him a loopy smile. "Wonderful."

He pulls back, matching my smile. "Thank you."

"For what?"

He kisses along my neck and shoulders, still marked by the ropes. "For this."

My hands free, I run them up his chest and tug him against me. "Anytime you want to tie me up and give me a mind-blowing orgasm, just let me know."

He huffs out a breath, thumb trailing over my shoulder. "We're not done."

I quirk a brow. "No?"

"Not even close."

He slowly tugs my dress up my body, his gaze darkening with each inch of exposed skin. His hands move to the fastenings of my bra, unclasping it and pulling it off in one swift motion before taking my right nipple into his mouth and suckling gently. I arch into the sensation and moan softly as his deep humming reverberates against my chest.

"Fuck," he growls, a dark edge to it. "I can't be slow." He searches my face. "I need to fuck you right now."

"Yes, green. Whatever, please." Words tumble from my mouth, and he guides my back against the wall. Buttons pop and clatter on the floor as he struggles to get his shirt off fast enough. He shoves his pants down and the second he's naked, he has my legs wrapped around his waist and his cock notched against my entrance.

He enters me in one fluid thrust, and I have to breathe through the burn as my body works to accommodate him. He buries his hand in my hair, loosening the braid, and pulls my head back, exposing my neck to his bruising kisses as his cock slams into me mercilessly. There's no hint of my controlled dominant River—he's completely lost in the moment, and I dig my nails into his shoulders, encouraging him.

"Fuck." River groans against my neck, thrusts turning jerky as he chases his release.

I reach around him and trail my finger down his spine, through the crack of his ass, and he growls low in his throat, bucking into me as he fills me with his hot cum.

He holds me in place, breathing hard against my neck as he catches his bearings. He trails open-mouth kisses over the sensitive spots he left and slowly lets my feet descend to the floor.

River runs his thumbs along my jaw, stopping at my temples, and curls his fingers around the back of my neck. "You're the best thing that ever happened to me."

My heart swells, and I can feel three words pressing at my throat to escape, but he's already backing up, letting the cool air come between us.

There's no lying to myself. I'm in love with both of them.

# CHAPTER 54
## ALEX

LUCAS: So how are the love birds doing?

Me: Fuck off.

Jax: Must be serious. You always talk.

Me: How are Sidney and Piper doing? You guys still getting it on in public?

Jax: I'm going to kill you.

Lucas: I'm closer.

River: If you don't like questions, stop asking them.

Jax: Don't worry, we get it. We were just checking how serious it's gotten.

Me: Dead fucking serious.

The locker room reeks of stale sweat, Gatorade, and the musk of unwashed equipment. I drop my head against the wood partition separating my locker from River's.

Our girl was still dripping when River brought her home last night, and I enjoyed every second of licking her clean. Fuck, the things those two do to me should be illegal.

Everything was great until Coach decided to run the early practice from hell. My quad muscles twitch randomly, letting me know exactly how much they hate me right now. Sweat drips from my hair and burns the corners of my eyes, but I'm too exhausted to move.

The second I can get the two of them back in bed, I'm forcing them to take a fucking nap. *Guy's got to rest.*

"Here," River says from beside me, and I peel open one eye. He's holding a damp cloth and a bottle of water. It's fucking adorable.

I gulp down half the water, never breaking our stare, and a cheesy grin forms on my face when I spot the pink flush crawling over his cheeks.

I run my tongue over the bottle spout and marvel at the way River's eyes darken, pupils blown. I lick it again, and he groans, throwing the cloth.

I catch it millimeters from my face, busting out in a laugh, and give him a wink. "Thanks for taking care of me."

He leans in closer, closer than he should be while we're surrounded by our teammates, and there's a low rumble in his chest. "Always, Baby."

My dick's instantly hard, and I have to shift my legs to hide the giant tent in my boxers. Fuck me. He's really getting off on this.

A hand lands hard on my opposite shoulder, and I shoot a glare at whoever the hell's touching me.

"You two aren't subtle." Lucas looks around the locker room, where all the other guys are purposely not looking at us. It's my turn to blush. "I can practically feel the vibe coming off the two of you."

I shrug him off. "Whatever, buddy. Good practice out there."

Lucas had been on fire on the ice. Nice crisp passes, massive speed, he's a fucking beast in the arena. "Thanks. So Piper tells me Mia's got some kind of black-tie event?"

"Yeah?" I hedge.

"You going?"

"We're going," River responds immediately. Turns out it's easy to get an invite if you donate enough.

"Good," Lucas says, a fucking devious look on his face. I absolutely don't want to know what it's about before he smirks at us. "Did you get her a dress?"

"Um, no? Should we have?" I ask.

Lucas's brows pull together in pure judgment. "Your girl is broke. Get her a fucking dress."

River cuts in, surprising me. "I already have a plan."

My attention snaps to him. "You do?"

"*We* do," he clarifies, a small smile curling the side of his mouth.

———

"Not a chance." I grasp Mia's hand before she can pull her blindfold off.

She's twisting her neck, as if a different angle will allow her to see where we're going. "Is this necessary?"

River's sitting on the opposite side of her in the black sedan and leans in so his mouth brushes her ear. "You're doing so well, Love. Just a little longer."

Fuck me. A shiver runs through Mia, and my dick's rock fucking hard. I glare at him, and he gives me this mischievous grin that knocks the air from my lungs. I almost rip Mia's blindfold off so she can see what we've done to our reserved boyfriend. Not that he's ever called himself that.

We pull up to an old brick building that houses the luxury dress shop. It has these looming columns covered in vines, leaves and moss that look like they've been carved in marble. Orange sunlight flickers against their tall, arched glass windows.

River gets out first, reaching in to help guide Mia after him, and I follow, bracing her back as she finds her footing on the sidewalk.

"Can we take this thing off now?" she asks, a delicious pout on her lips.

"Only if you promise to put it back on later," I murmur against her neck and smile as her skin erupts in goose bumps. Oh, our girl likes that.

"I don't know. I kinda want to see River use it to tie you up," she purrs, and my eyes snap to River's heated ones.

He raises an eyebrow in question, and I have to adjust myself in my pants before this becomes indecent.

*Jesus fucking Christ.*

I run my tongue along my lower lip and bite it, wanting him to be just as insane as I am. "Only if you're good."

Both River and Mia suck in sharp inhales. River gives me a look that lets me know I'll pay for that later.

*Looking fucking forward to it.*

He takes care not to pull at her hair as he unties the fabric from around her head and lets it drop.

She searches his face, a soft smile on her lips. "What are you two up to?"

He cups her jaw and runs his thumb along her cheekbone. "I told you. We're taking care of you."

She scrunches her nose but knows better than to argue. "Lead the way."

Mia's head darts from left to right as she looks at the dresses in the shop. The walls are lined with shelf after shelf of bespoke dresses, each one a different color than its neighbor. Each dress glints and shines with intricate beadwork.

I can see the second Mia registers that this is the type of store where nothing has a price tag, and I wrap my arms around her from behind and kiss just below her ear. "Let him do this for you."

She huffs out a breath. "You've already done enough."

I chuckle, smiling against her temple. "It'll never be enough. Get used to it."

She tilts her head, about to reply to me, but a

woman wearing a burgundy straight-line dress walks up to us.

"You must be Mr. Davis and Mr. Grayson. And this is Ms. Brooks."

"Doctor," River and I cut in at the same time, causing Mia to laugh.

"I'm so sorry. Of course. Dr. Brooks," the stylist stutters and tries to backtrack, looking uncomfortable as hell. A part of me wants to say something quippy to ease some of her embarrassment, but I fucking know River put down Doctor.

Mia breaks free from my arms and holds out her hand. "I'm Mia."

"Stacey." The stylist shakes it, visibly relaxing, and gives Mia a warm smile. "I hear you've got a special event coming up."

The stylist's genuine excitement gets her back in my good books, and I preen over Mia. "She landed a position at Boston General Hospital, and now she gets to go to a fancy black-tie dinner. Have you heard of the Center-Ice Challenge?"

Stacey's mouth falls open in surprise. "Yes! Our whole team did it last weekend."

"That was all Mia." I tug Mia's back to my chest and rest my chin on her shoulder.

"No shit?" The professional mask the girl wore drops, and she smiles wide.

"It's not a big deal," Mia says, earning a side-eye look from River.

"Are. You. Kidding. Me!" Stacey cuts in. "This is a huge deal! The little girl I'm helping has already contacted me, and she asked if I'd come help her pick out the pattern. *Me.* She's so adorable—you should freaking hear her sing."

We let Stacey get lost in going on about the kid she matched with, and I take the time to watch Mia.

A smile takes over her face. Her cheeks have a light dusting of pink, and her eyes sparkle as she listens to the excited stylist. My heart pounds in my chest, the rhythm offbeat as I look at just how perfect our girl is.

Stacey's hand goes to her cheek. "Oh my God. I'm sorry, I got carried away there for a minute. I pre-picked a few dresses for you, so if you'll follow me, I have a room set up."

"Let's go," I say, and Mia takes a slow breath and lets it out as if this is a giant pain in the ass, and I love her for it.

———

Mia comes out of the dressing room in her fourth dress of the night. They've all looked amazing on her, but something is never quite right. It's like they're trying to overpower her instead of letting her shine through.

"What do you think, love?" River asks from where he's sitting on the sofa, elbows propped on his knees.

She turns in the three-paned mirror, checking herself out, and shrugs. "It's pretty."

"Try another one, Kitten."

"It's fine," she says, but she doesn't look like it's fine. She's got *meh* written over her face.

"You guys have been so patient." She hesitates.

River stands and closes the few feet between them, clasping her jaw. She looks up at him with round doe eyes. "Stop trying not to be a burden. You have nothing to worry about. I have nowhere I'd rather be than right here with you."

She relaxes into his touch and shrugs. "Okay, well, then this isn't the one."

Mia disappears back through the curtain into her dressing room, and I stand. I walk through the lines of dresses, letting my fingers trail along the soft fabric, and stop dead when I spot one in satin gold.

There's just something about it.

I grab it from the rack, pass a curious River, and whisper through the dressing room curtain. "I found your dress," I say confidently.

The curtain peels back a few inches, and she peeks around the edge. "Did you now?"

I can see her reflection in the mirror behind her, and it takes everything in me not to back her up against the glass when I see she's only in a thin black thong. I tilt my head up to the ceiling and close my eyes.

This girl is going to be the death of me, and I'm apparently going to love every minute of it. I swallow hard and hold out the dress. She grabs the hanger, hand barely visible, and the dress disappears with her.

I walk back to the couch, collapse next to River,

and take a long drink from the water Stacey provided.

"What was that about?" River asks.

"You'll see." No sooner are the words out of my mouth than she glides in front of us. River's mouth drops open before snapping shut, and his Adam's apple lifts and falls.

*Right there with you, buddy.*

She's fucking stunning. The gold satin drapes over her curves like liquid and pools around her feet. She pulled her hair up, revealing the curve of her neck and the low-cut square neckline that shows off the top of her cleavage.

I'm done under when she spins. It's completely backless, except for a few thin gold chains, and I'm suddenly fighting off caveman thoughts. There's something entirely too appealing about hiding her away and fucking her in my den for a few months.

She clears her throat. "Sooo, what do you think?"

"I think you're going to get me in trouble," River replies. "And I think I'm going to like it."

Remembering that she needs to like the dress too, not just us slobbering over her, I ask, "What do you think?"

She does a spin and has a heart-melting smile. "I love it."

*My thoughts exactly.*

## CHAPTER 55
# RIVER

ICE CLINKS against my glass as I take another sip of my whiskey and look around the venue. The grand ballroom of the hotel is decorated with golden drapes and oversized chandeliers. It's filled to the brim with rich old white guys in tailored tuxedos, their arms around stunningly beautiful women who were clearly several decades younger than them. My nose burns with the overly sweet smell of flowers and expensive perfume.

We'd picked out Mia's dress two days ago, and I've been dying to see her in it tonight.

Piper showed up early and ran us out of Mia's apartment so she could help her get ready.

I haven't seen her since, and it's killing me.

A server approaches me, but I hold up my near full glass in dismissal. I've purposely propped myself in a position where I can see the entire room but out of the way enough not to be bothered.

Alex is front and center, chatting up one group of

potential sponsors, and they all laugh at whatever he's saying. No matter where he is, he's always been able to command a crowd. He's dressed in a perfectly tailored black tux that's just tight enough to show off the muscles shifting in his back. He chose to wear the tie we'd blindfolded Mia with the other night, and all I want is to wrap it around my fist and pull him to me.

He's sexy as fuck. If I wasn't so anxious for Mia to get here, I'd be trying to find a hidden spot to drag Alex into.

We'd decided to take separate cars, to keep the illusion we aren't anything more to each other than acquaintances.

I ignore the dull ache beneath my ribs, and I take another sip of my drink, the smooth liquid burning down my throat. I hate being her secret. Not when I want to scream we're together at the top of my lungs. Tell every single person I meet that I'm obsessed with *the* Dr. Mia Brooks.

She doesn't need that right now. She needs me and Alex to support her, and I'll be anything she needs me to be.

Gold flickers in the corner of my vision, and I turn to watch her walk in. My breath hitches in my throat, and I grip my cool glass harder to stop myself from going to her. She's a fucking vision in the dress. It drapes over her curves, revealing all my favorite spots. I want to trail my hands down her satin-clad sides and devour her mouth in front of everyone.

Instead, I down my drink and wave at the server,

grabbing another. It's going to be a long fucking night.

As expected, she's immediately enveloped by the crowd, smiling strangers wanting to meet the creator of the Center-Ice challenge. It's been so successful she's become a local star. I'm unbelievably proud of her.

I follow Mia with my eyes through the crowd and rely on the glimpses of gold to keep track of her as she moves between the attendees like she's made for this.

I can hear Alex's booming laugh from here. He's with a new group of investors, and he already has them charmed, shaking each of their hands. I can tell the second he spots Mia because he turns and walks away without a word. He prowls through the crowd, moving closer to her, following the same intense pull that I feel.

Alex stops ten feet away, jaw tensing as he watches her flitting from person to person. His eyes shoot to mine, and his frustration meets my own. It's easy to keep us a secret when we're mostly tucked away at home; it's physically painful not to be able to go to her now.

To know that it would hurt her if we said fuck it and gave in to what we want.

Her.

*Us.*

I move along the back wall, making my way closer to them, when a prickle crawls up my spine. I turn just in time to see Jason walk in. The girl on his arm looks like a cheap Mia copy. Pale blonde hair, flush complexion, and I'd bet my bonus she's got green eyes. Even with all the similarities, she doesn't come close.

Mia had warned us he may be here. His dad's a large investor in the North American medical field, but that didn't stop the anger from licking up my spine. I stalk through the crowd, staying out of his line of sight and waiting for the perfect opportunity to corner him. He's not fucking this night up for her.

It takes another twenty minutes before he heads to the bar alone, and I cut him off. "We need to talk."

"Pass." He raises his brow with a look of disdain like Alex didn't have him choking against a wall the last time we met.

"It's not a request." I hold up my hand, gesturing toward a dark area sheltered from the rest of the room by a black partition.

He laughs but looks unsure. "You wouldn't do anything here."

"Fucking watch me."

He swallows and moves toward where I herded him.

"I know you've been texting her. I thought we said to stay away from our girl." My voice is cut low and menacing.

Fear flashes in his features, but he covers it. "I knew that slut was fucking you both."

My fist connects with his sternum, and he collapses forward, fighting for breath.

"Call her that again. I fucking dare you."

"Sorry." He rasps out the word, still gasping.

I grab his collar, dragging him up so he can look in my eyes when I say, "You will back the fuck off, or I'm going to fuck your shit up. I don't like people fucking with what's mine."

He laughs. "She's going to ditch you, then come running back to me. You'll see."

Clenching my fist in his collar, I give him a hard shake so I know he's giving me his full attention. "She. Will. Never. Take. You. Back."

"Everyone is going to think you're a fucking fool," he sneers.

"It's funny how you think people's opinions mean anything to me when it comes to her."

# CHAPTER 56
# ALEX

RIVER'S DISAPPEARED, leaving me to do whatever the hell I want. At least for now. I don't even bother trying to stay away from Mia, slipping through the crowd and closing the remaining distance between us. She looks at me with wide green eyes but doesn't shift away, instead introducing me to the woman she's standing with.

"I'm sure you know Alex Grayson, star forward for the Boston Bruins. He's been a huge help supporting the Prosthetics For Kids charity."

"Yes, I've seen you in the videos. Excellently done and such a large donation." The woman across from her smiles at me. She looks to be in her late fifties or early sixties, and she's rocking it. Silver hair pulled back in a sleek style, black dress that doesn't cling to her but looks perfectly together. She's a silver fox if I've ever seen one.

"Alex, let me introduce Julia Garner, the CEO of Casper Developments." Mia bites her bottom lip, but

I can still make out the hint of a smile she's trying to hide from catching me checking the matron out.

Fuck me, I'm standing in front of a real-life billionaire.

I plaster on my most endearing smile. "You know how it is. I believe in this charity, so I have to put my money where my mouth is. I've been extremely fortunate, and it's really the least I can do." I purposely focus the conversation around myself so she doesn't feel like I'm calling her out, but she also hears the message I'm laying down.

"Unfortunately, I'm not sure I can pull off the whole soaked look," Julia says.

Time to throw on the charm. "I wouldn't say that. I think you'd look good soaking wet."

The woman's cheeks flame red, but I can tell she liked receiving the compliment.

She arches a perfectly shaped brow. "You know, most men wouldn't say that to me."

I shrug. "Most men are idiots."

She laughs. "Okay. Challenge me." She says it to Mia, who's now grinning.

"I challenge Julia Garner to the Center-Ice Challenge."

"I accept and pledge five hundred thousand." She tosses Mia a playful wink. "Can't let these young boys show me up."

I swallow hard. Holy fucking shit.

"Uh…thank you…oh my God." Mia stutters out her gratitude.

The woman waves her off with a conspiratorial

smile. "I'm going to go see who else I can rope into this. I bet I can get a few of these old men to play along." There's a gleam in her eyes, and I don't doubt her for a second.

Mia and I are as alone in a room full of people as we can be, and her face is lit up. "Five. Hundred. Thousand." She practically levitates off the ground with her excitement.

"That's only the beginning, Kitten. Hell, I'd be surprised if she doesn't collect a few million tonight on her own."

Mia looks stunning, painted in gold, pale blonde hair tumbling from where she's pinned it up. It's making her look ethereal and putting every other woman here to shame.

*Fuck*, I want to kiss her.

I blow out a breath and give her a lopsided smile. "You look beautiful."

Her gaze travels from my patent leather shoes up my suit-clad thighs, and pauses on the tie I chose.

Her cheeks grow an adorable shade of pink. "You should talk. You look good in that suit, Alex."

I smirk. "I know."

"Have you always been that cocky?" she asks playfully.

"Ever since I've been this pretty."

"What am I going to do with you?"

I lower my gaze, biting the side of my lip. "Whatever you want."

Her chest freezes for several seconds before she

shakes her head like she's waking up from a dream. "Behave."

"Around you? *Never.*"

She throws her head back and laughs, and I eat it the fuck up. If I do anything in life, let it be making this girl happy.

I lower my voice. "When I get you home—"

Mia's face registers surprise where she's looking over my shoulder.

I turn, following her gaze, and spot a guy I'd been chatting with earlier. James McKay—turns out he's a huge Bruins fan.

"Do you know him?" I ask.

"Jason's dad," she whispers, and my head snaps her way.

"You've got to be shitting me."

The blood drains from her face, and a spark of anger starts in my chest, rapidly growing into rage. That fucker is the one who got her fired?

I grab Mia's hand and practically drag her through the crowd. She doesn't say anything as we approach Jason's dad.

Thinking about Jason makes my mouth taste sour, and I fight the urge to spit my disgust.

James looks back at me. "Hey, good to see you again. I was just telling my friend here we should get box tickets."

Mia tilts her head to the side. "But you don't live here."

He looks down his nose at her. "Miss. I have several offices. Nothing's far when you own a plane."

I want to hit him for his tone of condescension, but I've got bigger plans. "I want to introduce you to my girlfriend, Dr. Mia Brooks."

James tilts his head to the side, like he's trying to place her. It only takes a second for recognition to settle in. "The girl who dated my son to get a job, then stole from the hospital?"

A low growl rumbles in my chest. "No. The girl your sniveling son's practically stalking. Won't listen to the word no—I sure hope you didn't teach him that. He thought he could manipulate her into taking him back by getting her fired."

The man's eyes shoot wide but quickly narrow on Mia. "That's quite the accusation. Do you really expect me to believe you?"

"I have proof that he's stalking me." She holds out her phone, but James doesn't take it. Mia bites the corner of her lip. "If I can get you definitive proof that he's the one stealing from you, what would you do?"

There are several moments of charged silence before James replies. "If you can gather proof—real proof, mind you, no hearsay—I'll get you your job back."

A rock drops in my stomach, and nausea burns my throat. That job had been her dream, and here it is on a silver fucking platter. I want to beg her not to take it. Say I need her here, but I could never do that to her.

"Thank you, but I have a family I love here." The

words tumble from her mouth, and she instantly blushes, eyes snapping to mine.

Is she talking about us? My pulse thunders in my ears, the world tilting around me, and I want to haul her over my shoulder, find River, and get the fuck out of here.

James studies her before replying, "That's your decision. I can promise you if you provide me with the information, Jason's behavior won't go unpunished. Now, if you'll excuse me, it's time for my speech." He hands her his business card, then leaves abruptly.

"I need you to come with me." My voice comes out in a strangled whisper.

I don't know if it's the desperation in my voice, but she follows without a word. There's a door off the back of the room, and I sneak us both in.

It's a storage room, filled to the brim with different-style chairs and extra tables stacked over each other half haphazardly. The only light comes from above, tall flickering bulbs casting everything in warm shadows.

"I'm sorry," she rushes out. "I shouldn't have said that. We haven't even talked about it."

I cup the sides of her face, cutting her off with a swift kiss.

"Mia, I love you."

"You don't have to say that just because I did."

"Are you kidding me? You've buried yourself so deep inside me that there's no way to know where my love for you starts and where I end. It's one and the same. You're all that I am, and I'm so fucking grateful to have you. *I fucking love you."* I coat my words in sincerity.

"You love me?" Her voice breaks, and my ribs squeeze around my heart.

"Always." I crush my mouth against hers and groan when she instantly opens for me. She tastes crisp like champagne, and as I devour her mouth, I back her against the wall beside the closed door.

Her hands bury themselves into my hair, pulling me harder against her. Like she's desperate to close the space between us. I break apart, kissing along her jaw and down the column of her neck.

"Say it again," she breathes, tilting her head back against the wall, making room for me.

"I love you." I graze my teeth along the shell of her ear, smiling as goose bumps erupt under my touch. "I love you, Mia."

Her grip tightens in my hair, yanking me back to her lips. She devours me with needy, desperate kisses that I return with equal desire.

Her nails rake down my neck, and her hips rock against me, searching for friction. Doing my fucking best not to ruin her dress, I pull the hem above her hips and lift her until her legs wrap around me.

Her mouth breaks away from mine with a hungry moan.

"I need you, Mia. I need you so fucking much. I need you right now."

She rolls her hips against my hard cock in response. "Yes! God yes."

I grip her ass with one hand, pinning her between the wall and me, then rip her underwear at the seams and tuck the remnants into my pocket. Pushing my pants and boxers around my ankles, I nestle my cock against her entrance, barely entering her. I pause, my mind swirling. This should be romantic, not some back-room fuck. Our chests heave against each other's, and her brilliant green eyes meet mine.

"I love you," she says, voice sure, and shifts to bury my cock into her core. I buck, entering fully, unable to stop myself.

"We'll do this slow and sweet later," I promise.

She bites my lower lip. "Shut up and fuck me."

I groan against her, losing my last vestige of control, and thrust into her. Her moans grow louder as her back pounds against the wall, taking every ounce of me. I capture her needy sounds with my mouth and tingles start in the small of my back, traveling down my hips. My dick grows impossibly hard as my orgasm begs to be released.

*Like fuck she's not coming with me.*

I drop my forehead against her, saying between gritted teeth, "I'm fucking close. Come with me."

She nods her head, hissing in each breath. I slide my hand up her thigh and circle her clit with my thumb. She cries out, back arching off the wall, and trembles in my arms as I draw small patterns against her. I listen to the sounds she makes, moving quicker or slower until her moans break and her orgasm rocks through her.

My hips jerk unevenly as I follow her over the edge.

Dizzy from my release, I press my chest into hers and bury my face into her neck. Her heart's pounding, matching mine beat for beat as we both come down from our high.

I lower her legs to the floor and smile at her rosy cheeks. I pull out my phone, snap a pic of my cum running down her leg, and fire it off to River before fixing the hem of her dress.

**Me: Getting cleaned up. Meet us out front, we're getting the fuck out of here.**

**River: Leave it. If you're going to fuck our girl without me I want to taste you on her.**

My dick's already half-hard. These two are going to be the death of me.

Mia lifts up on her toes and whispers against my mouth. "I love you."

My eyes close, and my chest clenches as I let the words seep into my soul. "I love you more."

———

I pull the sheet over Mia and River, covering her naked back. They'd collapsed into exhaustion a few minutes ago after our third round. He's holding on to her with both hands, and her face is pressed hard into his chest like they can't get close enough to each other.

My chest is so tight I can hardly fucking breathe watching them. I dreamed of this—of course I fucking dreamed of this—but I'd been terrified to hope. Being with them feels like I stole the answers to happiness, and I refuse to give them back.

I've never felt as free as when Mia said she loved me. It was like the entire world clicked into place except for one piece. River's hair tumbles over his forehead, and I reach over to push it from his face. I'm deeply, *irrevocably* in love with him. I think I've always been in love with him, and I'm not sure I can survive him not loving me back.

# CHAPTER 57
# MIA

THE LAST SEVEN days have been a blur. Alex and River have been busy with their hockey practices while I'm running around at the hospital, starting my new job. I miss them, but they more than make up for it at night.

It's supposed to be my day off, and I groan when I receive the text from Gerard saying he's in town and wants to meet.

I look at my reflection in the mirror and cringe. Rummaging through my closet, I finally settle on a sleek light gray dress with a square-neck collar and a simple black piping detail. My hair is hastily twisted into something resembling professional, like I'm trying to cram weeks of primping into seconds. With a steadying breath, I grab my bag and make my way to the lobby.

After a fifteen-minute Uber ride, I exit the elevator on Gerard's office floor. The receptionist gives me a worried look, but Gerard's already calling me in before I can ask what's happening.

He's at his desk, his gray hair pushed off his face, but his usual warm smile is missing. "You know Jason McKay."

My head snaps to the spare chair on the side of the room, and I come face-to-face with my ex. Acid burns the back of my throat, and I hiss at him, "What are you doing here?"

Gerard cuts in. "Jason has brought to my attention your unprofessional behavior." He holds out two pictures. One of Alex and I stepping into the back room at the gala, and the other reveals us leaving. Dread forms knots in my gut. The hem of my dress is askew, and my hair is scrunched up in the back from where it was pressed against the wall.

"I warned you this wouldn't be acceptable. I'm sorry, Dr. Brooks, but Astrocorp will be pulling all funding to Prosthetics For Kids."

My vision swirls, and I lock my knees to stay standing. "What? No, you can't. I did everything you asked. We've got more funding; it's gone national. We're so close."

Gerard looks sympathetic but unmoving. "I assure you, we can. Astrocorp cannot be associated with this level of scandal once it breaks out."

Jason smirks at me and pops a piece of gum into his mouth.

My despair flashes to anger, and I step forward, placing both hands on Gerard's desk. "How would anyone find out?"

Gerard huffs out an exasperated breath as if he's speaking to a child. "If Jason spotted you, no doubt countless more did."

I don't bother explaining to him the only reason Jason saw us was he was probably stalking me at that party. Hell, I wouldn't put it past him to hire a professional.

"That's it? After everything?" My eyes burn with angry tears that I blink away.

Gerard lifts a brow and steeples his fingers, his expression clearly stating he's done with me. "That's it. You can go."

I turn toward Jason, closing the distance between us, and jab my finger into his chest. "You are going to regret fucking with me, Jason. I'm done playing nice."

He barks out a laugh. "Yeah, what are you going to do?"

I smile, knowing I'm going to come through on this promise. "I'm going to ruin you."

His eyes flash wide, but I'm already turning away before he can say anything. I give him a little wave. "Enjoy the freedom you have left."

I glance back at Gerard. "I appreciate you putting your neck out for me in the beginning and everything you did, but you should know there's nothing wrong with my relationship. The Prosthetics For Kids campaign has been more successful than I ever could have dreamed. It's gone viral nationally, quadrupling what you offered and it's growing every day. It's because of them. It's because they believed in me while you doubted me every step of the way. You're blowing the chance at being a part of something amazing."

"Dr. Brooks, Mia. I never wanted you to fail." Gerard says, looking less sure than he did a second ago.

"Don't worry about me, I don't need your funding anymore."

I wink and shove through the doors and stride to the elevator, head held high. Pushing the button, I replay the last few minutes and sort through my emotions.

There's a loud buzz in my veins, and my pulse beats in my ears, but there's no hint of disappointment. I stood up to my asshole ex, and I'm going to do everything in my power to take him the hell down. I step on the elevator and smirk at the receptionist watching me with curiosity.

Just as the door is about to close, Jason dashes through the narrow opening, a smirk spreading over his lips. Rage bubbles in my chest as he blocks my exit.

He stands menacingly over me, his dark eyes narrow and piercing. He speaks slowly, deliberately, as if tasting each word carefully before he spits them out. "You think you're so smart going to my dad. Like you have the upper hand." His hand shoots out towards me, but I react quickly and slap it away; his face contorts into a sneer.

"What do you think your guys' coach will think

when he finds out they're fucking you? Hmmm, do you think it's good for their wholesome image?"

My heart drops and a band tightens in my stomach painfully.

"It would be so fucking easy to let these photos leak." Jason grins maliciously at me, his sharp teeth glint in the light. "I bet they'd even pay me for them."

Anger crackles beneath my skin. I fucking hate him. I want to scream and rail and spit in his face. This is all just a game to him, but Alex and River are my whole life.

Jason raises a brow, seemingly sure of himself with each move that brings me closer to the corner he backs me into. Tears prick at the back of my eyes in that moment; hatred coursing through my veins. I take a deep breath, swallowing down my rage knowing that if I don't give him what he wants then Alex will bear the brunt of it.

Humiliation flares inside me as the weight of my helplessness settles over my shoulders. I hate Jason, he makes me feel small, helpless. The polar opposite to how Alex and River make me feel. No matter how much I want to rage and scream, the only thing that really matters is them. I swallow down my ego clenching my fists and plead hoarsely, "Please don't do this, I can tell your dad I lied about everything. That I was just jealous."

A smirk appears on Jason's face. "Too fucking late, Mia. I'm going to make you pay for everything you've done."

The ever tightening band in my chest snaps, taking all reasoning with it, and I snarl through my teeth. "What I've done!? WHAT. YOU'VE. DONE. You egotistical asshole." I growl out the words, blood flooding my veins and before I can stop myself I'm gripping his suit lapels for stability and driving my knee into his dick.

He grunts, folding in half wheezing, followed quickly by the satisfying sound of dry heaving.

"You'd think it wouldn't hurt so bad with how small it is." I scoff.

"Fucking bitch." He hisses out, but doesn't look up. He clearly has no idea what to do with me when I'm no longer afraid of him.

The bell chimes, and the door opens behind him. He barely glances at me as he escapes like the fucking coward he is.

I stand, back pressed against the wall, and just let the last few minutes settle over me. From the disappointment of losing the sponsorship... To how good it felt to threaten Jason in that office. To... My blood drains from my face remembering exactly what he said.

*"What do you think your guys' coach will think when he finds out they're fucking you? Hmmm, do you think it's good for their wholesome image?"*

Guilt twists my stomach as my world crumbles. I know how important becoming captain is to Alex, how important their image is to their team. Now Jason is going to ruin all of that because of me. The realization washes over me like an icy wave, sapping away any courage I had. How could I ever tell them?

I don't go home. *Home.* Like I have any right to call it that.

Instead, I find a small diner to sit in and let what Jason's about to do bury me.

How am I going to tell them what I've done?

My phone vibrates in my pocket, and I hesitate to check it, knowing who it is.

**Alex: How'd it go, Kitten?**

After five minutes of not responding, he texts me again.

**Alex: You still in there? Text me when you get out.**

I order a meal so I can stay and push the food around my plate, but my stomach is too twisted to eat.

**River: Mia. It's been an hour. Where are you?**

**Alex: Just text back so we know you're okay.**

**River: We're cutting practice short. You better be at home.**

Knowing they'll get in trouble if they leave, I type out a quick message.

**Me: Sorry, lost track of time. Everything's good.**

If I see them, I'll fall apart, and they'll want to comfort me. Jason's going to wreck Alex's chance to become captain, and it's *my* fault.

An hour goes by, and my phone buzzes again.

**Alex: We're home. Where are you?**

**Alex: Mia, you're worrying me. Tell us where you are, Kitten.**

**River: What's wrong?**

He always knows when I'm not okay, but this time, I can't let him fix it.

My phone rings with a call, but I don't answer, muting it instead. I need to figure this out. I need to make this okay.

I dial Sidney, needing my friend.

She answers immediately. "Hello?"

"Hey."

"Where are you? I just got out of parliament, and I have about a million missed messages from your guys."

A sob breaks from my chest.

"Mia, what happened? Tell me."

I break down and explain everything. She listens without a word, letting me get it all out.

"So, to summarize," Sidney starts in. "Your asshole ex cost you your sponsor and now is going to try to ruin Alex and River's image, and you think they'll hate you for that?"

"I hate myself for it. I should've known it would go this way."

"Don't you think they should have a say in this? This isn't university. Alex and River are grown-ass men. Get your ass back home and tell them what happened." She's using her professional voice, and I sniff. "Get your ass home, Mia, or I'm going to fly down there and make you."

I rub my hand over my face and take a deep breath. "Okay."

"Text them before they send out a search party."

Her voice is lighter, with a hint of a laugh, and I relax a little more.

"Love you, Sidney."

"You too, babe. Now, go figure this out. And Mia…"

"Yeah…"

"We're going to bring Jason down."

A spark comes to life, and I'm able to take a deep inhale.

She hangs up, and I exhale, sending off a quick text.

**Me: Coming home.**

**Alex: Thank fucking God.**

———

Alex and River are already waiting for me in the hall. Alex walks up to me, immediately wrapping me in a hug, but River keeps his back to the wall, arms crossed protectively over his chest. He's watching me, teeth clenched.

Tears slip over my cheeks, and Alex leans back, brushing them away with his thumbs. "What happened? Who do I have to kill?"

A watery smile pulls at the corner of my lips. How am I supposed to tell him that I messed everything up?

"Let's get inside," River says and walks in without looking back. There's a frigidness to him that I know I deserve.

I bury my hands in Alex's hair, pulling him closer

and lift onto my toes, kissing him with everything I have. Not stopping when my lungs scream for breath and my head grows dizzy. If this is our last kiss I'm going to memorize every second of him.

He pulls back, his gaze roaming over my face, and his brows pinch in the middle like he doesn't like what he sees. "Mia." he whispers as he cups my neck in his hands.

My chest aches at his gentle touch, and I can't stop the tears from leaking down my face. I want him, *them*. I struggle against the unfairness of it all. They told me their coach threatened to trade one of them if Alex couldn't clean up his image. Jason is a lot of things, but he's right about this. Nothing screams playboy like hooking up with the creator of the charity he's working with. It'll be everywhere. Everything he's done will be overshadowed by the delicious gossip that he couldn't keep it in his pants. They don't know how much more this means. All they'll see is Alex Grayson being everything they think he is. I grit my teeth. They don't know him. Not like I do. I can't let their coach trade him. The idea of being the reason they're separated is like a lance to my gut. The only chance they have is to end things with me and for how much it hurts I have to let them.

Alex catches a tear with his thumb, and I can't stop myself from leaning into his touch. His throat bobs when he swallows hard, and worry settles over his features. "Why did that feel like a goodbye, Kitten?"

I fight back a sob and answer him truthfully. "Because when I tell you what I did, you're going to let me go."

His head snaps back like I slapped him. "Never."

My chin trembles as I desperately want that to be true. I break from his hold and walk through their door, ready to get this done so I can go curl up in a ball and fall apart in private.

River's leaning against the kitchen island, his arms crossed as he takes me in. I desperately want to steal a kiss from him. To feel him wrapped around me, and store the feel of him away to take out and remember him at night.

He doesn't move to close the distance between us. He's always been too observant, able to read me like a book. Alex joins his side, looking at me with unease.

River lifts one brow, tilting his head to the side. "Tell us what happened, Mia. Because I don't believe for a fucking second you'd hurt us."

My teeth snap together, not expecting that, and I roll my lips, taking several breaths before getting it over with. "Jason's going to go public with our relationship. It'll probably be plastered on every news station shortly."

Alex laughs, actually laughs, and his posture relaxes as relief visibly washes over him. "That's it? I've been dying to tell everyone about us."

My brows pull together, and I shake my head. "But your coach said you need to have a clean image, or you won't get the captaincy. You could get traded!

Pretty sure fucking the charity coordinator you work with counts as dirtying your image."

He closes the steps between us and meets my gaze head-on. "Listen to me, Kitten. None of it matters. Not my career, not the game. Especially not the fucking captaincy. Not compared to you. Not compared to this." He gestures between River and me. "People are going to think whatever they want. There's no changing that." He runs his thumb under my eye wiping away a tear. "We make our own rules, Mia. It's what we think that matters. It's what we choose that makes a difference. And I choose us. And I'll do it again and again. Damn the consequences. As long as I have both of you, I have everything I need. My question is, do you choose us?"

The world tilts, and I suck in a breath, tears pooling in my lashes. "Of course."

River walks up to us, and Alex makes room for him to wrap me in his arms. He stares into my eyes. "The biggest mistake of my life was letting you walk away. I should've fought for you then. Like fuck I'll make the same mistake now."

His mouth crashes to mine, and he kisses me until my lungs burn. He pulls back and stands shoulder to shoulder with Alex. "You're ours. We're yours. Always have been and always will be. There's no changing that. I love you."

*I love you* replays in my head, and I'm frozen in place.

They don't care. They don't care about the scandal.

Tears pool in my eyes, overflowing the rim. "Say it again."

"I love you."

"Even when I mess everything up?"

Alex wraps me in his arms from behind and buries his face in the curve of my neck. "Especially when you mess everything up. Not sure you've noticed, but we love fixing things for you."

River's movements are hesitant, and I realize I haven't said it back. I grab him by his crisp white collar and pull him in close.

"I love you. I love you both so much it hurts. I loved you when it was still the most reckless thing I could do. When I knew my heart would be ripped out. When I thought it might break me. But how could I not when it's you?"

# CHAPTER 58
# MIA

"I GOT IT!" Sidney squeals through the screen of my iPad the second I answer her FaceTime. I'd set the tablet on the kitchen island in order to make my cereal and pause mid-pour as her words register.

"What do you mean *you got it*?" I ask.

"Check your email. My guy came through. It's freaking gold, Mia." Sidney glows with excitement that was quickly spreading to me.

A thrill travels down my spine as I tap the screen, opening my inbox and spotting the email marked as "Smoking Gun."

Quickly opening it, my mouth drops open as my eyes travel over the words.

"How did he get this?" There are paragraphs of information interspersed with graphs and forms, all leading a trail from several hospitals to Jason's bank accounts. This is so much bigger than I thought.

"This is definitely a don't ask, don't tell situation," Sidney replies with a beaming smile. "Do you think it's enough?"

I nod, still stunned as I scroll through the seemingly endless proof. I flip the screen so I can meet her eyes, and a smirk pulls at the corner of my lips. "Oh my God. That asshole is going down."

Alex walks up behind me, wrapping one hand around my middle and the other on the counter. "Hey, Sidney. What are you doing to our girl here? Only we can make her this excited."

"It's not my fault I'm better at it." Sidney grins.

Jax's head pops into view. "Happy for you, Mia, but I just got back from playing away, and I'm going to be stealing my girl back."

"I just need another minute—" Sidney's cut off when Jax lifts her over one shoulder and leans closer to the camera.

"Keep us updated. I can always pay him a visit if this doesn't work."

"It'll work," Sidney replies from where her head is hanging behind him. Jax spanks her ass and grins before ending the call.

Alex rests his head on my shoulder, looking at my iPad. "Will it be enough?"

I show him what I have, and his grip tightens on me.

"Oh yeah, he's totally screwed." I break from Alex's grasp and head toward our room. "I just need to grab something."

The second I enter, I'm met with a dripping wet River, naked except for a white towel around his waist. My mind blanks as I take in his flexed muscles and the light dusting of hair trailing down from his navel.

"Need something, Love?" River asks, snapping me out of my daze. His light and playful tone warms my chest.

I close the distance between us, place my hands on his hot skin, and lift up onto my toes to capture his mouth in a gentle kiss. "I'm about to cause some chaos. Are you with me?"

"Always, Mia. I'm always with you." River's chest vibrates under my touch.

"Good, because I'm going to need your help."

I go through my purse and pull-out James McKay's card. There's no doubt in my mind he handed it over not thinking I'd use it. Joke's on him though.

I forward the email and dial before I can chicken out.

"Hello." A deep masculine voice I instantly recognize as Jason's dad comes through the phone.

"Hi, this is Doctor Mia Brooks. You know, the girl your son tried to frame." I push the words out. My lungs struggle to expand as my nerves start to take over.

Strong arms wrap around me, and River's mouth drops to my opposite ear. "Breathe, Love. You've got this."

I take a deep breath and tune back into what James is saying.

"Since you're calling me, I expect you have some

proof to back up your allegations. I assure you, Ms. Brooks, I will not take this lightly. For either of you"

I stand taller. "It's Doctor Brooks. I've already emailed them to you."

He's quiet for a minute before making a surprised, muted sound only to reply, "I'll be in touch."

The phone goes dead.

That's it? He'll be in touch.

Alex enters the room, holding up the iPad to River. "You should fucking see this. Boy is fucked," he says gleefully.

I look back at the guys. "I think the wait is going to kill me."

Alex lifts me over his shoulder and spanks me hard on the ass.

"Don't worry, Kitten. We'll keep you distracted."

———

One week after sending the information to James, I cross one stiletto-clad ankle over the other and watch the door from my seat in an overly expensive modern chair. Jason's dad contacted me yesterday to set up a meeting in his Boston office.

He's sitting at his large steel desk, hands clasped in front of him, a stack of incriminating documents on the table.

Apparently, he'd gone through the files, and even though I'd obtained the information through a shady channel, it was enough for them to follow through on their side.

Turns out, Jason had been stealing a lot more than what he'd pinned on me. He's been taking pills from each one of the hospitals his dad works with. Including the two located right here in Boston. Which is how I found myself dressed to kill in a black power suit, waiting for Jason to walk into his father's office.

Nerves prickled under my skin all morning with a nervous anticipation for this confrontation. For months, I wanted to have the upper hand on Jason, and now that I finally have it, it's sort of terrifying in an absolutely amazing way.

Both Alex and River have been nothing but supportive, giving me encouragement to come in here and witness Jason's downfall.

There's a light knock on the door, and an impeccably dressed man steps in. "Your son is here."

"Send him in," James replies, eyes already narrowing on the entry.

Jason strides in, a smile on his face. "What's with the emergency meeting, Dad—"

He freezes when his eyes meet mine, and I can't help the mischievous grin from curling my lips.

Jason pales as the blood drains from his face. "What are you doing here?"

I stand and walk toward him, placing a sympathetic hand on his shoulder and plastering on my most condescending smile. "I told you you'd regret fucking with me. This is me not playing nice."

"Son, come here," James commands, and Jason

shakes me off with disgust before approaching his father's desk. He's about to sit down when James stops him.

"No need to sit. This won't take long." He holds out the file, and Jason takes it, flipping through the contents. Sweat forms on his temples, and the back of his neck turns a bright red.

Jason's head snaps up. "I'm being framed." He looks at me. "She's a lying bitch. She's done nothing but beg me to take her back."

I snort but don't stop him from digging his own grave.

"This is a setup. You know I wouldn't do any of this," Jason pleads with his dad, giving him a look that no doubt got him out of countless things before.

James stands from his desk. "You had everything you could ever need, and yet you still chose to steal from me. Tell me why."

"I didn't," Jason replies weakly.

"Do. Not. Lie. To. Me." James's voice booms through the room.

"Come on, Dad. You know I wouldn't. Why would I?"

James shakes his head in disappointment and hits a button on his phone. "Send them in."

The door opens, and two officers step through. They walk up to Jason, who spins away.

"Do not touch me," Jason hisses.

The second cop grabs him by one wrist, and Jason tries to squirm away, but the officer already has him cuffed. "Don't make this harder than it needs to be."

Jason looks at me with hatred. "You can't do this."

"I assure you, I can." I repeat back Gerard's words from when he pulled his funding. "I hear theft of that amount is a felony. I hope you like the colors in prison."

"You fucking bitch—" Jason tries to lunge at me only to be held in place with a sharp tug of his wrist.

The officer cuts him off, leading him out of the room while reading him his rights. "Jason McKay. You have the right to remain silent. Anything you say can be used against you in court. You have the right to talk to a lawyer for advice before we ask you any questions. You have the right to have a lawyer with you during questioning. If you cannot afford a lawyer, one will be appointed for you before any questioning if you wish. If you decide to answer questions now without a lawyer present, you have the right to stop answering at any time."

"Don't drop the soap!" I call after them just before the door clicks closed.

"I owe you an apology." James says from behind me, his voice a cool professional that makes it hard to decipher.

I spin to face him, the clacking of my high heels echoing off the walls. And shrug. I really don't care about anything this man thinks. "Consider it forgiven." Then I push through the door, a freedom settling over my shoulders.

A few moments later, I step out of the elevator into the lobby. Alex and River are standing nearby with wide grins on their faces as they watch a police officer lead Jason away in handcuffs.

Alex is carrying two bouquets of helium balloons that read "Lock him up" in bright red lettering.

A laugh breaks from my chest, and it takes me a second before I can say, "What are you doing here? I thought we were supposed to meet back at your place?"

Alex motions toward the window where officers are leading Jason away. "Couldn't miss the show!"

River envelops me in a side hug and plants a kiss on my temple. "I'm so proud of you."

I sink into his chest, comforted by their presence. In that moment, I realized how truly lucky I am to have them both in my life.

I look up, resting my chin on his chest, and grin. "We did it!"

"Nah, Kitten." Alex cups the back of my neck. "You did it…well, Sidney helped. Do you think she'll want a present?"

River shakes his head. "There's nothing she wants that Jax hasn't already gotten for her."

Love swells in my chest as they joke around me. "What's next?"

River brushes a loose strand of hair behind my ear, a warm smile tilting his mouth. "We go home."

My heart swells, and I have to fight against the burning in my eyes.

*Home.*

# CHAPTER 59
# MIA

ALEX AND RIVER hold my hands as we stand in front of a crowd of reporters. Misty gives us the thumbs-up from where she stands behind us. Piper, Lucas, Jax and Sidney watch from the side.

Misty thought the best way to go about this was to get in front of it and she set this all up like it's no big deal. To my surprise Alex and River were more than willing to get it all out there. No matter how many times they prove it, I'm still surprised when they put me first.

We're in the arena press room, and I'm one hundred percent sure she didn't get permission for any of this.

"What did you call us all here for?" a reporter in the front asks. They all look eager for the story.

Alex steps forward. "We've been keeping a secret that needs to come out. That we honestly should've told you from the beginning."

There's a low hum as they all whisper amongst

themself.

River takes the microphone from Alex, surprising us both. "We did something we technically weren't supposed to. Something we were warned off of, but honestly, it was impossible not to. This is Dr. Mia Brooks. You may know her as the creator of the Center-Ice Challenge that Alex and I helped support. What you don't know is the two of us are absolutely in love with her."

The crowd grows loud, to the point I can barely hear the next question. "Isn't it irresponsible to get involved with someone you work with? It looks unprofessional to me."

River's face looks feral as he says, "I honestly don't give a shit what you think. Not when it comes to us, to them."

Warmth fills my chest, and he wraps an arm around me. If we go down, we're going down together.

The reporter steps back, nodding along like he respects it. Alex grabs the microphone. "I hope you caught your sound bite because we won't be talking about it again. What I do want to address is how Astrocorp dropped their funding to the Prosthetics For Kids charity the second they found out about our relationship."

The crowd changes from curious to mad swiftly, and I know Alex has them on our side.

He continues. "Losing the main sponsor has obviously hurt the charity's progress, but there's something we can all do about it. I challenge everyone watching this to participate in the Center-Ice Challenge, then I want you to challenge everyone you know. Help make a difference."

A sour-faced reporter is up next. "Don't you think you're being selfish? Hurting your career, losing her sponsor. Do you think it's worth it?"

Alex grins. "Abso-fucking-lutely."

Misty steps up, grabbing the mic, and my shoulders relax. "That's it for questions. Thank you all for joining us on such short notice."

She ushers us out of the back door, the noise from the room cutting off when it closes.

Damon Everette, the owner of the Bruins, is leaning against the wall watching us. The guys freeze beside me before stepping slightly in front, as if blocking me from whatever he's going to say.

"I'm not sorry," Alex says. "Take the captaincy, trade me. I don't care."

The man looks over the three of us, and then his attention lands on Misty. There's a slight blush curling up her neck and pinkening her cheeks as he spends several seconds too long watching her.

He surprises us. "I'd be more pissed if you didn't stand up for yourselves. If the press tries to spin this badly, I have faith Misty will fix it. Now, get out of here before I change my mind."

That breaks us out of our trance, and Alex leads me through several halls out the back exit, where Sidney, Jax, Piper, and Lucas are waiting for us.

Jax smiles wide, all dimples. "It's about fucking time."

# CHAPTER 60
# RIVER

I WAKE to the smell of bacon frying and whispered voices. I roll over and check the clock. It's well past ten. I can't remember the last time I slept like this. Always the first one up and dressed for the day.

I kick my feet over the side of the bed and pull on a pair of Alex's sweatpants and his T-shirt from last night. The scent of coconut and salt fills my nose, and I remember all the positions I'd had him in. I clench my teeth together and enter the hall, needing to be close to them.

I pause, leaning against the wall, as I spot Mia smiling in the kitchen. She has a spatula in her hand and a streak of flour across her cheek. She looks fucking delicious in my crisp white dress shirt, my boxers peeking from where she's left the bottom unbuttoned. I have to bite back my groan, not ready for them to see me yet.

She's looking up at Alex with wide doe eyes like

he hung the fucking moon for her, and he's staring right back with just as much love.

Crookshanks, who moved in when Mia started staying here every night, does figure eights between my ankles, meowing at full volume. I pick him up, and he nuzzles his head under my jaw, purring against my chest.

"Look who's finally awake," Alex says, smirking at me from behind the counter. He shifts, and the muscles of his bare chest tense and flex as he passes me a freshly brewed coffee when I sit at the island with the cat curled in my lap. He's wearing a pair of navy blue ball shorts, and I can just make out the outline of his—

"Pancakes?" Mia asks, sliding a plate in front of me before I can answer. The two of them look like they're up to something.

"Thanks." I take a bite, humming at the sweet taste of maple syrup. She walks around to my side of the island, and I wrap my fingers under my shirt around her waist. "Come here."

The cat jumps from my lap as I twist on the stool. Mia's searching my face, clear green eyes catching on mine. She takes a deep breath. "Alex and I were talking...and...what do you think if we both move in here?"

Warmth radiates in my chest, and I pull her onto my lap, capturing her mouth in a deep kiss.

She's breathless when I pull away. "Is that a yes?"

I glance between her and a nervous-looking Alex.

"I don't know how this is even a question." I kiss

Mia's temple before settling her feet to the ground and walking around the island. I set my coffee cup on the counter and back Alex into a corner.

I search his gaze, the worry clearly written across his features.

"What's wrong?" I ask.

He looks at his feet, the wall, then the ceiling. Anywhere other than at me. I grasp his jaw, grabbing his attention. "Tell me."

"I know you don't like to talk much, and I just wanted you to know…I love you…and…I hope you love me." There's fear in his eyes, and his words crack on the last vowels.

Shock registers through me, and I grip the back of his neck, closing the distance between our mouths. I kiss him long and slow, devouring every sound he makes before pulling away, chest heaving.

"Of course, I fucking love you. I fucking breathe because of you. And my heart beats because of her. You never have to doubt that. This. Us. We're everything."

# EPILOGUE

## NINE MONTHS LATER

### MIA:

I BEND AT MY KNEES, and crouch down to get my fingers under a cardboard box marked *LIVING ROOM* in black Sharpie. Sweat dampens the hair that escaped my ponytail and lies damp against my neck.

The moving van is nearly empty, and my arms shake from the weight as I haul the box to my chest. I swallow hard, looking down the narrow ramp and brace myself to cross it.

Ahead of me is our new home. We'd looked for several months, and nothing felt right until this came on the market two doors down from Lucas.

I knew the second I saw it that it's perfect for us. The straight lines and wood accents reminded me so much of Napa the air caught in my lungs and memories of sweat coated skin filled my thoughts when we pulled up to tour the place and River put in an offer that same day so large there was no way the owner could turn it down.

I wobble, leaning a little too far to the right, the steel ramp rocks beneath me, and I lose my balance. My stomach jumps into my throat, but strong arms grip my hips, lifting me, and the box easily in the air, placing me softly on the ground.

Alex smiles down at me. "Easy there, Kitten." He grabs the box from my tired grip and tucks it under his arm like it weighs nothing. "You're special cargo."

My heart is still racing from my near fall, but the way he's looking at me quickly has my heart skipping for a completely different reason. The air around us grows thick, and the magnetic force between us has me lifting on my toes, lips brushing his—

"Knock it off you two." Lucas calls, walking up the death ramp, and rolls his eyes at us. "At least wait until you've got your own room."

I can feel my cheeks heat, but Alex just gives him a cocky smile.

"Mia, take a break with us." Piper says, Sidney following close behind her. They sit on the oversized wood swing. The large mattress makes it more of a bed than a bench. A thrill shoots through me–at what we could use it for–that I immediately stomp down.

I glance up at Alex, who leans in and kisses my temple. "We've got this, go sit down. We need you well rested for the plans River and I have tonight."

Heat floods my core, and he gives me a smile full of promises, knowing exactly what he's doing to me.

It's fine, I can play right back. "I don't know. I'm feeling pretty tired, might call it an early night."

He trails his fingers along my jaw to where my pulse pounds in my neck and his eyes darken. "Good luck with that, Kitten."

"Hey, you two. Knock it off." Sidney echoes Lucas, holding two large glasses filled with golden liquid.

I roll my eyes at her and say to Alex. "We have to behave, or River will make us pay for it later."

Alex groans deep in his throat, his fingers wrap around my hips and tug me to him, crashing his mouth to mine. He kisses me like he owns me, like it's the only thing he needs and doesn't stop until my lungs burn in my chest.

He pulls back, smirking. "That's half the fun."

Spanking my ass, he directs me toward the girls who are now cat calling us.

I cross the manicured lawn, walk up the four wooden steps and take the beer Sidney's holding out for me, before collapsing on the swing beside her. I run my hand over the plush cushion, noting there's at least another foot to my right before the armrest.

"It's freaking hot out here." I take a long drink and hum at the back of my throat as the sharp taste cools me down.

"That's one thing to call it." Piper chuckles, and Sidney joins her.

"How did you two get out of working?" I ask,

and drag the cool glass, wet with condensation over my cheek, relishing in the feeling. I'm not sure what made me hotter, that kiss or the fact that it's a million degrees out here.

Sidney kicks off the ground, causing the swing to rock and leans back into the pillows. "Same way you did. Need your girl nice and rested for the night."

I snort. "You are way too open about that."

"Oh, please. Like you didn't just suck your boyfriend's face." Piper chimes in.

I'm about to answer her when a shirtless River steps out of the house. He's less than ten feet away, and I can see every detail of his sweat coated chest, the valleys and hills of his abs glistening in the sun.

My mouth waters as I take him in. He's wearing a pair of Alex's black ball shorts low on his hips, revealing the corded v of muscles that disappear into the waistband, and a stylish pair of running shoes.

A clanging noise from near the truck draws my attention, where I find Alex looking at River with the same lust filled gaze I am. He'd fallen back into the side of the truck, chest rising and falling rapidly.

River quirks an eyebrow and gives Alex a knowing smile. He's been smiling more often, and it never fails to enrapture me.

Alex snaps out of his daze, and he returns River's look as he sets down the box, and rips his own shirt off his back, with one hand revealing his sculpted chest.

River makes a pained sound beside me, swaying

a bit on his feet. Holy shit, if we don't hurry this up, these two are going to put on a show for everyone.

"Is it just me or did it just get one-hundred times hotter out here?" Sidney asks, eyes bouncing between River and Alex.

"You better be talking about me, Trouble." Jax comes up behind us, leaning forward as Sidney tilts her head back, and places a kiss to her forehead.

She gives him a sheepish grin. "Of course." her gaze roams over him. "Remind me why you're wearing a shirt?"

He laughs and pulls his own off, and Sidney immediately bites her lip.

I look between the guys and the girls and know there's no way we're getting anymore done today.

I stand, and walk to River, doing my best not to drool all over him. "Everything okay in there?"

His eyes are black pools when they meet mine. "Just finished setting up the bedroom."

Alex starts walking toward us. "It's late. We have the truck until tomorrow. We should start then."

This was met by knowing laughs, but Alex strolled straight for River and I, not paying anyone else any attention.

My cheeks heat, and I smile at Sidney. Jax and her are staying with Lucas and Piper for the weekend.

If I was embarrassed by how my guys are acting, it's gone the second I see the way Lucas and Piper are looking at each other.

I hope they're on different floors because it's about to get loud at their place.

"See you guys tomorrow," River says, entwining our fingers as he pulls me into the house.

My eyes widen as I walk through the arched entry doors. To the right, a winding staircase curves gracefully leading to the second floor where our bedroom is. While an intricate chandelier made up of lanterns hangs low over the threshold.

The tile, hard under my feet, is made from black slate that's been polished until it shines.

The living room is designed with River's dark, brooding color palette in mind, but the wonderfully comfy furniture blends seamlessly with Alex's masculine style.

I'd spent weeks working with an interior designer to make sure we perfectly tailored all aspects of this home. A hum tingles in my chest knowing I achieved the perfect concoction of our personalities. Everything from the warm wood accents and crisp white countertops felt like a piece of all three of us.

## ALEX:

I watch Mia light up as she looks around our new place. She gets this way every time she walks in, and a ball of warmth fills my chest.

A lot of amazing things have happened over the past year.

I landed the captaincy.

My parents came to my Captaincy celebration dinner after Mia showed up to their place and berated them for how they treat me. She put up with none of their bullshit and had them nodding their heads and repeating apologies.

Hell, we won the Stanley cup.

But none of it compares to the feeling of moving in with the two of them. It's like the final pieces are clicking into place and there's no doubt in my mind, they're mine forever.

Mia managed to make this place a perfect blend of all three of us, and from the second I walked through the doors, it felt like home.

I lean in close, placing a kiss to her temple, before dropping lower, running my lips down the shell of her ear, catching her earlobe between my teeth. She gasps, fingers digging into my thigh, and I spin her to face me.

I don't waste time, closing the inches between us. I haul her chest against mine, and eat the sweet moans she makes as I let my hands travel up her hips, gripping her perfect ass. She's panting when I kiss down her neck, licking off the salty taste of sweat.

The door clicks closed behind us and River steps into my back, causing my muscles to stiffen.

There's no telling what he has planned for the two of us. He never fails to keep it interesting, and I let him take the lead.

He places kisses between my shoulder blades, shifting upward, and grazes his teeth over my shoulder. A shiver runs through me, and I grip Mia's ass harder, earning a soft moan. River's fingers graze my sides, goose bumps erupting in their wake, and wraps his hands around my front until his fingers dip barely an inch under the waistband of my shorts.

Mia leans back, making room for him, and watches with heated eyes as River runs his finger teasingly over my skin until I'm rocking my ass against his hard length.

"Your cock's aching for me isn't it, Baby?" River's deep voice vibrates through my back and my dick jerks painfully.

I nod my head, and suck in a breath, making more room for his hand. A low growl rumbles in my throat when he doesn't lower it further.

"Tell me how hard you are." he demands.

I inhale sharply "So fucking hard."

"Good boy." He reaches down, grasps my cock, stroking it, before running his fingers over the tip and dragging the pre-cum gathered there down over my shaft.

I groan. *"Fuck-please-I can't-I need."*

River bites my neck, then soothes it with his tongue.

"On your knees." For a second, I think he's talking to me, but Mia's the one to drop to the ground in front of me.

She's making quick work of my shorts, pushing them around my ankles and makes a pained sound when she's level with my weeping cock. She looks up at us with round eyes, her pupils taking over everything but a sliver of green. Fuck she's pretty like this.

River strokes my cock in unhurried motions and guides it to rest on her mouth. He paints her lips with my pre-cum, and my balls tighten at the sight of her, ready for whatever he asks.

River directs her. "Open, tongue out."

She opens wide, doing what he said, and River tugs my cock by the base until the head's resting against her tongue.

He squeezes my cock once more before letting go and growling into my ear. "Fuck her mouth."

Mia and I both groan and my hips rock forward automatically. Her moans vibrate around me, and I dig my fingers into her hair, as I push deeper with each thrust. She gags, and I back off but she follows me shoving me deeper. *"Fuck, Mia."*

My knees start to shake as I pound into her greedy mouth, and just before I fall forward, River bands an arm around my chest, holding me up, then grips my throat, restricting my airway.

My head buzzes, the world closing in on me as Mia sucks me harder, taking me deeper until her throat closes around my tip. The breath deprivation mixed with her warm mouth around my cock has me busting down her throat right here in the entryway.

River's still holding me up when Mia licks my cum from her lips and stands in front of me. "That's one room."

*Jesus Christ.*

River steps around me, shoving his tongue into her mouth, tasting me on her. He groans low in his throat before tossing her over his shoulder and taking the stairs two at a time.

Her giggles are cut off when he smacks her ass,

the crack echoing through the room, replaced by her moan.

I follow after them, smirking at Mia from a few steps below, and she grins back. We are definitely down for whatever River has in mind.

We walk into our room, the curtains are drawn closed, and only a hint of light streams through the corners. It takes a second for my eyes to adjust and when they do, River pushes Mia into my arms.

"Strip her down and put her ass up on the edge of the bed."

Goddamn that visual alone has my cock hardening again.

## RIVER:

Fuck. I want to make this good for them, but I can already feel my control slipping. Watching Mia take Alex's cock as he thrust deep in a punishing rhythm had my dick aching for my own release.

I clench my quads, fighting my own desire as I watch Alex strip her down and place her where I instructed.

I have to take this slow, so it's good for her. Stepping beside a naked Alex, we both stare at her glistening pink pussy. He's gently stroking his rapidly harding cock and his tongue wets his lips. He looks fucking ravenous, and the feeling is mutual.

She's soft and soaking for us, but she's not ready for what I have planned.

I kneel at the end of the bed, my height lining me

up with her pussy, and spread her cheeks wide as I lick up her slit. I groan as the taste of her floods my mouth and bury my tongue into her core.

She cries and rocks against me, like the good fucking girl that she is.

I lift my mouth and push a finger into her before she can complain. Quickly followed by another. I take my time, coating my fingers in her wetness, then pull back and add a third. She tightens around me, resisting as I stretch her wider.

"Breathe, Love. I need you to relax."

She slumps down onto her forearms, taking several breaths and her pussy loosens, letting me pump all three fingers inside her. I scissor them, pressing against her g-spot until she's rocking back against me.

I press a fourth finger slowly into her, and she gasps in a sharp inhale, body working to accommodate the invasion.

Alex is the one to praise her. "Fuck, Kitten. Your pussy is so pretty, stretched like that."

A soft whimper escapes her mouth, but she doesn't tense as I work my fingers in and out. She's so wet it's dripping down my palm, and I use it to ease my way deeper.

She's panting, mouth wide open, as incoherent noises escape her lips.

Alex is stroking himself harder, dick inches away from my face, and I grab it with my free hand, taking it deep into my mouth and humming around him. He bucks, groaning, fingers instantly in my hair as I work them both in tandem.

I pop his cock from my mouth, needing him hard for what's coming next.

"Rub her clit." I command Alex through clenched teeth, and he immediately has her rolling her hips in circles, my fingers stretching her impossibly wide.

She clenches around me, body squeezing as her release crashes over her, and she cries out loud before collapsing to the bed. Her body's trembling when I flip her onto her back, slip my hands under her arms and lift her to the head of the bed.

I look back at Alex's darkened gaze, he's stroking his cock again and it's dripping from the tip.

"Get under her and shove that cock in her pussy."

He smirks at me. "Yes, Sir."

His words have my control fraying and my head going dizzy. There's nothing quite like having this big powerful man at my mercy.

Alex climbs over her with a soft smile, and she lets out a surprised giggle when he rolls them until she's on top, chest to chest.

"Like that, Kitten?"

Her response is turned into a whimper when he slowly guides her down onto his cock. He pumps into her in slow, even movements and arches a brow in question to me. *What's next?*

I strip out of my shorts, and shoes, and catch Alex staring at my cock. He wants this as badly as I do. I crawl onto the bed beside them, but further back so I can reach where they're connected and

# ALSO BY

Rule Number Five

Book 1 in the Rule Breaker Series

<u>READ NOW</u>

I had my whole life planned out... until I met a hockey player obsessed with breaking all of my rules.

## READ NOW

In a world where Omegas are cherished, Alphas are revered, and Betas are forgotten I wouldn't have changed a thing.

Growing up in foster care, my friends and I took care of each other. Ares, Killian, Rafe, and Nox, were my everything: my first loves, my only family, my pack. Until the same night they told me we'd be together forever, I presented as an Omega, and everything changed. By Jessa Wilder & Kate King

Made in the USA
Monee, IL
02 September 2024

65080321R00293